HYDE

AN URBAN FANTASY

BOOK I

LAUREN STEWART

Cover design by Olivia Rivers
Edited by Red Adept Publishing
Formatted by IRONHORSE Formatting

Other Titles by Lauren Stewart
Darker Water, Once and Forever #1
Unseen, The Heights Vol. 1
Unearthed, The Heights Vol. 2
Hyde, an Urban Fantasy
Jekyll, Hyde Book II
Strange Case, Hyde Book III
The Complete Hyde Series Box Set
No Experience Required, a Summer Rains Novel
Second Bite

ReadLaurenS@gmail.com
www.ReadLaurenS.com

ISBN-13: 978-0-9881701-1-7

DEDICATION

For those who want to reach for their dreams without compromising who they are. Remember: not everything is worth fighting over, so pick your battles wisely. And once you do, make sure you kick some ass.

...I thus drew steadily nearer to that truth, by whose partial discovery I have been doomed to such a dreadful shipwreck: that man is not truly one, but two.

There was something strange in my sensations...an unknown but not an innocent freedom of the soul. I knew myself, at the first breath of this new life, to be more wicked, tenfold more wicked, sold a slave to my original evil...

Robert Louis Stevenson
Strange Case of Dr. Jekyll and Mr. Hyde, 1886

PROLOGUE

Fifteen years ago

He woke up to the screaming. His mom's. Different this time. More fearful. More frantic. He ran to the door and threw it open. His sister barred his way, somehow knowing what he planned to do.

"Move, Shelly!"

"No, Mitch," she said, her eyes wide. "Don't. Don't go in there. It'll kill you."

It. The beast. The creature that had been part of his life for as far back as Mitch could remember. Even longer for Shelly and his mom. They never talked about it. As if pretending it didn't exist made life easier. Life wasn't easy. Life was terrifying.

Something had to change.

His mom's screams were louder. And then they stopped. Mid-cry, they just stopped. He pushed Shelly out of the way and ran down the dark hallway toward the living room.

"Mitch, no!"

Too late. It was all too late.

His mother lay on the tile floor. The only part of her still moving was the blood pooling beneath her body.

The beast stood above her, huge, smiling, blood splattered across its neck and chest. It raised its head slowly. There was a flash of recognition in its eyes, then it blinked, shook itself like a wet dog, and launched toward Mitch.

Mitch dove to the side. The beast barreled by him, into the hallway. Toward Shelly.

"Help!"

Her cry slammed into his mind, his heart. "Shelly!" He grabbed his baseball bat from the entryway and ran.

The beast had her pinned in a corner. "Are you afraid, bitch?" it growled. "You should be."

Mitch swung the bat. Three years of little league and the last two of high school ball packed into one hit. Then another. But the hall was too narrow.

The beast shoved Shelly against the wall and then flipped around, laughing darkly. "That all you got, boy?"

Mitch swung again and again, sometimes making contact with an arm, a shoulder, stepping back as the beast advanced, toying with him. The bat's length the only thing keeping the bastard from reaching him. Back into the living room, it pawed, trying to grab Mitch's inadequate defense. If it caught hold, if it backed Mitch into a wall, everything would end— Mitch, Shelly, everything.

A blow to its head stopped its laughter, a quiver rippling through its body. "Come here, you little prick!" it roared.

Mitch aimed high for another hit to its face, one step closer to use the full force of the weapon. The bat rebounded in his hands as it struck flesh, sending a shooting pain through Mitch's arms and shoulders.

Again, he swung. Again, he struck.

The beast stumbled, put its hands to its ears, still cursing. Another strike landed. Then another. The beast sank to its knees, its growls turning into grunts of pain.

Mitch lifted the bat above his head. His legs were numb, his upper body vibrating as he pounded all of his anger, all of his fear, into the monster lying at his feet.

"Mitch," his sister begged. "Please stop. Please."

He didn't. He couldn't.

"Stop! It's dead. Stop," she said, weeping.

He felt her arms around his waist, holding him, pulling him back from the edge. Finally overcome, the bat fell from his hands, and he let her guide him a few steps backwards. His foot caught on the rug and he sat down hard, Shelly sliding down beside him.

She crawled on her knees until she was between him and the bloody bodies on the floor and hugged him tightly.

Over her shoulder, Mitch stared at the creature. Watched it change, shrink, diminish. Until all that was left was the lifeless body of his father.

Their father. Dear old Dad. A man they had both hated. A man who had been filled with evil when he was human. Doubly so each time he transformed into Hyde.

Shelly held Mitch's shaking body in her arms, stroking his hair, making shushing sounds, telling him it would be okay.

Would it? Would it ever be okay? He slumped into her. "Oh, God, Shelly, what did I do?"

"You *had* to do it, Mitch. You saved me…saved *us*. We can be happy now."

Happy?

"He was a monster." Her words stung.

"Don't say that," he whimpered.

"But he *was*. He was evil. He *had* to die."

"*Please*, Shelly, don't say that," he said through his sobs, his eyes still locked on his father. "Because…that's what *I'm* going to be."

She stiffened, and then hugged him tighter, slowly rocking him back and forth. "No, we won't let it. We'll figure something out."

It was too late. His transformations had already started. Not as violently as his father's—not yet—but they'd begun. When his tears blurred the image of his parents' bodies, he rested his head on Shelly's shoulder and cried.

"You'll never be a monster, Mitch."

"I already am."

CHAPTER I

Fifteen years later

Eden's heart was the only part of her not completely frozen. Her pulse pounded in her ears, easily doubling the beat coming from his chest. His muscular arms wrapped around her while he slept and she panicked. Her mind screamed, "Run!" but the rest of her body wasn't listening. As if it wanted to stay right where it was.

She hadn't sleepwalked in eight years. She knew that. And it had never been like this. She would have remembered waking up in a room she'd never seen before.

With a man she'd never seen before.

Naked.

Especially a man who looked like he did. Waking up next to *that* would be a memory you'd hold onto. Peaceful beauty that seemed impossible in the real world. Yet there it was.

And here *she* was. Naked. Lost.

He stretched as he woke up. "Hey, I'm glad you stayed," he whispered. The stubble on his chin scraped her forehead followed by a soft brush of his lips. His fingers curled around a lock of her hair. "Huh, your hair looks different. I thought it was red. That's the last time I drink…whatever it was I was drinking." His voice was low and guttural, as was his laugh.

He adjusted his body toward her, holding her close to his chest. "Listen, I wanted to tell you…last night was—I've been going through a lot of—I just want to say—Fuck it. Never mind." He ran a hand through his hair. "What time is it?"

As he rolled his body on top of hers, she stared up at his profile. He was all hard angles—jaw, nose, cheekbones. The only softness in his face was his lips. Okay, maybe his eyes, but she wasn't a great judge at this particular moment. No, she was more of a panic button permanently stuck in the '*on*' position.

His dark hair fell forward, and he shook it out of large hazel eyes to look at the alarm clock. "Wow, forty-five whole minutes of sleep. I feel like a new man. Wanna feel?" With a small grin, he took her hand and pulled it under the sheet covering them.

Eden stopped her hand before she touched the erection already pressing against her thigh. *I am not that kind of girl!* Except that it seemed she *was*…or *had* been at some point she never wanted to remember.

"What's—?" He let go of her and pushed himself up from her body, his brow furrowed. "Why are you looking at me like that?"

Her mouth opened and closed as if she was trying to clap with it. *Yay for me*, she whimpered silently. She swallowed. "Did we—?"

He studied her face. "Did we what?"

How could she discuss something all evidence suggested they'd done, but she didn't remember doing? "You know." *Yeah, that was perfect, Eden. Very clever. Geez.*

"In every possible way." The smile filled his face, making his eyes dance and the corners crinkle. He brushed a fingertip across her lower lip and leaned toward her. "I have never—" His brow tightened again, and he tilted his head. "Stop looking at me like that. It's weird."

His words freed her body from its stupor, and she pushed

against him. "Get off me, old man!"

"Old man? Ouch, that hurt." He rolled to the side and laughed. "When they say it's all downhill after thirty, I didn't think they meant it quite so literally."

She lunged out of the bed, grabbing a pillow on the way to cover her naked body. Getting a longer-distance look at him hurt more than it helped. He was fantastic looking. Not old. Mature. Early thirties maybe? Again, her judgment shouldn't be trusted—she was actually attracted to a naked stranger who she'd seemingly already had sex with. Yeah, *so* not part of her usual M.O.

"Wait," he said. "Are you really upset? Oh, shit. Did I do something unbelievably stupid while I was asleep or something?"

You mean, like have a one-night stand that may have included more horizontal positioning than actual standing? Oh, God. "Leave me alone." Voice controlled. *That's a good sign you're still sane. Isn't it?* "I don't know who you are."

He sat up and took a long breath, his nostrils flaring and his eyes thin slits of anger. "Somehow I doubt that's ever stopped you before."

"I've never...I...I have a boyfriend." *Kind of.*

"Oh, okay. I think I get it. This is one of those 'I was so drunk' things, right?" He shook his head. "It's not my fault," he mimicked in his falsetto.

She should run. Run as fast and as far as possible. But then she'd never know what happened. Not to mention that he'd probably enjoy watching her butt bounce as she ran away. "How did I get here?" She waited for a reply that never came. All she got was an incredulous look and an eye roll. "Have we ever met before?"

"Why bother asking? If we had, you'd just pretend it didn't happen anyway." He pinched the bridge of his nose. "Next time you decide to pull the 'I'm not responsible for my actions' thing, don't let everyone in the club watch you pole-dance on the bar and jump all over me. It isn't helping your case." He gathered the taupe sheet into a loose ball and threw it at her.

Eden dropped the pillow that barely concealed her and wrapped the sheet tightly around herself. "I have no idea what you're talking about." She swallowed, wondering why she felt the need to explain anything to him. "I sleepwalk sometimes."

His laugh echoed off the high ceiling. "Come on, don't do that. That's just stupid. Totally ruins the whole night. A night I wanted to remember. For a long, long time."

"I...I...don't remember." She hated the stutter of her voice, hated her lungs that seemed incapable of full expansion. "Was I...drinking?"

"Okay, fine." He threw his hands up, the movement tightening his abs into six perfect squares covered with a small path of hair trailing down to his— *Oh, boy.*

"Listen lady, it's already ruined, so let's go whole hog. You were the craziest, *soberest* lay I've ever had. If that was you sleepwalking, I'd like to take the waking version out for a test drive as soon as possible." He dropped the volume of his voice as she skittered backwards toward the door. "So much for my charming wit." He bowed his head—"Thank you for the lovely evening"—and tipped an invisible hat. "It was a pleasure. Too bad it had to end like this."

"I don't do this. I must have been sleepwalking." Even *she* had a hard time believing it. It was probably the lamest excuse ever given. But it *had* to be true, there was no other explanation. Even if she *was* the type to end up in a stranger's bed—which she wasn't—she had no memories of anything they'd obviously done. Was this some kind of prank? Was someone about to jump out of the curtain with a camera and scream, "Gotcha! Now can you sign this release form"? She looked hopefully at the window drapes. *Please.* She wasn't that lucky.

And, oh yeah, the soreness of her muscles was probably due to all of the mountain climbing she didn't remember doing. Looking back to the man in the bed, she decided *no one* was that good of an actor. A Roofie? No. How could he have given her a Roofie when she'd gone to sleep last night locked inside her apartment? *Oh my God.* Somehow she'd REM'ed her way into his bed.

"Whatever," he muttered. "Let me know if you're ever ready to join me in the real world. The entrance is way over there somewhere." He motioned toward the door.

"What does that mean?"

"It means leave. Now. Good to meet you, good luck with your boyfriend, and get out." He flopped back on the mound of pillows.

Eden's legs were already jogging toward the door when she thought about what she was wearing. She pulled the sheet tighter around her and turned back to him with as much dignity as she could muster. "Um...where are my clothes?"

Without lifting his head, he pointed to the far side of the bed. "Your skirt is over there. And your bra is probably out in the hall. Under my pants," he grumbled.

She tripped on the sheet as she shuffled over to grab the black skirt off the floor. On her way to the door, she stepped over five empty condom wrappers, cringing at each one.

There is no way this is my life. She couldn't even do five *push-ups,* and she assumed sex took at least *some* upper body strength. Embarrassed by imagining she'd just laid there and made him do all the work, she slammed the bedroom door behind her.

As she walked down the wide, dark hardwood hallway toward the staircase, she reached down and snagged her bra by a strap, not touching the pants that were lying on top.

Then she heard him call out, "If you want your panties back, they're probably still hanging on the doorknob."

Eden slipped on her skirt and bra and began checking all the doors, first upstairs and then downstairs, passing through room after room of contemporary, elegant opulence mixed with sloppy, careless bachelor. She ran through everything she remembered about last night. *Home from office hours.*

Last day of school. Mac and cheese for dinner. With little sausages— Oh, God, don't think about sausage! She found one shoe in the foyer and kept searching for her other shoe and her undies.

Watched a rerun of Bones *because nothing else was on.* The black granite countertops in the kitchen were layered with Styrofoam take-out containers and half-filled glasses except for one side of the island. *Put on pajamas. Not clothes, pajamas. My light blue ones.* Broken dishes and utensils littered the floor next to the island, covering her other shoe as if it had fallen off right before everything on the counter was swept off in a hurry.

Could this get any worse?

She flipped around and hurried back into the living room. Her shirt was lying over the back of a leather couch. *Brushed teeth. Washed face. Then sleep. Sleep! Where is my stupid underwear?* She gave up looking and headed for the front door. *No club. No alcohol. No man. Definitely no man.*

She left the sheet at the base of the stairs and stepped out into the light of a new day. *Oh my God, what's wrong with me?* Her underwear was right where he said it'd be—she just hadn't expected it to be hanging from the knob on the *outside* of the door.

⌁⌁⌁

After he heard the front door slam, Mitch pounded his head into the pillow. *Damn it. Damn it. Damn it.* He'd thought—

Agh! No, no thoughts were involved at all. He'd *felt*. Damn it, he'd felt more last night than he'd ever—

Agh! Besides the sex—which was incredible—he'd felt connected to someone. Someone who seemed to *know* him in some bullshitty cosmic sort of way. Someone who wouldn't judge him but just *be* with him.

The booze had built up the fantasy in his mind. The perfect woman—soft everywhere a woman should be and tight everywhere else, uninhibited, knows what she wants and where she wants it. Funny when she spoke—which wasn't often—different from anyone he'd ever met. Thick, long hair he'd thought was red, but turned out to be a rich, dark brown. Either way, it was beautiful. Full lips, mind-blowing body.

Yeah, right. The perfect woman. He was a heck of a judge of that. Turns out, she was even more fucked up than he was. If that was possible. Which it wasn't. Hell, maybe they deserved each other. Of course she was crazy—there was no way the same woman could be his perfect lover and be sane, too.

He shouldn't have gone out last night. He kept his liquor cabinet well stocked. People in mourning over a family member should not get soused around other people. Or pick up strange, gorgeous women and have wild, hot, most definitely consensual sex all night with them. Especially people like him. Not that there was anyone like him. Bad idea all around. But those few hours had given him a reprieve from himself, from who he was, *what* he was. And that was good. Very good.

He'd even been *nice* to her. Holy shit, when was the last time that had happened? Nah, it was a good thing she was nuts. Certainly safer…for everyone.

He got up, showered, dressed, and headed out, stopping only briefly to stare at every place they'd been—walls, doorways, stairs. Why'd she have to ruin it with a lame excuse like she was sleepwalking? Fuck, the least she could have done was come up with a better lie. *Sleepwalking, my ass.*

He hit the office at 9:15. Not too late. Jolie was already sitting at her desk, typing something. Her coffee-brown hair was wrapped into a bun that bounced slightly when she looked up at him. She raised an eyebrow, looked at her Gucci watch, and went back to work. She had a knack for looking busy whether he'd given her anything to do or not. Maybe she really *was* working—he had no idea. He was just glad to have her running his life since, obviously, he was doing a shit-poor

job of it. Maybe he should have her vet any future women he
planned on taking to bed. Get rid of the psychos before they
had a chance to mess with his head.

"Good morning, Mitchell."

"Do I look old to you?"

"What?"

"Old. Do I look like an old man?" He watched her
expression change as she struggled to figure out what the hell
he was talking about. "Is thirty the new sixty or something?
What? You follow that kind of shit." *Damn it, thirty-one isn't
old.* "Never mind. What's doing today?"

Jolie gave him one last look of "what the—?" and then
pulled out the day planner that held *her* brain and *his* life. She
read off a short list of clients who had appointments today and
what she'd arranged in terms of his travel itinerary for his
upcoming speaking engagements.

"They want to change the date for your speech to the
MemCo execs. I told them it was impossible."

"Why?" He picked up the cup of coffee she brought him
every morning and sat down on the edge of her desk.

"The new date is the third."

"Oh. Yeah, that would not be good. Well, if that's when
they want to do it, they can find someone else."

"They wanted *you.* They've already given your book out
to all the VPs in preparation for your talk."

"Golly, it's too bad I can't be there. I guess they'll actually
have to read it now, won't they?"

She tilted her head in annoyance. "Mitchell, I *get* that part
of the reason you are so successful is because, for some
reason, your clients respect the fact that you don't give a damn
about them, but there's a limit."

"Is there? It seems to be working really well so far."

"Shockingly, you're right. But, yes, there is a limit."

He shook his head. "No limits, Jolie. There are no limits in
business. Or life. You should read my book."

She sighed and looked down to the planner. "MemCo is

trying to reschedule the meeting—"

"See? It works."

"They are *trying*. But aren't happy about it. Something about wherever else you need to be cannot possibly be more important than they are."

"Well, I'd like to see their faces if I actually *did* show up on the third. Then we'd see how unhappy they can be." Or how terrified. Or, possibly, how dead. He stood up and walked into his office.

Jolie followed him in. "Mitchell, the police called."

His steps faltered. He rubbed his jaw. It was like a bear trap he needed leverage to open. "What did they want?"

"They put a new detective on the case. He wants to ask you about her again."

He forced himself to quell the hiccupping of his breath. But the images of Shelly's body—broken and bloodied, leaning against his back door casually as if she'd just sat down to wait for someone—for him—came flooding into his mind. He couldn't make it to his desk. He sat down hard on the long, white couch against the wall and waited for his guilt to go away. Until the next time it appeared. Like in about ten minutes from now.

"Okay," he said.

Jolie sat next to him, so close her knee hit his. She took his hand and squeezed it between hers. "Mitchell, they believed me. You're not a suspect any more. The new guy probably just wants to start from scratch, or to ask about anyone who might have wanted to hurt her, since they've run out of leads. It'll be okay."

He pulled his hand out of her grasp and stood. He owed her. Big. But he would never understand why she'd done what she did. She'd put herself on the line with her lie, and sometimes he wished she hadn't said anything at all.

Every day part of him considered going down to the police station and turning himself in. Too bad there were those other parts of him—one that knew she'd be brought up on charges too, just for providing an alibi for a guilty man. Another that feared the carnage he would create if put in a prison cell with other men, before spending the rest of his life in a lab somewhere, being poked and tested.

And then there was the side that, even knowing the evil inside him, still couldn't believe he'd killed her. What kind of a man would kill his own sister? Whether he'd been something else at the time or not.

CHAPTER II

"What do you want?"

"You need to work on your telephone etiquette. It stinks."

"I don't have time for this. Tell me what you want."

"Your goody-two-shoes isn't so goody anymore."

"What are you talking about?"

"Eden Colfax—Jekyll0026. She switched. Should we start calling her Hyde now? What number are we up to?"

"No, Eden Colfax isn't a Hyde, she's a Jekyll."

"She *was* a Jekyll, emphasis on the 'was.' I saw her last night. Her handler is out of town so, as a good little employee, I kept an eye on her. Last night she left her apartment. And she definitely acted more like a Hyde than a Jekyll."

"That's not possible."

"So pole-dancing and practically screwing someone in public is just another facet of her good side? Interesting."

"How long has her handler been gone?"

"Ten days."

"She's been without any serum for ten days?"

"Tops. Before he left, he dosed a few jugs of milk. But who

knows, maybe she suddenly decided she was lactose intolerant."

"Ten days. That doesn't make sense. Did you switch the serums? Give her handler the one meant for Hyde0016 by mistake?"

"I would never make that mistake." *Oh, shit. Did I? No.*

"Of course, you wouldn't. Mixing up the two serums would be colossally stupid. You're not colossally stupid, are you, Cabot?"

"No..." *Asshole, I'm not.*

"Then I want a full report in my inbox in twenty minutes. Exactly what you saw, what she did, and who she spoke to."

"She did more grinding and pawing than speaking."

"Fine. Then tell me exactly who she...grinded."

"She seemed to home right in on our boy, Mitchell."

"Turner? Now, that is interesting. He was in his human form?"

"Obviously. Hyde isn't due for another few weeks. And it's not like I'd let him out on the town."

"Did Turner recognize her?"

"No, I don't think so. Of course, I was hiding behind a curtain the entire time."

"Poor you. What happened?"

"He took her to his house. And, while I have no proof, I'm fairly certain it wasn't to show her his decorating prowess."

"Are you suggesting that they went there to have sexual intercourse?"

"Yes, that is what I am suggesting." *Idiot.*

"That just might be good news."

Not really. "Also, a new detective is investigating the death of Mitchell's sister, Shelly."

"You mean the murder, don't you? Or have you already blacked out that little mistake?"

"It was self-defense."

"So your very tardy report stated."

"A very tardy report that the board quickly signed off on. And, anyway, why do you care? You guys wrote her off years ago."

"She didn't show any capacity for transformation, but we hadn't written her off. She had the susceptibility markers and was being used."

"As a broodmare."

"A crude but accurate comparison."

"So find another."

"Do you think it is easy to find these people? People we can use for the trials? It took us years to find someone other than her brother to impregnate her."

Eww. "Wow, thank god you found another Hyde or your newborn guinea pig might have had some kind of defect."

"Your sarcasm is tiresome. Send me that report."

"Fine. But it will be short unless you want to hear all the gory details."

"I'll speak to someone about the detective. Is that it?"

"What about his dosing schedule? And what should I do about Eden until her handler comes back?"

"I'll check on it. Expect an answer later today. Oh, and Cabot? The next time you have something to report, follow procedure and write me an email. I don't enjoy having my time wasted."

"You betcha, boss."

$$\text{-}\psi\text{-}\psi\text{-}\psi\text{-}$$

Eden stormed into her apartment and locked the deadbolt behind her. For once, the tiny, two-bedroom, one-bath apartment didn't make her feel claustrophobic. The walls that usually felt as if they were closing in on her were exactly what she needed. Something small and familiar to surround her with a sense of safety, regardless of the truth of it. This place had never been her *home*, though she'd tried to make it one for her and Carter. The cheap, secondhand furniture in various shades of greenish brown and the appliances in 1970s almond yellow were a comfort compared to the modern chic she'd just left. The devil-you-know sort of thing. The devil-you-don't-wake-up-naked-next-to sort of thing.

After a quick glance at the door to Carter's room, she ran through the kitchen to the bathroom. Carter wouldn't be home for another two weeks, but she still shut the door before ripping off her clothes and tossing them into the trash. Despite the scalding water pouring down on her, she shivered, scrubbing her body clean.

She took the showerhead off its clip, turned the spray from "rain" to "pounding," and aimed it between her legs. The water punished that sensitive area he'd been inside of. What had she done to end up at a stranger's house with no memory of any of it?

The sleepwalking had started when Eden was thirteen and disappeared by seventeen. So much of it was lost in her subconscious. Even back then, what she supposedly did or said bothered her, but ultimately didn't matter. It wasn't as if she killed people in her sleep.

She knew it had started again, but this? No. Six years. It had been six years with no more waking up in the kitchen with crumbs on her pajamas, surrounded by food that would normally have made her gag. Six years of knowing she'd still be in her bed in the morning and not in another room. And the entire twenty-three years of her existence of never waking up with anyone. While the life she'd *thought* she was living crumbled around her, she remembered what it used to be.

Good times, good times. Four foster homes. A group home. Lots of tears. Confusion. Dread. She'd started sleepwalking in foster home number two. Or was it three? Shortly after it had become a regular component of her nights, her state-assigned social worker sent her to a therapist. The shrink had said that her particular sleep disorder usually occurred in younger children and disappeared by adolescence. Therefore, his theory was that Eden's issues involved something deep and dark from her past. Apparently, by thirteen, kids in the system were supposed to have worked all that stuff out and be *normal*. Yeah, right. Eden had confessed that the deep and dark thing was probably the sound of her foster father slipping into her room after everyone else in the house went to bed.

The therapist had cut the session short to make a phone call. Eden hadn't even gotten to the 'it's all my psycho mother's fault' discussion. Isn't that what one was supposed to tell a shrink—true or not? Granted, in Eden's case, it was undoubtedly part of it.

Eden had been placed in a different home immediately, but the sleepwalking came with her. Then, one more foster home and two group homes later, it just stopped.

Until now.

A few days before, she'd woken up fully dressed, the front door partway open, mud on her shoes. It had scared the living heck out of her, but nothing in comparison to this.

God, when will Carter come home? She slumped down against the edge of the bathtub and slid the rest of the way, curling her legs to her chest as the water shot up toward the ceiling. She didn't even bother to wipe the wet strands of hair from her eyes.

How could she tell him what she'd done? Their relationship wasn't a romantic one, but for some reason she still felt as if she'd cheated on him. The idea that Carter had been with other women didn't bother her at all—it was totally understandable. She had no claim on him, no reason to expect his fidelity. Of course, she'd never had any proof that he was sleeping with or dating anyone. He kept that part of his life to himself. They'd been 'together' for years as best friends, roommates, codependents, but she'd have to be completely delusional to think he was celibate. Like she used to be. Did it count if she hadn't done it knowingly?

She climbed to her feet and turned off the water. Wrapping a towel around herself, she trudged into her bedroom and put on some clothes. A turtleneck and long pants in the summer, as if covering her body would lessen her vulnerability.

Carter might not answer his phone, but hearing his voice on the voicemail recording would be something. Something to reconnect her to reality. He picked up on the third ring.

"Hey, babe." His voice felt like a blanket, a warm, thick cover to hide under.

"Carter? Can you talk?" The shaking started again, forcing her to hold the phone tighter to her ear.

"What's up? Are you okay?"

"I am now. I—I need to talk to you about something."

"I only have about two minutes. We're heading into class. What's wrong?" Two minutes to bare her soul, put some of this weight onto his shoulders and let him obsess about it until he got home...or decided not to come home at all. Pass the Crime Tech exam and stay in Key West.

"I'm not sure you want to know," she said. "When are you coming back?"

"A week and a half more of classes, and then we have the wrap-up sessions. I come home on a Monday, I think. Then I'll be prepping for the forensics exam and hopefully be doing some slave-labor interning at the station in Ft. Lauderdale. My flight info is on the calendar. Is everything okay?"

"Ye—No."

"What is it? You sound upset."

She couldn't lie to him, the feeling of nausea she'd had since this morning gaining strength. "I'm having sleep issues." *Well, that's the understatement of the year.*

"Oh, crap. That sucks." Relief filled his voice and she hated the sound of it, knowing that once she told him everything, she'd never hear it again. "Well, stop eating all of my ice cream before bed. Too much sugar isn't good for you."

She didn't think it was possible to smile again, but she felt the corners of her mouth lifting. "I only had a little."

"And no caffeine after noon. Maybe a warm glass of milk before bed would help you sleep."

"I need to get more. The ones we had went bad."

"Both of them? Are you sure?"

"I'm a smart girl, Carter. I'm pretty sure milk shouldn't be chunky."

In the background, metal met metal and a voice called out, "Carter! Hand-to-hand training. Let's—" The voice sounded muffled as if Carter had covered the phone.

"Carter?"

"I gotta go, Eden. Class is starting."

"They teach hand-to-hand training to forensic students?"

"Um…yeah. That's what we call protocols for Chain of Evidence. You know, a cop's hand to my hand to a lawyer's hand."

"Oh. That's—"

"Listen, I'll try to call you tomorrow. You sure you're alright?"

"I will be. No worries." Her belly tightened painfully. Maybe after she'd fallen asleep last night, and before having boatloads of sex, she'd stopped off for bad sushi.

"That's my girl. I love you, but keep your hands off my ice cream, would you?"

"I lo—" She stopped herself just in time. Now was not the time to say something she'd never said before. "Have fun."

"I will."

He hadn't heard her first words, which was good. He'd probably jump on the first plane back if he heard her say them. After a quick goodbye, she dropped her cell phone on the nightstand and changed into sweats.

Wanting to get the smell of sex out of her pores, she went down to the little workout room tucked in a corner of the apartment building. Calling it a gym was a stretch. All marketing. It looked a heck of a lot better on the brochure. The room was bare save for two cardio machines, a bench, some free weights and a couple lifting bars. It wasn't fancy enough for Carter, didn't have a big setup, locker room, loads of sweaty men and a boxing ring like his did, but it was good enough for her.

In fact, the fewer shirtless, sweaty men she saw, the better. Because then she'd probably start comparing them to the guy from this morning, and none of them would measure up, and she'd keep feeling the feelings that she was feeling and—

She ran. Sure, it was on a treadmill, which meant she wasn't actually escaping anything, but it helped her focus. One foot in front of the other. A slow release of the soreness in her muscles as they warmed. Forced thoughts about puppies and shoes overtaking the brief images of *him*.

After a long workout and another shower, she crawled into bed. Her bed. No one else's. Not even Carter's. Her hands gripping the covers, she closed her eyes. On her way into the bliss of sleep, she vowed to only rest during daylight hours. If *that* was what happened when she slept at night, she'd have to find a way to become nocturnal.

And she succeeded. For three nights, she drank pot after pot of strong, bitter coffee, keeping herself awake with long conversations about nothing at all important with slightly bewildered classmates and with marathon TV-watching sessions. Reality television was a sure-fire escape from reality. Those people were crazier than she'd ever be. Oh God, she hoped so. Her eyes ached, but she only allowed herself short thirty-minute naps throughout the day. Never at night. Nights were frightening. And so long. So very long.

Skipping all the sex scenes, she'd gone through seven trashy novels, her exhaustion leaving her with no recollection of what they were about. She wasn't even sure if she'd actually *read* the words and not just turned the pages at regular intervals.

Foreign images occasionally flashed through her mind. Bizarre images, troubling ones. *A woman wearing red, her back to a door, her hair so dark it looked black against her fair skin, her eyes closed.* Then another. *Inside a club with crowds of people raising their hands above their heads, smiling, bouncing in unison.* And somehow even more disturbing were the ones of the man she'd woken up next to, his hands on her, hands in the process of making her body feel incredible. The puppy-thoughts weren't working anymore—she needed to come up with a better alternative. *But what's sweeter than a puppy?*

On the fourth night, she put a horror movie into the DVD player. Not the best choice for someone who was currently *living* a horror movie, but at this point, adrenaline was the only way to stay awake. The never-ending nausea kept her from drinking more coffee and her friends were starting to wonder why she had suddenly become so friendly. She blinked and…

Jerked them open again. The scene in front of her wasn't of lustful vampires and sassy heroines, it was a garden filled with beautifully manicured hedges and trimmed grass. As her heart took a flying leap into her throat, she looked down to where she was sitting. Flagstone steps. Their sharp edges settled into beige mortar. No people, thank God. No bed. As she jumped up, she saw the large, wooden door. The same door her underwear had been hanging from a few days ago. She sprinted across the lawn, out onto the street. She knew her way home—she'd made the trip just the other day.

At least she was *wake*-walking this time. And clothed. Horrified, but thankful she'd ended up *outside* the house and not in it—or with someone *in* her—she made her way out of the coastal Lighthouse Point neighborhood without seeing anyone. This was South Florida, so no one but tourists left their air-conditioned homes or cars to tackle the humidity. As she crossed Federal Boulevard into the lower-income area of Pompano Beach, her shoulders slumped.

Maybe she *was* going crazy. Great, she could get her own show. Too bad her mother wasn't still alive—it could have been a mother/daughter train wreck on Bravo. She reminded herself that she'd been through harder things. And had come out okay. She'd be okay. She would. Probably.

Maybe she'd have to ask for help. Not something that came easily to her. Carter had always just offered, in return only wanting what she was unable to give him—her heart, her body, herself.

CHAPTER III

Safely inside her apartment, she started to take off her clothes. But stopped. These weren't *her* clothes. The short skirt and tight tank top were *way* too skanky to be part of her wardrobe. She pulled off the thin, burgundy jacket, turning it to examine the tag. Sure, as if she'd find a note that said, "The jacket you are wearing belongs to," with a name penciled in. Where the heck had it come from?

Her hand gripped something stiffer than the fabric. Reaching into the pocket, she pulled out an off-white cocktail napkin. "Static" was written in gold cursive script. Under that, someone—*me?*—had written a phone number. Local, but no name. She turned the napkin over and swallowed hard as she read what had been scribbled in the same handwriting as the phone number. When she could no longer bear to look at her own name on the thing, she flipped it back over, read the phone number again, and reached for the phone.

"Good morning, Mitchell Turner's office. How can I help you?" an airy voice asked at the other end of the line.

"Um…Good morning." Eden took a deep breath to regain control of her vocal cords. "I…um…need to speak to Mr.—" She'd missed the intro. "With Mitchell."

"Of course. Are you already a client?"

"No."

"Let's see." The sound of pages turning. "He could fit you in on Thursday morning at 11:30."

"Is there anything sooner? I really need to talk to him."

"Hmm…He is pretty busy. He has a half hour this afternoon, but if that isn't long—"

"That's fine. I'll take it." A half an hour should be enough time to introduce yourself as a total moron, shouldn't it? A hello-help-me-figure-out-what-the-heck-is-wrong-with-me conversation with a total stranger?

"At one o'clock?" the woman asked.

"One is fine. Thank you."

"I just need your name and phone number. If you will be billing our services to your company, I'll need that information as well."

"No, it's just me." Wondering where she would get the money, Eden gave the woman the information she'd asked for. Then the line went silent. Had the woman hung up already? "Hello?"

"I'm still here. Eden Colfax. Okay, Eden, we'll see you at one."

"Wait! What…um…what does Mitchell actually do?"

There was a pause on the other end of the line.

Eden imaged the woman rolling her eyes and taking an eraser to her name. "I'm not selling anything. I was given his name by someone who thought he could help me."

"Who gave you his name?"

Good question.

"We like to thank clients who refer people to us."

"I'm not sure. I didn't get her name. She seemed to think Mitchell could help me, but I wasn't sure of his exact job title." Not a lie. A carefully crafted truth to cover her ignorance. Was that a lie? *Yes, Eden. I think that constitutes a lie.* Her stomach dropped a bit, and she silently whimpered, '*But I never lie.*' At least, she never *used* to lie.

"He's a life coach," the woman said. "Do you still want the appointment?"

A life coach? Yeah, she sure as heck could use one of those. "Yes, please. One o'clock. Thank you." Eden hit the end button so hard the phone bounced out of her hand onto the floor.

For the next half an hour, she wondered what a life coach would be able to do for her and who had stuck that napkin into her pocket. She'd be okay. She'd be okay. Some life coach named Mitchell was going to help. Maybe. Unless another woman named Eden had stuck the note in her pocket before lending her jacket to a nearby sleepwalker.

Sure, that made *much* more sense.

Eden got to the life coach's office at 12:45 and sat on the edge of her chair for the next ten minutes. The walls of the building were glass, the majority of it clear. The only opaque one held the door she assumed led into Mitchell Whoever's office. That made Eden even more nervous, imagining that some stranger was staring at her from the other side, judging her before they'd even met. Continuously. Unlike the beautiful woman at the reception desk who judged her *briefly* with every glance.

The woman, who dressed more like a socialite than a secretary, smiled politely whenever she caught Eden staring. "He'll be with you soon."

"Thank you." Eden flipped through one of the business magazines from the end table and tried not to squirm. She scratched her neck, wondering if her nerves were making her break out in hives.

"Let me check if he's ready for you." The woman stood up from her desk, slid her hands down her pencil skirt, and went to the door. She was probably desperate to get the hive-covered wreck out of the waiting room.

And, quite frankly, Eden was too. The faster this was over, the more likely she was to recover. Eden jumped out of her seat and followed.

CHAPTER IV

Mitch was sitting at his desk with his lunch spread out in front of him when he heard a knock on the door. "Come in."

Jolie stepped partway into the office. "Mitchell? Your—"

The door opened farther, allowing Mitch a full view of who was standing behind her. When the woman saw him, the color drained from her face and her jaw dropped slightly.

He stood up from his chair. "Oh, shit." And then he laughed. "Change your mind?"

Jolie was probably getting dizzy from turning her head so quickly back and forth between him and the girl. Both women had the same expression of surprise, but, unlike Jolie, the supposed sleep walker looked like she'd flee if he blew air at her. Tempting.

"Or maybe you came up with a better excuse," he said.

She looked at Jolie. "No, I'm here for...something else."

Jolie smashed her lips together briefly and then said, "Your one o'clock is here." She stepped back to let the girl pass. Which she did...reluctantly.

"Thanks, Jolie. I got this one." *Had this one, actually.* Mitch sat back down and threw a few fries in his mouth as Jolie glared at him and slowly shut the door on her way out.

He wondered if she'd be pressing her ear against the door. But with the shades drawn across the one-way glass walls, he couldn't check. Not that he cared that much. Or expected the girl's visit to be a long one. "What do you want?"

She was openly gawking at him, breath shallow, one arm crossed over her chest, the other caressing her shoulder. Her gaze ran over him, then darted to the couch, giving him the feeling she'd like to see him stretched out naked on it.

Flattering, but he'd learned his lesson from their last meeting. "What. Do. You. Want."

She jolted at his words, blinking rapidly and dropping her arms. Yep, he'd been right. On the couch. Naked. He could tell from the depth of her blush.

"You're the life coach?" she asked. Her voice was how he remembered it—during daylight hours—nervous and unsure. Nothing like the husky pitch she'd had the night before.

A nod was all she was getting from him.

She took a few steps toward him and stopped. "So what? Do you just tell people what to do?"

Ah, hell. He was feeling generous. She could have another. Nod.

"And they pay you for that?" She widened her stance as if she was gaining confidence and power right before his eyes. He'd fix that.

"Correction. You should have said: *We* pay you for that."

"Not unless—"

"What are you doing here?" He studied her, visions of their night together mixing with the image she presented today. It didn't jibe.

"I found this."

He took a quick glance at the small square she held out toward him, recognizing it. "Static. Where we met. Nice club. Nice napkins. Very sentimental of you, but I don't collect crap. Is there anything else?"

"I found it in my pocket this morning."

"Fantastic," he said with a mouthful of food.

"Do you know who wrote this?" She stepped forward until she was a foot away from his desk.

"Wrote what?" He sighed. "Give it to me." He put down his burger, wiped the grease off his hands with his own napkin, grabbed the thing from her outstretched hand, and read the scribble. "That's my phone number, but I didn't write that. The handwriting's too girlie. Since I'm guessing you wouldn't be here asking if *you'd* written it, I'll go with 'someone else'. Who knows, perhaps another fine lady jotted it down before you threw yourself at me. I don't remember. Did you mug her?"

"I found it in a pocket...of a jacket I don't own."

"I'm confused as to how this pertains to me."

"Look on the back."

He flipped the napkin over and read aloud, "He'll know what you are, Eden." He handed it back to her. "I help lots of people—that's the kind of guy I am," he said without a smile. "I don't know an Eden."

"I'm Eden. That's me."

"I thought your name was Chastity."

She raised her eyebrows. "*No.* I'm pretty sure it's Eden." The tone of her voice was stronger, more confrontational.

He liked that. Damn it, he shouldn't like that.

"So?" she asked.

"So, what?"

"So...do you know what the message means?"

"No idea. Maybe you should ask the girl you mugged." For some reason, she made him uncomfortable—and Mitch didn't *do* uncomfortable.

"I didn't—" She let out a long sigh of impatience, tapping her hand on her thigh. "Geez, and you were so nice to me the first time we met."

"Oh, so you remember now, do you?"

Her lips came together and she glared at him. "I meant the *morning* we met."

"I was, wasn't I? Well, I was even nicer the night before,"

he said, smirking.

"And I'm sure it was all very altruistic. I've already nominated you for Man of the Year." She sighed again. "I didn't come here to argue. Or to discuss your skills in the bedroom."

"Too bad. I was just about to cancel all of my afternoon appointments."

She glared at him. "You're not going to help me, are you?"

"Nope." He took another bite, praying she'd leave. "I'm going to eat."

She grimaced and peered over the lid of the Styrofoam box that held his lunch. "What is that?"

He swallowed and looked down, really seeing it for the first time. "Uh, let's see." He pulled it apart. "It's got bread, a couple sad-looking vegetables, and *this* has a slight resemblance to meat. So I'm going with 'it's a burger.'"

"I would have pegged you for more of a granola-eating, slave-to-the-gym kind of guy."

"Why would you think that? You've been to my house."

Her gaze traveled rapidly across his chest to his bicep then to his face as a blush planted itself firmly onto her cheeks. Damn it, it made her even more attractive.

"I didn't look in your refrigerator," she said.

"Why would you? Your panties weren't in there."

She caught her flinch quickly and looked straight into his eyes. "Do you always push away people who come to you for help?"

How could she get under his skin so easily? What the hell was he doing? Playful banter was one thing—playful banter with someone you'd almost lost yourself to was something too stupid for words.

Alright, little girl, get ready for the real me. "Of course not. I'd never be able to make a living. I only push away those people I've stuck my dick into." He felt a grin lift the corners of his mouth as her embarrassment grew.

"Wow. You're a real charmer, aren't you?" She tossed her

head, her hair falling around her shoulders, her eyes narrowing. "Too bad I was asleep through the entire *ordeal*. Does that happen with a lot of your bedmates?"

"Oh, so that was you sleeping, huh? Is that why you were such a shitty lay?" As he watched her eyes get three times larger, he thought how she'd been the most incredible lover he'd ever had. And that connection he'd felt...

She stepped backwards and blinked rapidly, tears beginning to pool.

Damn it, another thing he didn't do—regret his words. "Ugh, stop." He leaned back in his chair and tossed his napkin onto the desk. "Do you really expect me to believe you were sleepwalking? The whole time?"

The tears went away. "No. I don't *expect* you to believe anything. But I was."

How did I get messed up in this? "Here." He grabbed a yellow Post-it note, flipped through his address file, wrote down a name and number, and handed it to her. "Try her."

She took it from the edge as if she was afraid to let their skin touch. "Who is she?"

"She's a psychiatrist. I don't do that sort of thing."

"What *do* you do?"

"Well," he said, popping both eyebrows excitedly, "normally, on Mondays, I serve ice cream to orphans. Wednesdays are my 'Come in for some quick hypnosis' days. And the rest of the week"—he dropped the silly act—"I tell people to get off their fucking asses and do whatever the hell it is they want to do." Mitch dragged his eyes away from her and tried to focus on one of the files lying in front of him. "For $300 an hour. You can pay up front."

"But you didn't do anything for me."

"You are taking up my time and a small amount of space in my office. Tell you what, I won't charge you for the whole hour."

"Well, if I'm paying, I'm staying." She plopped down into a chair and glared at him.

"Suit yourself." He went back to pretending to work, fighting back his smile—the proof that he wanted her around. *Stay away from her, man. You don't need this kind of complication.*

He shuffled paper and she fidgeted in her seat for ten excruciatingly long minutes.

Thankfully, she broke first. "You're really not going to help me?"

"Aside from the fact that I'm not the kind of help you need, I've worked very hard to get to the point at which I can choose which clients I take on. I do not choose you."

She stood up, her stance wide. "Fine. Then I'm not paying." She stormed out of the office and slammed the door in the exact same way she'd left his bedroom.

Was she actually going to pay for the fifteen minutes she was here? Mitch picked up his cold burger then dropped it, laughing to himself. *Oh, the games people play.*

Ten minutes later, a tall, mean-looking SOB walked through the door with Jolie a few steps behind him.

Gotta get that fucking intercom fixed.

"You're a busy man, Mitch. I couldn't get an appointment." He walked into the office as if he owned the place, and Mitch was confident enough in his manhood to admit that the guy took up more space than most. He made Jolie look like someone who'd shop in the kids' department at the mall. Dark eyes matched his hair, which wasn't much more than a crew cut.

Mitch didn't stand. "It's Mitchell, or Turner, or Mr. Turner. Hell, I'll even take Señor Turner. But not Mitch." Only two people had ever gotten away with calling him Mitch, and they were both in the ground now. "And you are…?" Not a client. Which made him either a telephone repairman or the new cop on his sister's case. Not a tough guess.

Great. As if his day hadn't been dramatic enough already.

Jolie stayed close to the man and mouthed, '*He's the cop.*' Her eyes darted between the two men, her expression changing from a silent apology at Mitch and a lustful gaping to the cop. Good thing Mitch couldn't care less. Although she really should be doing it on her own time.

"Detective Landon. I'm here to talk about your sister's murder."

"You have a card, Detective?" Mitch motioned to the chair that the little sleepwalker had just vacated.

The cop handed him a business card of cheap, thin stock and terrible lettering.

"What happened to the other detective, Nick?"

The man tilted his head at the use of his first name and claimed the chair, stretching out his long legs in front of him. Jolie took the other seat.

"He retired unexpectedly. I got some of his more colorful cases." He nodded at Mitch. "Such as yours."

"You mean, my *sister's*. Or am I still a suspect?"

"You have an alibi, don't you?" His smile was more like a sneer. "However, I like to start fresh."

"Fresh away," he invited. Mitch usually welcomed a challenge, but he sensed that Landon was a worthier adversary than anyone else he'd crossed. Not to mention that Mitch was, in fact, probably guilty and needed to be careful.

The detective checked his notes. "Your assistant, Jolie Cabot, who I believe is you"—he glanced at Jolie—"stated that you were together the night your sister was killed. Is that statement something you're sticking to?"

"Yes," she said. "He was with me, but we're no longer seeing each other." She leaned forward, flashing the cop a shot of her cleavage.

Mitch could have caught a swarm of bees in his mouth with the way it dropped open. Why'd she have to offer that last bit of info? Unless... He saw the way she was watching the cop, practically licking her lips. Oh shit, this was getting even more convoluted.

"We went back to his house in the morning and found her body," she said.

Landon's eyes went back to Mitch, waiting for his agreement perhaps.

So Mitch gave it to him. "We found her, I flipped out, tried to…I don't know…bring her back to life." He felt his lip start to tremble at the memory and rubbed his jaw to stop it. "But she was already dead."

"And that's why you had so much blood on you? Because you tried to resuscitate her?" His questions weren't really questions, more like statements of facts he didn't quite believe.

Mitch cleared his throat. "Yes." Blood, *yes*, there had been heaps of that. Shelly's blood covering him. He'd wanted it to be his own. Would have given anything to trade places with her.

"Was your sister visiting a common occurrence? At that time of night? Time of death was between, what, three and five?"

"Early riser, and she practically lived there," Jolie answered for him. Which was good, because at the moment, Mitch was still there on the doorstep, at Shelly's side. "It didn't matter what time it was, she'd stop by whenever. She had a key,"

He'd woken up confused in the upstairs hallway, Jolie's arm around him, helping him walk. The chains he'd gone to sleep wearing were broken, the door of his cage wide open. There were lines of blood on his chest, almost as if they'd been painted on. Jolie's panicked voice telling him Shelly was dead. That Hyde had gotten free. He'd shaken her until she told him where Shelly was and then stumbled down the stairs in a fog to find her body. Even as he'd tried to start his sister's heart again, he'd known that she was gone.

Landon flipped through a few pages in his notebook. "They found the key on her body. Was the house broken into? Anything taken?"

Mitch shook his head. "No."

"But you told the officers on the scene that you believed it was a robbery attempt."

"What else could it have been?" Jolie asked.

Landon shrugged. "You tell me." When no one responded, he continued. "Is there anyone who wanted to do you or your sister harm?"

"I piss off a lot of people. But would anyone want me dead? Doubt it. Want *her* dead? No way." She'd been a saint to his Lucifer, living the kind of normal life he'd never have. It was almost as if she was doing it for the both of them.

"What about—?" Jolie started. Her eyes widened as the two men focused on her. Then she seemed to relax, enjoying their attention as if they were at a bar discussing which of them she'd go home with instead of talking about death. "What about Leanne Tate? She might have wanted you dead."

"Who's Leanne Tate? Did you tell the other detective about her?" He flipped through his notebook again.

Mitch tried to catch Jolie's eye, cursing her for bringing an innocent into the situation. But she was looking at the cop.

"Leanne is one of Mitchell's ex-clients. She has"—Jolie gave him the international look for 'whacked'—"issues. She was absolutely obsessed with him for a long time."

"But I haven't seen her for a few months, Jolie." *Fuck, why'd she have to bring Leanne into it at all?* Liars were liars, the guilty were guilty, and innocents should stay the hell away from all of them. Though truthfully, he imagined Leanne was part of the first and second groups most of the time.

"Was she ever violent toward you?"

Shit, the detective would find out eventually. "A few months ago she attacked me in the parking garage. But it was no big deal."

"Mitchell, it *was* a big deal." She looked at Landon. "I was at my car and saw the whole thing. She wanted to hurt him."

"Did you file a report?"

"Jolie did, but…" He shook his head.

"You don't think it was her."

"No, I don't." Mitch was really struggling here. He wanted

the police to figure it out without getting anyone else in trouble. Not sure how that was possible since Jolie had stuck her nose and her questionable integrity into the whole thing. What if it *had* been someone else? Could Leanne have done it? Probably not. But he hadn't been human at the time, nor had he had any flashbacks of the actual murder. The only thing he knew for sure was what happened after he'd come back to himself, naked and bloody, Jolie panicking next to him.

"Leanne Tate. I'll check her out. Is there anyone else who might want to hurt you?" Landon looked at Mitch. After Mitch shook his head, the detective looked at Jolie.

"What about the woman from earlier?" she asked. "What was her name? She looked kind of angry."

Mitch didn't give a name. In fact, the faster they stopped talking about her, the better. For all sorts of reasons, among the most obvious was because, "I only met her about a week ago." Had it been a week? Longer? Nah, he'd been grieving the six-month anniversary of Shelly's death when he'd slept with the woman. And then more drama had ensued. "Not to mention, I don't think she'd be capable anyway, she's too...scared of her own shadow."

"Anyone else?"

Mitch shook his head for what felt like the fortieth time, so Landon looked to Jolie for an answer. She shook her head too, possibly at a loss as to who else she could falsely accuse.

"Your sister was pregnant at the time of her death. Who was the father?"

Mitch wished he would stop calling her his sister. It was making the situation even more painful by bringing back all the emotion he so carefully tried to tuck away. "I don't know. She didn't tell me she was pregnant. I only found out when the cops told me about her autopsy." God, he hated that word being connected to the only person he'd ever loved.

Landon asked more questions and somehow they were answered—some by him, others by Jolie. He couldn't keep track. His mind was miles away.

The week before Shelly had died, she'd been laughing, hobbling into her apartment, just back from the hospital. The leg she'd broken skiing wrapped in a white cast. That kind of shit happened to normal people. He'd carried bouquets of flowers from her friends and her bag since she hadn't yet mastered walking with a cane. After working so hard to convince her to rest, the doctor had given up on the idea of crutches. She hated the cane too, but she used it. That clacking sound as she walked would be forever branded on his eardrums. He tried not to think of the sound the cane might have made each time it had struck her flesh. Before it—and probably *he*—killed her.

"We're done for now." The detective stood and closed his notebook. "Thank you for your"—he hesitated—"honesty."

Jolie straightened her skirt as she stood, still beaming at the guy as if he cared about the caps on her teeth. "You'll let us know if there's anything else?"

"Oh, there *will* be something else. A lot of something elses. I feel like I should tell you that I believe about half of what just came out of your mouth." His stare rested on Mitch.

Mitch got the feeling the man ended every one of his interviews with that line. "Half? Is that about average?"

Landon smirked, nodding his head in a way that said, *touché*. "Occupational hazard. I never believe anything anyone says. So, actually, half is pretty decent."

"Then I'll be satisfied with it."

"I couldn't care less about your satisfaction. I'm more concerned with what happened to your sister. The *whole* truth."

"And nothing but the. Right?"

"I'm not going away, Turner. I'll be in touch," Landon said, his jaw tight, "with each of you. Separately."

As Jolie followed the guy out into the waiting room like a puppy chasing a lion, Mitch called out, "Can't wait!" She threw him a dirty look and shut the door behind her. Two minutes later, she returned, looking frustrated.

Mitch stopped pretending to be able to focus on work. "Your flirting wasn't as effective as it usually is."

She sighed and lay down on the sofa, crossing her legs at the ankle. "I know. Why is it that all the men I *want* seem to be the only ones incapable of seeing my charms?" She gave him a look.

If she was waiting for a compliment, she'd be waiting a while. "Perhaps they can see through to your true intentions."

Why she put up with him, he'd never understand, but she leaned back against the arm of the couch and said, "Yeah, that could be it."

CHAPTER V

A nudge against her thigh jolted Eden awake. A quick glance around let her know she was no longer in her apartment and that someone wearing dark gray slacks and black shoes was shoving his foot into her rear end.

"Why are you here?" Same doorstep. His voice. His aggravated, impatient, gravelly-sounding voice.

Eden looked up as he nudged her again. "Okay, enough. I'm awake."

"When you visited my office the other day, did I accidentally say I couldn't wait to see you again? Because if so, I left out a word. I meant to say: I can't wait to see you *never* again."

"I'm sorry." *Why here? Why him? Couldn't I have ended up somewhere else? Like—oh, I don't know—my own bedroom?* Something was drawing her here. For some reason she could fathom even less than why he was still kicking her. "Hey, I said enough! Believe me, this is the last place I'd want to wake up."

"Old excuse, get a new one. Don't you have a home? Or a job?" He grabbed her by the arm and hauled her off the flagstone step.

"I was a T.A." As soon as she was upright, she tore out of his grip and dusted off her bottom.

He glanced at where she had her hands, then at her chest, and smirked. "T and A, huh? Makes sense."

As repulsive as the idea was, she knew his sarcasm was all bravado. *How* she knew it was still a mystery, however. "I'm so sorry to disappoint you, but T.A. stands for 'teacher's assistant.'"

"Oh. Then go play with the little snot-nosers and leave me alone."

"College students can wipe their own noses." *Usually.* "Are you this condescending to everyone?"

"Yes. Don't you have morning classes?"

"It's summer."

He looked around, squinting in the sunshine. "Ah, so it is."

When she started law school in the fall, would she still be waking up on doorsteps? *His* doorstep? *Just living the dream, aren't you, Eden?* Would his foot be her alarm clock every morning? His strong features, slicked-back hair, and athletic body be the first thing she saw? It was a great view, but not worth the attitude that came with it.

She couldn't deny her attraction to him, even as unlikable as he was, which, quite frankly, was a lot. But neither could she believe the attraction was merely sexual—he was like a magnet, one she couldn't avoid or escape from. Eventually she was going to smack into him even harder than she imagined they had during the night, thankfully, still hidden deeply in her subconscious.

And one or both of them was going to end up *very* bruised. She had to stop that from happening.

"Mitch," she said.

"No." He arched his eyebrow and shook his head as if in warning.

"What? I haven't asked you for anything yet."

"That's not my name."

"Fine. What should I call you? Dickhead?" The word left

her mouth before she could stop, her heart pounding even faster. "Sorry, I didn't mean that."

"What? Calling me a dickhead? I am one." He cocked his head to the side. "Or worse."

"True." But cursing was one of the many things she didn't do. Not that she cared when other people did, but long ago, she'd made a list of things *not* to do. A list solely based on what she hated most about her mother—sober or stoned. Not cussing was the second simplest thing on it. She'd *thought* sleeping with strangers was the first. *Huh. Perhaps it was time to look at that list again.*

"I don't cuss," she said.

"Ever?"

"Never."

"I'm not even sure 'dickhead' is a bad word. It's just two nouns stuck together to describe an asshole." His hand flew up and he pointed at her. "There you go! Asshole, try that one. Still two nouns, but 'asshole' has more punch."

"I don't cuss."

"You got some strange kind of morality going on in that head of yours, lady. Call me whatever you want. Just not 'Mitch.'"

"Fine. And it's 'Eden.' Not 'lady' and not whatever name you called me the other day."

"Chastity? That's what you told me to call you."

"No, I didn't."

"Yes, you did."

"No, I—" She clamped her mouth shut. Too bad she needed this snot-noser's help. "My name is Eden. Please call me that."

"I don't plan on calling you anything. Other than 'gone' or 'what the fuck was I thinking.'" He brushed past her and headed toward the silver Jag in the driveway.

Eden raced after him. "Mitch— Mitchell?"

He didn't stop.

"What-The-Frig-Was-I-Thinking!" she called.

He stopped and then turned toward her. He was scowling and his jaw was twitching, but he *had* stopped and turned.

"You have to help me," she said. "I'm being drawn to you."

He shook his head. "I don't owe you anything."

"She's leaving me on your doorstep every few days. You don't think that means something?"

He stepped forward so fast, he nearly knocked her off her feet. "She?"

She stumbled, but caught herself before she fell. "What?"

"You said 'she' is leaving you. *She* is leaving you on my doorstep."

"I did." It came out as a statement, not a question, as it hit her. There was another person inside her. She wasn't just sleepwalking.

"She." It sounded...right.

"You have a partner in psychosis? Someone to drop you off, then drive you home when you're done annoying people? Well, believe me—it's time to call her for a pick-up. Because I am done, I'm over-done, I'm done-r than anyone has ever been done. I hope you both have great lives"—he shook his head and crossed the driveway to his car—"somewhere far, far away."

She was bringing Eden to Mitch. And *she* must have a reason.

Unblinking, Eden watched him drive away. She kept staring at the end of the driveway long after he'd gone, her eyes dry and scratchy. Unsure what to think, what to feel, or how to react, she eventually decided it might be a good idea to walk home.

She. Well, didn't that just throw things completely out of whack? Into a whole new sort of whack, actually.

Only one more week until Carter got home. He'd take care of her, stop her from leaving the apartment, help her figure out a way to stop what seemed to be memories—that couldn't possibly be—from showing up in her head. Every day, the visions gained detail, gruesome detail, whenever they appeared. Eight more days. Eden only needed to last eight more days.

Who is she? became the mantra of the slow walk home. Days later, she was still asking the question.

CHAPTER VI

Mitch yawned as he walked through his office building's empty parking garage to his car. Fucking time zones. Fucking teleconferencing. Why do the Japanese need coaching anyway? *They are kicking our Armani-covered asses.* And he was very confident that his expertise was less than apparent after midnight. Visions of a hot shower and a soft pillow danced in his head like the sugarplums of some shit-sappy story his parents had never read to him as a child.

He dropped his briefcase next to the car and stuck his keys into the door lock before realizing that, um, yeah, he lived in this fucking century and could have started the damned thing from fifty feet away.

"Hey, Handsome." Female voice. Dark somehow. How else had he described it? Yeah—husky.

He turned toward her as she stepped into a beam of light from overhead. "You are a troubled, troubled girl, you know that?"

"Thank you." She wore a blood-red micro-mini skirt and a tight, black halter top. Hips swaying and sexy, long, curly hair bouncing, she slunk toward him like a leopard stalking its prey through the fucking Serengeti.

He fought his own urge to pounce. "For what?"

"For thinking I'm trouble."

"I didn't say—" He shoved his hands deep in his pockets. "Yes, you are trouble too. Are you here to pay your bill? Because Jolie can take care of that in the morning."

"My bill?"

"I can't think of any other reason you'd show up again. You know I'm not very nice, right?" He kept his eyes on her face, and away from the soft flesh pushing out of her top, and geared up for his most patronizing tone. "This makes two sessions. And you've now wasted sixteen minutes of my life. Since you can't replace the time, I should at least be compensated for it."

She didn't stop until she was inches away from him. Jesus, she smelled good—like lust and chocolate in just the right proportions. And her eyes were unnaturally light, a blue so fair it bordered on silver. The garage might have been dark, but he'd have to be brain dead not to know they weren't this color in his office a few days ago.

What, does she wear colored contacts as part of her harlot costume for hitting the town? "Ah, are you playing the bad girl again? I'm not interested in repeating that mistake and getting sucked deeper into this. Go find other prey. I'm sure it won't take you too long."

"I want you." Her focus wasn't on him, just his body, as she pressed closer.

He reached farther into his pocket and tried to move his cock which was now so hard, she'd be skewered if she moved another centimeter. "Not going to happen." *Ignore the pounding of your heart, Mitch. The surge of adrenaline in your veins, the almost-compulsion to be near this woman. Man up, for Christ's sake!*

"But I want you," she breathed.

"No." Just as he thought he'd never actually said that to a woman before, she grabbed his shoulders and slammed him back against his car. As he hit, the thought and word preceding it flew out of his mind. "That was unexpected."

She pressed her body against his and ran her hands roughly over his chest, yanking his tie loose.

He grabbed her wrist and pulled it off his body. She fought his movements, her bicep straining, but he was stronger. *Careful, asshole, she's dangerous.* Their eyes locked. Both of them were breathing hard—though not from the physical effort. No, this was far more primal. A need. And not an acceptable one.

He let out his breath when she took a step back. Then inhaled sharply as she slid down to her knees and nuzzled his cock through his pants. He took her head and pushed it away from him. She tugged against his grip until all he held was her hair, wrapped around his fingers.

She looked up at him and dragged her lip through her teeth. Then she leaned forward, his hands slipping to the back of her head but still pulling tightly. She let out a little gasp and the corner of her mouth lifted in a grin. Not a grimace, a grin.

Oh, shit.

She reached behind her and put one of her hands on his, guiding him, creating more tension on her hair. This time her cry was at least half moan. "That hurts," she whispered.

He didn't move. "Tell me to stop." *Oh, Christ, tell me to stop.*

"No."

He'd never let himself go there. Causing someone pain reminded him too much of Hyde's desires. Gave the bastard more power over the man. So what the hell was Mitch doing here? Handing his power over to her?

"You don't want me to stop, do you?" he asked.

"No."

"Tell me what you *do* want."

"More."

This is very bad. With his heart thundering in his chest and his cock beating against his pants trying to escape, he knew he was in trouble. What was it about this girl? Every cell in his body stretched out, begging him to follow her down the rabbit hole, and to a few other holes. '*Do it,*' they shouted. Every cell but the gray ones of his brain. Those all screamed, '*Stop!*'

"Fuck it." He went with the majority. Mitch hauled her up, one hand still fisted in her hair and the other on her arm. Without letting go, he brought her to him, slamming their bodies together. He kissed her hard, mouths already opened. Tongues dragged across teeth, teeth bit into lips. A total fucking mess of power, submission, domination, and control.

Until this moment, he hadn't realized how much he missed the connection they'd had the night they met, the freedom he'd felt. No thought, only desire. It scared the shit out of him. But it hadn't been like this—no pain, no violence. Just gratification.

He caught her tongue in between his teeth and held, hoping to stop her...to stop himself. Her muffled moan reverberated inside his mouth, bouncing off his palate and knocking out any common sense that remained.

Without breaking apart, she unclasped his belt and tugged his pants open so hard, he heard a rip as the clip popped off and the zipper's jaw yielded. His hands flew down to cover hers, stopping her from taking his cock in her beautiful little hands.

"I don't deserve this," he said, not knowing if he was being punished or shooting a 'thank you' out to the whole fucking universe.

"What does *deserving* have to do with anything? We're alive. That's the only important thing." Her smile was so beautiful it hurt him. Since he held both her hands, she stretched out a finger, tickling the head of his erection with tiny circles.

He should have stopped her. But all he felt was her hands guiding his as they drew out his belt. He should have found the strength to stop *himself* as he lifted her up, carried her to the hood of his car, and set her down, spreading her legs around his thighs. He stared into those eyes that were ice blue yet warm and open to him, wondering what the hell he was doing. He should have been stronger. Instead, he raised both of her hands and wrapped the belt around her wrists, pulling the leather tight to secure them.

She opened her legs wider, and he remembered the power she'd struggled to hold over him in his office. How much he'd enjoyed watching her fighting for it. So where was that girl now? And why the fuck wasn't he running away?

She scooted toward him, her skirt riding up. She wouldn't need to wonder where her panties were tomorrow morning—she'd left them at home already.

Until now, he'd never been in a fight he knew he'd lose. "I am a weak, weak man."

Her head tilted. "No, you're not. You're strong. That's why you were chosen. Because you're worthy."

Worthy? Me? He went numb at the word. A word he'd never expected to hear out of anyone's mouth, not about him. *Tempt not a desperate man.* Especially not a man whose inhuman side was so very close to the surface, struggling for freedom. But, damn it, in this instance they wanted the same thing, for very different reasons. Hyde wanted to fill her body, Mitch wanted *her* to fill his soul.

"Mitch?"

His emotional orgasm interrupted, he said, "Yeah?"

She crinkled up her nose. "Will you fuck me now?"

He thought about it for approximately 1.4 seconds. "Yeah." His hands dug into her hips as he pulled her closer.

"Wait," she said. "I want you behind me."

That he could do. He hauled her off the car and flipped her over, pushing her forward onto the hood.

Her bound hands were visible above her head, her fingertips white from grasping at the smooth metal. She arched her back and lifted her ass up like an offering.

With one hand on the small of her back holding her from wiggling too much, he ran the other up her inner thigh and under her skirt until he felt her wetness warm his fingers. When he moved higher, she arched even more, encouraging his hand to go back down to where it had been. He flipped her skirt up and looked at the pale perfection under his palm. He rocked his hips forwards and backwards, barely brushing himself across her ass. Every touch sent a jolt of anguish down his body—knowing he shouldn't be here but unable to stop. He could feel Hyde pushing toward the surface. What would happen if he gave the bastard what he wanted? What both of them wanted?

When he went for the condom in his wallet, she raised herself onto her elbows, pressing back into him. "She likes you, but she'd never let you have her this way."

His body clenched. "What?" He pushed her against the car and leaned in close, ignoring her moan. "What did you just say?"

"Miss Sensible Pumps. She might have the same ass, but she'd never let you use it like this."

Holy shit. What am I doing? This is all kinds of wrong. She's just some messed-up girl. Who has a great ass. And knows how to work it. How to work mine, too. Shit. He stepped back and pulled her skirt down. "Get off my car."

She turned, her breath shallow. "Do you want to go somewhere else?"

"Yes. But not with you." Mitch shoved his traitorous dick back in his pants and zipped them up as well as he could with a broken zipper and no hook. "Give me your hands. I need my belt back."

She stood frozen in front of him, her head tilted. "But you want me."

He caught her wrists before she twisted them away and unwound the belt. "I don't know why you are torturing me like this, but it's beyond old now. Go home. No, better yet, go check yourself into a psychiatric center." The keys were still hanging from the door. Mitch yanked them out and slid into the seat, tossing his belt and briefcase into the back.

He stopped. *This girl is going to get ripped apart acting like this. Fuck, imagine me being the good guy.* "Get in, I'll take you."

"Where?" She walked around to the other side of the car.

"To the asylum."

Her eyes looked like blue-diamond solitaires surrounded by some freaked-out whites, and she bolted.

Mitch jumped out to run after her, thought better of it, and got back in, slamming the door and driving in the direction she'd run. *Okay, probably wasn't the best moment for sarcasm.* Two hours later, he was still canvassing alleys, side streets, and parking lots. He gave up looking at dawn.

CHAPTER VII

"This had better be important."

"Common courtesy states that you should say hello before making any rude comments when someone calls you."

"And protocol states that our communications should be via email, so what do you want?"

"*Your* girl visited *my* boy last night."

"Did they have intercourse? What forms were they in?"

"Oh, so now you're glad I called."

"Answer the question."

"Questions. Multiple. No, they didn't have sex. Almost, but not quite. He was human, she wasn't."

"That's not good enough. Their union should be encouraged. However, we are considering the possibility that one or both of them are less fertile in their transformed states."

"So what do you want me to do about it? Get Chastity to stand on her head after they screw? Maybe I could hold her ankles for her." *It would give me a chance to slam the bitch's head into the floor a few times, too.*

"I find no humor in that suggestion."

As if he found humor anywhere. "Oh, I know. Why don't I suggest something that seems to work for millions of unhappy teenage girls—doing it in the backseat of a car?"

"The subjects should be encouraged to copulate in their human forms."

"Gosh, that sounds so romantic. I can just see it now: 'Hey, Mitchell. I'd like to encourage you to copulate with the little bitch while she's her goody-goody self, and not the bad girl who throws herself at you all the time.' Great idea, boss."

"If you are unable to do what is required, I'm sure we can find someone who can."

Prick. "You made *her* virtuous and *him* into exactly the type of man a good girl would never give it up to. And I'm supposed to get them together? No one could do that."

"As I'm sure you've noticed, Turner is a highly attractive male. Obviously, part of her seeks him out. All you have to do is get her *other* part to agree."

But he's mine. "Yeah, easy-peasy. I'll see what I can do."

-ɅⱯⱯ-

That girl was driving Mitch nuts. He spent the weekend cursing his life. And everyone left in it. And everyone he'd ever come into contact with. Until, bright and early Monday morning, someone came crashing through his waiting room like a bat outta hell. Damn it, he'd have to take a break.

The next thing he heard was Jolie shouting, "Don't go in there!"

Very professional. When his office door opened, he understood Jolie's sentiment. He pushed his chair back from his desk and stood. "Get out!"

The woman, whatever her name was today, marched in. Her hair was in a ponytail and she was dressed in some fashion house's Demure, Dull, and Dowdy Daywear Line, but he didn't have to see her ass to recognize her. Sadly, his cock didn't either. *I have no fucking control here. When did that happen?* He lowered himself into his chair to hide his groin.

"Please, you have to help me," she said.

"Should I call the detective, Mitchell?"

He blinked, refocusing to see Jolie at the door. "No, not him." Then back to the troublemaker. "Get out before I call security."

"Why would you call security?" she asked, bewildered.

"Because there is no way in hell I'm ever coming close to you again after Friday night."

Her brow furrowed. "Ooh-kaaay. I have no idea what you are talking about, but that's not why I'm here."

"Why are you here? To punish me?" Jesus, he'd just recovered from her last visit. He would never be comfortable walking through that parking garage again.

"No, but I guess I could give it a try?" The pitch of her voice rose and her face looked like someone had taken a crayon to it and colored in the lines with confusion. "But only after you help me."

"Why me?" He put his hands together in a pyramid and looked up to a God who always seemed to screen his calls.

"That's what you do, isn't it? Help people? I'll even pay you this time."

"Mitchell? Should I call someone?" Jolie asked.

"No. She'll leave, won't you?"

"Um…no."

"It's fine, Jolie. She'll leave when *I'm* through with her."

Jolie rolled her eyes as she left, shutting the door behind her. Mitch stared at the woman, considering how to permanently get rid of her. Rudeness hadn't worked, putdowns, condescension, sardonicism. Christ, what was left?

Hell, she's a crazy person. One should ignore crazy people. Especially people with as much crazy as she has. He dropped his eyes to his desk, having forgotten what he was working on.

She was impossible to ignore. "Do you do any other kind of stuff for people trying to get their lives together? You know, like those 'You can be anything you want to be' or 'You're strong enough to do anything' kinds of things?"

He slowly brought his gaze back to her face. "Do you honestly think I would say any of those things to anyone?"

"No." She shifted her weight from one long, shapely leg to another. "But you help people be stronger, right? Decide what they need to do...to get their act together?"

"Stop stammering and get to the point."

"I want you to hypnotize me. You do that, right? I know today is usually your 'Ice Cream for Orphans' day, but I thought...since you're here..."

"Why?"

"Why are you here?" She shrugged. "I don't know. If I had to venture a guess, it would be because you ran out of either ice cream or people to treat like crap."

"Why do you want me to hypnotize you?"

She took a deep breath and squared her shoulders. "Because I think I'm going crazy, and I need you to find out if I am. Saturday morning I woke up at my house—"

"What a *crazy* coincidence—so did I."

"While you are oh-so-very amusing, I seriously doubt that your front door was..." Her mouth twitched like it had something to say, but needed time to find the words. She'd already wasted enough of his time.

"Your front door was what? Open? Covered in take-out ads? What?"

She mumbled something that might have been, "Torn apart," but Mitch couldn't make it out. He waited for her to say something that made sense.

Her pause was a long one. "I think there are two of me."

Maybe the asylum idea shouldn't have been a joke. He ran a hand over his face. "What are you talking about?"

She wrung her hands as she spoke, her expression a mixture of confusion, discomfort, and determination. "I think that, in my head, there's *me*. And there's *her*. Two of us."

He studied her. She was tough—he'd give her that. Putting up with him wasn't easy. Two of her? Thinking back to the two sides she'd shown him, the theory that she could be divided like he was passed through his mind but didn't stick. Nah, no one was like him. No one. Especially not *her*. She was too nice, too *good*. No, this one was just a screwed up little girl with daddy issues. But what if...?

"Why me?" he asked.

"Because I trust you." She blinked. "Well, no. That's *totally* not true. But you've met her, and you won't be surprised. You know her. I don't."

"I only know that you seem to enjoy being one person and then another." He gave her a thumbs-up sign and a shit-eating grin. "Loads of fun."

"You still think I'm faking? I'm not faking, I'm crazy!"

He agreed in part, but crazy people don't know they're crazy. Usually. "You're not crazy. You're just young and in need of some serious help."

"That's why I'm here! Do you think it's easy for me to ask? I went to a doctor after we...met, and he completely blew me off. He told me I shouldn't watch TV before bed, that it will pass. But it *won't* pass. So I'm asking the last person in the entire world I want to ask. You. Will you please help me?" Pain, manifesting itself as tears, dripped down her cheeks.

No, he couldn't *let* himself. Mitch swallowed, afraid of what she might do to him, to his life. "Stop it. Go buy a diary," he forced out, tapping his pen on the desk. "If you really think you have multiple personalities, you should go see the psychiatrist."

"I can't," she whispered, dropping her head forward. "I think she may have killed someone."

Mitch froze. "You what?"

"I think she may have killed someone and, if I go to the shrink, she'll have to tell. They'll just lock me up in a psychiatric center or prison. I have to know...one way or the other. Then, if I *know* I did it, I'll turn myself in to the police. I promise."

"I'm really not interested in your ethical dilemma. Why do you think you…*she* killed someone?"

"I'm having visions. Images of walking around. Doing things. Doing"—she wrapped her arms around herself—"you. But it's not me, it's like I'm having out-of-body experiences."

Kind of sounds familiar, doesn't it, Mitch? No, damn it. That's impossible. "When you're having these 'experiences,' are you on drugs?"

She flipped her head up and shook it. Once. "I don't do drugs."

"Then they're dreams."

"They aren't dreams, I'm awake. They're like…flashbacks."

Mitch had flashbacks—the cage, the bars, the ceiling, sometimes of Jolie, but none of the night Shelly died. "And you've had flashbacks of killing someone?"

"No. Not the actual killing, but seeing a woman's body, her face, her blood. Then, when I woke up on Saturday, I found another note. In the same handwriting as the napkin I showed you, except this time it was written on a newspaper article. I don't *get* the newspaper, Mitch. I don't." She shivered. "It said, 'Mitch can help,' above a picture of the woman from my visions."

"What woman?" His heartbeat sped up…

"Her name was Shelly DuPont. She was murdered about six months ago at her brother's house somewhere in Lighthouse Point."

…and then it dropped. *Holy, hell.* After their father died, Shelly had used their mother's maiden name, but Mitch kept his father's, to remind him where his evil had come from. "You think you saw her murder."

"I don't know. I thought that you could help me see more. Please," she begged.

If he could get into her mind, would he see one like his?

He'd never thought of hypnotism as a tool for himself. Never had anyone he trusted enough who could do it. Never thought of teaching Shelly or Jolie how.

"Fine," he said, his mouth suddenly dry.

Her chest rose and fell with a deep breath. "Really? You'll help?"

"And then you'll leave."

She nodded. "Then I'll leave. Just ask her about what I'm seeing. She'll tell you. She seems to like you. Well, either you or your doorstep."

"Yeah, she told me something similar about you the last time I saw her." Christ, did he actually just say 'she'?

"You saw her again? She came to you? Did you...?"

"Fuck her? No. I don't play with women who have more issues than I do. Not twice, anyway. Why do you think she likes me?"

"Really?" She crossed the room and sat down. "If you're fishing for a compliment right now, it's not going to happen."

Yeah, that was a stupid question. "Make yourself comfortable."

She leaned back, her head resting on the top of the couch, her legs crossed.

He moved a chair close to her and sat down. "You're sure about this?"

Her eyes were large and scared. "Yeah. I can trust you, can't I?"

He took his time before answering. Could she? No. He could barely trust himself. At least not when *she* was around. He'd do it, find out if she knew something about Shelly's death, and then kick her the hell out of his life before it was too late. If it wasn't already too late.

"Only for this," he said. "Not anything else, you understand? You should *not* trust a man like me."

"Okay." Taking a quick breath and exhaling slowly, she folded her hands together and put them on her lap. "What do I do?"

He looked around for something shiny she could focus on. He picked up a shit-stupid award he'd gotten for being a bang-up guy and looked at the bottom. Yeah, it'd work.

He stuck his head out of his office. "Jolie, don't bother me for a little while."

She looked up at him and rolled her eyes, still holding the phone to her ear, and mouthed, '*How long*?'

He shrugged. "When's my next appointment?"

She looked at her watch, said, "I will give him the message," into the phone and hung up. "You have thirty minutes until Mr. Somners comes."

"That'll do." He slammed the door on her irritated expression.

Turning back to his pro-bono client, he said, "I shouldn't be the one to do this. A lot of people are better at it than I am."

"Are you better at it on Wednesdays?" Eden asked with a nervous grin.

"What?"

"Wednesdays are your 'Come Get Hypnotized' days, right?"

Huh, she actually listened to the bullshit that came out of his mouth. That was new. "I lie. A lot."

She nodded. "That's not terribly surprising. But if you can do it, I want you to."

"I've only done it a few times, mostly as a parlor trick, so I may not be able to get you under."

"Well, thanks for trying."

"Don't thank me yet." He sighed and then went through the steps—carefully explaining what he would be doing, what she should expect to happen, and a few of the questions he would ask.

CHAPTER VIII

They didn't teach hypnosis in college, at least not the one he'd gone to. He'd figured it out with how-to manuals, obsessed with how the brain works—conscious and subconscious thought. He'd practiced on classmates. Much to the frustration of the few male friends he'd had back then, he drew the line on the nearside of a con to get into girls' pants. He preferred his women conscious, not to mention responsive. But all that had been years ago.

Sure hope to hell I remember how to do this.

He kept his voice slow and melodic as he led her step by step into a deep relaxation. Understandably, it took a little while before her muscles started to release and her eyes closed. Even *he* wouldn't dare get too comfortable around a guy like him. But, once she let go, she seemed very susceptible. It was almost too easy.

Okay, looks good so far. Now what to ask. "Who are you?"

"Eden. Colfax." Her voice was dull, emotionless, empty.

Mitch wasn't sure what conclusion he'd be happy with—that she was faking the whole thing, was on drugs, was suffering from multiple personality disorder, or that she was divided like him. No, definitely not the last one, that was for damn sure. He'd never wish that on anyone. But she was right—something was bringing them together. He didn't believe in coincidences, just really fucking awful karma. You get what you give.

He decided to start with some easy questions to verify that she was really under before he got to the tough stuff. "What color is your underwear?"

She didn't answer right away, but there was no telltale blush on her cheeks he assumed would've shown up if she was awake. "Pink."

Yeah, that sounded about right for her. Pink. Interesting. Strangely, also a turn-on. *Focus, moron.* "Tell me about your parents."

"I don't have parents."

"Are they dead?"

"My mother is. I don't know about my father."

"Do you do drugs?" He watched her face for any reaction, but it was peaceful, beautiful even.

"Never."

"Who is Chastity?"

"I don't know."

"Do you really believe you've been sleepwalking?"

"Yes."

He rubbed his palms together. "Okay. How many times have you woken up in a different place from where you went to sleep?"

She paused, and he wondered if she was counting.

Shit, he was doing this wrong. "Has it happened a lot?"

"Yes."

"Aside from being in a different location, how do you know?"

"I see flashes of doing things, like memories that never were."

He took a deep breath. *Now comes the hard stuff.* "Picture what the woman you saw looked like. Where she was. Where *you* were. Can you see it?"

"Yes."

"Good. Tell me what you see."

"She is in a doorway, leaning against the side, sleeping."

Sleeping? He wiped his forehead. "What does she look like?"

"Long hair. Black or close to it. Pale skin. Red shirt."

Mitch didn't know if Shelly had been wearing red that day. Everything in the memory seared into his brain was red. Blood red. But he didn't know how much of that was real.

"Is there anyone else there?"

"Yes. Another woman. Pretty. Wearing a green shirt and tan pants. High heels." That could have been Jolie.

"Anyone else?"

"A man. But she can't see his face."

She?

Before he could ask which 'she' Eden was speaking of, she spoke again. "His face is hidden by the bushes in front of her. His body is tucked in towards the sleeping woman."

Me. That was me. Or him, maybe. No, he needed her to go back further. "Go back a bit. To before the woman was…sleeping. What do you—does *she*—see?"

"The pictures are all jumbled. I don't know which comes first. She saw the sidewalk, stores, the house, the lawn. I think she went around the side, but I don't know why."

She twitched. Then a full-body jerk and a whimper.

He leaned forward and held her hand, ignoring the current he felt as their skin touched. "Eden, you're okay. You're safe. Nothing bad is going to happen." He squeezed her hand, stroking the back of it. His stomach dipped as he thought, *Please, don't let anything bad happen to her.* He dropped her hand and sprang back from her, his heart beating a rhythm foreign to him. *Focus.*

"Tell me what you're seeing," he said, adjusting himself further back in the chair.

"Nothing. All she sees is the woman sleeping. They can't wake her up," she said, shaking her head.

He was nauseous. "Did you touch the woman? To make her go to sleep?"

"I can't see it, don't know if she moved. It's just flashes. But I don't think so."

No matter what questions he asked, what way he phrased them, she didn't—or couldn't—answer differently.

He lifted his hands off the arms of the chair. They were sweaty and stiff from gripping so tightly. She'd picked the wrong person to come to for help. The one person who would've given anything for a 'yes' answer. So he'd be able to pass his guilt off onto someone else.

After a few more questions that got him nowhere, he said, "Tell me about the other flashbacks. How they appear and what you see."

For ten more minutes, she spoke of broken images, random people, various places, but nothing tangible or even truly understandable.

As far as he could tell, and Eden seemed to know, she wasn't a murderer. If she knew more than she was saying, he didn't know how to get it out of her. She'd seen something— Jolie, Shelly. Maybe Hyde, maybe him. But did that mean she'd *done* anything?

He needed to think. To know. One way or the other. His hope that she'd been involved wasn't enough. There was definitely some freaked-out shit going on here—her use of pronouns was too messed up to be normal.

Multiple personalities. Had to be. Could another personality be responsible for Shelly's death? Could he keep Eden close enough to figure it out? He needed to keep his mouth shut until he could figure it out, keep her guessing. But that would also mean she'd be close enough to cause more problems with Hyde. *Fuck.*

Ready to bring her back into consciousness, he stopped to look at her. She was so relaxed and peaceful, as if she was just taking a nap. As if they were regular people. Sitting on his couch as if she was his.

Whoa, where'd that come from? He wasn't that guy. He wasn't even the kind of guy to be satisfied with a quick peek into a stranger's medicine cabinet. No, he was the kind of guy who picks the lock, empties all the bottles onto the counter, pockets the good ones—with zero intention of actually taking them—and then puts all the rest back into the wrong bottles. *That* was him. Who he made sure he was. Who he forced himself to be.

But she trusted him. Okay, fine. He wouldn't try to lay down some fucked-up posthypnotic suggestion just to mess with her. That would be immature. Instead, he'd just ask her *one* inappropriate question. *One.*

"Go back to the night at my house. Do you remember us being together?"

"Yes."

He knew it. She hadn't slept through that. Okay, did he say *one* question? He'd meant two. "What do you see? Feel?"

"Afraid."

He swallowed. He couldn't stop there. *Three questions, just three.* "Why are you afraid?"

"I don't know how she got here. Why I woke up in your bed. What you did."

Four. "So, I don't scare you?"

"No. You're mean, but you don't scare me."

Understandable. "Go back a bit earlier. What else do you see? Feel?" He lost count what number he was up to.

"How you look. Peaceful. How I feel. Disgusted."

"Why do you feel disgusted?"

"Because I wish being here had been my decision, but it wasn't." Her breath hiccupped. "Carter's going to be so upset."

"Who's—?" Nah, he'd used up all his questions. And he really shouldn't be doing this to her. He had a conscience. He just tried very hard to ignore it most of the time. It won this round.

If only she'd stop mumbling about some guy named

Carter.

Bringing her out of hypnosis, he made sure she would feel relaxed, peaceful...and forget those last few questions he'd asked. It wouldn't work, but...

Here's to hoping.

Damn it, why did he even *care*?

━╢╴╟━╢╴╟━

Eden opened her eyes, the weight of her relaxation still gently molding her body to the couch. Mitch was staring at her, his eyes soft. A wave of connection passed between them. Like a warm bath after a winter rainstorm. She soaked in it, gaining the strength he offered.

What would he do if he *knew* how he was looking at her? So peaceful, accepting, open. Did he know that he was showing her his soul? That she could see it in his expression— in the warmth of his eyes, the slight tilt of his head, the tiny curve of his mouth?

No, he didn't—he couldn't. He was dangerous. Not dangerous *to* her, dangerous *for* her. She shouldn't get too close. He'd warned her time and time again. She shouldn't be feeling like—

"So?" she whispered, blinking, wondering how deeply into her *he* had seen.

He looked surprised when she broke eye contact, then confused as if *he* were the one who'd been hypnotized. "Nothing. It didn't work. It was just you." He stood quickly and turned away from her. "And you didn't admit to murder. You can go now."

"I don't remember very much—just a few images. Is that normal?" she asked, ignoring his oh-so-polite dismissal.

"As normal as anything is about this situation," he grumbled. "It depends on the person and the emotional connection they have with what we discuss."

Emotional connection? Great. Of all people, she'd told

him things she was emotionally connected to. *That's just great.* She felt her cheeks warm. "So what did we 'discuss'?"

"Your honor is intact. I didn't ask any embarrassing questions about how you lost your virginity. I stuck to the topic."

Thank God.

"You fall asleep, and then you wake up. The flashbacks are just random sights, but nothing about actually murdering anyone. Maybe you're right. Maybe you're sleepwalking."

Then why did she end up at his house so often? Why was she finding notes saying he could help if he couldn't?

She was on her own again. "Thanks for trying." She unfolded her legs and stood. "Just—"

"What?" The impatience was back in his voice and his expression.

Feeling the heat of her cheeks intensify, she said, "If she comes to see you again, please don't sleep with her."

He saluted. "Request granted."

Eden had her hand on the doorknob when he called out, "Oh. You can be anything you want to be! And you're strong enough to do anything!" And then he laughed.

"You're a jerk."

"Absolutely."

"Just when I thought you were human," she said, sighing.

"Who's Carter?"

Eden stopped the door from opening and looked back at him. "Carter? How do you know about Carter?"

"You mentioned him while you were under."

"Carter's my..." *My what, Eden? My best friend who wishes I felt for him more than I ever could? My roommate who needs to move on and find someone else to love because I never will, at least not in the way he deserves?* She swallowed. "Carter's my boyfriend. What did I say about him?"

"You kept repeating, 'He's good.'"

"Oh. Well, he is…good."

"Then make sure he keeps you in at night."

Eden looked at him one last time before she left. The wall he hid behind was even thicker than hers. But she'd seen through it, catching a glimpse of the man who was trapped on the other side. Had she let Mitch into her in the same way? No. If Carter couldn't get through, no one could.

CHAPTER IX

Mitch sat on his desk after she'd gone, wondering why his heart had clenched when she'd said the word 'boyfriend.' *Damn it, I better not be getting soft.* He'd been soft once. For him, it had ended badly.

For his father, it had simply *ended*.

Mitch still felt the blood on his hands. He always would. Even though the world was better off without his father in it, no longer able to terrorize his family or anyone else he came in contact with. And the lesson Mitch had learned was twofold. First, he'd learned that dear ole Dad had passed down his tainted gene for evil, and, second, that the only way to control that evil was to let it out early and often. Before it had time to build up. Lash out at people verbally, so Hyde wouldn't hurt anyone physically.

Mitch had spent the last fifteen years of his life making a conscious effort to keep people away. The more human he let himself be, the harder it was to keep Hyde quiet. It was all about control.

Every waking moment. Every glare, putdown, and sarcastic comment he put out into the world kept Hyde under control. Vent it out slowly, every day, so Hyde would only be able to break loose once a month. Never be kind. Never be empathetic. It was the only way people would be safe. Well, *that* and the cage.

He thought of Shelly—how she'd understood what he was, why he acted the way he did. Despite all of it, she'd loved him. And he'd repaid her by layering her blood on top of their father's. He covered his face with his hands, smothering himself in *her* memory and *his* guilt.

Jolie poked her head into his office. "Mitchell?"

He jerked up straight. "What?"

"Geez, take it easy. I just wanted to ask what that was all about."

He'd have thought she'd know better than to ask. But no, her pert, little nose seemed to have an abundance of initiative lately. "She's a kid. Needs help. I tried. Unsuccessfully. The end."

"Be careful with the good-guy act, Mitchell. We both know what a bad idea that would be."

"Indeed we do. But, seeing as you're the only person here for me to lay into, are you sure *now* was a good time to remind me?"

She rolled her eyes. "Fine. You can 'lay into' me later. But only if you take me out for an expensive dinner first."

"Nice," he said, smiling. "Although, in case you don't remember, we tried that. It didn't work out." It had been a long, long time ago, and they'd both gotten over it—him about sixty seconds after he told her, her...who knew? But she'd moved on.

He took a deep breath and reclined in his chair. "What's next? Another psycho for me to deal with?"

She pursed her lips together. "Actually...Leanne keeps calling. I'm guessing the detective spoke to her. Now she wants to speak to you."

"Fantastic. Thanks for telling him about her, by the way." The sarcasm rolled off his tongue so easily. "That was sweet."

"FYI, I'm saving your ass here, so a little appreciation

wouldn't be out of line."

"What does 'FYI' mean?" He smiled. *Damn, that was fun.*

Her eyes flashed in frustration before narrowing into a glare.

"Phone's ringing," he said.

She looked behind her, obviously so focused on being pissed off she'd missed it. "We're not done with this."

"Didn't think we would be." *Or ever will be.* Her lie, her continued lying, bound them together in a way he was extremely uncomfortable with. "Hey, Jolie," he called out as she went to her desk. "Call someone about the intercom system again."

The call rang through to his office. He hated not getting a heads-up about who was calling but supposed it was better than her sticking her nose into his office every time someone called or came in.

He sat back and pressed the flashing button. *Good things—flashing buttons. Very clear.* "Mitchell Turner."

"Mitchell, it's me."

Yes, he recognized the voice. A woman. Not clear enough. "Ah-ha," he said, remembering Jolie's comment and the attitude she'd left his office with. "Leanne. What do you want?"

"Why did you sic the cops on me, Mitchell? I didn't do anything to you."

"*Lately*, Leanne. You didn't do anything to me *lately*."

She paused.

He wondered how much time it would take for her brain to start functioning again. "It was great talking to you again, Leanne. Take care." He lowered the phone to hang it up, which was good because she started yelling so loudly his eardrum would have burst had the receiver still been near his head. He ignored the nonsense she was spewing and spoke loudly and firmly, not really caring if she understood him.

"Leanne. I didn't tell the cops about you. But the police report—that I didn't file—is public record. Not to mention they only had to walk down the hallway to find it at the station. If you believe"—*like I do, but don't want to*—"that you've done nothing wrong this time, it won't hurt for them to ask you some questions. Then we can both get on with our lives. Separately. FYI"—he kind of hoped Jolie heard that part—"This is not an invitation back into my life. You're on your own. Don't call again." Then he slammed the receiver down onto the cradle and yelled into the waiting room, "Thanks, Jolie."

Was it possible that Leanne or the girl had been involved in the murder? Jesus, that would be good. Shelly and her baby were already dead, the damage done. But if it hadn't been his fault? Yeah, that would be really fucking good. He'd be able to grieve without the guilt. He'd had no memories, no images of Hyde killing her. Hell, maybe this detective would be smart enough to figure out what Mitch couldn't. *Yeah, either way it'd be really fucking good.*

CHAPTER X

Eden pored through old biology and freshman psychology textbooks, scoured the Internet, and thought more about her mother than she had in years. The research gave her no rationale for what was happening to her. Her mother had died when Eden was eight and before that hadn't spent much time sober. She'd never known if her mother's erratic behavior was due to a mental illness or the drugs.

Her mother had been involved in some kind of trial, some kind of treatment center, but Eden had always assumed it was for the drugs. What if it wasn't? Maybe her mother had passed down a form of mental illness. But nothing made sense.

Nothing felt true.

When her head was close to imploding, she quit thinking about it. Carter would be home in a few hours. Not that he would know anything more than she did, but at least she could count on him to keep her safe at night.

She checked the arrival times on the airline's website obsessively. Then, after the flight info switched from "in transit" to "landed," she started pacing, silently cursing the driver of the shuttle van bringing Carter home so slowly and dragging out her anticipation.

Her heart lifted when she heard the click of the door lock. *Thank God, he's back.*

Carter walked in with a question on his face, turning the doorknob on both sides. He studied the door the apartment building's superintendent had fixed with duct tape.

"I'm glad to be home, but what happened to the door?" he asked.

She didn't answer—she was too busy staring at him. He looked older, tanner, more mature. Since he'd only been gone about three weeks, her perception could have been playing with her mind. But he looked more manly, like someone who could keep her demons at bay. His blond hair was still shorter than she liked it, a requirement of his dream job, the one he could never have. He'd cut his hair before he knew he would never be allowed into the Police Officer Training Program. Until he could prove his epilepsy was under control, he was ineligible. And he was running out of medications he could afford to try.

So he'd changed course and gone to school aiming for something unsatisfying but similar. Unfortunately, the Crime Tech Department had nearly the same physical requirements as the police academy, including the bad haircut. Crew cut aside, he was still gorgeous. And the years of physical preparation for his eventual disappointment had made his shoulders broad, his chest hard, and his hips slender. He probably didn't mind the female attention his physique garnered.

Six years was a long time to be celibate. It worked for her, but she assumed he found comfort in other women's arms. Or legs. Or other parts.

Shaking off the thought, she jumped into his embrace, throwing her arms around him. He dropped his bag and grabbed her before they both fell over.

"Geez, Eden! It's good to see you too." He laughed into her hair and held her tighter than she deserved.

"I missed you!" Pressed up against him, she felt a spike of

heat in her core. That was new, uncomfortable. Could that have changed too? Did she...*want* him?

Carter carried her to the couch and set her down, then sat down beside her. "I missed you too, babe."

With the separation of their bodies, the sensation disappeared. Maybe she'd been wrong—maybe she was just happy to see him in a totally platonic way. Yeah, that was probably it. "Liar. You were too busy to miss me."

"Never." He pushed a lock of her hair off her cheek, brushed his fingers along her jawline—somehow a motion too intimate for the relationship they shared.

She didn't want to push him away, but she couldn't help scooting back a little and folding her legs in front of her, creating needed space between them. "How'd you have time to get a tan? I would've thought they'd keep you in a lab, bent over a microscope the whole time."

"What can I say, after three weeks in the Florida Keys? You get tan just walking from microscope to microscope." He laughed.

"Well, you look great," she said, her eyes roaming over him.

He blushed.

"So what was it like?" she asked. "Tell me everything, but leave out the boring bits."

He shrugged. "That doesn't really leave much to tell. Training. Books. Lectures. Lots of yelling and putdowns for reasons I still don't understand. Very military-esque. How about you?"

Her insides froze while she struggled to not let it show on the outside. "Well..."

"You haven't been sleeping, have you?" Cradling her face in both hands, he ran a thumb under her eye, studying her. "What's going on?" He always saw right through her.

Darn it. "Well." She bit her lip, took his hands from her face, and held them. "I kind of started sleepwalking again. I think I've been— No, I *know* I've been going outside."

He grimaced. "Yikes."

She tilted her head back and forth like it was no big deal. "Yeah. I woke up somewhere kinda bad." *Kinda bad, Eden? Really? Is that the best way to describe it?*

"Where?"

She took a deep breath. "Don't be mad because it wasn't deliberate. I was sleepwalking…or something like it." *Oh yeah, that was a great set-up.*

His eyes grew and his mouth opened as if he was planning on eventually using it, but had forgotten how.

Don't think, just spill. Get it out fast, like ripping off a Band-Aid. "I woke up with a man. I don't know how. Or why. But somehow I met him"—her heart was now emulating the same rhythm as when she'd actually been in Mitch's bedroom—"Well, maybe 'met' is the wrong word because I didn't actually *meet* him now did I? Since I was asleep." Little smile—a lousy attempt at making this an amusing little anecdote. "In a club. That I don't remember going to. And it seems we went to his house and…" *Oh God, please don't make me say the rest.*

While she'd been speaking, or blabbering, his body had stiffened and pulled away from her. "Is this some kind of joke?"

Should she have started with a joke? Give him a giggle before dropping the bomb? *Dang it.* She hid her face behind her hands and noticed the sweat on her palms. "Sadly, no."

"You *sleep-screwed* some guy?"

Nausea hit her like a ton of bricks. "I believe so, yes," she whispered.

"That's the truth? You were asleep the whole time?"

She peeked out between her fingers. His expression was that of someone who was desperately trying to believe the unbelievable. Which she could understand—she felt the same way. "Let's go with 'not consciously.' But yes, I swear to you. That is the truth."

"And he was a stranger?"

She nodded from behind her hands.

"Once."

"One night. But it seemed like we...um..." Did he really need a tally of how many condoms they'd actually gone through? Yes, because not telling all the truth was the same as lying. "There was evidence of mult—"

Carter threw up his hands to stop her. "One *night*, right?"

She swallowed, thankful he didn't want to know every gory detail. "Yes."

He sighed and looked away, rubbing his hands together then running them through his hair and resting them behind his head. "Are you alright?"

Her shoulders dropped with her hands. "You believe me?"

He nodded. His mouth was still tight as if he was having trouble with it, but really, could she ask him to be totally normal after a confession like that? "Unless you're a totally different Eden, I believe you. You don't lie."

She stared at him with her mouth slightly open. His reaction was so fast, so perfect, she almost couldn't believe it was true. "You're right: I don't lie, and *you*, Carter, are magnificent."

He smirked. "Be that as it may, I'm never letting you out of my sight again. Got it?"

"I would expect nothing less." She tackled him again and held on to the best man she'd ever known, and who she'd never deserve. It felt like dreading a dentist appointment for weeks, and then that morning, the receptionist calls you to tell you the doc has to reschedule.

Although, after hanging up, you realize you now have another few weeks of anxiety.

She'd tell him about waking up on Mitch's doorstep later.

CHAPTER XI

Jolie cursed when she saw the caller ID. He wasn't supposed to call her, *she* was supposed to call *him*. Now she knew how *her* boss felt. "Welcome home, Carter." She stifled a laugh.

"Eden's been sleepwalking. Is that supposed to happen?"

Jolie kept her voice low. The door to Mitchell's office was closed, but she couldn't take any chances. "No. Did she drink the milk you left for her?"

"She tossed it because she thought it had gone bad."

Probably the serum's fault. She sighed. "You shouldn't have left."

"Going to the police academy training was part of our arrangement. You set it up, for shit's sake." The carrot. All he had to do was keep dosing the girl and he got a free pass into the police academy. The Clinic provided a new health history and gave him the meds he needed. No records. No fuss. But leaving to do some stupid police scuba-diving course shouldn't have happened.

"I did my part," he grumbled.

"Not if she didn't drink the milk, you didn't."

"Do you have any idea how long I have been giving her that medicine? I left for a couple weeks—with *your* okay—

and it all goes to hell. You *said* she would be alright."

"She's fine, isn't she? Alive and well?"

"Alive, yes. Well? Not really. She's freaking out because she doesn't remember anything. But she woke up in some guy's bed. Eden wouldn't do that. She wouldn't." His voice was tinged with panic. It was like dealing with a toddler who'd lost his sippy cup. "Why did she do that? What's going on, Jolie?"

"You need to calm down. They don't know, but they're looking into it. They'll figure it out, don't worry. But don't give her anything until they've decided what happens next."

"I'm worried about her. Maybe I should tell her what's wrong with her."

You have no idea what's wrong with her, kid. "No, do not do that. She won't understand. Even if she did, how do you think she'd feel about you lying to her for so long about the"—she stopped herself before she used the correct word with him—"*medicine* or about your career path? Do you think she'd just forget about it and throw you a party for getting into the police academy?"

He didn't respond.

"Listen. You are helping, okay? We are all trying to figure out what's happening. But if you tell her about the *medicine*, she might not take it anymore and then who knows what she'll do. This is for her own good." The lies came out so easily. "If her behavior changes again, don't do anything other than call me. If she wants to leave the apartment, don't try to stop her. Just call me. Right away. I will take care of her from there. Got it?"

"I guess so." His words were eased out of him as he settled back into his necessary denial. He took a breath. "When can I see you?"

"Soon. Call me if she changes."

And I will babysit the bitch.

"Oh, Christ. We agreed that you'd leave me alone. How'd you forget after only a couple of days?" He was kicking her again. Probably enjoying himself too.

She scooted away from his feet.

"Oh, right," he said. "Short-term memory loss. Got it. Next time, at least bring me some breakfast."

Ignoring his attitude was becoming almost second nature to her. "Why do I always end up here?"

"Because you have some *serious* issues. Ones that I can't help you with."

She got up and followed him to his car, keeping her gaze away from his hips. Which didn't stop her mouth from watering—he had magnificent shoulders. What the heck? Was she in heat? "Wait up! There has to be a reason why she keeps coming to you. What's happening to me?"

"No idea. Leave me alone."

"Did you see her last night? How'd I get onto your doorstep?" She wouldn't cry. She wouldn't. The last time she'd cried in front of him had given her chills. Worse than the disgust he'd shown at her tears, for a moment, she'd seen misery in his eyes. Not going to happen again. "Please. I don't know what to do."

He stopped without turning. "It's called 'somnambulism.' Not common in adults, but it happens."

"This isn't just sleepwalking. I sleepwalked when I was a teenager, this is more than that. Way more."

"Ah, two years out of your teens and look how wise you are."

"Five. I'm five years out of my teens."

"Pardon my rudeness, I should have guessed. Seeing how well-adjusted you are."

She had to walk around him to see his eyes, which seemed to be very interested in his feet. "If I don't figure this out, I'm just going to end up like a newspaper—on your welcome mat every morning...Grandpa." Eye contact. Finally, an insult that bothered him.

"Did you just call me Grandpa?" He sighed and scrubbed his face with his hands. "Are you schizophrenic? Have anxiety? Migraines? Tourette syndrome? Depression? Are you on any medications?"

Eden shook her head in rhythm to his questions. "That's quite a list. Do you have a lot of experience with sleepwalkers?"

"None, but I know how to use WebMD."

"You looked it up for me?" Wow, the man actually had the ability to be considerate. Though he could certainly use more practice at it.

"No. For *me*. Needed to know what kind of stalker I was dealing with. Do you use recreational drugs?"

"Ne-ver," she said, cutting the word in two with a machete.

"Then it's D.I.D."

"D.I.D.? No, I'm not a multiple personality."

"Oh, well since you seem to know all of the things you are *not*, why don't you use that big brain of yours to figure out what you *are*."

"I can use WebMD too. People with dissociative identity disorder don't have flashbacks of what their other personalities have done. Nor do they get…" Her voice trailed off into nothing with the knowledge there was no way she could tell him without receiving a mountain of ridicule and humiliation in return.

"Spit it out already. My attention span doesn't reach full capacity before ten-thirty."

She willed him not to laugh. It wouldn't work, but she willed it anyway. "Nor do they get superhuman strength."

See? Didn't work. His laugh reached Cleveland. "So you're superhuman now, are you? Cool. Do you have x-ray vision, too? What color's my underwear?"

"I'm not talking about x-ray vision."

"Obviously not. Or you'd know I don't wear underwear. You're a terrible superhero."

"Does anyone find you amusing?"

He grasped his heart. "Ouch. You're a *mean* superhero. Fine, tell me all about your incredible powers."

"I broke my door down a few nights ago."

Blinking, he asked, "Why'd you do that?"

"To get out. Our door lock is the kind that you have to use a key for both sides and, apparently, while I'm unconscious, I'm not smart enough to look in my purse. After I woke up on your lawn, I went home. The door was in the hallway. A normal person can't kick in one of those locks. And I don't— I don't think I could even pick up that door now."

His brow furrowed and he leaned up against the car. At least he was listening, listening intently. "Is your boyfriend alright?"

"Yes."

"Well, where was he?"

"He was—"

"Wait, let me guess. He was sleeping, wasn't he?"

She clamped her jaw shut and waited for his little rant to be over. It might take a while, because he seemed very amused by her situation.

"You supposedly ripped a door off its hinges, and he slept through it, right? You guys are a heck of a pair—he sleeps through doors breaking and you sleep through sex. Just with me or with him too?" He quit talking, so she assumed it was finally her turn to speak.

"We—"

"No"—he threw his hands out to stop her—"forget I asked. My ego can't take it. I'll ask one more time: Do you do drugs?"

She waited for him to start monologuing again. He looked at her impatiently.

"Oh, is it my turn now?" she asked. "Are you *finally* allowing me to speak?"

"Only if you say something intelligent."

"Wow. You are so good at being cruel. I *get* that you don't

like people, that you don't like *me*. But what about you? Do
you hate yourself as much as you hate the world?"

He was still, his face a mask, probably considering which
insult to throw at her next. Maybe he'd go lowbrow and call
her fat. Or say she dressed badly. Nothing had changed. He
would never believe anything she said, never be willing to
help her.

"Me or the world?" His grin was sad, bitter. "There's no
comparison." He pushed himself up and flicked his head to
the other side as he opened the car door. "Get in."

She flinched. What? No snappy, demeaning comeback?
She was sure he hadn't run out of insults. "Why?"

"You want my help? Fine, I'll help. But it's a limited-time
offer, and I make all the rules."

"How surprising," she muttered. But she'd take the deal.
What other choice did she have?

"Get in. And don't call me Grandpa."

"How old are you?" She skittered around the back and
jumped in before he could change his mind.

"Thirty-one."

"Hmm," she said, attaching her seatbelt.

"What? I'm thirty-one."

"I believe you."

A tight-lipped grin spread onto his face. "Aha. Anyone
over thirty is ancient, right?"

She didn't comment.

"I need directions."

"I don't even know where we're going." God, why did she
trust him? He'd been very clear that would be a mistake.

"Your house."

"Why?"

He threw the car into reverse and pulled out. "I want to see
this tissue-paper door you took apart and take some
measurements. I'm going to buy you a present."

"What? A straitjacket? I'd probably take a medium,
depending on the cut."

He smirked. "No straitjacket."

"Turn right at the light. Some chains? For my wrists?"

"Thought about it."

"A cage?"

The corner of his mouth twitched. "In a manner of speaking."

She gripped the door as he took the corner. "In *what* manner of speaking?"

He didn't answer. Which was not a good sign. Her imagination went into all sorts of nooks and crannies of horrendous plans he might have.

"I can't be tied up," she said. "I don't want to be tied up." Never again.

He watched her, waiting, like a rattlesnake in the grass. Would she hear the warning rattle before he struck? No, he was too smart to give himself away.

Despite the danger, Eden smiled at the image of him shaking his tail. *That might be something worth seeing.* She looked out the window. Geez, where were these thoughts coming from?

"Why doesn't your boyfriend keep a better eye on you? Keep you so busy at night, you don't want to leave the house?"

"Relationships are complicated."

"Not all of them. For instance, our relationship is very simple. You are annoying; I am annoyed. See? Totally uncomplicated."

"Each time we're together, I'm shocked at how much easier it is to ignore your rudeness," she said, turning back to him. "Go left on Federal and then take the first right. If I'm so annoying, why are you helping me?"

"Aside from the fact that you won't leave me alone?"

"Yeah, aside from that."

"I would've thought you wouldn't care about *why* I helped you, just that I did." Mitch's eyes never left the road. "Not that it's any of your business, but I knew the woman who you claim to have murdered." His knuckles were white on the steering wheel.

"Oh, I'm sorry." *He knew the woman?* She leaned forward to look at him. "Are you...emoting?"

"Hardly."

She righted herself in the seat again and faced forward. Of course, he wasn't. Mitch didn't *have* feelings he couldn't control.

"Were you in love with her?" she asked.

"Again, not your business."

"It's the building on the left. Park in front." She took a breath and prepared to ask a question she wasn't sure she wanted the answer to. "Mitch, do you think I murdered your friend?" Her heart felt like a dirty napkin someone had wadded up...

"Sister."

...and tossed in the trash. She didn't look at him, didn't touch him. This was Mitch, not anyone else on the face of the planet. His rules were different. "She was your sister?"

"Indeed." He put the car in park and slid out.

She opened her own door, using it to steady her nerves. "Why are you helping someone who might have killed your sister?"

"I intend to find out if you're right."

Over the top of the car, she asked, "And if I am?"

"If you are?" He slammed the door and looked right into her eyes. "Don't worry, Eden. It will happen so fast, you won't feel a thing." Then he turned and walked toward the dilapidated apartment building.

She shuddered. "Yeah. This is totally uncomplicated."

CHAPTER XII

How do you respond to a threat like that? Should I send a 'thanks for the warning' card? A fruit basket? Eden was way out of her comfort zone, way out of her *dis*comfort zone, too. Nah, he wouldn't kill her. He probably wouldn't even hurt her ...too badly. She was *nice*, and, while nice people often end up last, they don't inspire violence in others.

It just wouldn't happen. But maybe she should say something to him. Just to make sure.

"Don't you think we should talk about this a little?" She ran to catch up with him.

The look on his face hadn't changed—severe, hollow, dark.

And so she chickened out. She silently led Mitch to the second floor. He was five steps behind her when she got to the door of her apartment.

Her shoulders drooped and she turned around. "I have to go downstairs to get the key. Sleepwalkers—or other personalities—don't like to carry purses, it seems."

He stepped to the metal railing, giving her more than ample room to pass. She was at the stairs when she heard Carter's voice behind her.

"Hey."

"Hey," Mitch replied.

She turned back to see them staring at each other—Carter filling the doorway, looking wary, Mitch leaning against the rail, looking bored.

"Can I help you with something?" Carter asked.

"It's me!" She ran back. "I didn't think you'd still be home. Carter, this is Mitch. He's the guy I told you about." *Oops, that could have been handled more delicately.*

Carter's eyes bulged. Then they narrowed. Eden stood between the two men, her body being swayed side to side by the shots of testosterone they were firing at each other. She grabbed Carter's arm for balance. And to keep him from attacking. Mitch didn't move.

With her eyes, she pleaded for help.

Carter acquiesced. "Boy, have I been dying to meet you, Mitch."

Mitch pursed his lips together. "Don't call me—"

"Oh, he goes by Mitchell," Eden said in a rush. *Wow, what fun. Why didn't I do this sooner?*

"What, I can't call you Mitch?" Carter taunted.

"Not if you like the way your pretty little head sits on your pretty little shoulders."

"Really, boys? I'm not a basketball and this isn't the school grounds. So knock it off." She pushed Carter backwards into the apartment, his bodyweight heavy against her palms. "Carter, I told you what happened. There's no competition here." After a pause, she felt him relax under her hands.

"Why are you here?" Carter asked Mitch.

Mitch sauntered through the door. "I'm buying your girlfriend a present."

Carter leaned forward again.

"I said knock it off!" She glanced at Mitch. "Both of you. Carter, he's here to help me. I got out again last night."

Carter's brows came together. "Shit, I thought you'd gone down to the gym. Sorry."

She lightly stroked his arm. "It's not your fault. And Mitch is just here to help. That's it. Tell him, Mitch."

Mitch sighed and looked around the living room. "Yep. I'm just the hired help. Without the hired part. Today I'm just a wallet." He turned around and knocked on the wooden door, smiling. The area surrounding the knob was still wrapped in duct tape. "You guys know someone busted up your door, don't you?"

"I fixed the deadbolt," Carter said, glaring. "And the new door is getting here either today or tomorrow. I'm not a magician." He looked down at Eden. "We don't need his help."

"We need all the help we can get. It will be fine."

"He'll help and then he'll leave, got it?"

"I swear to you—he'll leave." She saw the bag he carried and his uniform—navy blue sweatpants and t-shirt with "FLPD" in white lettering written across his broad chest. "Did you get the internship at the station?"

His smile was proud. "Yeah, but I don't start for a few more days. The final exam is on Saturday, so today is just a study group. Then I'd planned on working out. But I'll reschedule."

"No, you should go. I don't think we'll be long. And Mitch knows he's not my type." *When I'm awake,* she added silently. "Right, Mitch?"

"This keeps getting better and better." He stuck out his hand to Carter. "I'm not here to screw with your territory, man. Aside from some bars and another door."

Carter reached around Eden and shook Mitch's outstretched hand, holding it a little too long. "You help. And then you leave," he growled.

"Great!" Eden brought Carter's face down to hers and kissed him, almost on the lips. "Have a good day."

"We'll talk soon. Keep your phone handy." He walked out, twisting to keep his eyes on Mitch until he was walking backwards.

"Study hard." Eden shut the door after him with a smile she hoped said, 'You can trust me.'

Mitch laughed as he took off his suit jacket and sat on the couch. "You got one hell of a boyfriend there."

"He's a good guy, so don't make fun of him."

"I'm sure he is." His smile disappeared. "Are you in love with him?"

The question he had no right to ask hung in the air between them.

With each blink of her eyes, she wished she could break the hold Mitch had on her. It didn't work.

"I'm...with him." Once spoken, the answer she'd felt compelled to give left her embarrassed and ashamed. She hurried into the kitchen for some water.

"That's it? You're *with* him?" he called from the other room, his voice getting louder as he followed her.

"It's the truth." Why had she brought Mitch into her home? Her home that had a bed in it.

He leaned on the fridge, his shirt pulling across his chest. "Fair enough. But he's in love with you."

"What?" she asked, refocusing her eyes.

"He's in love with you."

"Yes. At least, that's what he tells me."

"Oh, the poor boy." His laughter filled the apartment, making her cringe.

Jerk. "Stop laughing!"

"I can't." His carefree smile hid none of the wickedness in his eyes.

Stupid, gorgeous jerk. "I shouldn't have told you," she grumbled, filling two glasses from the tap.

"Why did you?"

Because that is who I am. "You asked." She handed him the glass. "And I don't lie."

"Everyone lies."

"I don't."

"Ever?"

She shook her head. "If I'm not honest, then how can I expect other people to be honest with me?"

After one last chuckle, his mouth settled into a smirk. "You can't. People lie. Whether you accept it or not makes no difference. All it does is make you a willing participant in your abuse."

She set her glass down on the counter, his words stinging her ears. That couldn't be true. She'd built her entire life around the idea that the only thing she could control was herself—her actions, her words. And, if she did the right thing, other people would somehow treat her with the same respect. But it wasn't true, now, was it? Her decency made no difference at all in anyone's life but hers. And, oh, what a life it was turning out to be.

"Okay, let's get to work." He left her where she stood and went back into the living room. "You got a tape measure?"

Amazed how quickly one phone call to Jolie and a Visa card worked, Eden stood in her refurbished prison apartment. Mitch had gotten security bars installed on her windows and a new keyed lock on her new door. In a day. Man, she needed an assistant. And a whole heck of a lot of money.

"Even your superhuman strength can't get through this one." Mitch winked at her and knocked on the new metal door. There were two deadbolts, but he handed her only one key. "Call Carter and tell him to come to my office to pick up the other key on his way home."

"Why do I only get *one*?"

"That's the point of the bars, Eden. You *do* understand that, don't you? You can sleep tight knowing you'd need a crowbar to get outside." He grimaced. "You don't have a crowbar, do you?"

⌁⌁⌁

After leaving Eden's apartment, Mitch spent the rest of the day worrying. Not something he was accustomed to doing about someone other than himself. The idea that Eden was like him was unfathomable. Impossible.

She was *pure*.

Fuck, she probably brought sandwiches to the homeless or took in stray animals in her free time. He'd know if she struggled to keep her evil inside. He'd have seen it on her face—the weariness, the pain. Just like he saw in his own eyes every time he looked in a mirror. No, she was nothing like him. She was better.

After his last client left, Mitch sat down on the edge of Jolie's desk and watched her work.

Without lifting her head, she asked, "Do you need something, Mitchell?"

"Nope."

She pushed back from the desk. "Then I'm free to go?"

"You are. I'm gonna stay awhile."

Her eyes narrowed. "What's going on? I never leave first."

"A guy should be dropping by pretty soon to pick something up."

"Wow, could you be any more vague?" She picked up her enormous purse and stood. "Who is he?"

"My new BFF."

"Aside from the fact I'm absolutely shocked you even *know* that expression, I'll remind you that you don't have an *old* BFF."

"True. Then he's my first. I love to try new things."

She shook her head as if something had come loose. "No, you don't."

"Also true. I'd *love* to love trying new things."

"I'll see you tomorrow, Mitchell." She left, still shaking her head.

Mitch spent the next twenty minutes trying to decide which kind of asshole he wanted to be to the guy.

Carter came in, full of the kind of feigned arrogance Mitch thought of as 'Rookie Know It All.'

"So I'm just supposed to lock her in every night. *That's*

your great idea?"

"How else do you propose to keep her from leaving the apartment?" Leading him into the office, Mitch didn't ask him to sit. Carter probably wouldn't have anyway. "Because, obviously, the technique of sleeping next to her and being aware she's leaving hasn't been successful thus far."

"I don't sleep—" He clamped his lips together and looked around the office. "I'm on meds. They make me sleepy."

Mitch raised an eyebrow. "Meds, huh?"

"I don't do drugs. They're for a medical condition."

Why he was helping a delusional girl and her sick-and-clueless boyfriend was an utter mystery to him. He gestured to a chair. "She says you're a good man."

Carter skipped the one Mitch had pointed to and sat on the couch, spreading his legs wide. "That's nice to hear."

"That she thinks you are or that she told me?"

"Both, I guess."

"How did you two meet?" When he got a glare instead of an answer, Mitch continued, "If I had an olive branch, I'd offer it to you, but since I'm all out..." He held up his palms. "I'm just trying to help. She needs help, you know."

Carter nodded, let out a deep breath, and scratched his forehead. "I know. But I don't think it should come from you."

"Fair enough." Mitch wasn't good at this kind of shit—getting people to *share*. Especially people who hated him even before they met him. No, that usually happened right *after* the introductions. And his technique for life coaching had nothing to do with people opening up emotionally. He taught his clients how to be aggressive, take no prisoners, feel no empathy for others. They paid him well for something that came naturally to him.

"I was gone," Carter said. "You know, when you and she— When it started happening. I was at the Police Tech Academy in the Keys. If I'd known"—Carter shook his head sadly—"I wouldn't have gone."

"Do you believe her when she says she was

sleepwalking?"

"I believe she believes it. Eden doesn't lie."

"She really never lies?"

"Never."

"How is that possible?" Mitch leaned back in his chair. "I lie before breakfast. And, if no one else is around, I lie to myself."

"That's exactly why you should leave her alone. It's hard for people who haven't grown up in the system to understand. At eighteen, the state dumped us with nothing but ourselves. They wiped their hands and waved goodbye. At that point, we each had to make a decision about which path to take. Eden is on the extreme of one of those paths—no lies and no deceit. Period. End of story."

"That's not the end of this story, I hope. Because it sounds unbelievably boring."

"She was right—you are an asshole."

Mitch flinched, impressed. "She said that?"

"Not as colorfully, but, yeah, she did."

"Huh. I wasn't sure she'd noticed."

"Leave us alone, man. She doesn't deserve this." Carter leaned forward, resting his elbows on his knees, but his body was still on edge. Ready to attack if given the slightest provocation. "She's the best person I've ever met. That's why I believed her when she said she wasn't really there that night…with you. Something else was going on. I don't know what *was* going on, but I know that she would never put herself into that position willingly. So, either you are a master manipulator or she was out of her mind. Literally. So which is it?"

Mitch looked at the guy. The rookie had been replaced by someone who was genuinely afraid. For someone he was in love with. *Wonder what that would feel like.* "While I consider myself a good manipulator, if she really is who you say she is, I'm not *that* good."

"That's what I was afraid of."

"How long have you guys been together?"

"Together?" Carter chuckled weakly. "That's complicated. We've never really been *together*. More like two people occupying the same room but being in totally different places." He adjusted himself, obviously uncomfortable with the direction this conversation had taken. "Shit. I think you just manipulated an answer out of me that I didn't want to give."

"I told you I'm not that good at it." Mitch shrugged, giving the guy a break instead of an asshole comment. "How'd you two meet?"

"She considers me her hero." Not an answer, a challenge.

"That's a big job title. Congrats. So, how long have you held that position?"

"About six years or so." With a sigh, he seemed to finally give in to Mitch's nagging and answer the question instead of deflecting. "Okay. We were living in the same group home. It was, like, her first week there, I think. One day, I'm on the phone with a friend and I walk into a room where four guys have her backed into a corner. It wasn't hard to figure out what they were planning to do, so I told the guy I was on the phone with to call the cops."

"Did they kick your ass?"

"Yep."

Protecting a stranger. Would Mitch do that? Could he *let* himself do that? "You *are* a good man." *A fucking Boy Scout.*

"Yeah, right." Carter picked at a thread on his sweats. "I come out of it looking like some big hero because I yelled three words into a phone." He sighed. "Ever since then, she sees me as her protector, like her big brother."

"People rarely sleep with their big brothers."

"It's not like that. We don't—" His lips slammed together, and he reddened.

Mitch would have given anything to know what the guy was about to say. *They don't what?* Because if that sentence was going to end with, 'fuck,' 'sleep together,' or 'put tab A into slot B,' *that* was something Mitch wanted to hear. He watched the Boy Scout's face take on a deep burgundy hue.

Holy shit, they don't? Six years and they don't? Sure, it had been years since Mitch and Jolie had been horizontal, but neither of them had any romantic feelings toward the other. Jesus, six years of friendship with someone you *want* but can't have? It was proof that men and women *can* be friends, even when one of them spends that time crossing their fingers and hoping.

"She knows I would die to keep her safe," Carter said, "and I'd like to think she'd do the same for me."

Mitch put up his hands, palms out. "If she treats you like a big brother, why are you in love with her?"

"Anyone who's ever spent five minutes with her knows why."

Their eyes locked, an understanding passing between them. An understanding Mitch didn't think he needed. Or wanted.

"But you already know that, don't you?" Carter asked, his jaw tight.

Yeah, Mitch knew. Wished like hell he didn't, but he knew. "Don't worry about it," he said. "She thinks I'm too old."

"How old are you?"

"Thirty-one."

"Oh."

Fucking kids. "And I'm not a good man."

"Yeah, kinda figured that. So you'll back off? Let me take care of her?"

"Sure, why the hell not? I already have a job." Mitch held out the key.

Chapter XIII

----- Original Message -----
From: "JCabot" <jcabot@theclinic.net>
To: "The Clinic" <rwhittley@theclinic.net>
Subject: Project Hyde-0016

As repeatedly stated in my many, many previous emails, Det. Nick Landon has been observing Subject Turner's activities. Considering the situation and the relations with Subject Colfax that I've been assigned to encourage, it is very likely that Det. Landon will witness a transformation at some point. Why aren't you more concerned about this?

If nothing is done soon to protect Hyde-0016 from exposure, I will assume it's my responsibility to make sure attention is drawn away from Turner.

----- Reply -----
From: "The Clinic" <rwhittley@theclinic.net>
To: "JCabot" <jcabot@theclinic.net>
Subject: Re: Project Hyde-0016

We are in the process of pulling the detective off the case; however, it is taking a bit longer than we hoped. Do not do anything until you hear from us, Cabot.

*"'Do not do anything until you hear from us'?" Too late,
jackass. You should check your precious inbox more often. If
I'd called, it wouldn't have happened, and I wouldn't have
ruined a perfectly good dress. Now it's too damned late.*

⌇⌇⌇

"What the fuck!"

Eden opened her eyes, thinking the same thing, though
she'd never say it. Only a few days later and she was on his
doorstep again, obviously her favorite place to sleep. Even
though her back was aching and she probably had creases on
her face from the brick façade she was leaning against.

Mitch hauled her up and dragged her into his house. Not
the direction he usually pushed her—which was *away*. He
pulled her upstairs and into his bedroom.

"No!" Still dazed, she fought him the whole way. She tried
to gather her legs under her so she could scramble away, but
he was moving too quickly. Past the bed. She clawed at his
arm. "Stop it! Let me go!" Into the bathroom.

"What the hell did you do, Eden?" He dropped her arm
without warning, and she pitched sideways onto the vanity,
directly in front of the large mirror hanging over the sink.

Hearing the shower turn on, she gripped the edges of the
sink and stared at herself in the mirror. Red-brown smudges,
approximately the size of one of her fingers, drew three short
lines across each cheek and one traveling from her hairline to
the bridge of her nose. Like warrior paint. One of the lines was
thicker than the others, and the blood had dripped down and
dried near her jawline. She slowly let go of her death grip on
the porcelain and turned her hands over. The color on the tips
of each finger and her right palm matched the marks on her
face. More splotches were scattered on her arms and legs.

"Are you hurt? Does anything hurt?" Mitch's hands were

on her again, roughly turning her toward him and tearing off her clothes.

She wasn't hurt. It wasn't her blood. She barely noticed his eyes traveling over her naked flesh as he turned her. When he touched her face, she flinched.

"Eden, we need to clean you up. Come here." He ripped off his jacket and shirt, tossing them onto the floor, and kicked off his shoes.

Tremors started in her legs, multiplying in speed and force as they moved up her body.

"I'm going to pick you up now," Mitch warned. He lifted her stiff body and cradled her to him. She wanted to burrow her face in his chest but couldn't twist her neck.

He shifted her in his arms and took both of them into the steaming water.

She felt him start to put her down. "No!"

He stopped and held her as her body came to life and melted into him. They stayed there, water pouring down, soaking them both, his hair sticking to his strong cheekbones and into his eyes. She took one of the hands she knew belonged to her, but no longer had control of, and brushed a lock out of his eyes, stopping when she realized she might leave behind a trail of fear in the wake of her touch.

Finally, she let him set her down. He gently wiped her cheeks and forehead with his thumb, wiping away tears and someone else's blood. Then he lathered soap between his palms. His hands traveled across her skin—her chest, arms, neck. She arched into his touch, momentarily closing herself off from a reality she felt smothered by.

She watched him crouch down to rub her legs, felt her breath grow shallow and quick. Their eyes met and his mouth opened slightly, letting out a long sigh.

"Eden, I—" He shook his head, water droplets scattering from his hair. Then he tentatively took her by the hips and nudged her back—away—toward the hot pounding of the shower.

She closed her eyes and moved into the direct pressure of the water, letting it rinse away a sin she had no memory of committing. She felt his fingers run through her hair and hold the nape of her neck. Once her heart resumed a more normal rhythm, she stepped closer to him and opened her eyes, looking up at him.

"You shouldn't have washed me," she whispered. "The police needed that as evidence."

"Listen to me." His tone was steel. "At this point we know nothing. Something happened, but it could have been anything—a fight or a dead dog, for fuck's sake." His fingers dug into the back of her neck.

"No, I should be locked up. It's not safe for me—or for anyone else—to be out."

"So you stay here with me. I'll take care of you."

"I need to find out what she—what *I* did."

"You were right the first time, Eden: What *she* did." He brushed his hand across her shoulder. "You're shivering. Are you cold?"

Eden shook her head. He reached around her to adjust the water temperature anyway. When he leaned back, she grabbed him around the waist so he wouldn't go too far. He was solid, real. And she needed something real to keep her standing.

She rested her cheek against his chest, pressing the length of her body against his, enjoying the closeness, feeling the stoking of fiery heat between her thighs, hotter than the water that rained down on them. Which led to more disgust at herself.

This wasn't her, who she was. None of it.

He held her tightly while she cried.

Wrapped in a thick towel, she watched Mitch search his closet and dresser for something she could wear. She ended up borrowing a tank top that smelled clean, like him, and workout shorts that hung down to her knees even after she'd rolled the waistband four times.

What had she done? And to whom? Her brain wasn't

functioning properly. She'd been so secure knowing there was a right and a wrong answer to every situation. But not knowing what was going on threw that totally out of whack. If she'd done these things consciously, there would be no question. She'd go to the police immediately.

No, that wasn't right. If she'd been conscious, she would never have done any of this to begin with.

Without a word, Mitch took her bloody clothes out of the room, as if seeing the evidence would remind her of something she didn't remember to begin with. She was done trying to convince him she hadn't been conscious. He either believed her or he didn't. She wanted to think that he did. Knowing that he was helping a possible murderer get away with a crime was incomprehensible, even for him—someone who saw everything in shades of gray. Or maybe black. But never white. Nope, not Mitch.

Mitch could feel Hyde's eagerness, his anticipation of freedom. It hit him in the gut, right below where Eden had rested her head in the shower. Where her tears had fallen.

He was getting too close to her, wanting to be more than he could be. For her. *You are walking a thin fucking line, asshole.* The faster he was out of this, the better. Get her out of this mess and say *sayonara.* Yeah, right.

"Fuck." Mitch speed-dialed Jolie, holding the phone between his ear and shoulder while he tucked away the bloody clothes he'd pulled off Eden. He'd burn them later, but not while she was around. She was still reeling from her image in the mirror, from the blood on her hands. He'd told her that they'd find out what happened before he handed her over to the cops. He'd been lying about the second part of that. Although, if she decided to turn herself in out of some kind of twisted sense of ethics, he couldn't stop her.

But what she needed was psychiatric help, not judicial. His

mind going over the last few weeks, he was convinced she had two distinct personalities. If there were more, he hadn't met them.

"Good morning. Mitchell Turner's off—"

"It's me."

"Mr. Schmitt has been waiting for twenty minutes," Jolie said, her voice dropping to a whisper. "Where are you?"

"Tell the lazy bastard to get back to work. And tell him that's a direct quote from me. Cancel everyone else on the schedule today because I'm not coming in. Tomorrow too, Joles. Then I need you to do something for me."

"You always do. What's up?"

"Wait until Schmitt leaves and then call all the hospitals and emergency clinics within five miles of my house."

"What is going on?" He heard the nervousness in her voice.

"I'll tell you when I know. Ask them if anyone came in with a knife wound last night or early this morning. Actually, a knife or a bad beating. But try to be subtle about it." Conning an answer out of an exhausted nurse wouldn't even be a challenge for Jolie. He knew firsthand how well she lied.

"What's happening, Mitchell?" Her voice was sticky, each word bleeding into the next. "Is someone there with you?"

"Just do it, Jolie. I'll explain when I can." *Maybe.* Before she could argue, he hung up.

She'd do what he asked. She always did, anticipating his needs and controlling the circus that followed in his wake. If there was a body, she'd probably volunteer to mop. Like she had with Shelly. She'd offered to help him hide Shelly's body after he'd murdered her.

"Don't call the cops, Mitchell. They'll put you in prison," she'd said. And then they'd find out about him and what he became. He'd called them anyway. Who the hell else would punish him? But she'd stepped in and saved his ass again, cleaning and dressing him as if he were a child. And, when the police finally arrived, she'd offered up the alibi that they'd been at her house all night. So no jail time, no prison full of the carnage he would create, and no aftermath in a fucking lab somewhere for the rest of his existence. *Was that what friends are for?* he'd wondered after his brain had started working again.

And now he was doing the same thing for Eden, minus the beast, of course. Just a sick girl who, for some unknown reason, was drawn to the one man who wanted to help her as much as he needed to get rid of her.

What a fucking mess. Yeah, she was right—relationships are complicated.

Jolie called back and told him three people had been admitted into North Broward Hospital with bleeding wounds, but all had known their attackers or had done it to themselves. Ignoring the questions that came barreling across the phone line, Mitch hung up. It was time to take a drive. A nice Sunday car ride around the neighborhood to search for a body or a pool of blood. *Happy, happy days.*

He found Eden lying on the couch, covered by a throw blanket.

"I'll be back in a little while," he said.

"Where are you going?" She sounded like she was on the edge of a cliff. But at least she was no longer falling.

"Just a quick trip around the area to see if I can find anything."

She threw off the blanket and stood. "I want to come."

"No, you stay here."

"Maybe I'll remember something. Please, I need to go. I need to...*know*." She looked at him with eyes full of fear, but fighting desperately to control it, the corners twitching slightly.

"You don't get out of the car, you understand?"

She nodded and slipped on her shoes—the only piece of her clothing he'd been able to wipe the blood off of. As soon as he could, he'd get her some new shoes and burn the old ones with the rest of her clothing.

Taking side streets and driving through alleyways, neither of them spoke. After a half an hour, they saw the caution tape.

Two police cars blocked the alley behind Static. A crowd peered over the tape, kept back by a uniformed officer. A news media van was pulling away from the curb. Mitch parked a half a block away.

"Stay here. I'll find out what happened." He waited for her response. When he raised an eyebrow and said, "Eden, you stay here," she finally agreed with a quick nod.

Twenty feet from the car, he heard her door open behind him. "Damn it, go back."

She didn't. She jogged up to him, shaking her head. "I can't."

He could drag her back to the car, but with the crowd within sight, he'd just bring more attention to them. The point was to just check things out, scratch this site off the list and keep looking. He turned around and started walking again, with her at his side. "Don't say anything. No talking, crying, screaming, nothing."

They joined the group, and Mitch pushed his way in. Eden followed through the opening his not-so-polite elbows were creating within the mass of gawkers. Thirty feet beyond the line of tape, more police—some in uniform, some not—and the coroner were standing over a body, now covered with a sheet. Not a good sign. Whoever had covered the body had been lazy—a dirty tennis shoe stuck out.

Small. A woman's.

He held Eden's arm and squeezed a warning. One of the plain-clothed investigators glanced back. It was good ole Detective Nick Landon. Recognition flashed in his eyes and he walked toward them.

Damn it. As badly as Mitch wanted to throw it in reverse and get the hell out of there, it would only pique the detective's curiosity more.

"Well, hello there, Turner. What are you doing here?" He held up a finger. "Wait, let me guess. You were going out for brunch and just happened upon our little crime scene here."

Mitch dropped his grip on Eden's arm. No need to draw attention to her.

"What? You lose a contact or something?" The detectives hid none of his condescension. The crowd pulled back from them.

"I'm just here to gawk like everybody else, detective," Mitch said.

"Uhhuh. Sure. It's a pretty gruesome scene. Kinda like another I've seen in pictures recently. What do you know about it?"

"Well, I'm guessing that the plastic sheeting isn't covering someone's pet. *And* that the city's finest aren't going to be available for brunch any time soon. Am I right?"

"Where were you last night? Between"—he checked his notes—"eleven and one o'clock."

Mitch sighed with relief. He had an alibi, and the cop hadn't noticed his companion yet. "Babysitting some clients. We were drinking at Heavenly until the place closed down. They make a mean martini. You should try it."

"I might do that. Head over after I'm done here. Check the place out. Think they remember you being there?"

"I'm sure they remember my credit card. And me signing the bill. Will that do?"

Landon clenched his jaw. "Should do. So, what, you're just taking a midmorning stroll with your date?" He threw a pointed glance to Eden.

Damn, why couldn't he have dealt with one of the other detectives? One of the more jaded and less observant ones. "Just taking her home."

"Were you with him at the bar last night, Miss…?"

"Yup, she was."

Landon stood close to Eden, staring down at her. "What's your name, Miss?"

"Eden," came out as a whisper, but she matched the intensity of the cop's gaze, pound for pound.

"Will anyone remember you, Eden?"

"I don't—"

"She'd be hard to miss," Mitch said. "Don't you think?"

After a quick glare at Mitch, the cop looked down to what Eden was wearing. "Nice outfit. Not really up to the dress code at Heavenly, though."

"You interested in ladies' fashion, Detective? I didn't know." Mitch's words brought Landon's eyes back to where Mitch wanted them—away from Eden. "I don't judge, don't worry. But red wouldn't bring out your eyes. You should stick to the blues, maybe greens."

"I like you, Mitch." He smiled when Mitch grimaced. "I think I *will* try one of their martinis. It's tough to find a place that makes them right." He glanced back toward the crime scene, and then turned to Eden.

"Give me your phone number. Just in case I need some fashion advice. No offense to yours, of course, Mitch."

"None taken, Nick."

Landon's pen was ready and quickly jotted down the number Eden gave. Damn it, she'd probably given him the right one. There was no reason to make the cop's job any easier.

"I spoke to that ex-client your secretary told me about," Landon said. "What was her name again? I forgot."

Mitch wondered if the playing-stupid thing worked well for the cop. Maybe he'd have to try it for himself sometime. "Jolie told you about Leanne, I believe."

"Hmm… Was that her name?"

"I don't trust anything that anyone says either, Nick."

Landon smiled, not bothering to look guilty. "Right. Leanne, Leanne Tate."

His chest tightening, Mitch looked at the body again. Was that Leanne's body under the sheet? Is that what the cop meant?

"Something wrong, Mitch? You look pale."

He swallowed. "I'm fine. I just don't know how you do it,

Nick. Deal with death every day."

"It's tough, but I try to stay focused on the good I'm doing. Taking down the evil, you know?" He paused, studying Mitch's face. "I'm about to leave. Would either of you like to have a drink with me at Heavenly? Think they're open this early?"

"Not gonna happen. But thanks anyway."

"That's too bad. I was hoping to have a casual drink with a friend."

"A friend."

"Sure. I'd like to discuss which politician my friend has in his pocket."

What did that mean? "What are you talking about?"

"Do you think I'm stupid, Turner? When I get a call to drop your sister's case, wouldn't you think I'd be just a little bit curious about *why*?"

Mitch paused. What the hell was going on? "So someone else is investigating the case?"

Landon's mouth pinched together as if he was tired of the game. "No, Mitch. The whole case. Congratulations, it's done."

That made no sense. He didn't know any politicians. And he sure as hell hadn't done anything anyone would owe him for. "Why?"

The detective shifted on his feet uncomfortably. "Who'd you call in a favor from?"

He shook his head. "No one." He wasn't a suspect anymore. That should make him happy, shouldn't it? Not chuck a stone of paranoia into his belly. How long had he been silent? Too long, obviously, since the cop looked as confused as Mitch felt. "I guess I have a secret admirer."

"Sure you do. I'll be checking really hard on that alibi. Then maybe we'll see if your secret admirer helps you out on this one as well." Landon bowed a short dismissal and walked back to the body.

CHAPTER XIV

The drive back to Mitch's house was a long one. Somehow what had only taken a short time to travel the first time seemed an eternity to Eden now.

Mitch's finger tapped the steering wheel. "You know you didn't do it, don't you?" he blurted.

She kept her eyes on the road. "*I* didn't, but maybe *she* did."

"She? Your other self?" He waited while she slowly nodded. "I need to figure something out, but right now, I don't think she did it either."

She. Her not-better half. Yes, *she*—her other personality. With symptoms Wikipedia didn't mention. Hurray, she'd get to add them to the website's list of screwed-up things to look for if you think you might be going insane.

"A few days ago you thought I was faking," she said spitefully. "And *now* you think you know what she's capable of? How'd that happen?"

"I just do. I don't know what's happening with you, but I can't imagine this other personality would go that far. She's never shown any signs of violence, other than—"

She whipped her head to look at him. "Other than what?"

"Never mind," he mumbled.

"No, you need to answer the question." Eden was so sick of his half answers, half-truths, half bull. "Other than what?" she yelled.

He nodded stiffly, the muscle in his jaw twitching. "Okay, fine. She's kinky. She likes it rough. She'd live on all fours if she could, waiting for someone to spank her and tell her how naughty she's been. Are you happy now?"

Her hands clutched the armrests, knuckles white. "No, I'm not 'happy now'! She may have left someone dead in an alley. How could I *possibly* be 'happy now'?"

"Stop yelling at me," he said, breathing hard. "All I'm saying is that I just don't think she could. She's someone who gets what she wants without having to put in too much effort."

Eden threw herself back against the seat, disgusted. Whatever she'd done to him didn't seem important compared to what she may have done to that body in the alley. Whatever it was had left him standing. Breathing. And still endlessly frustrating.

"Well, I'm glad you seem so sure," she said through a clenched jaw. Eden didn't know how she felt yet. Her brain couldn't reconcile the idea that any part of her would be capable of that, even subconsciously.

"You need to get some help, Eden. Some psychiatric help. Did you ever call that number I gave you?"

"I thought I could deal with it on my own." Which wasn't true, now was it? She'd been hoping Carter and Mitch could deal with it for her. "Plus...the shrink didn't have any openings for a week." Eden fully realized that he'd given her the card well over a week ago and if she'd have made the appointment back then, she might already know what was going on with her. And all of this might not have happened. *I need to seriously reevaluate my decision-making skills.*

"Let me call and see if I can get you an appointment."

What would happen if she let someone into her head? Someone who would have to notify the authorities if her other side confessed to murder. At least in prison, *she* couldn't hurt anyone else. If *she* had been responsible. "Okay."

As they pulled into Mitch's driveway, Eden asked, "What is that cop going to do when he finds out I wasn't with you last night? You shouldn't have lied." *I shouldn't have let him.* "Are you going to get in trouble?"

"Nah. You look enough like Jolie to make it plausible. She was there for most of the night."

"Wearing red?"

"Yep."

"Quick thinking. You're a very good liar."

"And don't you forget it." He parked the car and waited for her to follow him before going into the house. "You should stay here tonight. Carter's a worse babysitter than I am."

⌇⌇⌇

Mitch told himself Eden didn't do it. She *couldn't* have done it. Her teary eyes, pale skin, and slumped shoulders told him she didn't have the strength to pull someone down and kill them. Chastity, her other personality, wouldn't have either—unless she fucked them to death.

Not much he could do about it anyway. *Here and now, Mitch. What can you do here and now?*

The girl needed help. Why he was offering it, he had no clue. Another bad idea. A habit he didn't seem to be able to break around her. He already had the detective's attention and now he was acting as if that just wasn't enough. *Sure, let's go wandering through crime scenes involving murders similar to the one you're a suspect for. Of course, why didn't I think of that sooner? What a great fucking plan!*

Even more bothersome was not knowing who had told the cops to back off Shelly's case. He felt his control slipping—the control over his life. That other people were determining his fate was abhorrent. Some unknown person had stopped the police from investigating him. Who the hell would care enough about him to fix a mess he'd created? He had no fucking idea how to find his silent benefactor.

And this girl. This girl who couldn't help herself was making him feel protective, making him care, making Hyde push harder against Mitch's gut to be free. She needed to go away. Before the beast came out and hurt her.

This was more than playing with fire. This was playing chicken with a lit fuse, deluding himself that, when it reached his skin, it wouldn't burn him and everyone around him.

No, it was time to pass her off to someone else. Someone who actually could help her with the let's-talk-it-out part, the craziness-in-the-head part. He took his phone into the backyard, past the pool and into the pool house. Hiding in his own fucking territory.

He dialed Margaret's personal line.

The psychiatrist answered on the second ring. "Hello?"

"Hey, Doc. It's Mitchell Turner. I need your help." *Ugh, that felt awful.*

"I didn't think I'd ever hear those words come out of your mouth, Mitchell."

He imagined her sitting in her office, lightly laughing at him. "Me neither. But I do."

"Would you like to set up an appointment?"

He'd given up on psychiatry long ago, at least for himself. Even Margaret Simonetti couldn't help him dispose of anger issues he didn't want to get rid of. *Couldn't* get rid of. Especially when everything he'd told her had been a necessary lie. "No. Well, yes. But not for me."

"Is it for Leanne again? I don't think she'll want to come back, Mitchell. She wasn't particularly happy in therapy."

Mitch thought about the last person he'd referred to her. The same person Jolie had given the cops as a possible suspect in Shelly's murder. The same person who might have started today lying under a coroner's drop cloth.

He swallowed. "No, the appointment is for someone else."

"Another client of yours?"

"Kind of, but this one's not crazy." He scratched his head. "Not *technically* crazy, just the normal kind. And she sure as hell isn't obsessed with me. Well, not in the same way."

"I'd be happy to meet with her. But I'm also concerned with you and why you seem to attract this type of woman into your life."

He knew she was teasing him. That's why he held onto her number—she could deal with his personality without wanting him dead.

"It's my get-the-hell-away-from-me attitude that drives them nuts." *Sometimes literally.* "I'm considering that as my next book. A guide for men."

She laughed. "Sadly, I'm sure it would be a bestseller. Does this woman want to come see me, Mitchell?"

"'Want' is a strong word. Sees the potential benefit? Yeah. I think she might be a multiple."

"Really? A D.I.D.?" Her voice was bright, as if he'd just presented her with diamonds. "What makes you think so?"

"She can tell you all about it. What kind of meds do you use for that?" His hands traveled to his gut and punched. Hyde, his ever-present, never-welcomed companion was aching to get out. "Never mind, I'll let you deal with her. I'd like to wipe my hands as soon as possible. When can you get her in?"

After he hung up, he flipped on the news, looking for any information on whoever had been murdered in the alley. His thumb punished the up arrow as he cursed the stupid cable company for offering too many damn channels. He stopped when he saw the backdrop of a local news station. Headlines from across the country were ticker-taping across the bottom of the screen, but all he saw was the alley. The alley he'd just left.

And then a shot of a face, a mug shot. The woman looked emaciated. She had spiky bleached hair, pasty skin, dark circles under both eyes, and a ring through one nostril. At one point, she might have been attractive, but not in this picture.

It was as if she'd tattooed 'Junkie' on her face, chest, and arms. The police's number placard was tilted, possibly too heavy for her to hold straight. The message under the picture was a name, not one he recognized. Didn't recognize the face either. When the screen changed back to a shot of the alley, Mitch raised the volume.

A deep voice spoke steadily, but Mitch only heard pieces. "...Police say...between eleven and one o'clock...violent attack...Static...if you have any information, please call—"

"Yeah, right." He clicked the television off and tossed the remote onto the couch. It hadn't been Leanne. *Hallelujah.* Not that he enjoyed the idea of someone being murdered, regardless of their life choices. But the body he'd seen not being Leanne, not creating another connection back to him or back to Eden? *Let me hear you say Amen.* One problem gone. How many did that leave? One. One huge problem in a gorgeous, little package.

He'd get rid of her after cooling off a bit. Right. The next time he saw her, he'd...

Fuck. What was he thinking?

CHAPTER XV

Within the safety of Mitch's house, Eden let herself take full breaths again. She'd been walking around with a pain in her belly and head for weeks, as if something was trying to claw its way out of her. *It's not me. I didn't kill anyone.* What was happening to her couldn't be happening.

It was like a horror movie where a demon possessed the heroine's body. If that *someone else* had killed the woman in the alley, what the heck was Eden supposed to do about it? If this *was* a movie, a hero would come and rescue her, ripping the evil out of her with voodoo or spells or something.

She seriously doubted that Mitch knew any magic. Or that he'd want to be her hero. At least she still had Carter, good, reliable, honest, *non magical* Carter. She should call him. But what would she say?

Mitch left her alone for most of the afternoon, just checking on her from time to time. Probably to make sure her head hadn't done a 360 on her neck. She searched the house for her bloody clothes, but he'd put them someplace she couldn't find. Wandering through each room, she decided that he must have put them into the only room upstairs that was locked.

What a surprise—Mitch has secrets. Then she went to look for him.

She found him outside, in a large pool that looked like it was cut straight out of *Home and Gardens Magazine*. Rocks jutted out of a waterfall at the far end. A small cabana with glass doors stood on the opposite side. She sat down on a lounge chair and waited for him to surface.

When he did, his hair stuck to his forehead, down into his eyes until he pushed it back. As he climbed out of the pool, she saw water pour off his chest, droplets clinging to it and his abs.

Holy goodness, he was exquisite.

"See anything you like?" he muttered, his voice taking on a tinge of gruffness.

Jumping off the chair, she blinked herself out of her daydream, and brought her gaze higher.

What am I thinking? "Yeah. It's a beautiful pool," she said, her cheeks burning.

He grabbed the towel off the chair she'd been sitting on, reaching around her to get it. "Not what I was talking about."

She scooted out of reach. "I'm…um…I'm going to head back inside."

He caught her wrist and spun her back around. "It's okay not to be good *all* the time, Eden."

"I know that," she sputtered, trying very hard not to look at his chest or lips, or— Dang it, there was no safe place to look. Nowhere that would stop the heat creeping through her body. "And, obviously, I'm not good all the—"

He pulled her into his chest.

"Stop!" She threw her other hand out, feeling his abs tighten under her palm. "Stop!"

His breath was warm on her cheek. "Please excuse my rudeness."

She swallowed, but didn't pull away. "You're excused."

They stayed there, stuck together, his wetness soaking through her clothes, bringing the heat of his body along with it.

Wanting to be close to him, to any man, was new to her. With everyone else, she'd always kept a bubble of personal space around her—one that was large and somewhat unwieldy. But not now. *Why not now?* Why not with Mitch?

"Carter…" If she could only get rid of the breathiness of her voice. "He…"

"He what, Eden?" The grip on her wrist turned into a caress, moving up her arm, over her shoulder to her neck.

"He's…a good guy."

Mitch stepped back, leaving her cold and wet. "And I'm not. Right. Wise decision." He nodded once and walked back to the house. "Good luck to you both."

Not sure why she wanted to explain anything to him, she followed. "I don't want to hurt him."

He spun around as she closed the French door behind her. "You don't think you hurt him every time he's around you? Every time he sees what he can't have? You don't think that hurts?"

"Carter understands."

He looked around as if he was searching for a way to escape. "No man understands that." He moved forward so quickly, she stumbled back into the door. His breath came faster, matching hers. Inches away from her. "No man…" he whispered, his eyes focused on her mouth.

"He understands I'm not ready for that kind of relationship. Carter has never made me feel guilty for choosing to be a virgin."

Mitch clenched his jaw and then inhaled sharply. "A virgin? I beg to differ. Or didn't we go over that?"

She hated him—his constant belittling, cruelty, desire to humiliate her. "You slept with *her*, not with me."

"She *is* you."

"No, she's not."

"I see. So virginity is a mindset then, is it? Fine. But it's gotta be confusing for you."

Dragging her stare away from his chiseled body didn't help. Her eyes were brought to his mouth. She leaned forward, unable to control the desire to run her finger, and then her tongue, across his lips.

"Perhaps you'd like me to help you remedy that quandary?" he asked, his voice a gravelly whisper.

"Yes," she begged, shocked at her own words.

He jolted backwards. "What did you say?"

She wasn't sure which of them was the most surprised. But neither did she care. "I said yes. Should I have added 'please'? Yes, please, Mitch." As if she wasn't in control of her own hands, she grabbed the only thing she could—the waistband of his swim shorts. She yanked him toward her, challenging him. Taking back the power he so easily brushed away from her. "Rock my world, Mitch. Give it to me just like you gave it to *her*."

He put his hand over hers, trying to pry her fingers off. "Enough. Go home, little girl."

No, that wasn't good enough. Not anymore. Not ever, but now she was just desperate enough to ignore the lines she'd always drawn for herself.

Take, Eden. Don't think. Don't judge. Take. As if some part of herself had finally woken up and was telling her what to do.

"According to you, we've already been there," she said. "Except I can't remember, so show me." The words coming out of her mouth were foreign, like someone had reached into her mind and plucked out thoughts she had but would never have owned up to. "Show me so I can stop wondering."

"You can't be serious."

"I *am* serious! Ever since I woke up in your bed, I've wondered. So show me!"

"No. You don't want me."

"I don't lie." It was true—she wasn't lying. She wished she was. She wished she could control her own voice. "And I know what I want."

"But you don't know what you'll get."

"Treat me like you did her."

He shook his head. "You're not her. You'll never be her."

She felt her brow furrow and tears form. "Oh, that's it then," she whimpered. *In a competition with myself and I still lose. That hurts.* "Then close your eyes and imagine her if it helps. Close your eyes, and I'm her."

"I don't want *her*." Their lips collided, knocking her back against the door. He was so warm, so safe. She'd take all he gave. His tongue danced on her lower lip until she opened up wide, bringing him further in.

CHAPTER XVI

He was lost inside her. Christ, she was everything. How could she not know that? He poured his frustration into the kiss, feeling her grasp his shoulders and pull him closer. Her hand touched the scars on his back, flinching, and then traced them with a fingertip as if accepting them as part of him. Reminders of who he was. And who she wasn't.

He'd never treat her like Chastity because she *wasn't* Chastity. She was simply and perfectly Eden this time. Someone who should be adored and loved and...who he wasn't good enough for. It hit him like an anvil, throwing him back from her.

He broke the kiss, righting her with one hand on her shoulder as he backed away. *What am I doing bringing her into my life? Punishing her? For what? Wanting someone like me. Who the fuck am I to be punishing anyone?*

"What's wrong?" Her voice was low, guttural, incredibly sexy. "Is it the scars?"

"This is a mistake." He shook his head and forced himself to take a few steps away from her. "This can't happen."

"Why?"

"I can't be with you. You need someone *better*."

"Hey, *I'm* the one with the issues, remember?" Her chest heaved, nipples hard through the wet tank top she wore. "How could you possibly top what I have going on?"

"You don't know what kind of a man I am. What I've been through. What I've done."

"I went through four foster homes and two group homes. I know a lot more than you think I do."

"About what, Eden? What do you know?" His gut tightened seeing the confusion and rejection on her face.

"I've seen evil. I've seen people do horrible things. I didn't have a chance to just be young, to direct my own life. Now I do. Now I can be whoever I want to be. What's wrong with that?"

Push her away before it's too late and you can't let go. He was so good at that. Years of experience. *Do it!* "Right, your life was so hard. You don't know what hard is. What evil is."

"Oh, my life was peaches and cream because I wasn't beaten? Other things are just as bad."

His anger flared—that she'd seen into him, that he couldn't help being what he was. He lunged toward her, pressing her against the door again.

"Trust me, Eden, you do not want to play 'Whose Childhood Sucked More' with me. You won't win."

"Are you sure about that?" Her eyes widened, the look in them intensified.

And then he saw them change.

⌐⎺⌐⎽⌐

"Oh God, no," he said, his voice crumbling. He took three hurried steps backwards, his eyes showing more white than pigment. "What color are your eyes?"

"Brown. Why—"

"Fuck, fuck, fuck, fuck." He paced short lines in front of her, accentuating each repetition of the word with a head bob or hand throw, glancing briefly at her between each one. His agitation fed hers.

"What? What's wrong?" she asked.

"Go look in the mirror."

"Why are you freaking out?"

"Hers are blue." He scrubbed his face with both hands before looking at her again. "Hers are blue."

"*Hers*? What do you mean? How do you know that?"

He stopped burning tracks into the tile and turned to her with a panicked look. "I'm sure I saw them once or twice before I flipped her over. Or maybe it was while she was on top."

Back and forth, back and forth. Would this game between them ever end? "Do you think being crude will drive me away?"

"I sure as hell hoped it would. It worked on everyone else. But you...now... Jesus! Just look in the goddamned mirror."

He resumed his freak-out as she went into the formal dining room. A long, wooden table took up most of the room and was stacked high with paperwork and random folders. It might have been used once, possibly twice, but unless Mitch was using the thing as a recycling bucket, it had been a long time ago.

In the mirror that took up most of the long wall of the room, Eden stopped just as she saw her reflection along the side. Then she took a tentative step forward. Another. Stretching her neck out to get a better view, but not willing to get too close.

To her own reflection.

The ice-blue eyes that stared back at her were like none she'd ever seen before. Certainly not on her own face. Was she looking at herself or at her other side? The person who she couldn't control and didn't know. Like she was seeing the eyes of some kind of evil twin. Except she felt no change within herself, no sense that this other...self was trying to come out. Nothing but the same ache in her belly she'd been feeling for weeks, accented by a new stabbing sensation she'd thought was the pain of Mitch's rejection.

Oh God, is that part of it?

Her face looked the same, but her eyes... As she took another step closer, they began to muddy, darken. Her normal mocha-brown color swirled and chased the glacier blue until her true color was all that remained.

In the background she heard Mitch still cursing to himself, mumbling and chuckling flatly.

"Damn it, I told myself you were wearing colored contacts. Fucking stupid. I'm so fucking stupid!" His voice broke. "I *knew*. Goddamn it, I didn't want to know, but I knew. Shit!"

She couldn't break the lock between her eyes and their counterparts, framed in the glass by a face she recognized as her own. A face she knew. A person she knew. "What just happened?"

"It happens every four days, right?" His voice dropped in volume and pitch as his speech turned from cussing to actual words. "The sleepwalking?"

She glanced at his reflection, then did some mental calculations. There was a pattern, not a perfect one, but definitely a pattern. But she'd just blamed it on the fact that she'd spend the first three days after an episode souped up on caffeine and paranoia. Then, by night four, she'd been too tired to resist sleep's temptation. And surprise, surprise, she'd wake up surrounded by different scenery. Who was stupid now?

But a four-day cycle? No, the brain didn't work like that. People didn't work like that. "How did you know?"

"So that makes..." He squinted and looked up. "Wednesday night. Great. Tell your boyfriend to expect me."

"Where?"

"At your place. We're gonna have us a slumber party." His eyes flashed, and he lifted his hands up as if he was shaking imaginary pompoms. "Yay." Then he dropped the goofy act and left the room, mumbling, "Gotta cancel that appointment with Margaret now. Shit. Call Jolie. In the daytime? Shit. I've never changed…"

After one more pause to look at herself, to see if she was still *her*, she followed. "Aren't you going to tell me what just happened?" Her voice was raw. "Please?"

He took the stairs two at a time, stopping to look down at her from the landing above. "I need to check on something first. You've never seen your eyes like that before, right? Never napped during the daytime and woken up somewhere else, or done anything that would tell you you've been sleepwalking?"

She shook her head. This was impossible. The mind didn't work like that. Every four days in a pattern? That didn't happen. Eyes changing color like that?

"What is happening to me?" she asked, her voice nothing more than a whisper.

He stepped away from the banister, out of her view, and then popped back. "Oh. And keep Saturday night open too."

"What's happening—" She raised her voice so he would hear it. "What's happening Saturday?"

"Something you need to see."

She wrapped her arms around herself, suddenly feeling very alone at the bottom of a very big canyon. "Can I bring Carter?"

There was a long pause before he answered. He sneered down at her, a dimple appearing on his right cheek. "Like I care. Sure, bring the Boy Scout. But he goes at eleven."

Mitch was leaving her without any answers. How could he do that? After a kiss that had finally made her think they'd connected.

"What for?" she asked. "So I can get a repeat of today? The kiss was great, but totally not worth the whopping dose of humiliation that came afterwards. And my eyes…" She blinked away the tears that ached for release.

"No kissing, no humiliation, hope to god not the eye thing. I need to show you something." His intensity flowed past the railing, down the stairs, leaving her standing in a puddle of it.

She lowered her head. What could top today's adventure? Eden wasn't sure she wanted to know. No, she was *sure* she didn't want to know.

He sighed, leaning against the railing. "Look, you'll be fine. For the next few days you'll be fine, I'll— *We'll* figure this out. On Saturday. Okay?" He paused, perhaps waiting for a response. "Please, Eden. It's important."

She took a deep breath, the inhalation lifting her chest and her chin up. At least she looked tough. She just hoped her voice wasn't going to be as shaky at her stomach felt. "So show me now."

"I can't. It has to be Saturday. Saturday I will show you who I am."

CHAPTER XVII

Eden had always valued honesty, always believed it was the only absolute. Black and white. Easy to understand and, thus, to follow. Until now. Honesty is impossible when you don't know the truth to begin with. And for Eden, the truth was tucked so deeply into her subconscious, she couldn't even begin to understand it.

When she got home, Carter was already gone. She found her cell phone and saw that he'd called nine times since the morning. The messages he'd left increased in volume and worry until he was practically screaming. She stopped listening and called him.

He picked up on the second ring. "Oh, thank God. Are you alright?"

"I'm fine. I'm at home. How did I get out last night?"

"Have you seen the dryer?"

"The dryer? Really? 'Hey, babe,'" she mimicked, "'I know you got out last night and may have gotten into terrible trouble, but I'm outta socks so could you finish my laundry for me?'"

"Check the dryer, Eden."

"Fine." Eden stalked through the kitchen into the small

alcove that housed their washer and dryer. The machine was pulled away from the wall. Peering over the heavy appliance, she saw a hole in the drywall where the hose was ripped out. The vent it fed into was torn apart, leaving a gap big enough for her to fit through if she'd really squeezed. It led outside. To the second floor. *That's quite a jump.* Enough of a jump, she almost felt the need to make sure her legs weren't broken. Chunks of drywall were on the ground on both sides and powdered chalk covered the floor. "I did that?"

"If it wasn't you, then… Eden, where did you go?" he asked. "Where were you all day?"

"I was with Mitch."

"Damn it! What did you do?"

She knew what he was insinuating. Why was he more concerned that she'd been with Mitch today than that she'd broken out of their apartment and gone who knows where last night? Now that he knew she wasn't dead, he didn't care about what had happened. Only that Mitch had been involved.

Her nostrils flared. "You want to know what happened with Mitch? You *really* want to know?"

"Yeah, I really do. You have no idea how worried I was about you. Did he do anything to you?"

Eden swallowed the words she'd been about to spit out. He was just worried. "No, he didn't do anything to me. He… He helped me. When are you coming home?"

He sighed. "Hopefully, around eight. I've been looking for you all day. I'm at the station now with a missing person's report in front of me. Now that I know you're okay, I have to make up some of the time I missed."

She wondered why he hadn't gone to Mitch's to see if she was there. Then she remembered the trip to the crime scene. Maybe Carter had just missed them.

"I'm glad you're alright, Eden. I love you."

The pause was a long one. She didn't know what to say.

"I'll see you later," Carter said, letting her off the hook.

"Yeah, I'll see you later." She hung up the phone, plopped

down on the couch and cried.

After two and a half days of considering what to tell Carter about what had happened, Eden still hadn't told him. As they'd patched up the wall, reinforcing the area with metal sheeting, and tried to act as if nothing had changed, their conversations were stilted. Formal. Uncomfortable.

Was what she'd done with Mitch cheating if the only reason she and Carter were together was habit? Or comfort? She had no romantic feelings for him, so, no, it wasn't cheating. However, she was learning that there was always another side. Less black and white, more shades of gray.

When she'd told him about sleepwalking and finding herself in Mitch's bed, she'd been horrified because of her behavior and because of their unspoken expectations, but not because she felt like she'd cheated. Well, other than on herself.

Carter had feelings for her—he'd never been shy about them. So her being with someone else would hurt him. And that's what she'd done. Hypocritical? Absolutely. But for so long, they'd been in these roles with each other. Crazily unhealthy roles, if she thought about it. Which she had been. Constantly. Since leaving Mitch's house.

So she had to tell him. And let him punish her in whatever way he deemed fit. That was his right. That was right.

The days dragged by as she waited for a knock on her door. The police would find something at the crime scene, or Mitch's fake alibi for her would be revealed and they'd come for her. A week ago, the question of whether or not she should go to them first wouldn't have even given her pause. She'd have told them everything and let them figure it all out. But now, not knowing what she'd done, not believing it was possible for her to murder someone, made things fuzzy. She'd always trusted her intuition, and it was insisting that she hadn't killed anyone.

So she'd wait. Wait for the cops to tell her. Wait for her other personality to appear again or send her a flashback of what had actually happened. Wait with a heart that felt like it was wrapped in chains that tightened with every beat.

Thankfully, she was lying down when the flashback slammed into her head. If she hadn't been, she would have ended up on the floor.

An image seen from down the alley. *Two women—one light, one dark. A body on the ground, surrounded by blood that looked almost black.* The next image was tighter, as if the camera in her mind had been lower, closer to the blond woman's body. *A hand—*mine?*—touching a puddle of blood.* Then nothing.

Eden wiped the hair off her face. Her forehead was damp. If she could trust what she'd seen, she—Eden or the other person inside of her—hadn't done the killing. It wasn't what she'd seen. Oh God, how she wanted it to be true. She dialed Mitch's number.

"Did it happen again?" His voice was frantic, confused. "It hasn't been four days."

"What? No. Mitch, I don't think I killed her. I'm not sure, but I don't think I did it."

"That's great." He didn't sound as if he believed her revelation. "How'd you figure that out?"

"I had a flashback. I saw her hand touch the body, but she didn't kill her. Mitch, I really don't think she killed anyone." The more times she said it aloud, the more her mind accepted it as truth, the more her voice bounced with relief.

He didn't respond immediately. "Good news. But I'm still coming over tonight. There's something I need to see. If I'm right, then remember the way you're feeling right now. You're gonna need to remember that."

"I don't think I murdered that girl anymore. It's going to take a lot to bring me down."

"Sure. I'll be there by ten." He hung up.

She waited anxiously for Carter to get off work. Putting it off this long had been wrong enough. She'd tell him what happened at Mitch's house. Come clean. About everything.

And then, finally, let him know Mitch would be over to stay the night for some reason she couldn't quite fathom at this moment. But her jerk-of-an-unpaid-life-coach seemed adamant, and he wasn't the type of man to go out of his way for anyone unless there was a very good reason. Her eyes changing color was definitely a good reason.

Flipping through countless websites, still searching for an explanation for her eyes, she sighed. None of them mentioned anything about pigment changes of the iris in adulthood other than gradually during times of great hormonal shifts. Admittedly, her hormone levels had definitely peaked at Mitch's house, but none of the other conditions were present at the time. Pregnant? Nope. Gradual? Big nope. She cursed Mitch for withholding the knowledge that he seemed so confident of having yet was so unwilling to share until it suited him.

I'll be fine for a few more days? Gee, Mitch, thanks for the intel. And for being so forthcoming. If he doesn't start coughing up answers pretty soon, I'll... What could she do? Beat it out of him? Yeah, right. She was powerless to do anything. And it felt awful.

When she heard the click of the deadbolt, her heart doubled in speed. She tried to convince herself how happy she was that Carter was home and they'd have a chance to talk.

"Hey." He threw his bag next to the door and tossed a package wrapped in brown paper into her lap. "Did you order something?"

"No. What is it?" It was rectangular, heavy, about the size of a half-sheet of paper, and at least an inch and a half thick.

"Don't know. As I was coming up here, a bike messenger dropped it off. Seriously, who hires a bike messenger to deliver something?" He flopped down on the couch next to her.

She shrugged and flipped it over. Aside from her name and their address, there was nothing else written on it—no return address information or any indication of who it was from.

"Think it's a bomb, Officer?" She smiled and shook it. Nothing rattled.

"Not an officer. But I have enough powers of deduction to…deduct"—he smiled, switching into a bad impression of Sherlock Holmes—"that this is not a bomb but a book, my dear Watson."

"Yeah, not loving the impersonation. You do a terrible English accent."

He clutched his heart melodramatically. "Alas, there goes my career on the stage."

"Super alas. Tis true. So tis not a bomb?" She laughed lightly, appreciating his attempt at normalcy—tragic accent or not. Maybe, at least in part, things could go back to the way they used to be.

He pressed his lips tightly together and held his breath as if he was really trying to come up with a witty answer. Then he blew all the air out, shook his head sadly, and said, "I got nothing. Just open the thing, would you?"

Eden set the package on her lap, ripped the paper down the center, and peeled it back. Both of them stared at an old-looking—like, *really* old-looking—green cloth-bound book. There was no decipherable title on the cover, just worn cloth with an occasional hint of gold lettering as if it had been well worn and well loved. She glanced at Carter, who shrugged and scooted closer to her, putting his arm around her shoulders.

She opened the book to the first page, careful not to push the binding too far. A piece of thick stationery with a sharp, gold line across the top covered the title page. Obviously Carter read faster than she did, or was certainly less patient and had skipped to the end, because his arm came off her shoulder. And he moved to the opposite side of the couch before she'd even started reading.

Read this before I come over for our sleepover. It's my personal copy and is a first edition, thus making it worth more than you, so take good care of it. No highlighting, no dog-

eared pages. Got it?

"Mitchell Turner" was embossed in gold leaf at the bottom. She looked at Carter and grimaced at the invisible steam she imagined was coming out of his ears. "I need to tell you about the sleepover thing. Does it help if I tell you that you're invited?"

He grunted something incoherent.

Angry at Mitch for leapfrogging over news she'd planned a careful and delicate discussion with Carter about, she grabbed the thick stationery and crumpled it in her fist. The title was now exposed, sending a chill down Eden's spine, followed by a rippled spasm in the muscles of her back.

Strange Case of Dr. Jekyll and Mr. Hyde

That was just mean. Mitch was playing with her, the jerk. She closed the book, trying to decide if it was seriously worth something or if he'd bought it at a flea market and would just laugh when she told him she'd tossed it out the window.

Picking it up, she felt something slick underneath. She slid it to the side and saw another—a bright yellow and black striped, very new book. She set the older one on the coffee table and took a good look at the second.

Cliffs Notes on Stevenson's Dr. Jekyll and Mr. Hyde

Underneath the title was a Post-it, its yellow only slightly lighter than the book's. The handwriting was the same as that on the stationery.

Wasn't sure you were a reader. If you aren't, give me back the original immediately. You can keep this one.

Okay, now that's just offensive. He was messing with her *and* he thought she was borderline illiterate. "Gee, thanks," she said to the Post-it. She picked up both books and stood to bring them to her room. Which, evidently, was the wrong thing to do, because Carter started cursing.

"Jesus, Eden! What is going on with you two? He's giving you gifts, like, continually."

"He's given me bars on our windows, an old book he wants back, and a three-dollar cheat sheet. I don't think those really count as gifts."

"So nothing is going on between you guys?"

Oh, boy. The timing to start this conversation could have been a heck of a lot better. Like maybe while he was asleep or drunk or something. "Um…nothing *much*."

The snap of his jaw clamping together gave her hope that he wouldn't have anything else to say. Maybe they could move onto watching television or something that took no mouth movement at all.

Sadly, that wasn't the case. He struggled for a moment and ended up speaking through his teeth. "Is all of this *his* fault? Is he doing something to you?"

"Of course not." She laughed at the idea of Mitch with crazy mad-scientist hair, sitting in a lab, brewing up some kind of potion like the doctor in *Jekyll and Hyde*. "What could he be doing to me?"

He held her eyes, his own sad and filled with regret. "I don't know." Then he shrugged and went into the kitchen. "Tell me about the sleepover," he called out over the sound of a beer being opened.

"Did I mention that you're invited?" Why wasn't she telling him? Being honest about everything? Because it would hurt him? Or because it would hurt them both?

CHAPTER XVIII

Wednesday was normally Eden's get-comfy-on-the-couch-and-catch-up-on-trashy-television night, not her sit-stiffly-on-the-couch-with-two-men-and-be-the-main-event   evening. But there she sat, across from Mitch and next to Carter, her back sunk deeply into the cushions of the green secondhand piece of junk Carter had bought a few years ago.

The memory flashed through her mind—Carter waiting for her to say she hated his first attempt at making a home for both of them, looking at her anxiously. Kind of like he was looking at her right now. Except back then, he'd also had an apologetic expression, as if what he'd bought wasn't good enough for her.

And just look at us now. Another pair of peepers had been added to the mix—Mitch's bright hazel ones. Two sets of eyes staring at her, waiting for… She had no idea what they were waiting for. She broke the awkward silence. "So? What now?"

Mitch was the only one of them who appeared halfway relaxed, leaning on the arm of the worn blue and green side chair. "You sure you want him to be here?" He flicked his head toward Carter.

"I'm not leaving you alone with her," Carter said.

Eden was so tired of their territorial squabbles. "I don't even know what's supposed to happen."

"You need to sleep," Mitch told her.

Eden sighed. "Yeah, like I can sleep with you two staring at me."

Standing up, Carter said, "Maybe you should take a sleeping pill or something."

"No. She can't. She can't be sedated."

"Why not?" Eden asked. He didn't answer. Not surprising.

Carter flopped back on the couch grumpily. "What the hell are we doing here?"

Mitch didn't look at him. "You'll see."

"This is beyond insane."

"You got any board games?" Mitch asked.

Eden and Carter glared at him.

He shrugged. "What? They're called '*board*' games for a reason."

She refused to go to her room—the idea of them staring at her lying on her bed was even less appealing than this.

After what seemed like hours of trading glances, shifting positions, and grumbling about the uselessness of the evening, they were all showing signs of fatigue. Eden yawned. The men popped to attention, waking her up more than a fistful of NoDoz would have.

Mitch stood and wandered around the apartment, stretching. "Did you get the books?"

Eden sighed inwardly, risking only a sideways glance at Carter. "Yes," she whispered, feeling ridiculous. *As if I'm hiding anything from anyone.*

"Did you read one of them?"

"Yes." She knew he'd assume it was the dumbed-down one. Which it wasn't. She had some pride, after all. Especially when someone was silently challenging her. Of course, she hoped he didn't ask which one she'd read because then she'd have to tell him the truth and risk upsetting Carter even more. Although Carter would never guess that, by choosing to read the original story and staying up until the early hours of this morning to do so, Eden imagined herself closer to Mitch somehow. No, it was better to let Mitch assume she took the easy way out.

"What'd you think?"

She blinked, ignoring Carter's stare. "Of what?"

Mitch's eyes narrowed. "Of the book."

"Good versus evil. Crazy doctor with a monster inside of him that keeps popping out whenever it wants to. Good story. Read it in high school, I think. Sad ending."

Truth was, the story had given her chills. Why had Mitch given it to her? She wasn't being doped. Sure, after reading the book, she'd vowed to never again drink anything green. But being short, hairy, and evil? No. Her other personality wasn't evil, just horny. And creepy. Not evil. Eden hoped. And there was a reason *Jekyll and Hyde* was found in the fiction section of a bookstore. It was fiction. But it had given her chills nonetheless.

Both men looked at her but said nothing. Which was really the biggest favor she could've asked.

Another uncomfortable hour passed. Then a few more.

⌁⌁⌁

After Carter slumped farther down the high back of the sofa and nodded off, Mitch watched Eden struggle to keep her eyes open. He wanted to tell her to stop fighting the sleep but knew it was only a matter of time. Fifteen minutes later, she gave in. He watched the subtle lifting and lowering of her chest as her breathing slowed.

Then her body started to move in a totally different way. She arched her back, untucking her ankles from under her ass, rubbing her hands down her thighs.

After a moment of indecision, Mitch nudged Carter awake. She wanted the Boy Scout in on this, so if he freaked out, that was *her* problem. "You won't wanna miss this."

"Go to hell." Carter barely opened his eyes, readjusting himself. Then he caught sight of Eden's flowing form and was wide awake.

Her body squirmed, shifted, arched. She let out a long moan as Chastity broke free and came out to play.

"Fuck, that's hot," Mitch muttered.

"Shut the hell up. She's just dreaming." Carter scooted away from her, perching himself on the arm of the couch. "Why are we even—?"

She tugged her shirt over her head, tossing it to the floor and ran her hand over her bra, unclipping the front closure. Tight, full breasts bounced out, freed.

Mitch shook his head. "And you slept through that?"

"Shit! What is she doing?"

Her hair lengthened before their bulging eyes, changing from its normal dark brunette into deep scarlet curls. She slid her shorts down her hips, taking her panties along with them.

Completely naked, Chastity opened her eyes—now a pale, pale blue—and looked at them both, a wicked smile showing off her pearly whites.

"Take your clothes off, boys."

Carter looked like he was about to bolt. "What the—?"

"Hello, Chastity."

"Hi, Mitch. Can I have you now? Both of you?"

Carter's breath came out in gasps. "Oh, fuck."

"Yes, please." Her voice resumed the lower pitch Mitch recognized from their previous encounters.

"Chastity?" Mitch walked around the small, wooden coffee table and reached into the bag he'd brought with him.

"Yes, Mitch."

"I'm going to tie you up."

"Okay."

Carter jumped off the couch. "No frigging way."

"Chastity wants me to"—Mitch shot a look of warning at Carter but kept his tone calm as if speaking to a child—"don't you?"

"Yes." She offered up her wrists, grinning.

Mitch pulled out a pair of metal handcuffs. He scanned the room, looking for something strong enough to hold her. "Let's go into the bedroom."

Carter pushed Mitch away from her. "Get the hell out of here, you bastard!"

"Listen, you little prick. You wanted to be here." He didn't have time to play nicey-nicey with the guy. Chastity was too unpredictable at this point. "You go along or you leave."

"I'm not going to let you do anything to her."

Chastity focused all her attention on Mitch, apparently unhappy with Carter's attitude. "Can we fuck now?" She followed him into the bedroom, squeezing his ass as she ran past him and jumped up on the bed, stretching her arms above her toward the scrolled, wrought-iron headboard.

Carter followed in a daze. "Eden doesn't cuss."

Mitch closed one side of the cuffs onto Chastity's thin wrist, wrapped them around the thickest piece of iron, and carefully clamped the other side onto her. "She's not Eden. Are you?"

"Hell no." Her brow furrowed as she watched Mitch step back to where Carter stood by the door. "Mitch?"

"I'm going to be right over here, watching you, babe."

"Don't call me babe."

He held out his hands, as if talking someone down off the edge of a building. "Okay."

"Call me bitch." Chastity giggled and tossed her head back. Her dark red hair spread out on the pillow.

Mitch thought she looked like an angel might—if the angel had fallen very hard into a very naughty position. *Focus. She's not just one of the hottest things you've ever laid eyes on. She's cursed.*

Just like you.

Carter stumbled back, hitting the doorjamb. "This is what's wrong with her. When she doesn't get—"

"Get what?" Mitch snapped.

"Rest. When she doesn't sleep."

That made no sense. Mitch studied the guy. "Are you in shock?"

"I can't touch myself." She writhed on the bed, flipping over and sticking her ass in the air. Then she tugged against her shackles.

Mitch blew out a breath, hoping it would force his lungs to refill. "And you fucking slept through this."

"Touch me." She pulled against the straps, getting increasingly angrier. "Fuck me! Hurt me! Do something!"

Mitch knew it would happen, knew she'd be upset at being trapped, caged. He'd felt it himself. "How do you feel, Chastity? Are you in pain?"

"I want to be. Please!" she cried.

Mitch held Carter back from rushing over to free her. "Did you hurt anyone, Chastity?"

"Yes."

His grip on Carter's arm tightened, no longer to keep Carter back but to steady himself. *What if—?* "Who did you hurt?"

"You."

He sighed. "Did you hurt anyone who didn't want to be hurt?"

Carter turned, wide-eyed, toward him. Mitch just shrugged.

She yanked back from the headboard. The metal creaked but held. "Why are you talking? I don't want to talk. I want to fuck." Her voice came out as a screech.

"We will…" The word—one that he'd never called anyone, yet had no more meaning than any of the others he'd used countless times without thinking—felt so wrong suddenly. He knew he wasn't talking to Eden, but still had to force it from his mouth. "Bitch."

"Like hell," Carter growled.

Mitchell elbowed him hard. "But not yet. First we talk."

"I don't want to talk anymore," she whined.

"It's turning Carter on, though. He wants to hear more. Don't you, Carter?"

"No! What's wrong with her? Is this her other personality? She said—"

"Afraid not. She's something else entirely."

"I think— I need to breathe." Carter put a hand across his mouth, turned, and ran out of the room. "Don't you— Don't touch her, goddamn it!"

Mitch heard Carter cursing to himself in the living room, his words cut off by what Mitch could only assume was dry heaving. But Mitch stayed focused on the woman—*No, the Hyde*—in front of him. "Chastity. Tell me. Tell me who you hurt…besides me."

"You liked it, didn't you?" she purred.

"Very much." He swallowed. "Too much."

Her face turned into panic. "Mitch? She's—"

"She's what?" He approached the bed, sensing her fear but not knowing its cause.

"Mitch! She's coming back! She's coming back!" Her shout turned into a whimper. "I don't want her to come back yet."

He glanced at the window. The light of dawn peeked through the window shades, slowly bringing Eden back with it. From behind him, he heard Carter come back into the room.

Mitch sat down next to her and reached out to stroke her head, wondering if Hyde was like this. Did the bastard feel fear before he went back into the pit he came from?

"It'll be okay, Chastity. We can play next time. Okay? We'll play next time. Next time you come out."

"Promise?"

He nodded. "Promise."

"I don't want her to come back, Mitch." Chastity's abs jerked as she tried to fight something she had no control over. No control whatsoever.

"You bastard," Carter growled from the doorway. "What did you do to her?"

"I didn't do anything to her, man. Nothing at all." Mitch kept a hand on her hair, stroking it as Chastity went back into whichever hell she came from.

Eden jerked her eyes open and saw Carter taking a handcuff off her wrist, his hands shaking. She ripped her arm away from him. "Carter?" When he didn't look at her, she glanced around the room and at herself. She was on top of her bedspread, the throw blanket from the living room laid across her naked body. Her lower lip trembled, but she didn't cry.

Rubbing her aching wrists, she saw that both of them were red and raw. "Did I—? Did she...?"

Carter didn't say anything, just looked at her with a face filled with sorrow.

She sat up, her heart pounding against the cage that held it. "Carter? What happened?"

He stood, still silent.

"Tell me what the hell happened!"

He flinched at her words, stumbling back a step.

Mitch came into the room and leaned against the doorframe. "He thinks you have multiple personalities."

"Do I?"

"Nope."

"What happened?" She looked back and forth between them, then stopped at Carter. "Did I do something to you?"

He dropped his eyes toward the floor and shoved his hands deep into his pockets.

She held the blanket tight to her chest and looked to Mitch for an answer. *Yeah, because he was such a reliable source of information.*

Mitch adjusted his pants. "Nothing a long, cold shower or some lotion won't fix."

"Shut up, asshole." Carter's voice held none of the conviction of his words.

"Carter?" she pleaded.

Mitch yawned and righted himself. "Well, my work here is done. Get some sleep. You need to be at my house Saturday by ten. Eden, pack an overnight bag. And, Carter, you aren't invited."

"There is no way in hell I'm ever leaving her alone with you."

"She won't change until Sunday, so you have nothing to worry about."

"Nothing to worry about? Seriously?" she asked.

"I meant about Saturday night." He studied her and asked, "You'd never let me get in your pants while you're *you*, would you?"

"While I'm *me*? So...she's real?"

"Sure as shit. Nothing will happen to her, Carter. Promise."

"Excuse me for not being impressed by your promises, Mitchell. You just promised her that you'd fuck her."

"Not Eden. Chastity. And I lied." He smirked. "I do that."

"Yeah, *that* inspires trust."

Eden couldn't care less about their testosterone-induced squabbles. *Why aren't they talking to me?* "Chastity's real?" It didn't make sense. First, Mitch says she doesn't have D.I.D., and then he tells her he saw someone else wearing her body.

"Carter will tell you all about her," Mitch said. "Won't you, Carter?"

Carter nodded slowly, painfully.

"Jolie will be with us all night. She'd never let me get within touching distance of your girl. Just ask her."

Carter flinched. "Jolie? Who's Jolie?"

"My assistant. Knockout girl—you'll love her. Ten o'clock then."

Mitch walked out, leaving her silently begging for answers. Why was he being so cruel? He taunted her, confused her, but never gave her anything.

Finally outside, Mitch let out the sigh he'd been holding the entire night. Damn it, he couldn't count how many times he'd wanted to just walk away since he'd figured out what she was. Knowing he couldn't. Not now. Hell, not before, either.

She wasn't someone a shrink could handle. And, maybe, just maybe, through her, he could understand more about Hyde. The beast that was a part of him but who he could never truly know. He ran his hands over his face, straightened his shoulders, and made his way back to the car.

In his worst nightmare, in his waking nightmare of a life, he never thought he'd meet another. And for that other to be someone like Eden? It was simply too much to stomach. He knew why he was being punished, but her? No, that wasn't right.

Only peripherally did he wonder how the conversation he'd just walked out on would go. How she would react to the truth. Because whatever Carter told her wouldn't be the whole truth. The Boy Scout was still in shock. She would have to come to Mitch for all the answers Carter didn't have.

And Mitch knew he'd have to tell her, come clean, share the knowledge of who and what *they* were. Relive all of the pain he'd spent years trying to forget. His father, Shelly, Hyde. All his dirty laundry would be brought out in a big pile for her to gawk at…and fear.

She never lied? Well, looked like it was now Mitch's turn to try it. *I love to try new things,* he lied to himself.

CHAPTER XIX

From: "JCabot" <jcabot@theclinic.net>
  To: "The Clinic" <rwhittley@theclinic.net>
  Subject: Hyde-0016
  I still have not received a response regarding a change in Turner's dosage schedule, nor any orders on what to do about Colfax. However, Turner's behavior has altered since the death of his sister and the repeated visits from Colfax. I've attached my notes to this email.
  Please advise.

$\sim\!\!\!\!\!\!\!\!\!\!\!\!\wedge\!\!\!\!\!\!\!\!\!\wedge\!\!\!\!\!\!\!\!\!\wedge\sim$

Jolie pressed send and then looked up to see Carter walking into the office. Damn it, how did he know where she worked?

"Surprise, surprise." He sounded angry and desperate. Looked even more so, slamming the waiting room door behind him. That was not good. "Can you imagine my surprise when I find out that this guy Eden keeps going to for help turns out to have an assistant named Jolie? 'Jolie' is hardly a common name. But there's no *way* that the Jolie *I* know wouldn't tell me she knows him, works for him, right? No way. And, look, here you are, sitting in his office like you belong here! What the hell, Jolie?"

"You can't be here. I'll call you later."

"I saw him leave. I know he's not here. So spill."

Jolie shushed him even though he was right—Mitchell wasn't in the office. He'd made a house call and brought his show on the road to a CEO who couldn't bother to come to the office. Normally Mitchell would have told the guy to buzz off using highly colorful language, but Mitchell was different now. *Without* Jolie altering the serum dosage in his coffee every morning. She had a feeling she knew why. And that scared her. He was starting to care about Eden, which meant Hyde might get stronger. So her theory went anyway—The Clinic not being one for explanations, or any information at all.

But Hyde's power wasn't what bothered her most. No, watching Mitchell change because of a woman other than Jolie herself stung.

"We can talk about this later, Carter."

"No, we can talk about this now!"

"That's a shame. I thought we might be able to meet somewhere more…comfortable."

"Talk. Now."

"Okay." She sighed and considered how much she could tell him. "Yes, I work with Mitchell. Yes, he suffers from the same *illness* that Eden does. And, no, he doesn't know about the medicine either."

His glare lessened as she came clean. Clean-ish. "So why does she keep going to him?"

"I don't know. It was probably some weird sort of coincidence. It's nothing to worry about." As his eyes narrowed, she realized why he was so angry. "Are you jealous?"

He didn't respond.

"You don't need to be jealous, Carter. Mitchell doesn't *do* relationships. If she hasn't put out by now, he's moved on. Frankly, even if she *has* put out, he's moved on. Trust me." She wondered if he'd buy that. It was something she'd believed for years. And then Eden had come along.

"I don't want to do this anymore," he said. "I want to quit."

Jolie looked at the poor, naïve little hottie in front of her, his eyebrows all squished up in confusion. She stood, went to the door, and flipped the dead bolt. Pulling the curtain panels across the glass walls, she put on her mask of seduction. It would work on him—it always did.

"Carter," she purred. "You can't quit. I need you. *We* need you."

His eyes roamed over her, filling with a different kind of need, but his head kept up its shake. "I can't. I saw her change last night. I saw her change, Jolie! I know I said I would help, but seeing her like that... She's a good person, Jolie. That was someone totally different."

Hips swaying, Jolie approached him. "She's a good person because we *make* her that way, babe." She pulled up his t-shirt. He didn't resist, lifting his arms from his sides to help her. "That's the only reason, you know." She undid his belt and slid her hands onto his hips, pushing his jeans and boxers down his thighs. "And I think you're amazing. I don't want you to go away. What would I do without you?" She ignored the 'no' that was apparent on his face, instead focusing on the 'hell yes' his cock was showing her. And that was all before she'd removed a stitch of her own clothing.

"I'm not an idiot, Jolie. I think you'll be just fine without me." While the look in his eyes surprised her, his words *stunned* her.

Damn it to hell, am I losing all my charm? "If you want me, you need to act now. In about another twenty minutes, Mitchell will be back." She took his hands and guided them under her skirt. "And I'll have to put all of this away."

"You think you can just screw me and I'll do whatever you

tell me to do?" His grip tightened, pulling her closer, but she wasn't winning. He looked angry, nothing like the puppy dog he usually was.

"Of course not." Sighing, she pulled back slightly and reassessed the game plan that had always worked with him. "I can't make you do anything you don't want to do. And making love with you has nothing to do with that." She looked up and blinked, hoping to locate a few convincing tears. "I can't believe you would even think I would do that to you."

He pushed her away and yanked up his pants. "I'm out. I gave her the medicine, called you so you could take over, did everything you asked me to. But I'm done. That stuff isn't even working anymore! She's changing. She's different now. And last night was frigging horrible, Jolie. Seeing her like that. She needs to get checked into that clinic."

Not 'that clinic,' Carter. 'The Clinic'—capital 'T,' capital 'C.'

"They can give her more medicine or try something else," he said. "I don't know what to do for her anymore. She doesn't even want my help. She wants *his*."

"He can't do what you can do for her. He doesn't *know* what you know. He *can't* know what you know. Do you understand, Carter?" She tried to keep her voice low and seductive while she laid down the threat. "You cannot tell him anything. Or the whole thing falls apart, and Eden will end up hurt." But if the truth came out, Eden wouldn't be the only one. They were all too mixed up in The Clinic's operation to come out of it unscathed.

Jolie grabbed his jaw and kissed him hard. He held out for a few seconds with a feeble effort to turn his head away. He started verbally protesting again when she moved her mouth to his neck, then his chest.

"Carter, stop talking. I get it. You don't want to be part of this anymore. But you absolutely cannot tell *either* of them anything. Okay? We can figure something out." As her mouth traveled lower, she glanced down at the carpeted floor and cursed silently, wondering how badly it would scrape her knees.

She had twenty minutes to change his mind.

–∿–∿–∿–

Standing on Mitch's front stoop, her hand aching from Carter's grip, Eden felt so stupid. It didn't take a rocket scientist to know something was going on. Something they weren't invited to. Spotlights shone into the front garden, lighting the walkway and doorstep she so often woken up on. Expensive cars lined the driveway, stuffed in like jewels in a…whatever the rich stored their jewels in. They'd had to park Carter's seven-year-old Cherokee halfway down the block, right behind a catering van. Yeah, that should have been her first clue.

It was too late now. She'd spent the last day and a half—ever since she woke up with wrists still stinging from the handcuffs and a best friend who wouldn't make eye contact with her—begging him to tell her what Chastity had been like. He'd told her enough to leave her wishing she could live in a cave for the rest of her miserable existence. But she knew he was holding back. She just didn't know what he was keeping from her. Something she'd done or something worse—like how he *felt* about the situation. So when she'd threatened to go to Mitch for some straight answers, she'd been shocked that Carter agreed. The expression on his face—one of disappointment, defeat—was something she'd never wanted to see, but had always known was coming.

She wondered if part of the reason he was holding her hand so tightly to his side was so he wouldn't have to look her in the eyes. "We should go. He's obviously having some kind of party. He's not going to be able to talk to us."

Recently-Turned-Mute Man said nothing as he drummed his fist on the door.

"This was a bad idea. I was bluffing. Please, let's go—"

The door swung open and a smiling Jolie, dressed in a gorgeous emerald-green cocktail dress, became an unsmiling Jolie.

"What are you doing here?" she snapped. At least the dress was still nice.

Eden tried the mute thing Carter had perfected and just shrugged, her face heating up.

"He didn't invite you, did he?" After a quick head shake from Eden, Jolie glanced behind her into the foyer. "You should have called first."

"I tried. When he didn't pick up, we thought he was avoiding our calls."

With the mention of 'we,' Jolie's eyes drifted to Carter, flashed, rolled briefly, and then drifted down his body. Probably not to admire his jeans, t-shirt, or tennis shoes. "Oh goody, you brought a date."

"We'll go. Sorry," Eden said. "Can you tell him that I need to speak with him as soon as the party's over?" She tugged at Carter, who seemed unable, or unwilling, to move.

"Jolie?" The door opened farther, revealing the host of the party they weren't welcomed to. Mitch wore a suit and tie— all black. All amazing.

Suddenly feeling very warm and very frumpy, Eden barely caught the gasp that was heading up her throat and pulled harder on Carter's arm. She needed to run for it before someone noticed her mouth watering.

Mitch turned to the party crashers and sighed, his expression making Eden feel even smaller than she already did. "I said *Saturday* night, not Friday."

"I know. Sorry, we were just leaving."

Carter held his ground, glaring. "She wants to talk to you."

"I'm sure she wants a lot of things, but that has nothing to do with what she'll get."

"It can wait until tomorrow." Eden's sweaty palm slipped out of Carter's.

He grabbed her forearm to stop her from fleeing. "No. It

can't."

"Fine. Come in." Mitch turned and walked deeper into the house. "But you can only have two hors d'oeuvres a piece. And keep your mitts off the shrimp puffs. They're for my paying clients."

Jolie grudgingly stepped back to let them in. "You're slightly underdressed, aren't you?" She turned her back to them and caught up to Mitch's retreating form, taking his arm and whispering in his ear.

As Carter dragged her inside, Eden glanced down to her black yoga pants and fitted t-shirt announcing she was an "Equality Fetishist." Suddenly her favorite statement t-shirt wasn't her favorite anymore. *Fetishist? Really, Eden. You thought that would have been appropriate even if there hadn't been a party? Around Mitch?* She shook her head.

They strolled through small groups of people in their finery, milling around the living room and discussing politics and functions Eden had never heard of. She was out of her element in an elemental way. With an occasional nod or comment to his guests, Mitch led the way through the house and out the French doors to the backyard pool area. There were even more people outside, smoking and drinking. The kind of people who chuckle insincerely only when they deem it absolutely necessary. Carter nabbed a glass of champagne off the tray of a passing server and chugged it. The group of four walked past everyone, stopping in front of the pool house.

With a small push, Mitch released Jolie from his arm and aimed her at Carter. She didn't look like she minded the pass-over. After a quick adjustment of her dress, she approached, stopping right in front of him.

"I'm supposed to keep you occupied. Carter, is it?"

Carter obviously appreciated the brunette's beauty, his eyes traveling down her body, but he kept his grip on Eden. "I'm not leaving them alone."

Jolie raised an eyebrow. "He doesn't bite. She'll be fine."

Sick of being spoken about like she wasn't even there,

Eden pried Carter's hand off her arm. "You agreed to come here. So let me talk to him."

"Which will give me a chance to get to know *you*," Jolie said, smiling. But it looked forced.

Carter bit his lip, gave Eden a look of warning, and walked back to the party with Jolie. Eden watched him grab another glass of champagne as soon as he was within striking distance.

"Why are you here, Eden?"

She flinched at Mitch's voice and turned toward him. "Carter brought me. Believe me, I don't want to be here."

"Then leave."

"You're a wonderful host. Is this your M.O. with all your guests?"

"Just the ones—"

She cocked her head to the side. "The ones you've had your...*junk* in?"

"My *junk*?" Laughing, he scanned the crowd behind her. "No. There may be a few of those I've had my *junk* in who I haven't kicked out yet. Though I try to keep my *junk* out of my business life. Thank you, by the way, for teaching me such a lovely expression."

Eden regretted not grabbing a drink on the way over. "Carter's not telling me everything...about what I did. Or what *she* did the other night."

"So much for honesty in paradise, huh?"

"He's honest. Just— He's obviously struggling with the situation."

"I love situational honesty." He glanced down at her t-shirt, then kept his eyes put. "I also love fetishists. Equality?" He shrugged. "Sure, why not?"

Eden wrapped her arms over her chest. "When the party is over, can we talk seriously? Carter's not going to leave until I'm smiling. Although the chance of me smiling after talking to you is pretty slim."

"I think I may have seen him smile at Chastity. Probably when she ripped off her top." He ducked down to catch her eyes, which were currently staring at his feet. "He told you about that, didn't he?"

"Yes," she whispered.

"That was my favorite part."

She brought her chin up. "That's great to hear, Mitch. Really. I couldn't be happier for you. Please, tell me all about it. Tell me how amusing I am to you."

He raised an eyebrow.

"No, I mean it," she challenged. "Tell me all about it. But skip the naughty parts."

"What else is there?" His grin was wicked.

She growled inwardly. "I really don't need to hear your opinion of my body. Do you think you can control yourself long enough to tell me what she's like otherwise?"

"It'll be tough." He rolled his eyes at her glare. "Alright, funny girl. What else do you want to know?"

Would he finally give her some answers? "How did you know she would come out on Wednesday? How did you know multiples work like that?"

"I don't. I have no idea how multiples work. But that doesn't matter because you're not a multiple."

She blew out her breath. "How else can you explain it?"

Sighing, he looked at the party guests and then shook his head. "Not now." He brushed her shoulder as he walked past her. "Come back tomorrow, and I'll tell you what you need to know."

She spun and jogged behind him. "*That's* no answer. Tell me now."

"Not yet, my dear. Enjoy the party. But be careful with the booze—you look like a lightweight."

"What is this for you? A dance? One step forward, two steps back. Information doled out only when you're in the mood?" No, that wasn't good enough. Not now that she was sure he knew far more about this than anyone else, especially her. "Mitch, tell me now!"

As they neared the pool, she caught his arm. He flicked it

out of her grasp. She stumbled sideways, caught her heel on the edge of a piece of flagstone, and felt herself lose contact with the ground. Sailing through space happened in slow motion. Her hands clawed at nothing but air until her back hit the water. The last thing she saw before completely going under was Mitch's surprised and amused expression.

Chlorine stung her eyes and nose as she righted her body, pushed off from the bottom and came back to the surface of the pool. She spit the water from her mouth and tossed her hair back. Everyone was staring.

I wonder if now is a necessary time to chuckle. Water dripped off her eyelashes, thankfully fogging the faces of the party guests.

Mitch didn't look at anyone but her, great guffaws coming from deep in his chest. By the time he'd stopped laughing, she'd swum all the way to the stairs in the shallow end.

He went into the pool house and grabbed a large, thick towel. When he returned, she was glaring at him from the top step, her t-shirt clinging to her breasts.

Handing the towel to her, he thought she looked like a wet dog. Like a gorgeous, wet dog. One he might cross the line into seriously sick fetish territory with. "Nice night for a swim, but I thought you came to talk."

"You mean you'll talk to me now?" she grumbled, keeping her voice low. "Gee, and all I had to do was make a fool of myself. Funny, I thought I'd already done that by waking up on your doorstep and repeatedly begging for help. You're a tough guy to impress."

He thought about what he could tell her. No, she needed to see it to believe it. Eden wouldn't be able to accept what she was unless she witnessed his transformation, saw something tangible, proof she could touch. Not that he'd actually let her touch Hyde—that would be tragic. But there was nothing he could say to make her understand. He could, however, give her just enough information to make absolutely sure she'd come back tomorrow night.

"Get dried up and... No chance you brought any extra clothing, is there?"

"Yeah, because I always bring along a dress on the off chance I fall into some asshole's pool in the middle of a party I'm crashing."

He smiled broadly and chastised, "Language, Eden, language."

She stopped wringing the water out of her hair and looked at him. "What did I say?"

"I think I'm rubbing off on you."

"Just what I always wanted." She stomped through the crowd of people still gawking at her, her pants sloshing from side to side, and went into the house. The thought that she was going to ruin his floors made his smile even bigger.

He saw Jolie and Carter tucked into an intimate corner, Jolie's arm resting nonchalantly on Carter's. Jolie shook her head slightly from side to side. As relaxed as her grip appeared, Mitch knew she was holding Carter back from the hero routine he desperately wanted to do. She mouthed, 'Should I go?'

Mitch shook his head, not wanting to interrupt what was looking to be a connection between his assistant and Eden's boy toy. *Two birds. And I didn't even need a stone.*

Wondering why he wanted to lessen Eden's embarrassment, especially since she'd probably never see any of these people again, he said to the crowd at large, "Anyone know a good mason? I need to have that patio leveled." Ignoring their muttered replies, he strode into the house, wondering what the soggy girl's next trick would be.

He followed the trail of water droplets. She must have tried every room before leaving a puddle in front of his bedroom door. Her last choice was the only room he'd forgotten to lock before the party. Throwing a party was bad enough, but the idea that people might get 'lost' and 'accidentally' be peeking into his life was absolutely unacceptable.

CHAPTER XX

As soon as she saw the knob turn, Eden cursed herself for not locking the door. Her eyes darted around his room for something to cover herself with, her wet clothes wrapped up in the towel at her feet.

As she reached for the bedspread, she saw Mitch's face, knowing that her expression matched his exactly—shock. Except his immediately turned into amusement, while hers stayed frozen. At least she still had her bra and underwear on. Wrapping her hands around her breasts, then her bottom half, then back to her chest did nothing but make his smile larger. She glanced down at her body and saw, with a large amount of horror, that her attempts at covering herself had only made her breasts press together and look fuller. So she dropped her arms to her sides and jutted out a hip, daring him to keep laughing.

"Please, keep fidgeting. It's improving the show," he said, chuckling.

She matched his stare, willing *his* to rise above chest level. "In case you didn't notice, my clothes got wet. I can't wear them."

"Too bad you didn't bring your overnight bag early. Make

sure you bring pajamas tomorrow. An old lady nightgown or something else that covers you from head to toe. I'm easily distracted."

She forced her hands to be still at her sides, fingers denting her thighs. "Since I won't be staying the night, I'm not bringing anything."

"Oh, you'll stay the night. So if you don't want to wear anything, I think you should know that I will be having very naughty thoughts about you."

"I said *bringing* nothing, not *wearing* nothing." Dang it, of all the men in the world, why was she only attracted to this one? He was her Kryptonite—weakening her knees, destroying her strength.

"My mistake." His grin stayed put.

"Could you please go tell Carter that I want to go home?"

"I thought you wanted to talk."

Somehow, her embarrassment made him chatty. Sadly, she seemed to be quite adept at providing comic relief for him. Might as well get something out of it herself. "I do." She glanced down at her wet things. "Can I at least use your dryer?"

"Don't have one."

"You don't have a dryer? How do you dry your clothes?"

"I don't. I send them out."

"Someone else washes your underwear?"

"Don't wear underwear."

"Right, I forgot." She rolled her eyes. "Then can I borrow a t-shirt or something? Or don't you wear those either?"

He wiped his mouth roughly. "Close your eyes."

"No."

"Close your eyes," he repeated, this time with more frustration.

"Why?"

His shoulders tightened. "So you can't see me staring at your tits. Jesus, just close your damn eyes."

She made a big show of it, closing them slowly and

completely before opening them a crack and watching him through her lashes. When he left the room, she flopped down onto the foot of the bed and pulled the duvet around her, happy with the knowledge that, when she got up again, there would be wet spots that matched her underwear and bra. Petty and childish, but still incredibly satisfying.

When he came back into the room, she shut her eyes again. "Yeah, like I didn't know you opened them. Well?"

"Well, what?"

"Open your goddamned eyes." He shoved a large white box out at her. "Take it."

She lowered the duvet and took the box from him. Inside was a black dress surrounded by red tissue paper. She pulled the dress out. It would be about knee-length on her and had black beads around the spaghetti straps and neckline. It was beautiful.

"Where did this come from?" she asked.

"I don't know. Jolie showed me a webpage, I picked one out, and she had it delivered."

"For me?"

Shaking his head, he said, "It doesn't match my pumps, so, yeah, I guess you can have it." His half grimace brought a dimple to his cheek. So the man did actually have the capacity to blush. But he still covered it with a thick layer of sarcasm. Being nice was definitely new territory for him. And not being suspicious of him was new to her.

"You got it for me. Why?"

He blew out a breath, obviously uncomfortable. "Since you don't seem to be able to leave me alone, I thought you might come tonight. In a brief moment of insanity, I even played around with the idea of inviting you. I assumed you would wear sweats or have to mug someone to get something suitable to wear. So I..."

Who was this man standing in front of her? She liked this side of him—it proved he was human. "It hurts you to be nice to me, doesn't it?"

His blush disappeared, replaced by a clenched jaw and a go-to-hell look. "You can wear it or stay here half naked, I couldn't care less. Of course, when the party is over, I'm going to come back here, see you in your underwear, and care very much indeed. Your choice."

Yep, it hurt him. She smiled. "Thank you." She held the dress over her bottom as she headed into the bathroom to put it on.

"Whatever." His voice was muffled through the locked door. "I just figured that since you normally don't seem to care what you look like— No, that came out wrong. You don't spend a lot of time on your appearance. Christ, I'm dying here. Throw me a bone, would ya?"

She slid the dress over her head and stared at her reflection in the mirror. "You're a little late, but thank you."

"Late for what?"

"My birthday. It was two months ago." She walked out of the bathroom. The look on his face let her know he approved…and was definitely in pain. "Could you…um…zip me up?"

-ᴠᴧ--ᴠᴧ--ᴠᴧ-

Mitch wanted to chop off his hands and throw them to the dogs as he zipped up her dress. They were shaking harder than a paint mixer at Home Depot. *It's because of tomorrow. I'm nervous about tomorrow, that's it.* Had this happened the first time he'd shown Jolie all those years ago? No, he didn't think so. Damn it.

His belly convulsed as he felt Hyde slug him. His eyes rolled back, and his body fell forward. He threw out his hands to catch himself, knocking Eden onto the bed.

"Stop it!" she yelled, flipping over, ready to fight him off. When she saw his face, she scrambled farther onto the bed.

His stomach spasmed in rolling waves as he tried to control himself. "Get Jolie. Now!"

Eden jumped off the side of the bed. "Are you alright?"

"Get Jolie!"

He watched her run barefoot from the room, slip on the water at the door, and keep moving. *Not now. Not now.* He tried to slow his breathing, the pounding in his chest, as the beast within him clawed to get out. A few seconds later, he heard footsteps on the stairs but didn't know how many feet were making them. *Christ, it sounds like the whole fucking party.*

He was shivering from the effort of keeping Hyde down when he saw Eden and Carter following Jolie through the doorway. But it was working. The bastard inside of him was quieting, though not without a fight.

"Oh my God, Mitchell." Jolie blocked the other two from coming in, her arms posted at ten and two on the doorjamb. "It's not tonight. It's not supposed to be tonight!" Her voice shook from fear or shock. Maybe both.

"You need to get everyone out." His voice was strained but coherent. "Tell them I'm ill. Violently ill. Get them out and then hurry back up here."

She nodded and headed back downstairs.

Carter and Eden were frozen where they stood, staring at him like he was some sort of freak show. Which he kind of was. Or would be very, very soon.

Pointing at Carter, he said, "You. Leave. Now. And you"—he switched his gaze to Eden—"make yourself comfortable. Tonight's going to be a long one."

"I'm not leaving her with you," Carter said.

Eden turned toward him and pulled his face down to hers. "I'm fine. He's not going to hurt me, are you, Mitch?"

God, I hope not. "No. I promised, didn't I?"

Carter looked down at Eden's attire with a big, fat "what the—" in his expression, but didn't ask about where she'd gotten the dress. He slammed a fist against the wall. "You better take care of my girl, Mitch."

Your girl. Yeah, she sure as hell isn't mine. His tension

very high and his patience very low, he growled, "Don't call me Mitch."

"Why not?"

Now was not a good time to argue with the guy. But damn it, he couldn't stop himself. "My name is Mitchell. No one calls me Mitch."

"Eden does. All the time."

"No, she doesn't."

"Yes, she does. So does Chastity."

"Hmm…" He swallowed and then painfully shrugged. "Show me you got an ass like hers and I'll let you call me Mitch. Until then, it's Mitchell."

"You're such a dick. Just don't screw her over, man. She's been through enough of that."

As Carter huffed off, Mitch yelled, "Hope you had fun at the party."

Why today? For years it had been controlled—every five weeks like clockwork. Ever since he had accepted the evil inside of him and turned being a major asshole into a full-time job. Letting his anger out thirty-five days in a row had reduced Hyde's visits from every few days to one horrible night. Why now? What had changed? He put his hand up to his carotid and counted. Four beats in a row then a long pause when it should have been the normal two, break, two, break. Christ, what was broken? He was *awake,* for fuck's sake. He picked up the lamp from his nightstand, ripped its plug out, and threw the thing against the wall.

Eden gasped and ran from the room.

"Wait," he called out. He'd forgotten she was there. He stood up slowly, focusing on putting one foot in front of the other as he walked down the hall, unlocked a door, and went in.

Leaning on the one chair in the room, he heard Jolie's voice behind him, then the door closing.

"What's happening to you, Mitchell?"

"I don't know. So much has been going on lately. I just

don't know."

"You've been stressed out a bunch of times, but it's never changed the day." She opened a drawer in the antique dresser and pulled out a keychain and a large syringe. "I think we both know what's changed."

He whipped his head toward her, his voice cutting the air. "No, I don't think we do, Jolie."

She flinched, eyes huge. "Get in the cage. He's here."

He turned away and took a deep breath. "Sorry."

She was right—his vision was different, darker. He'd never felt Hyde come on so quickly, so ferociously. Usually, by this point, Mitch wasn't even awake. Was he seeing the world as Hyde did? Through Hyde's eyes? He shook his head to try to focus. "Lock me up and keep Eden occupied for a little while. Until *he's* ready."

Mitch ripped off his suit, dropping it on the floor as he walked into the cage. His prison cell—complete with wall-to-wall steel bars and a metal bed that was bolted to the floor—welcomed the beast within him. God, he hated his life. He sat down on the hard mattress and secured his ankles into the thick metal cuffs at the bottom corners of the bed.

Jolie set the keys on the small table next to the armchair. She walked to the cage, hesitating at the door.

"It's alright. I'm alright. But I don't know for how much longer." The pain had lessened, now just a growl versus a roar. "Maybe I'll have a good night's sleep here, and Hyde won't even make an appearance. Everything will be back to…normal."

She stepped in and gingerly took each of his hands, closing them into cuffs just above his head, leaving Hyde no way of hurting himself or anyone else. "You're being too nice to her. It's making you *better* during the times when you're *you*. And making Hyde much worse. It needs to stop."

He nodded, understanding why she waited until he was locked up before having this conversation with him.

"I don't know why you're even showing her. Or telling

her, for that matter." The volume of her voice increased and she used her hands to accentuate each point. "What if she goes to the police? Have you even thought of that?"

"She won't."

"Why not? How do you know that she won't be Miss Goody-Two-Shoes and tell someone?"

"I don't. Not for sure, anyway."

"Mitchell, this is a really bad idea. You need to stay away from her. Whatever her issues are or"—she took a deep breath and put her hands on her hips—"whatever is going on between you two is not worth it. You need to get her out of your system. Just screw her and then send her away."

Seeing Jolie lose her temper was a new thing for him. He'd given her plenty of chances to do so. But she'd never bit. "It's not—"

"Don't you dare tell me it's not her! You've been in control of him for as long as I've known you. You're a jerk. I know that. But then this chick starts coming around and you change. Christ, you're even nicer to me. That's how it works, isn't it?"

He nodded. "I think so." It was a theory he'd held onto for so long but had always been afraid to test. Now Eden was forcing that test.

"So why are you keeping her around? Why can't you just keep it me and—" She swallowed and looked at the door like she'd heard or seen something he hadn't. "Are you absolutely sure you want her here?"

"Yes."

"I want it to be on the record that I believe this is the stupidest thing you have ever done. And that's saying a lot."

"Duly noted."

"So what should I tell her once she sees Hyde?"

CHAPTER XXI

Eden found Carter pacing on the front lawn, obscenities hitting the air with every few strides. Headlights momentarily blinded her in succession as cars filled with confused party guests took impolite turns backing out of the driveway, an occasional blaring horn disturbing the stillness of the night.

"Carter?"

His body tensed even further when he looked up at her.

She jogged down the steps. "It's going to be okay. Jolie is staying too. I think he's just sick and wants me to wait around until he feels well enough to talk." Okay, so she knew there had to be more to it than that, but not knowing for sure brought her denial into full bloom. Enough impossible had entered her life, she held on to the wee bit of reality she could.

"If he touches you…"

"This isn't about touching me. This is about helping me, remember? He seems to know all about multiples and is the only help I have." When Carter flinched, she squeezed his hand. "I didn't mean it like that. It's just… You are my rock, but you can't always do everything for me. I need to figure this out for myself, and Mitch is helping me to do that. He's not replacing you."

"I know. I just don't like him. He's sneaky and…there's something wrong with him."

"There's a lot wrong with him." She smiled. "I promise I won't fall asleep. And I'll call you if anything weird happens. Okay?"

"I don't want to leave you. Eden, listen. There's this clinic. I think they can help you."

"Okay. Maybe. Let me hear what Mitch has to say first. Then I'll come home, and we can talk about it. I won't stay the night. Maybe Jolie can drive me."

He gripped her hands in his. "Make sure she stays close to you the whole time."

"You got it. I'll be stuck to her like Elmer's."

"Crazy."

She arched an eyebrow and grumbled, "Thanks."

He chuckled and gently lifted her chin. "I meant the glue— Crazy Glue. Elmer's takes too long to dry."

When his lips met hers, she blinked and then closed her eyes. He hadn't kissed her in a long time, like, a long, long time. She knew this was his way of claiming her, and she let him. He deserved more than she could ever give him. She wished it wasn't that way, but it was. One kiss was the least she could do.

But something about the kiss brought everything to bear— she was leading him on. She'd been using him, purposefully ignoring his desires. Because she was afraid that once she actually said the words, "I'm *never* going to feel the way you want me to. Never," that he would leave her. And she'd be alone. What kind of person would do that? What kind of person had she been this whole time?

She let him kiss her, knowing that it was goodbye. She needed to push him away—not physically, emotionally. But it would take a big push. And she knew exactly how to do it.

He pulled back and rubbed his lips together as if he was still tasting her. "Thank you."

She nodded, saddened by the fact that while he was kissing

her she was thinking of another. Not for her—for him. She thought about the beautiful woman whose hip she planned on spending the evening attached to. Maybe Jolie would be able to give him more than she could. They'd obviously been attracted to each other—Eden had seen it when they met. Maybe it was six years too late, but she would step aside and get him to focus on his own needs for a while. She smiled at him. She'd make him find his own happiness and be someone else's rock. It was the twenty-fifth hour.

He gave her hand one last squeeze and headed down the driveway. "Be safe, Eden. And stay close to Jolie. She'll protect you."

"I will."

It was encouraging that he seemed to click with Jolie so well. Yep, Jolie was the perfect choice for him. Once he'd gone around the corner and she couldn't see him anymore, Eden turned back to the door.

Jolie was standing there, watching her. Or watching them. And whatever she'd seen didn't seem to have made her happy. The scowl on her face made Eden unsure if she'd have a friend tonight.

Eden made her way back to the house. "Did I do something wrong?"

Jolie walked away from her. "Come on."

With a glance up the stairs, wondering why they weren't going back to Mitch, Eden followed Jolie into the kitchen like a puppy without a home. The caterers had left their gear and extra food on the counters. Jolie must have been screaming.

"Jolie?"

"It's nothing personal, Eden. I just don't know why he's telling you at all."

"Since I have no idea what's going on, maybe we should go check on him and ask."

"In a minute. I want to get a drink first." Jolie grabbed an open bottle of champagne and a tall glass from one of the cabinets. "You want some?"

Eden gaped as Jolie filled the glass to the rim. "Sure, but a little less than that—like only a *half* a gallon."

Jolie shrugged, grabbed a small cup, and filled it halfway. "Here. You'll probably need more, though." She took a large gulp.

Eden took a sip. The bubbles hit her nose and she tossed her head, trying to shake them out.

"Not a big drinker, huh?" Jolie asked.

"Not really. Never tried champagne either."

Jolie turned the bottle around and looked at the label. "Nice one to start with." Then she tipped it over and let the remainder drip into her glass. "So…tell me about yourself."

"Um…" Eden thought about what she could tell this woman, who obviously didn't like her, something trivial but that sounded important. "I'm starting law school this fall."

Jolie coughed on her bubbly. "Law school?" She laughed. "Really?"

"Is that funny?"

Jolie's smile faded. "No, not particularly. It's just so…*ordinary*. Are you going to chase ambulances?"

She hadn't even started school and lawyer jokes were old. "Nah, I don't run fast enough."

"So what kind of law are you going to do?"

She knew Jolie didn't really care, so she kept it simple. "I haven't decided."

Jolie yawned. "What else?"

Eden didn't know what to offer up that wouldn't bore Jolie further. Then she remembered what she'd been considering a few minutes before. "Carter's funny. He's nice too." She looked at the other woman expectantly.

"Yeah, he seems like he is. Have you been together long?"

"We're not really together. Not in the traditional sense, at least." She traced a finger around the rim of her glass. "We have a weird relationship."

"Sounds familiar."

Eden didn't know what that meant, but she continued.

"We're friends—best friends. We met during a tough time for both of us and have each other's backs, you know what I mean?"

"Exactly." Jolie finished her glass and went to the fridge in search of another bottle. "Damn, those people can drink."

Eden glanced behind her and saw a cardboard box stamped with the same name that was on the bottle. She peeked inside and pulled out a full bottle, holding it up like a prize. "Ah-ha! We might need to ration it though, there's only one more in the box."

"Warm champagne—my favorite."

When Jolie grinned, Eden joined her, happy she'd broken through a chunk of the ice that stood between them.

"I really shouldn't let you drink too much. Mitchell wouldn't be happy." She covered the bottle with a cloth towel and popped it open, sending a spray of champagne foam into the towel and onto the floor. Looking at the mess at her feet, she whispered, "I won't tell if you won't," and winked.

Eden followed her into the living room, where Jolie topped off both their glasses, sat down, and put her feet up on the coffee table.

"Make yourself at home. I do."

Eden sat back into the leather couch, brushed off her bare feet, and awkwardly put them on the table. "Do you spend a lot of time here?" she asked, wondering why she felt a competitive clench in her chest.

"I practically live here. I'm more like his wife than his assistant." Jolie cocked an eyebrow and tilted her head. "Minus the sex, of course."

Eden covered her sigh of relief with an, "Oh."

"We're kind of like you and Carter are, I guess. Friends with*out* benefits. But Mitchell and I have very few secrets between us."

Eden's cheeks heated. What did Jolie know about the secrets she kept from Carter?

They drank in silence, Eden taking tiny sips and Jolie

emptying her own glass at least two more times.

"So, do you think Mitch is feeling better now?"

Jolie furrowed her brows. "Feeling better? You really don't know, do you? Oh boy, are you in for a surprise. Shall we go check on him?" She stood, shook the empty bottle, and then set it back down. They went to the kitchen to grab the last bottle before heading upstairs.

Eden held the banister for balance. She had no idea how Jolie could be in heels and not need something to hold onto. They passed Mitch's bedroom and stopped in front of the third door down—the one that was always locked.

Jolie put her hand on the knob and her ear to the wood, listening. "Yep, he's ready. Are you?"

"Ready for what?"

Jolie swung the door open, giving Eden a full view of the only room in Mitch's house that she hadn't been into. Her mouth fell open when she saw the cage. Seven or eight-foot-tall bars, each one over an inch thick. "What the—?"

Jolie crossed the almost barren room and peered through the bars. "Shhh. Let him get a little rest."

Eden slowly walked past the armchair toward the cage. Mitch was sleeping, his arms and legs strapped down to each corner of a metal bed. And he was absolutely naked. She looked away, thought how ridiculous she was acting in the face of something so totally bizarre, and looked back.

The first question that popped into her mind was beyond stupid, but she asked it anyway. "Why is he naked?"

"He hates to rip up his good clothes."

"What does *that* mean?"

"You'll see."

"See what?"

"Shut up and sit down. The show's about to begin." Jolie backed up to the armchair a few feet away from the cage and then patted the upholstered arm. "Only one seat. We'll have to share."

"If this is some freaky sexual thing, I am *so* not into that."

She turned to leave.

"Get over yourself. Sit down."

With denial becoming a rapidly fading oasis, Eden perched herself on the thick arm of the chair obediently. A small wooden table was on the opposite side. It held a keychain with two keys—probably belonging to the padlock on the door of the cage and the cuffs—and a large syringe filled with clear fluid. Eden suddenly felt nauseous. How did she get mixed up in all this? All she wanted was a simple, boring life—no craziness, no drugs, certainly no split personality. That shouldn't have been too much to ask for. To expect her life to be.

Mitch's body started to jerk, his back arching and his chest billowing out as if he was trying to breathe but could only gasp.

Eden leaned forward, blinking uncontrollably, as her mind tried to reconcile the image of his muscles growing and gaining more definition.

"I love this part," Jolie said breathlessly.

Eden flipped her attention to the woman.

All Jolie needed was a box of popcorn and a soda. Her eyes were rapt and shiny. She must have felt the weight of Eden's gaze because she glanced at her. "What? I like watching him. Sometimes I spend all night looking at him." She smiled and shrugged. "It's not like he remembers anything when he changes back."

Changes back? Eden turned toward the cage when she heard a moan. "Oh my freaking God." She stopped breathing.

Mitch had grown. Inches. In every direction. Less of the mattress was visible as if he'd gotten taller. The normal definition of his muscles had become bodybuilder-like, veins barely contained by his skin. His enormous biceps clenched as he pulled against the straps binding his wrists. Then his quads gathered to tug at those on his ankles. His moan turned into a growl.

"Ta-da. Are you impressed?" Jolie clinked the bottle to her

glass, and then skipped the middleman and took a swig straight from the bottle.

Eden couldn't feel her body. "He changes—" She stopped, wondering if Mitch had told Jolie about Chastity. Until she knew for sure, she'd kept her mouth shut. "What is he?"

Jolie's eyes roamed around Eden's face, studying her. "He calls it his 'Hyde.' Like Jekyll and Hyde."

The book. This is why he'd given her the book. Which meant that Chastity was... "How often?"

"How often does he come out? One night. Once a month or so."

"Is it like a moon thing?"

"You mean like a werewolf?" She laughed. "No. It's a Saturday thing. Every-fifth-Saturday thing. Doesn't cripple the social life too much."

This is what he wanted me to pack an overnight bag for. To see this. "Wait. It's Friday."

"Yes, it most definitely is Friday." Jolie's tone showed her frustration.

"So it varies? But you said—" She shook her head. "I don't get it."

"That makes two of us, kid. I've known him for almost fifteen years and *him*"—she nodded her head toward the writhing creature in the cage—"for a little less. It's never happened on a Friday before. Or a Thursday. Or Monday. Or any other day of the week. Until now."

"So why'd it change?"

"You'll have to ask him about that." Resentment or anger made Jolie's lips tight and her voice staccato, so Eden decided to drop it.

It felt so strange to be talking about him as if he wasn't in the room. "Does he always chain himself up like that?"

"Yep."

He yanked against his bonds, letting out another growl.

Eden fought her inclination to take a closer look, her body swaying back and forth with the effort. "He looks like he's in pain."

"I don't think it's pain, just rage." She slapped Eden's leg. "Why did he want to show you?"

"He didn't tell you why?" Eden asked.

Head shake. "You're not going to tell me either, are you? Fine. We all have secrets, don't we? From each other. From ourselves. Ain't life grand?" She rolled her eyes and shrugged. "You are pretty. I can see why he likes you so much."

"He hates me."

"Oh. Right. I guess I must have read that wrong." She leaned back and took a long swig of champagne.

Eden looked back at Mitch. Or, at Hyde. In addition to an increase in muscle mass, another part of him had increased in size. His erection stretched to his belly. She looked away, feeling guilty for her invasion of his privacy and wondering what Chastity would be thinking if she were here. Was this what she was like? Was this what Carter hadn't wanted to tell Eden?

"Is he always naked?" Eden asked. "Couldn't he wear sweats or something?"

"Maybe he doesn't like how his ass looks in sweats. Are we done with the stupid questions now?"

A voice came from the cage. "I can smell you." Not Mitch's voice. Nothing like Mitch's. This one was lower, gruffer, meaner-sounding. "Sex." A long sniff. "Two sexes. One different. *Niiice.*"

Eden's stomach took a free-fall to the floor.

"Release me so I can be close to that glor-ri-ous smell."

Jolie's cheeks were flush, her chest lifted. When she saw Eden looking at her, she relaxed and scratched her temple.

"Let me go, lambs. I'll be gentle. I'll take one of you. Then the other. All night. Let me go." He waited for a response that both women didn't give—one because she was terrified of what was in front of her and the other perhaps because she knew that he was lying. "Fine. Leave the straps. Just come in here and keep me company. Sit on my cock and let me come all over you. Fuck. Me." The bass in his voice echoed off the ceiling and sent vibrations through Eden's body.

Eden felt Jolie's hand clutch the fabric she was sitting on. The woman rose on her seat like she wanted to go to him. *How can she possibly be turned on by that?* The only hormone flowing through Eden's body was adrenaline.

He sniffed the air again. "Fear. Could do something with that, too." He jerked against all four cuffs, contracting every muscle, again and again and again. "Let me go! I'll fucking tear you apart! Let me go, cunts!" He strained his neck, using all his force and slack in the straps to lift his head.

When she saw the color of his eyes—like glaciers, like shadows on a snow-covered peak, an only slightly darker color than she'd seen in her own eyes just a few days before— Eden flinched back, falling into Jolie's lap. But she kept her stare on the monster in front of her.

"Oh. My. God." She'd never sleep again.

CHAPTER XXII

"Before you yell at me for calling—I don't have a computer handy, so deal with it."

"Are you drunk?"

"Not completely. But I'm on my way."

"This is extremely unprofessional."

"No, telling you that you are a sniveling, little worm of a boss who is asking me for the impossible would be unprofessional." *Laugh.* "Oops."

"I'm hanging up on you now, Cabot. If you are very lucky, I won't tell the board about this conversation. Call me when you're sober. No, email me when you're sober."

"Wait! Don't you want to know what they're doing right now?"

Sigh. "Talk."

"He turned a day early and is showing her Hyde. I think he wants her to know the *real* him. Isn't that sweet?"

"Hardly. They need to have intercourse, not share information. That could be dangerous. Stop them."

"You want me to get them to screw but make sure they don't speak to each other? *Très* kinky, boss."

"Sleep it off and, the minute he's reverted into Turner, start doing your job."

"I'll get right on that. Night, night."

Click.

Mitch knew it was morning. Not that he could see sunlight—the windows in Hyde's room had been boarded up long ago. And he was anything but rested. No, he knew it was morning because he was human again. He couldn't see Eden, but he heard her humming quietly. Hopefully what she'd seen last night hadn't driven her completely off the deep end straight into some sort of mumbling psychosis.

He called out, "Good morning. How was the show?" He heard her feet hit the floor and wondered if she'd gotten any sleep herself, curled up in the chair, or if Hyde had kept her attention all night.

She yawned, maybe stretched. "Fascinating."

"Where's Jolie?"

"She went downstairs a few hours ago. I think she got annoyed with all my questions."

"Jolie doesn't get annoyed very easily. You must have had a lot of questions." He saw her when she stopped just outside the bars. Jesus, she looked exhausted—pale skin, matching dark rings under her eyes. Or maybe that's what terror left behind on someone's face after they saw a monster.

She gripped the bars. "Does she know about Chastity?"

"Nope. That's your tale to tell. Not mine." He flicked his head to the cage's door. "She usually unlocks me. She left the keys on the table, didn't she?"

"Yeah, sorry." She ran out of his line of vision, and then ran back into it, gripping the keychain in her hand.

He wasn't sure if she was shaking or was just unfamiliar with industrial-sized padlocks and cages, but it took her a while to open it.

"How can you stay in there?"

"No choice." And he needed to get out of here as soon as fucking possible. "Not a lounge chair under an umbrella here. You mind?"

She stepped inside, her eyes taking turns between gawking at his body and trying to avoid it.

"And the performance continues," he muttered. "While I'd love to stay here spread-eagle all day while you ogle me, my arms are cramped."

She blushed. "Why don't you wear something when you...change?"

"We don't seem to like the feel of clothing." He'd used the word 'we.' Shit, that was something he'd never thought he'd do, but, strangely, it eased the weight in his chest at the same time. He wasn't alone anymore. "Carter didn't tell you about that part?"

"He told me." Avoiding his eyes, she bent over to unlock the chains on his ankles. "It'd be a tough thing to miss."

"What'd you think?"

"Of last night? You're a horrible, horny monster."

"Thank you. But what did you think of Hyde?"

"I'm guessing the crappy jokes are all yours." She hesitated at the locks binding his wrists. "But I'll ask anyway: You're really *you*, right?"

He nodded as she freed his hands. "If I wasn't, you'd be on the ground screaming about now." He rubbed his forehead. No pain this time. "You don't get headaches, do you? The day after?"

"No. You do?"

He nodded his head and then left it low to stretch out his neck. "But only recently. Last six months or so." Maybe it was part of the reason he'd transformed a day early, a symptom of losing control. "But not today. Hell, maybe I'm cured." Pushing himself up, he watched her. She was strong. Scared but strong. "You're taking this much better than I thought you would."

"I'm still in shock." She shrugged, a lock of hair falling into her eyes. "What now?"

"I take a shower—you're welcome to join me—and then we have a nice long chat. Over breakfast. I'm starving."

Jolie was sacked out on the sofa downstairs, her dark hair covering most of both eyes, strands of it blowing up and down with every breath. The empty champagne bottle was tucked between her hip and the cushion.

Eden tiptoed past her and went to look for something to cook for breakfast. She started by attempting to make a pot of coffee. There were so many buttons on the machine, she wondered if she'd brew coffee or a pot full of water. It was a gadget only rich people knew how to use. The whir of the beans being ground might be enough to keep her vertical until it was ready. Then, through some sort of miracle, the beans fed into the right place and, when she bent in close, the magnificent aroma of java hit her scent glands.

She should have slept, but there was no way she could. Mitch's Hyde had kept her transfixed all night. He'd growled, struggled, and spouted obscenities for hours. After Jolie left the room, Eden had curled herself up in the chair, wrapped her arms around her knees, and watched the freak show.

So she was paying for it now. Each eyelid felt like it weighed seventy pounds. She was nauseous and miserable. Her brain was so rattled, it couldn't seem to process what she'd learned over the past few days. A curtain had been pulled back, giving her an ocean view of who, or what, she was. But right now, her exhaustion left the vision fuzzy, blinding her, unable to assimilate the facts of what she'd seen and heard.

"Coffee," Jolie yelled from the other room. Eden took three mugs out of the cabinet.

Dragging her feet, Jolie came into the kitchen and flopped

herself onto a tall stool next to the center island. "I think I'm still drunk." She rested her elbows on the marble and leaned her face into her hands. "Please tell me you made a full pot."

"Um...maybe? At least, I tried to." She peeked into the carafe—"Hey, it worked"—and poured the dark, rich goodness into three cups.

Jolie shifted her face into one hand and stuck the other out. "Give it to me." She gulped the stuff down, even though it had to be burning a hole in her tongue. Unless she didn't let it stay in her mouth long enough to feel it and her throat was lined with some kind of fire retardant.

Eden took some cream from the fridge and still had to blow in her cup before she took a sip.

"Did you stay up there all night?" Jolie asked.

"Yeah."

She rubbed her forehead in between sips. "I remember the first time I saw him change. Freaked the shit out of me, honestly. I remember Shelly, Mitchell's sister, holding me put, petting my arm like I was some sort of flight risk. You know, the 'smile and nod' kind of thing."

Eden could have used some of that, but instead had been left huddled in a chair, too afraid to flee. "Why did he show you?"

Jolie raised her eyes to Eden's. "Because he trusts me." The squint of her eyes was not a reaction to the sunlight flowing through the kitchen windows. She was pissed.

"I didn't mean anything bad. I just meant that if he already had someone to lock and unlock him, I'm surprised he told anyone else." Okay, that was stupid. He'd shown Eden, so she'd just insinuated that Jolie was going to be replaced. Not a direction she wanted to travel in. "I didn't mean that either. I meant—"

Jolie released Eden from their eye-lock. "I know what you meant: Why did he tell me when he had his big sis? Why did he tell you when he has me?"

Eden nodded.

"You never met Shelly, did you?"

"No. She died before I met him."

"Mitchell wanted to make sure someone else knew about Hyde so she didn't have to do it on her own anymore. He didn't want her to be the only one."

"Why not?"

"Because he felt like two people sharing the burden was better than one dealing with the whole shebang." Jolie sipped her coffee. "Shelly was the one who originally told me, *chose* me. We were friends. A few months before she died, she told me she was pregnant and didn't want Mitchell to know until her belly started to really show. I took over all of Hyde's care so she didn't have to be near him. He might've hurt her. Accidentally, you know."

"And then she was killed?"

"Crazy world we live in, isn't it?"

"I thought at least one of you would've made me breakfast by now. What the hell have you been doing?" Mitch's hair was still wet from the shower. He wore jeans and a black t-shirt that showed off his chest and waist, reminding Eden of all that she'd seen of him last night.

She focused her attention on handing him some coffee. As he took the cup, their fingers brushed and she flinched backwards, sending the mug and its contents crashing onto the tile floor. Mitch didn't move even as the hot coffee splashed on his bare feet, his only reaction a slight twitch of one eye. Apologizing profusely, Eden ran for a towel and knelt down in front of him, wiping his feet and the floor.

"Jolie, go home." His voice was flat, dead sounding.

"Huh?"

Though she couldn't see Jolie from the other side of the island, Eden imagined the shock on her face mirrored her own.

"Go home," he said, without glancing at the other woman. "Eden and I have lots to talk about."

Eden stood and saw Jolie shove her stool back, her mouth moving as if she had lots to talk about as well. She clamped her jaw shut and stalked out of the kitchen. From the living room, Eden heard sounds of shuffling, clinking, and angry mumbling.

Neither of them spoke until they heard the front door slam. Mitch flicked his head. "Follow me."

CHAPTER XXIII

Eden trailed after him through the living room, up the stairs and back into…Hyde's room.

He leaned against the wall of bars and motioned for her to sit. "Tell me what you're thinking."

Perched on the arm of the chair, she stared into the cage behind him. "What I'm thinking? I'm thinking this is the best coffee I've ever tasted. I'm thinking that this room is a little drafty and it would be nice to have a sweater or something. I'm thinking…I'm..." She put her mug on the table, sighed, and ran a hand through her hair. Avoiding his gaze no longer possible—he wanted to know what was going on in her mind and she wanted to know the same about his. "I'm thinking about how stupid I feel. How much I thought I knew about the world. About myself. And how wrong I was about all of it."

"This is only one part of you. And definitely not the most important part."

Her chest felt closed in, locked, like she couldn't get a deep enough breath. "How do you deal with it?"

"How *I* deal with it is not how you should."

"But Chastity"—she put her hand to her chest, then out to him—"Hyde. We're the same."

"No, we're not. *They're* not. Chastity is liquid sex. Hyde is…not human. He makes her look like Mother Theresa."

"Except you only have to deal with him every five weeks, right? Chastity's like a terrible neighbor who keeps showing up whenever she feels like it. No, she's worse."

"And she's much more fun." He rubbed his wrists, still red and scraped from the cuffs.

"Why does it happen more often to me?"

He shrugged. "Chastity is *made* from concentrate. Hyde *is* the concentrate. He used to be like her—less anger, more sass. As life toughened me up, he made fewer appearances, but each one was more violent than the last. The way I figure it, making rage into a full-time job changes the frequency, but increases intensity. Know what I mean?"

Not really. "So that's why you're such a jerk?"

"Partly."

"And the other part?"

He smirked. "I enjoy it."

"How did you figure out what you are?"

"My father. He taught me everything."

"Can you teach me?"

"No." Then he mumbled, "You don't want to be like me."

She stood, suddenly furious that after all of this, he was falling right back into keeping things from her. Who else did she have? "That's bull. What I *don't* want is to be someone who wakes up covered in blood who thinks something inside of her might've caused it. Someone who never knows what her other half will do or where she'll go." She stifled her tears and pointed all her frustration at him. "If I can't get that, I'd at least like it to happen less frequently. So teach me!"

"I can't change who you are. I don't *want* to. My father changed me with his belt. With his fists. I'm not going to do that to you."

"Well, find another way! I can't do it without you. Should I just go out and pick a fight"—like she was doing with him—"so someone beats the tar out of me? Is your dad still alive?

Maybe he'll do it."

"It wasn't the beatings that did it." He kept his voice controlled, but he couldn't do the same with his eyes—they felt like lasers singeing holes into hers. "It was the darkness inside of me that it created."

She matched his anger, advancing on him until she had him pressing his back into the metal he leaned against. Perhaps in an attempt to control his own anger. "I'm loaded with darkness. Why hasn't that controlled it?"

He shook his head. "Whatever you've been through isn't enough. You're still good. You don't even lie, for Christ's sake. Not sure if the virginal attitude helps or not."

"A part of me played in a woman's blood, maybe more." She swallowed. "And she may have even killed your sister. What's darker than that?"

"She didn't kill my sister."

"How the heck do you know?" she screamed.

"Because *I* did."

She blinked, stunned. "You killed your sister?" Then she noticed his hands, gripping the bars like he was trying to stop them from shaking. Or striking.

His nostrils flared and his words barely made it out of his clenched jaw. "I woke with Shelly's blood dripping down my door, her body lying on my steps. Just like what you saw in your flashback. Chastity must have been there, must have seen me kill her." His jaw shook as if he was fighting against an impending breakdown. "I wanted it to be you. I really did. I wanted to believe it wasn't my fault."

"You broke out of the cage?"

He scratched his forehead. "Jolie thought she might not have closed the lock all the way. I thought the chains would hold him back. I was wrong. I have thicker ones now."

"Do you have flashbacks of it?"

"No, not killing her. No."

"So it could have been someone else. It could have been Chastity."

"No, it couldn't have been her. You wouldn't still be changing so often. It would've slowed down."

"Maybe you're wrong. Maybe one murder doesn't change anything."

"It did for me. It changed everything."

That stopped her. "You mean you killed someone before your sister?" She backed away, suddenly terrified of the man who, despite his cruelty, she was continually drawn to.

He laughed. "Why are you surprised? Or are you still under the mistaken impression that I am a good man?"

She shrugged, not knowing what she should expect from him. A good man? No, she wouldn't go that far. But a murderer?

"Hmm," he said. "It seems we both made some bad assumptions."

"Maybe we did."

He took a deep breath, wiped his forehead, and separated himself from the cage. "I need to sit down." After taking her place on the chair, he said, "My father's Hyde tore my mother apart in front of me. Tore her apart. She was trying to protect us.

"Before that moment, I don't remember much about him. Just rage…violence…terror. He could have had a heart, I don't know. Doubt it, but it's possible. There had to have been a reason my mother stayed with him, right?"

Since he was looking at the floor and not at her, Eden didn't respond.

"Before that I have memories of him being somewhat under control. Most of the time. He'd go out a lot, leave us alone—my mom, Shelly, and me. That was a lot better than having him around. I didn't recognize the pattern until a lot later, thinking back on it. Then just after I turned fifteen, I *turned*." He took a breath. "Every four days, just like you. Needless to say, we were all very disappointed."

Every word seemed to take concentration to release, as if he'd never said them out loud before. "I was soft back then—

beaten into submission. But then I grew up. Dealing with that rage, accepting it"—he pointed his finger at her—"and not in any way I would suggest, created more time between transformations, but not significantly. Not predictably. Not until my father died. Not until I killed him."

He looked at her, waiting for a reaction she was too exhausted to give, a question she was too tired to ask. He didn't offer her an explanation, a rationalization. Maybe because he thought she understood better than anyone else would. Not that he would have been right, of course, until she had seen the beast within Mitch firsthand.

He sighed. "After that I started to know when it was going to happen. I can feel it, feel *him*. And it's predictable now, every five weeks. One night every five weeks, I turn into a harder, angrier, larger beast than I am now. As if my nature took those other days and slammed them all together for one night of hell. And the rest of the time, I'm just a bastard. Who can control my urges…most of the time."

His eyes swept over her body, sending a chill through her. Pleasant and unpleasant at the same time. Desire and fear so close together, twisting around each other, moving as one.

"So what do we do now?" she asked, shivering.

"We? *We* do nothing. I'm done," he said, reclining in the chair. "Now that you know all I do, you're free to go."

"Are you kidding me? Now that I know, I'm on my own?" She wiped imaginary dust from her hands. "Congratulations, you're a monster like me, now go home," she mimicked. "Knowing the truth is just the beginning, Mitch. Once you know the facts, you figure out a way to change them." But he'd just accepted it and expected her to do the same.

"I told you about Chastity," he said. "Showed you Hyde, put bars on your windows, and a hell of a lock on your door. What the fuck else do you want from me?"

"I don't know." Tears of helplessness ran down her cheeks, feeling as if they were slicing her skin open as they flowed. What if there really was nothing she could do about it? About

any of this. My God, what was she going to do? "It's okay.
I'll be okay." She tried to speak with confidence, but couldn't
stop her lip from trembling. "I'll figure something out.
Thank—"

"Stop doing that." He motioned at her face. "Don't—Agh!
Alright! There's something else. Just turn off the sprinklers."
He went to the dresser and looked inside the second drawer.
"What the—?"

"What?" She approached him.

"I thought I had a lot more."

She peered around his broad shoulders, then gave up and
stepped in close to him. Inside the drawer were two vials of a
clear liquid—no labels—and two packages of syringes, one of
them almost empty.

She took three quick steps backward. "Oh, no. Not that.
I'm not touching that."

He picked up one of the vials, turning it in his hand. "It
will stop you from transforming. I don't use it—that's why I
have the cage and the cuffs—but I always keep some in a
syringe, just in case."

The shake of her head was more like a shiver than a sign
of disagreement. "I'm not doing it."

"Jesus, why are you so stubborn? I'm trying to help you.
Isn't that what you wanted? Don't you want it to stop?"

"Not with that."

"Look, you don't have to *like* it, but it's an option."

"Not for me, it isn't. My mom was a junkie." Her mind
flashed back to those days, more than a decade before, days
she hadn't revisited since she'd been placed in her first foster
home. Childhood memories that had all been shoved deeply
into the section of her mind that blocked out the most painful
of her life experiences. But now they began to crash into her
consciousness like a tsunami, tucked in between random
assaults, faces of those who had sexually abused her, and even
some happy moments with her mom during the rare times
she'd be sober.

Mom dressed like street trash, giving me a tearful kiss on my forehead before leaving the house at midnight, night after night after night. The sound of a slap I was too scared to feel after I hid her stash. I was, what, seven? The hands of a man the courts had trusted to keep me safe scraping my body. The look on Mom's face when I found her on the ground, the needle still dangling from her arm. For hours, I'd sat with her, trying to wake her up. Like some terribly cheesy movie-of-the-week sob-fest.

"No, I can't do that." Her own voice stopped the images from escaping any further. "I won't be like her." She forced them from her mind's eye, back into the box of darkness she'd do anything necessary to keep them enclosed in. "She's gone."

"It's okay," he whispered. "You're okay." At some point, he'd led her back to the chair. He was kneeling next to her and stroking her hair. "That's how she died?" There was a softness in his tone she'd not known he was capable of. Sadness in his eyes.

She nodded slowly, hammering another nail into the box with each downward motion. "I was eight. I woke up and found her." Drugs, not life, still filling her veins.

"Do you blame her or the drugs?"

Her head popped up. "What kind of a question is that?"

He shifted back onto his feet in a crouch. "Maybe she knew something you didn't."

"Like what? How to shoot up?"

"Maybe she was self-medicating to stop her transformation. Did you ever see her Hyde?"

"No." It was everything the disillusioned little girl inside her could hope for, and that part clutched onto the idea, hoping it was true. *I'm hoping my mother was a monster?* "She left me alone a lot. I always thought it was because she was trying to score more dope or…I don't know…selling herself to get more cash."

"Maybe she was." He shrugged. "But maybe her addiction

didn't start out as recreational."

No, it couldn't be true. "Once, in a rare sober moment, she told me that she wished she'd never started." Why did Eden trust him? She'd never even told Carter about her mother. Was it because she and Mitch shared a side of themselves no one else would ever understand? Or was it because, looking into his eyes, she saw a goodness he'd buried so deeply even *he* didn't know it existed? "Originally, it had been prescribed at a clinic—the legal stuff. Then when that ran out..."

He leaned toward her and cocked his head. "Prescribed for what?"

"I don't know. I was, like, seven when she mentioned it. And she'd already been using for years. The semi-apology stuck with me, but the rationalization didn't."

"The reason," he corrected.

"Reason, rationalization. What's the difference?"

"The difference is *why* it started. What made it start. If she self-medicated to keep her Hyde under control, when it started is *very* important."

Eden shrugged. "I don't remember and she sure-as-heck can't tell me, so it doesn't make any difference now, does it?"

He sighed. "I suppose not. It just would have been helpful to know. There are times when I think all of this is some kind of sick joke. Or someone's way of punishing me. It started with my father's genes, but sometimes—" He shook his head. "I can't deal with the what-ifs, I can barely deal with the what-now's. Was your mother good to you?"

"She was high all the time."

"But was she good to you?"

"Yeah... Mostly. That doesn't mean she transformed, though. She could've just been an addict like millions of other addicts."

"True. But it ran in my family, why wouldn't it run in yours?"

"Why would anyone like that reproduce?"

"Well," he said, breaking into the singsong of how a parent

would speak to a child, "when a man and a woman love each other, they *express* that feeling physically. Although, occasionally, the 'love' part doesn't apply, and they just want to get naked and fuck." He grinned like he was encouraging her to do the same.

Sure, like I can find a silver lining in this. "I was an accident. Some guy she screwed when she was high. Charming story to tell your kid, right? I think she might have snuck it in with the there's-no-Santa-Claus discussion."

"Until I changed for the first time, I never understood my father. I still would never have done what he did to us, but now I understand that he couldn't control himself. He should have left like your mom, or stayed in a cage like I do. Even when he was human."

"Did your sister change?"

"No. But she understood. She took care of me when I couldn't take care of myself." He looked up and blinked eyes that were shiny.

"It's okay to cry if you need to," she said softly.

"I don't cry," he said.

"Ever?"

"No."

"What? You don't have tear ducts? Or are you just an unfeeling bastard?" she teased, trying to remind him of the openness they'd had just moments ago.

"To my knowledge, I have tear ducts. So I guess that leaves us with the second option." As he shifted onto his feet, she saw his wall come up.

"Not even over your sister? Not once?"

"Maybe just once." Then he muttered, "*Or constantly.*"

"I'm sorry."

"Shelly was a good person—same genes, totally different result. She recognized the signs before I did. She found chains we thought would be strong enough and ordered the cage."

Eden didn't want to see him cry. One of them sporadically weeping was enough. Why? Because that would make him likeable, understandable. Because it would make this conversation real.

"So, did you buy that off the rack?" she asked.

He looked up and smirked, his eyes shining but not leaking. "It's built for large animals. Lions, tigers—"

"And bears."

"Oh, my." His smile was infectious. So they stood there, grinning at each other, ignoring the fact that neither of them would ever have a normal life again. That both of them were monsters.

"I can't imagine you watching that movie," Eden said.

He cocked his head to the side. "I have other interests, Eden."

"You mean, other than pissing me off and being a total jerk?"

"Well, those seem to be my favorites. But, yeah, I do have other hobbies."

She glanced away, and her gaze fell onto the table where he'd put the vial and where Jolie had placed a syringe last night. Her grin disappeared. "I can't use that."

"Then you need to stay here. Or, if that's…undesirable to you, at least make sure Carter knows what's at stake and stops taking whatever he's on that makes him too groggy to wake up when you change. Or he'll be the only one who ever sleeps again."

"Oh my God, Carter!" She jumped up. "He must be freaking out right now. I promised I'd come home."

Mitch's lips tightened. "Poor guy. He must have had a horrible evening."

She glared at him. "Leave him alone. None of this is his fault. He's been nothing but good to me."

"There's that word again—good. He's good. You're good. Aren't we all just…good."

"Not all of us."

He smirked. "Touché. Well, you'd better hurry home and tell all the good fucking news to your good fucking man.

Oops, make that your good *not* fucking man."

"You've got the jerk thing down pat, you know that?"

"Thank you. You might try it yourself—it would make you a little more interesting."

"Wow. Thanks for all the support and kindness you've shown me. But I think I've had more than enough of it."

"Then my work here is done." He bowed deeply. "You still know the way out, don't you?" The understanding was gone from his eyes, the kindness. He was a shell. A full-time bastard again. Dumping a bit of his anger out to keep Hyde from appearing. Eden accepted it, not wanting to experience Hyde's wrath ever again.

"What is the Clinic, Mitch?"

He blinked. "What did you say?"

"The Clinic. What is it?"

"I have no idea. Where did you hear that?"

"Hyde mentioned it. Right before he told me how attractive I was and how he'd like to see if I was just as attractive without my skin."

Mitch shivered and then his shoulders slumped. "I'm sorry, Eden. I'm sorry I showed him to you." When he met her gaze, his face was tight, controlled. He was so adept at putting distance between them. "It won't happen again."

"All of us hate to be caged, Mitch. For Hyde and maybe Chastity, it's necessary. But for the rest of us, it's a choice." Eden stalked out, wondering which choice she was making.

CHAPTER XXIV

Eden ran over the front lawn, but what she saw waiting just outside of Mitch's property made her slam on the brakes and skid to a stop. Carter was sitting in his car, tapping his hand on the steering wheel, glaring at her.

She walked sheepishly to the passenger side and slid in. "I'm sorry."

"Yeah."

"Have you been here a while?"

"Yeah."

"I'm sorry."

"You said that already."

"And I meant it. Both times. I should've at least called, I was just..."

His hand hit the steering wheel. "You were just *what*, Eden? Too busy? Too exhausted? Too naked? What?"

She'd pushed herself closer to the door with every accusation. The first two were true, but the last? It hurt just to think he'd believe that of her. Though she knew full well that only a few days ago, she and Mitch hadn't been all that far from what Carter was insinuating. If he hadn't stopped. If her eyes hadn't— "I'm sorry."

"Stop saying that!"

"We didn't *do* anything, Carter. I swear."

"So what the hell did you do all night? Play cards? Do each other's toenails? 'Cause, let me tell you, babe, I have a really hard time believing that dear ole Mitch likes making s'mores."

She wished she'd taken a moment before darting off to think about which parts of the night she could tell him. Not that she'd imagined him staking out the house, of course. But Mitch hadn't told Jolie about Chastity, and she was thankful. So was it fair for her to tell Carter about Hyde? Was that her 'tale to tell'?

"I talked to Jolie for a while. She was there all night, too." She swallowed, hoping he wouldn't ask her a question she'd have to lie to him about, knowing he would.

He stared at the steering wheel. "Did she give you some answers?"

"Yes, some." She knew he wanted more from her but dreaded going too far.

"Some. But not enough." He shook his head and traced the Jeep emblem with a shaking finger. "Did you talk to Mitch too?"

"This morning, yes. But he wasn't there last night. He left a few hours after you did and came back early this morning." Technically, that was true—Mitch had stepped out of his mind for the evening and left his body for Hyde to inhabit. But technicalities weren't what Carter deserved. "Can we go home now? I'm tired."

He didn't turn on the car. "Why am I forced to drag this out of you? What aren't you telling me?"

"Nothing." The word stuck in her throat. The first outright lie she'd ever told him. "We talked about Chastity. What she's like, when she appears. There's a rough pattern, you know? Every four days."

He studied her face, his eyes darting to her eyes, then her lips, then her body. "That's all that happened? All night?"

"That's it." The lie felt like a dry-swallowed pill, a rock

she struggled to swallow, slowly moving down her throat. And even though she could keep it down, she couldn't stomach it. "Really." She wished he'd stop looking at her like that, as if he could see the lies pouring out of her mouth.

He started the engine. "So what now?"

Eden forced herself to smile. *Move on. Pretend everything is okay.* "We go home, I take a nap, you make me breakfast, and then we mark every fourth day on the calendar."

"Not until you take that damned dress off and burn it."

She looked down at the dress Mitch had bought her. She'd completely forgotten about it. Just like she'd forgotten about Carter, her promise to return home last night, and, oh yeah, telling the truth. Well, she hadn't actually forgotten about that, had she? More like she'd considered it and then deliberately did something she knew was wrong.

Why was she lying for a self-proclaimed-and-proud-of-it bastard while hurting the man who sat beside her, who had stood beside her for so many years? To protect him? From what? The answer stung even more than the lie had.

Me.

She was protecting Carter from herself.

The drive home felt as long as the Mississippi River. As they pulled up in front of their apartment building, she touched his wrist, drawing a figure eight on it.

"Carter?"

He flicked his arm away, flipped the gearshift, and looked at her.

"I think you need to move on." She ignored his confused expression and continued. "I adore you, but I think it would be best for us to live apart from now on."

"Is this about him?" There was fire in his voice.

"No. It's not about him. At all. This is about you. You don't deserve this. To live like this."

"And *you* do?"

"No, I—I don't think I do either, but you can walk away. I can't. You can have a normal life."

His eyes shone. "Why would you ever think that I could walk away?"

She might have been out of tears. Or maybe she was just too lost and overwhelmed, but she had no reactions left in her to give.

He twisted in his seat and took her hand. "If you want to live apart because of any other reason, then that's...fine. But until this thing with Chastity stops happening, I'll be spending my nights with you, so deal with it."

Deal with it. Something she hadn't really even tried yet. Relying on Carter and then Mitch to help her through. She took a deep breath. Wasn't it time to start living her own life instead of having other people live it for her?

She pretended to nap for most of the day, not wanting to talk to him—to lie to him—anymore. He checked on her frequently, standing in the doorway to her room, not speaking or coming any closer. She hoped and feared that he was formulating a plan for a life without her.

When she finally got out of bed, she didn't ask about the dress. He'd stood right next to her when she'd thrown it into the trash. Since then the garbage can had been emptied.

Their conversations were stilted and awkward all afternoon. "Are you hungry?" "Not really," said by each of them to the other numerous times. That was pretty much it. Carter sat on the couch and punched the arrows on the remote incessantly.

Eden stared at the calendar posted on the fridge. His study group and workout schedule, the days he would go to the police station to intern, a dentist appointment next week, the day she needed to register for next fall's classes. All normal things. Her fingers gripped the dry erase marker.

Every four days. *Great.* How does one mark 'doom' on their schedule? A circle? A smiley face? She made a large 'X' through every fourth day. Her mouth dry, she counted 1-2-3-Chastity, 1-2-3-Chastity...

From directly behind her, Carter's voice sent a spasm

down her back. "You sure about this every four days thing?"

"Pretty sure."

His fingers tapped her shoulder, as if the body they belonged to wasn't sure they were allowed to touch. Or were afraid to. "Until we're sure, I'll stay here."

"Okay." Oh God, he was really going to leave her. She knew it was for the best. For *his* best. And it was bound to happen one day. She'd never be able to offer him what he needed, especially now.

He wandered back into the living room and flopped down onto the couch again, the light of the room changing as he flipped through the channels. It was getting dark outside. Night was coming. If Mitch was right about the pattern, tonight she could sleep. And tomorrow? Well, tomorrow was a completely different story.

It was like waiting for the guillotine blade to fall. Knowing that tonight, as soon as she fell asleep, she would be somewhere else, and Chastity would take over her body. Eden was so tired—she'd barely slept last night, flinching every time her eyes closed all the way. And she'd only gotten a minimal amount of sleep for days before that. Tonight wouldn't give her any rest either. *How can this go on indefinitely?* Her mind was already playing tricks with her, sleep deprivation leaving her unsure of what was real.

At ten o'clock, she started to nod off on a kitchen chair. She jerked up and went into the living room.

"Carter?"

He glanced up from the television. He looked as exhausted as she felt. She wondered how much sleep he'd gotten last night, or the night before while waiting for her to come home.

"Can you lock me into my room?"

He dragged his tall frame off the couch and followed her. She flipped the padlock on her window bars closed and climbed into bed, her heart hammering in her chest.

"Good night," she said.

His lips were pressed together as he started to close the door.

"Carter?"

He stopped and finally looked her in the eyes. "Yeah?"

"You mean everything to me. I love you." The words tumbled out of her mouth, words she'd never actually said aloud. "Not in the way I know you want me to, but I love you so much. I'm so sorry."

"Yeah." He swallowed, his eyes filled with pain and disappointment and goodbye. "I love you too, Eden." He was letting that part of his love for her go, she could see it. "I'll be right outside the door."

She heard the padlock snap shut. She was alone.

CHAPTER XXV

Mitch had spent the day pacing a trench into the floor. After about two hours of laps in the pool and an hour pounding on the treadmill, even exercise couldn't distract him anymore.

The Clinic. He needed to know if Margaret had ever heard of it. If a shrink as well-connected as she was didn't know, then it didn't have anything to do with psychiatry. He left a message on her voicemail. When Eden had told him Hyde mentioned it—or cursed it or groaned it—a spark had lit inside him. He'd heard the name but couldn't place it. A pharmaceutical company? Low-fucking-cost vaccination business? Doc-in-the-box?

Hell, it was probably just some company he'd done a lecture for at some point. Jolie hadn't answered her phone, either, so she was no help. He'd considered going to the office to look, but everything was on that stupid computer filing program Jolie had set up and Mitch had never bothered to learn how to use. That was what he had *her* for.

Night was coming. And he couldn't get his mind off of that damned girl. Thankfully, he trusted the locks more than that boyfriend of hers, so at least he knew she'd be safe. She was tough, he kept telling himself. He just hoped she was tough *enough.*

He knew Jolie had spoken the truth. Eden was at least part of the reason Hyde had come out early. It was the only thing that made sense. He'd let her inside of him, made him want to be a better man, and that was dangerous. For everyone. He couldn't be around her anymore. He needed to sink back into the cesspool of his old life. Pre-Eden. Get back to the good ole days of being a prick and not letting anyone close. That was safer.

A very long, very hot shower made it even clearer. He wrapped a towel around his hips and walked into his bedroom. Night was here. Shit. He'd taken a *very* long shower. The hallway was dark, but the stairway was lit, sending in just enough light so he could make it across the room.

He blinked, seeing the silhouette of a woman in the hallway. "Jolie? Is that you?" He chuckled at the idea that he'd just said a line from every slasher movie ever made. "Is anyone there?" Funny. Horror movies had nothing on his pathetic existence.

The curvy shape came closer, until it became more than an outline.

"Hmm…you're not Jolie."

She shook her head, but there wasn't enough light to see her eyes or her hair.

"Which one are you?" Not that it really mattered—he didn't want either of them here.

She ripped off her shirt and tossed it onto the ground.

That's an answer I can understand. "Good evening, Chastity."

She slithered into the room and walked a tight circle around him. Why had she come inside this time instead of just leaving Eden to wake up on his doorstep?

He needed to figure out what to do with her. But her hand running across his chest was very distracting. *Break contact, Mitch. Do something. What are you, fourteen?* He crossed his arms but couldn't seem to get his legs to work. "How'd you get out of her apartment, Chastity?" Damn, the feel of her breasts through the thin layer of her lace bra pressing against his arm was even more distracting. "You're going to have to find another part of the house to play in."

"Are you saying no to me again?" she pouted from behind him, the heat of her body scorching his back.

"I am."

She reached her arm around him, traced a trail down his abs, and settled her grip around his traitorous erection, the thickness of the towel providing too little protection. "But your cock isn't."

"Thankfully, my cock doesn't do all of my thinking for me. Please remove your hand." When she gave him a firm squeeze, he stifled a moan. He took her wrist and pried her fingers off him. "No means no, Chastity."

She pulled back her hand. "No one says no to me." Dumbfounded. "Why do you?"

The long version/truth wouldn't hold her attention. "Eden asked me to."

She huffed and came around to face him. "Eden asked you to? Oh well, if *Eden* asked you to! Anything for her." She stepped in close and whispered in his ear, "Would you say no to her?"

He said nothing. All he wanted was for her to get away from him. Far, far away from him.

Chastity threw her head back and laughed. "Christ, I hope you're a better liar in front of her. She'll walk all over you."

He ground his teeth together. He had nothing to prove to her. To himself? Now, that was a different story. One he'd deal with eventually, but not now. No, now was the time to focus on breathing and baseball.

"You obviously don't know anything about your other half."

She shrugged and ran her hand through his hair, down his back to the too-thin barrier of the towel covering his ass. "But I know all about men. About you. I know you have a fun side.

And a dangerous side."

Could she know about Hyde? Sense him? Or had she seen him?

Mitch took a step away from her grip. "What do you know about my dangerous side?"

"He's a lot more entertaining than you are. Why can't you be more like him?"

He fought the need to be exactly who this woman—or creature—wanted him to be, backing up until his thighs bumped the mattress. "Have you seen him?"

Her eyes flashed. "I'll tell you all about him, if…"

This wasn't going to be good. "If what?"

"If you play with me. All night, like a good boy."

He sat down hard on the bed, which she took as an invitation and wiggled over to join him. He barely got his hand out in time to stop her, his palm pressing into her tight belly as she leaned toward him.

"I haven't agreed to anything."

"Yet."

Jesus, she was so sure of herself. Or of him. *Damn it.* He shook his head. "I haven't agreed to anything. Period." Was he actually considering this? Putting out to get some information from her? The temptation was definitely there. But while he'd never met a promise he couldn't break, this involved Eden too. Chastity would be using both of them. How much did he owe the girl?

Chastity straightened, crossed her arms around her ample breasts, and tapped a foot on the hardwood floor. "This is boring." She had the attention span of a spaniel.

If he didn't say something soon, she'd just move on to other prey. Maybe he could use something other than his body and hers as leverage. "Alright, but not here."

She smiled, her tongue peeking out as she ran it over her pearly whites. "Where?"

"Follow me." As he walked by her, she grabbed the edge of his towel and yanked it off him, giggling.

"That was completely unnecessary," he grumbled.

"I know," she said, tossing the towel onto the ground and following his naked body.

He took her down the hallway into Hyde's room.

"I've seen this room before," she said.

He glanced at her, shocked. "When?"

She shrugged. "I get images of places she's been, the boring shit she does. Almost all of it is boring, I swear."

"You get to do all the fun stuff, right?"

"Sure. Lots." Her voice was lower than Eden's. And the more she spoke, the more Mitch felt like he was talking to a cast member of *The Real World*. Not that he'd ever really paid attention to reality television, or much of reality for that matter.

He led her into the cage. "What kinds of stuff?"

"Boys. Booze. Drugs. You know, the things that are—" Her eyes widened when she saw the straps. "Are you going to tie me up or can *I* do you?"

"What kind of drugs?" He cringed at the idea that Eden had been doing drugs without her knowledge. "Ladies first."

She ripped off her bra, slid her skirt down over her hips, and hopped onto the mattress. Spreading her arms and legs out to each corner, she asked, "What are you waiting for?"

He was waiting for his eyes to go back into their sockets. Yeah, and it would be nice if his cock would stop throbbing. *Damn it, focus.* "What kind of drugs do you do?" He ran a hand through his hair and bent down to attach the cuffs to her wrists.

She tugged against the straps, satisfied they were tight enough, and grinned. "Whatever I can, but never any uppers. That might wake her up and I would have to go away."

Interesting. "You're a smart girl."

"Yes, I am."

Not smart enough to know what I'm about to do, though. No, she definitely wasn't Eden. "What else do you know about her?" Aside from his rapid heartbeat and dry mouth, this was incredible. He was getting a glimpse into Hyde in a way he never thought possible. But he needed a cold shower. Maybe he could have one installed...

"I don't want to talk about her. I want to play."

He rubbed his face, thankful the sight of her body outstretched like that was gone even momentarily. "Now we play." He turned and walked out of the cage. With a quick glance to the table, checking to see if the keys were still there, he locked the door. "Chastity, have you ever heard of The Clinic?"

"Mitch, let me out. Or come in here." She yanked against the straps. "This isn't fun."

"What do you know about my Hyde?"

She clenched her jaw, squeezing the words through it. "Mitch, let me out!"

"Tell me what I want to know and I will," he lied. His heart was pounding, not from lust—which *was* present—but from misery. He tried to think of her as an animal that needed to be protected from herself. But she wore Eden's body, Eden's face. Everything but the hair and eyes. That's what he focused on.

Once she understood that he'd played her, she screamed at him for hours, shouting obscenities and threats, and tugging against the bonds with her entire body. Eden would feel it tomorrow. Eventually she calmed down and tried another tactic—manipulation. She rubbed herself on the sheet and arched her back, then contracted her hips up and down, dry-humping the stiflingly hot air of the room.

It was torturous for Mitch as well. He kept his hands gripped onto the arms of the chair, as far away from his cock as possible, and fidgeted, unable to leave even to go get some pants on. Both of them were sweating. He tried to get her to talk, but aside from all kinds of suggestions about how he could use her body, she stayed mute. Not what he'd hoped. She told him nothing about Hyde, what she'd done, or anything she'd witnessed. A total bust.

With one last struggle to free herself, she sighed, almost crying. "You'll be happy now, Mitch. She's coming back." Her eyes closed and her whole body twitched. Then she was still.

Mitch approached the cage and watched her. As her hair shortened and darkened, he waited. She was truly beautiful. He knew he shouldn't be a part of her life and at the same time wondered if that was possible. It was easier to blame it on Chastity, take no responsibility at all. Truth was, he wanted to be with her. And if he couldn't have Eden, then, at some point, he might convince himself that Chastity would be good enough. Hell, he'd done worse things.

In fact, at this very moment, he was considering one. He couldn't wait to get his hands on Carter. That fucking kid needed a wake-up call. Chastity could have ended up anywhere. With anyone. And Mitch had probably just burned a bridge to ashes with her. Next time she came out, she wouldn't come to him. Okay, decision made—he'd kick Carter's ass and convince Eden she needed to be caged. A conversation he *so* didn't want to have.

CHAPTER XXVI

Mitch saw Eden gasp, eyes wide open, and move to sit up. The chains stopped her, snapping her back to the mattress. Her scream was the most desperate and anguished sound he'd ever heard. Damn it, why hadn't he untied her instead of contemplating his own crap?

"Hey! It's me, Mitch," he called through the bars. "I'm gonna get you out, okay?" He ran to get the key, realizing he was still naked. What the hell could he do about it now? She needed to get out of there. He knew what it felt like to wake up trapped and held down.

She was struggling to get a full breath, panic filling her face and body. Clenching muscles that had spent the last seven hours tightened by someone else. "Get me out of here! Get me out! Please!"

He tore open the door and headed toward her wrists. "Eden, you have to relax your arms. I can't release the cuffs if you are pulling on them."

"Help me." Her eyes pleaded with him, tears dripping down her temples onto the mattress. "Please." Her pecs and biceps wouldn't let go as if she was frozen with fear. With his hands just above her arms, he hesitated, not wanting to be the one to hold her down.

"Do it. Get me out of here," she begged.

He pushed her arm down and used the other hand to release the cuff. With one hand freed, she relaxed slightly, enough to let him undo the other one. He tried not to think about his cock being so close to her head as he held his hips as far back as he could. Gee, had he caused enough emotional scars today?

Her breathing slowed while he undid her legs. As soon as they were free, she leapt off the bed and ran out of the cage, stopping with one hand gripping each side of the door to the hallway.

"I'm sorry, but I had to confine her somehow," he said. "It was the only way."

"I know why you did it. I just—I can't be...like that."

He picked up the skirt and bra Chastity had been wearing, wondering if they were Eden's or not, and handed them to her. "I'll be right back." He slipped past her into the hall and went to get her shirt and some shorts for himself.

Back in Hyde's room, Eden had already put on her other clothes. She took the shirt gratefully, mumbling "thanks," with her eyes lowered.

"Nothing happened between us, Eden. She came here and I locked her up. That's all."

She looked at his half-naked body with a serious look of doubt written across her face. At least he had pants on and was only *semi*-hard. A full erection would have been tougher to explain.

"Nothing happened. I was getting out of the shower when she came over. And I didn't want to leave her once I tied her up."

Since she flinched at his last sentence, he felt it wise not to mention the colossal hard-on he'd sported all night. *I'll leave that for another day. Today I already have too many awkward conversations planned for the two of us.*

"You hungry? Thirsty?"

"Thirsty." She nodded.

Downstairs, she gulped down two tall glasses of water before the questions started. Her voice was shy, tentative, as if she was refusing to believe they had each witnessed the other's worst moments.

"How did I get here?" she asked.

"I don't know." *But I sure as hell will find out. As soon as I can get my hands on that little shit of a boyfriend you trust so much.*

"Did she do anything to you?"

"Other than throwing some stones, an occasional stick, she didn't do anything. Don't worry about me."

"I'm not." She hadn't forgiven him. "I should call Carter. Tell him I'm okay and find out how she got past all the locks."

He gritted his teeth. "Why don't you stay here and rest? I'll go over there and talk to him. He's not working today, is he?" If he was, he'd have to come up with a clever way to hide the bruises.

"At the station? No, I don't think so, and definitely not for a few more hours. I should call him."

"I'll take care of it." He watched her rub her arms, knowing how sore she must be. "You take it easy. I'll be back soon."

Her head popped up as if struck by a new idea. "You don't think she did something to him, do you?"

"No, he's strong enough to take care of himself."

"She's strong too."

"He's stronger." *Probably.* "I doubt she touched him." Strange that it hadn't occurred to him. Although as long as the guy got a whipping, Mitch didn't care who did it. He imagined wringing the Boy Scout's scrawny neck with his sash of merit badges. "Get some rest."

He left her curled up on the couch, her legs tucked underneath her, hands clutching her glass, eyes dull and at half-mast. He hoped she felt safe enough to get some sleep. He locked the front door behind him, knowing that it would never hold Chastity in, but, then, Eden was nothing like Chastity.

His feet hit the pavement in front of her building at a jog, which quickly turned into an outright run. The stairs he climbed in twos. When he reached the second floor, he forced himself to slow down and breathe. The door hadn't been ripped off. *Not a good start for Carter.* If Mitch didn't see his unconscious body on the floor, he'd make sure it was there by the time he left the apartment. His fist hammered the door.

I swear to God, if he comes to this door with sleep in his eyes, he's dead. He heard the padlock being opened from the inside. Saw the knob turn. Readied his legs to pounce. It opened. *Fucking guy is yawning!* Mitch threw Carter back into the room and slammed the door behind him.

"What the—?" Carter yelled.

"How did she get out you lazy, stupid piece of shit?" He towered over the younger man, who was anything *but* sleepy now.

"Stop! Jesus." He held his hands out like he actually thought that was going to stop Mitch from hurting him.

Mitch had been hoping for an all-out fist pounding, but the guy wasn't fighting back. Ah, hell. That only mattered to honorable men. He coiled his arm for an uppercut.

"I dropped her off, man! I dropped her off at your house!"

Mitch's arm fell as fast as his jaw did. "You let her out? On purpose?"

"Yes... No. I didn't let her out. I brought her to you. I *gave* her to you." The words were forced through tight lips.

"What the hell is that supposed to mean?"

Carter slung his head forward and scooted back onto the arm of the chair he'd fallen against when Mitch had pushed him. "She attacked me. I didn't know what else to do."

"I don't see any bruises, so she couldn't have hit you that hard."

He shook his head. "She didn't hit me—she attacked me. Like...like...like she was going to force herself on me."

Mitch cocked an eyebrow. "So you decided to drop her off on *my* doorstep? What am I missing here?"

Carter sighed, stood up, and headed into the kitchen with Mitch following closely. He reached into the fridge and pulled out a beer. "Want one?"

Mitch glanced at the wall clock. 7:30. "Sure." They sat on opposite sides of the small Formica table and drank. "What, no toast?"

Carter ignored him. "About an hour after I locked her in, she started screaming—Chastity, not Eden, but I didn't know that at the time. Eden's really weird about not being able to get out of closed spaces. She gets really freaked out and panicky."

"Yeah, I know."

With a tilt of his head and questioning eyes, Carter continued. "I thought it was Eden. I really did. But then, when I opened the door... Obviously they're different."

"Obviously. Go on."

"She tackled me—kinda like you just did—and started saying things that..." He took a large swig from his bottle. "She's *Eden*, for Christ's sake. I mean, she *looks* like Eden, but she's so..." He shook his head violently. "She had her hands all over me and I couldn't make her stop. I didn't—"

Mitch nodded. He knew what Carter couldn't say out loud—he didn't *want* her to stop. "But you did. You stopped."

"Yeah, by practically hiding in my room! She started to swear at me and call me all sorts of names. And then she said she was going to get out. She was going to go to you. That you would 'take care' of her if I wouldn't."

"I'm still confused about why you would actually bring her to me. Especially after she said that."

"I thought about Eden. And, after all that she's gone through, I couldn't do that to her. I didn't trust myself."

"And I'm a better choice because...?"

"Because she's been telling me no for years. I'm very clear on where I stand with her." He looked up at the ceiling and a sad smile spread across his face. "Well, I am *now*. So if her other personality is going to use her body like that, it shouldn't be me she uses it on. If she just got out, who knows what she would have done or who she would have ended up with. So you were the only logical choice." He didn't say what Mitch knew Carter was thinking, but, for the life of him, couldn't understand.

"Logical choice," he muttered bewilderedly. "So you think Eden would be happier if she found out Chastity had fucked me."

"I don't know if I'd use the word 'happy,' but—" The guy struggled and then nodded. "Shit." He slammed his beer onto the table. "Yeah, I might use the word 'happy.' Plus, she already woke up next to you, so it wouldn't be as shocking the second time."

Mitch wasn't sure about either point. Although the second made a little more sense than the first. "She needs to stay with me from now on. In my house. Whenever she sleeps. You okay with that?" Though he'd asked the question, the answer didn't matter. But Eden would care, even if Mitch didn't.

Carter thought for a while, chewing on his upper lip. "Her idea or yours?"

"Mine. She doesn't know about it yet."

He laughed. "Good luck with that. I don't get a choice anyway. She asked me to move out."

"She what? Well, that was stupid. Did she have a plan for her evening hours a few times a week? Sure, that'll work. Hire a teenager to babysit her and listen to Chastity's screaming. Or maybe she planned on locking the doors and windows and swallowing the key."

"I told her I would be here when she changed."

"That worked almost as well as the babysitter idea."

"Give me a break! I didn't know what else to do. You seem to have all the answers, like it's something you deal with every day, but this is whack for me. Totally frigging insane. I'm fighting myself to stick around for her, but I'm losing the battle." The Boy Scout had a point—they didn't teach this kind of crap in the Police Tech Academy.

"I'm empty." Mitch shook the bottle and looked toward the fridge.

Carter drained his own and went to get two more.

"Alright," Mitch said. "This is how it's going to be: She sleeps"—he caught himself before he said 'with me,' which wouldn't help the tension level in either of them—"at my house. You do too. Every fourth day, you pack a bag and stay in one of my guest rooms. Lucky boy." He winked. "Bring your own toothbrush—I don't share well."

"That's hard to believe." Sarcasm helping him regain his composure, Carter slid the Heineken across the table. "Why do I have to be there?"

"Because you do." He lifted up his glass, toasting their new arrangement. "I didn't sleep with her, by the way."

Carter coughed, covering his mouth before he spit his beer all over the table. "Who stopped?"

"Who do you think? I did. Jesus, I'm not some kind of monster." He shook his head when he saw the way Carter's body finally relaxed and slumped back into the chair.

Mitch would have to come up with a way to explain the cage. Eden obviously hadn't told him about Hyde, and he'd like the guy to stay in the dark about that for as long as possible. Maybe a thorough cleaning, a pink couch, and a big, red bow on one of the bars would make it look brand, spanking new.

He would never be able to put those cuffs on her again, not after how scared she'd been this morning. But the cage would hold Chastity at this point. If it ever stopped being enough, well, they'd deal with that when it happened.

CHAPTER XXVII

For Eden, the next few days were either filled with anxiety or desperate attempts at normalcy. She saw her life as clearly as a book. The beginning, most of which she'd blocked out, had been traumatic, filled with hateful characters and painful drama. But until a month and a half ago, things had seemed to be working out, slowing down, with the potential of including a moderately happy ending.

And then Chastity came along. So the future? The future held no promise other than repeated visits to the cage, being taken care of by two men she'd never understand.

When Mitch had broached the subject of moving in with him—which was basically what it was, at least every fourth night—she thought he'd lost his mind. His voice had been so hesitant, his words...not so much. There were no other options unless she bought herself her own cage. And then what? Lock herself in permanently? Have a delivery guy bring a key to her in the morning, maybe with a pizza? She hated being dependent on anyone, but she could no longer ignore the fact that she'd been emotionally dependent on Carter since they met. She'd let herself become a perpetual victim and forced him into codependency. It was wrong. So much of this was wrong.

If her life was in tatters, she could accept it. Somewhere in her mind, she figured she deserved this. And Mitch? He was offering her nothing more than a prison bed. Whether that was enough for her or not didn't really matter.

Keep it just business. She laughed at the absurdity of that thought. The sound was foreign to her ears. When was the last time she laughed? Mitch was…a very confusing personality she tried not to spend too much time thinking about.

Carter was different. *Carter is—* She searched for a word other than the one that always appeared in her mind to describe him, the one Mitch had poked fun at with a steel finger. He was more than good, he was…*great*. Okay, that just sucked. Why was it so hard to pinpoint who he was? Why had she never thought of more than that before? He was honest, loyal, and brave. He was also too generous, with his life and his heart.

He'd never walk away, never open himself up to anyone else without a big shove. She could give him that. Having something to focus on helped push back the fear pulsing through her veins, taking a ride along with her infected blood. Yes, that's how she saw it—infected. With whatever brought Chastity out.

On day four, while Carter was at work, she dialed Mitch's office number.

"Good morning, Mitchell—"

"Jolie? It's Eden."

A sigh answered her across the line. "Mitch isn't here."

"That's okay. I wanted to talk to you."

Another sigh. "What?"

What had she done to piss the woman off so badly? "Are you doing anything tonight?" she stammered.

Jolie laughed. "Are you asking me out?"

"Sorry, but you're not my type. It's for…Do you remember Carter?"

"Yes."

"Well, he's too chicken to ask, so I'm going to do it for him." She played with a thread hanging from the couch, feeling like she was asking someone to the prom.

"Do what?"

Stop stalling and speak, Eden. "I saw the way you two got along at the party, and I thought you might want to continue the conversation you were having."

"You want me to date your boyfriend?"

"He's not my boyfriend."

"I don't date castoffs."

"You *know* he's never really been my boyfriend. Jeez, Jolie. Help me out here. I want him to be happy."

"You think *I* would make him happy?"

"It's worth a try. Maybe both of you could get something out of it." Eden waited for a response. And waited. She opened her mouth to declare the entire idea had been the result of a momentary lapse in brain function.

"Maybe," Jolie said. "He's not in love with you or anything, is he?"

"No." The lie came out so easily, it shocked her. She rationalized it by focusing on the facts: what he felt for her wasn't love—codependency and loyalty weren't the same as romantic love. And the person Carter loved was a fantasy, not who she really was.

"Does he know you're asking me?"

Eden imagined Jolie leaning back in her chair, deciding which questions to ask to make this more difficult. "No, he doesn't."

"So, what, you want me to pretend I never spoke to you and ask him out?"

"Yeah, but it seemed like a better idea before this call."

"He's younger and poorer than I usually go for, but he's cute." A pause. "Okay, I'll do it."

Eden let out her breath. "That's fantastic. Thank you."

"But I'm not paying. And I don't do Dutch."

"*Okaaay.*" That wasn't a concern—Carter wasn't the kind

of guy who would let a woman pay for anything. Now she just had to figure out a place for them to go. "Do you like movies?"

"No."

"Parks?"

"No."

"Restaurants?"

"As long as it isn't Chili's, that'll do. Are you going to chaperone?"

"No. And it won't be Chili's."

"Better not be, Eden."

God, the woman was more like Mitch than Eden had realized. "Don't tell him I asked you to call, okay?"

"I thought you didn't lie."

Eden took her time answering. "People change, I guess."

"Hey, Eden. I was just messing with you. We already spoke." She laughed.

Eden almost dropped the phone. "You what?"

"We have plans for tonight. But it was so fun to make you work for it, I couldn't resist. You're not mad, are you?"

As if she even cared. "Mad? Um…no, I guess not. Confused, yes. And glad. But that wasn't nice, Jolie."

She giggled. "I know, I'm sorry. I couldn't help myself. No hard feelings?"

"None." *At least no new ones.* "Have a good time tonight…and be nice to him."

"Oh, I will." She sighed, the giddiness of her big joke disappearing from her voice. "With us being out and Mitch being human, maybe you should go over to his house and ask him to keep you company."

That was unexpected. Eden had always thought the reason for Jolie's dislike of her was the time she spent with Mitch. Maybe everyone was changing.

"Yeah, I think I might." She didn't mention that she'd already set up a date between Mitch and Chastity. Thankfully, there would be bars between them.

"Oh, and he thinks it's annoying when women talk while

he's fucking them, so keep your mouth shut. Unless it's otherwise occupied." She chuckled.

Eden had no words to respond with.

"Another joke, Eden. I'm sure he'll be gentle with you. You've gotten under his skin. Maybe all the way to his heart, who knows? I think you'd make a"—she paused— "*magnificent* couple."

Not believing that in the slightest, Eden finally found her voice. "Thank you. But that's not going to happen."

"Why not? What are you, twenty-three? You're allowed to live a little. Have fun. I know I will."

After Jolie hung up on her, Eden wondered if she'd chosen the right woman for Carter. Or if Carter had chosen the right woman for himself.

Ever.

"Live a little," she repeated. It was a fairly new concept for her. She'd always prided herself on making the right decisions, being 'good' all the time. But that had nothing to do with 'living a little.' It never occurred to her to include that in her life plan. Would she be a bad person if she chose to sleep with someone she was incredibly attracted to and had feelings for? Sure, not all those feelings were positive, but, somehow, that made the idea even more intriguing.

Maybe Mitch was the one she'd been waiting for. At least he was honest with himself. Which was more than she could say for herself. Maybe denying her own wants and needs was part of why she was in this mess to begin with. Like Mitch had theorized about Hyde—if she let that emotion out in daily doses, it might keep it from dumping out all at once in the form of a redheaded menace. She knew where she stood with Mitch and where she would stand if they did come together. *If* he'd have her.

One step at a time. Cross one hurdle before worrying about the next one.

She waited about thirty minutes before calling Carter. She got his voice mail and left a quick message, letting him know that she'd spoken to Jolie. *True.* That the idea of a date had come up. *Also true.* And that he'd better pick a nice place to take Jolie to. *All true. Hurray for me.*

An hour later, he called her back, skepticism seeping through his voice. "Hey, Jolie and I spoke before I got your message. It took me a while to get my mind moving again and check my voice mail. So this is okay with you?"

Darn it, why did he still assume she had some sort of say in his love life? "I think it's great. It would be good for you to get out. And who knows what will happen."

"She wants to meet tonight, but tonight is…"

Tonight is Chastity's. "I know. I'm still not sure why Mitch wants you there, anyway. I'll be in a cage, for goodness sake. I'll talk to him."

"I already tried that. It's a condition he isn't budging on, but I'll be there by the time you go to sleep. Just stay up a bit later than usual."

Eden didn't say it, but she was glad Carter would be there. She needed a buffer between Chastity and Mitch, so Eden would know for sure that they didn't do it through the bars. The line went silent for so long, Eden thought they'd lost the connection.

"Eden, I should have checked with you first. I'm sorry. You sure you're okay with this?"

"Absolutely. Jolie is"—she struggled to find the right word—"a catch." *Kind of.* "But she doesn't know about Chastity so, if you can, could you drop her off before going to Mitch's? Oh, and whatever you do, don't take her to Chili's."

After he agreed not to bring Jolie to Mitch's or to any restaurant that had paper placemats, they said a quick goodbye, and Eden went back to worrying about what the evening held for her. What could she wear that Chastity wouldn't pull off? Nothing. She'd have to make the men promise to keep their eyes closed. Yeah, like that'd work. She repeated, "The human body is beautiful, and it's nothing they haven't seen before," to herself and hoped it would sink in before bedtime. Heck, she knew Chastity had displayed all of their parts to the men before, so her body was *definitely* something they'd seen before.

Since Carter hadn't moved out yet, and Eden wanted to be gone when he came home to get ready for his date, she left her apartment at six o'clock. The walk to Mitch's took longer than it needed to. She stopped to window shop without really seeing and watched people on the street whose biggest worries were what they would make for dinner.

She'd lost her appetite weeks ago. Well, she'd lost her appetite for *food* weeks ago, but her hunger for the man she would be seeing soon was starting to overwhelm her.

CHAPTER XXVIII

Mitch got home to find Eden sitting on his driveway. She stood and brushed herself off as he got out of his car.

"Reporting for duty, sir." A quick salute with the wrong hand and half a smile. It was nice to see her smile.

"Yeah." After days of wondering how he could keep her safe while still pushing her away, he was still no closer to an answer. Thank goodness he was a people person. *Riiight.* Maybe he could lock her up early and spend the evening in his room…jerking off.

She followed him inside, taking nervous little steps like she didn't know what to do with herself. Which made two of them.

"Carter's coming, right?" he asked.

"Later, yes. He has plans, but he'll be here."

"Plans, huh?" Mitch had his own plans—keeping the idiot awake even if it involved some *Clockwork Orange*-esque equipment.

She wasn't hungry, but he would force her to eat if he had to. Her eyes had dark rings under them and she looked thinner. In four days.

"Eat." He plopped a plate of leftover Chinese food in front

of her and sat down with his own. She picked at the chow mein until she succumbed to his glare and put a few noodles into her mouth.

"Do I need to tell you to chew?"

She shook her head and ate.

He shoveled some hard rice into his mouth and winced. "Yeah. Not good." Picking up both of their plates, he threw them into the trash and went in search of something palatable.

"How was your day?" she asked.

"You wanna play house? Fine. My day sucked. How was yours?"

"It sucked."

He smirked. "When do you go back to school?"

She blinked. "Um... Wow, I hadn't even thought about it. I guess classes start in late August, but I'm not sure I'm going."

"You want this to be your life? Make everything about *her*? That's a bad idea. It'll kill you." When she didn't respond, he went back to searching the freezer. "You like pizza?"

"Yeah. How do you do it? Have a day job, knowing what you are?"

He unwrapped the pizza, threw it in the oven, and turned the thing on. Preheating was for wusses. Burnt pizza was a delicacy. "First off, I don't have the four-day cycle, so that makes it easier. But even when I did, I still went to school, did dishes, brushed my teeth, same as everybody else." He shrugged. "You do what you gotta do."

"I need to be a bad person. Test your theory. I just haven't figured out a way to be bad."

He tried to hide his smile. "Okay, first lesson. Say 'fuck.'"

She looked at him doubtfully.

"What, you can't say it? It's just a word."

"I know. But I don't think that'll make me a bad person."

"Say it, then."

She gathered herself, sitting up in her chair like she was

about to address Congress. "Fuck."

"Nice. Now mean it."

She shrugged. "Mean it?"

"Use it in a sentence. Tell me to go fuck myself."

"Go fuck yourself." She giggled.

"Oh, Christ. You're a lost cause." He held a beer out to her. She declined. "Let's try something else. Lie to me."

"About what?"

"Ugh! This is impossible. How am I supposed to help you if you don't at least try?"

She pinched her lips together in thought. "You're an amazing man."

"That's better. How'd it feel?"

"I wasn't lying."

He coughed on his mouthful of beer. "Don't do that."

"What? Tell the truth?"

He couldn't move, his breath caught in his throat. Why was she making it so difficult to push her away? "I'm not—"

"I hate you."

He blinked, confused.

She grinned. "I was lying. I don't hate you. I probably should. No, I *definitely* should, but I don't. Let me try it again." She squinted her eyes, considering what to lay on him next.

"Lie about someone else. Not me." He didn't want to hear any more of her opinions about him. Ever again.

Her eyes dropped to the countertop. "I'm totally okay with what's happening to me. It's fine. I barely think about it at all. I'll have a totally normal life—husband who adores me, two or three babies, a dog, a cute little house, a job I love—the works." When she looked up at him, his heart broke, a reflection of hers. He knew her pain, though he'd never even let himself consider having those things she'd obviously dreamt of.

"That was good," he said.

"The pizza's burning."

"Okay." He took a breath, still holding her gaze. Then he smelled it. "Oh, shit. It's burning!" He threw open the oven door and, barehanded, grabbed the paper tray he should have taken off before cooking the damn thing. The burn hit him a second after. He dropped it, half on and half off the door. He grabbed a towel from the counter and caught about a third of the crust, the rest in a cheesy puddle on the floor. "Shit!"

"That's okay. I like burnt pizza. It's a delicacy." She leaned on the island and peered over.

"The pizza is fine. Kind of. It's the tray that's blackened. Do you like burnt paper?"

"It's my favorite."

"You're getting good at this."

"I know. I like it when my fucking pizza is fucking burnt." Her smile was like the first ray of sunshine after months of rain.

"Fucking beautiful." Oh, shit. He'd said that out loud. She was as surprised as he was. "The pizza. I meant the pizza— fucking beautiful." He hadn't convinced either one of them. Damn it.

"I can tell when you are lying."

"What? No you can't."

She nodded. "Yes, I can. You have a tell."

"What's a 'tell'?"

"Don't you play poker? A tell is a gesture or something that people can't stop themselves from doing. Whenever you lie, you do your tell."

"No, I don't." What had he done? What had she seen as his tell?

She shrugged, walked around the island, and started to pick up the pizza that he'd completely forgotten about.

He bent down to help. "I don't have a tell, and I wasn't lying."

"I think you lie so often, you don't know when you're doing it anymore." She ripped off a chunk of the pizza from the oven door and bit into it. "You're a great cook."

"Alright. Point taken. Now you can stop." Scooping the mess of cheese off the floor with a spatula, he dumped it in the garbage.

You gotta work on your poker face, asshole.

They spent the rest of the evening in front of the television, Mitch trying to hide his frequent glances toward her with awkward shifts of his body and feigned interest in the clock on the wall behind her. Eventually he realized the clock hands weren't moving and started checking his watch. *Excruciating.*

"Where the hell is your boyfriend?"

"He'll be here."

"It's ten o'clock!"

"Past your bedtime, Mitch?"

Huh, she really did call him Mitch. Why had he never noticed it before? Only two people had ever called him Mitch and gotten away with it—his father, because Mitch had never had a choice in the matter and from whom he'd learned to hate the nickname, and Shelly, because she was the only one who said it with love. *Whoa, stop that connection right there.*

"Don't call me Mitch."

Her eyes flashed at his tone. "Sorry, I didn't realize I was."

"Call your boyfriend and tell him to get his ass over here, *pronto.*"

"I can't. I don't want to bug him. He's on a date. He'll be here before twelve."

"He's on a date?" He felt his lip lift in a scowl. "I didn't know you had that sort of arrangement. Score another point to your inner bad girl." Two more hours of waiting. *Shit.*

She straightened. "He's not my boyfriend anymore. Actually, he was *never* really my boyfriend, so can we drop it?"

"Sure." It was nice to see some of her fire, her sass. He turned back to the television. "You watching this?"

"No."

He flicked it off and tossed the remote onto the coffee table.

"I hate waiting." She leaned back on the other end of the sofa, sinking into the cushions.

"Okay, lesson one and two you have," he said. "Let's move on to lesson three."

"What's lesson three? Stealing? Coveting thy neighbor's goods?"

"I suppose adultery is out of the question now that your boyfriend isn't your boyfriend, huh?"

"Is that lesson three? Sex?" There was an urgency in her voice, an intensity he hadn't heard before.

"No, that's lesson five." He laughed. "Don't worry, you have another couple of things to learn before you need to start panicking about that one."

"I'm not panicking about sex," she said, watching him, her eyes darting to his body. "I just think it needs to be with the right person."

"Wow, where you gonna find *him*?"

She paused, staring at him, not letting him break eye contact. "I already—"

He threw out his hands and stood to get away from her. "No-no-no-no-no, little girl. Do not say what I think you were going to."

"Is it so impossible to imagine?" Her whisper became louder, more confrontational, more entrancing. "I think I'm ready, Mitch. Are you?" She moved closer, advancing on him like a cat—slowly, but with far too much confidence for his liking.

What the hell? "Eden. Stop right there." Damn it, why was he always finding himself in this situation with her. Or with Chastity. It was like the body in front of him had its sights set on an invisible target on his chest.

"I want to—" She pressed her lips together and took a deep breath. "I want it to be *you*. I'm ready for lesson five, Mitch."

He bristled at that name, but not because it was unpleasant. And that scared the shit out of him. He backed away, bumping into furniture but unwilling to take his eyes off her for a second. The rest of his body had a different opinion, though. Every bit of him wanted to move forward and wrap itself around her, inside her.

"This is a bad idea, Eden. A really fucking bad idea."

She glanced at his crotch and blushed. "But it's not impossible."

He rolled his eyes and cursed his body. His ass hit the edge of a table. "Not impossible, but… What happens after? If we do this?"

She cocked her head to the side. "I don't know. I guess we go back to being who we are."

Who the hell are we? "Is this about her? About being bad?"

"Should I lie right now?"

He shook his head.

"This is about being honest. With myself. With you. And, yes, part of me is curious beyond what it would be like to really *be* with someone. It would be a huge bonus if she stopped showing up so often."

For once he was glad for her honesty. It didn't help him decide if this was a good idea or not, though. In fact, it made it a hell of a lot harder. "Just so we understand each other: I'm not the picket fence kind of guy. If that's what you're looking for, you better keep looking."

"I said I was waiting for the *right* guy, not the perfect one." She smirked.

His body hummed. Maybe this was right for her, but what about him? *What would I do after only one taste of her?* He closed his eyes. *Oh, shit. One taste. Shouldn't have thought of that.* Momentarily freed from his indecision, his thighs tensed and launched him towards her. He swept her up into his arms and slid them both onto the couch.

She grunted as they hit, the full weight of his body on top of her, her eyes wide with surprise.

"Are you okay?" he asked. The couch was soft, she was soft, but he was as hard as a steel post.

She gave him a small, nervous grin and as much of a nod as her position allowed. "Yeah. Just…be gentle, okay?"

He took a deep breath of the small amount of air between them, bringing her scent along with it. *Gentle. Okay.* Could he do that? Had he ever done that? "You can still change your mind." God, he hoped she wouldn't.

"I want to." Her face was flushed, her eyes bright and excited. She was so soft and receptive under him. Her body pressed against his, fitting with his like it had spent a lifetime there. "I'm just new at this."

He smiled at her beauty and lifted himself onto his hands, giving her a moment to breathe, hopefully not to reconsider. "Tell me something I don't know." He felt her body tighten under his, but not in a good way.

Her face changed—brow furrowed, eyes averted. "I—I never chose."

"Chose what?"

"To do it. It was never a choice."

Oh, shit. Now *his* body tightened, matching hers.

"They never gave me a choice," she whispered.

He pulled away with his eyes closed. "I didn't know."

She brought one of her hands to his shirt, clutching it like she didn't want him to move away. "How could you? It's not something I'd tattoo on my forehead."

Balancing on one arm, he took the other and pried her hand off him. "I'm sorry."

"You didn't do anything."

"But I did…with her." He climbed off her, sitting by her legs on the edge of the couch. Nice fucking guy. He'd almost taken her on a frickin' couch, for fuck's sake! Her first time, her first *willing* time. Jesus, why doesn't he just screw her in the backseat of his car? He didn't do romance, but the least she deserved was a man who'd make an attempt.

She sat up. "I sure know how to kill a mood, don't I?" Her

hand caressed his back. "I'm sorry."

"No need. It wasn't right to begin with. We shouldn't have even started. Not like this."

"I just wanted you to know that this"—she motioned to the two of them—"*was* a choice. I want to be here. With you."

He shook his head. "It's too complicated right now. There's too much going on."

She sighed but didn't move away. "So…am I off-limits again?"

He felt his heart rate slow while he thought, all desire fading from his body, replaced with disgust at himself and sorrow for her. "I don't know." He twisted his head to look at her and saw tears brewing. "Not off-limits. Just a temporary reprieve." Not wanting to see those tears crest her eyelids, he said, "You still have lessons three and four to work on." Not that he actually knew what lessons three and four even were.

"You wanna talk about it?" he asked the floor, not really wanting to hear what Eden would say but wanting to be there for her. Hyde jabbed him in the gut, in the back, scraping at Mitch's insides. He shivered. She was so fucking dangerous to him.

"No. I think I said too much already. But thanks for not being afraid of me."

"Afraid of you? Why would I be afraid of you?"

"No one wants to know someone else's pain or that there's darkness inside of them. But you…you make me feel like I don't have to hide anything. So thank you." Her hand curled around the nape of his neck, trying to turn his face back to her. He let her, part of him worried it had been Hyde's decision and not his. She leaned forward and kissed him. Gently. Two lips on two lips.

Hyde's tug faded away, the strength of each pulse diminished with every connection of their lips. He'd never been kissed with such kindness. The idea of taking her harder, asking for more, didn't appeal to him. That was new. He relaxed into her, lips separating only briefly, just to get a different angle, feel each other in another way.

She opened her mouth wider, the tip of her tongue tasting him lightly. He held himself back, following her lead, not groping her with his large hands, but caressing her arm, her shoulder, the bone leading into the soft hollow at the base of her neck, to her jaw.

The kiss held for decades, millennia, and neither of them seemed to want to move forward or stop. In the brief moments his mouth wasn't on hers, he realized he was speaking, whispering words unfamiliar to him—words of passion, beauty, and a white picket fence. All the things he wanted her to have. All the things he wanted to give her.

She answered with her own. "Stop...talking...you're going...to...regret...it later."

No, he didn't think he would.

Carter's voice rang in from the foyer. "Hey! Don't you ever lock your door?"

Mitch pulled back and stood, gaping at Eden, waiting for her expression to change into embarrassment or regret. It didn't. She looked like she'd just stepped out of an incredible dream, a smile dancing on those plump lips he now knew so well. She put her fingers to her lips slowly, just in time for Carter to enter the room.

His eyes darted back and forth between them, a suspicious haze in them. "What's going on?"

"Hey, Scout. How was your date?" Patronizing tone thrown out to Carter, eyes drawn back like magnets to her. *Damn it.* He forced himself to look away.

Carter glared at him. "Nice. It was really nice."

Mitch wondered if the sensation he felt on his lips was evident in their color or size. They still felt tingly and raw, as if every other nerve in his body had fallen silent or had all made a temporary move to his mouth. Did he look as flushed as she did?

Wait. Was he actually embarrassed in front of this kid? That had to stop immediately. "You get lucky?"

Carter's mouth tightened. He glanced at Eden and then shrugged, probably assuming what he'd thought had been happening between her and Mitch couldn't possibly have happened. Eden would never stoop so low.

"No, I didn't get lucky. I had to come back here," he challenged.

"Too bad. I'm getting a drink, anyone want one?" He hightailed it into the kitchen, furious that he felt the need to escape. He heard murmurs of the conversation coming from the other room and tried very hard not to follow it.

"…doing…was he..." in Carter's irritated baritone.

"…date?...sorry…thanks…" in Eden's lighter pitch.

Mitch started to hum. When that didn't cover their voices, he broke out into song. If nothing else, his tone deafness would scare them silent. "What'll you do when you get lone—" Bad choice. "Ain't no sunshine, when she's—" Another bad choice. *Jesus, why don't men ever sing about anything but women?* He flicked on the MP3 player built into the wall and turned it up high, sending out a violent boom of Eminem's tortured soul that covered the sounds coming from the other room.

"Perfect," he grumbled when a female voice claimed to love the way Eminem lies.

CHAPTER XXIX

Mitch had finished his first beer and was grabbing another when Carter came into the kitchen. The men nodded to each other, and Mitch handed the guy a bottle. "I hope you brought some more with you, because I'm officially out."

"Why do I have to be here?"

"Because I asked you to so politely."

Carter grunted. "She said you have a cage upstairs."

"I do."

"Should I ask why?"

"Special order. She'll be safe without being cuffed." He nodded toward the living room. "Is she ready?"

"She says she is."

"Wonderful. Let's go up."

Carter followed him into the living room to where Eden was sitting on the couch, wrapped up in the throw blanket. Mitch kept his distance, not wanting to piss the guy off any more than necessary. He needed him to take care of Eden when Mitch couldn't. It hurt to think about, but he knew there would be times when they both would change on the same night and he wouldn't be able to be there for her. So hopefully, her ex-boyfriend would be able to man up and stay alert. At least in time to let her out of the cage.

Eden stood and gave a weak smile. "I guess it's time, huh?" She led them upstairs, the blanket trailing behind her.

Carter gasped when he saw the cage.

Mitch rolled his eyes. "What were you expecting? A dog carrier?"

"No, I—"He was frozen at the door, seemingly unable to cross the threshold until Eden took his hand and led him to the chair.

"I'm okay with it, so you should be too. It's the best way." She glanced at Mitch for aid, but Mitch just shrugged. "The key always stays on this table. Always. When I wake up, one of you unlocks me as quickly as you can."

Mitch could see she was trying to control her fear, and Carter's attitude wasn't helping. "Get a grip, Scout. She'll be fine as long as one of us is here with her."

After a quick, tentative nod from Carter, Eden stepped into the cage and sat down on the mattress. She briefly looked for the cuffs, but Mitch had tucked them underneath the bed to avoid causing her more emotional damage. She mouthed, 'thank you.'

He kept eye contact with her while he shut the door and closed the lock.

A visible shiver went through her at the sound. "You'll tell him about the clothing thing if...*before* it happens?"

"He witnessed that last time, babe. But I'll explain. Don't worry, we'll both be here the whole time."

"So both of you will be staring at me," she muttered. "Great."

"No, I'll be covering his eyes and he'll be covering mine. Promise."

Her expression said, '*You're full of it, but thanks for trying.*'

She lay down and closed her eyes, sleep staying out of reach for a long time. He wondered what she was focusing on. Her breathing? Their kiss? Hell, why should he assume it meant as much to her as it had to him? He backed away and leaned against the wall behind Carter.

Her chest slowed its movements, letting them know she was nearing slumber.

Carter whispered, "What's with the clothes thing?"

"Chastity has very sensitive skin. When she comes out, she won't keep anything on for long. But then, you've already seen that." He tried to keep his jealousy from attaching to his tone. "You keep your eyes averted, you hear me?"

"I'm a man. That's a tall order, you hear *me*?"

Asshole. "Yeah, I hear you." She wasn't his. And she still trusted the Boy Scout. Mitch had to get on board with that. As much as he hated the idea, he knew that Carter was necessary.

When the moaning started, both men tensed. Her body clenched, arched, and shook. Her hands scratched at the clothing she wore, tugging her shirt up to expose a perfectly flat belly, the bottom edge of her light pink bra.

With a jerk, Chastity opened her eyes and stretched out her limbs. She yawned and sat up, as if she was waking up from a night of undisturbed rest. A flash of delight registered on her face when she saw them, then filled with frustration, focusing on the bars between her and her toys.

Carter stiffened, probably a second away from going to her, maybe to comfort her or maybe to bring a different kind of comfort to himself.

"Don't say anything to her." Mitch held Carter back with a firm hand on his shoulder.

She focused on Mitch, and he shook his head. After a quick lip pout, she called out to Carter, her voice silky and wanting. "Carter? Let me out. I'm scared." She held on to the bars and looked at him through her lashes, a fake look of fear on her face.

Carter pressed forward into Mitch's grip.

"She's lying. She doesn't feel fear."

With a quick glare to Mitch, she refocused on Carter and started to unbutton her shirt. "Carter, please. He's so mean to me. He does things to me, Carter. Bad things. Don't trust him."

Carter looked at Mitch, unsure.

Mitch knew he'd given no reason for Carter to trust him. "Scout, you handed her to me the last time she changed because you knew I wouldn't let anything bad happen to her. Remember that feeling. She'll do whatever she can to get free. She's not Eden."

"Shut up!" She tried to shake the bars of the cage without success. "Let me out!"

Carter jerked to the side and Mitch lost his grip. The guy fled, running for the door with Mitch close behind him.

"Where the fuck are you going?" Mitch shouted.

He stopped at the top of the stairs, his hand clenching the banister. "I can't see her when she's like that. I just can't."

"Tough shit, Scout. Let me lay it out for you. Your cute little girlfriend turns into a wanton pile of hormones stuck on the greatest pair of tits I've ever seen and an ass to match, right?"

Carter's nodding matched his breath—quick and erratic. "I guess so."

"No guessing. Do you understand what happens to her? It's not her anymore. Do you understand that?"

"Yes." His voice was shaky.

How could he get the kid to stay? What could he tell him? What would he believe? "Good. You also understand that it would be nearly impossible for a saint to walk away from her, do you not?"

"Yes."

"I am the last person on earth anyone would nominate for sainthood."

"Yeah, you mentioned that."

Mitch was glad to hear some resentment in the kid's tone. "So you have a choice. You stay, we have a couple beers, keep an eye on her, and end the night with indigo balls. Or, every couple of days, you fade off into happy-happy dreamland knowing that I'm banging your girl six ways from Sunday."

"You wouldn't." The glare in his eyes was exactly what Mitch wanted to see.

He smirked. "Why not?"

"You wouldn't screw with her, knowing that if she was herself, she wouldn't want you to."

Mitch paused, gearing up for the lie. "Maybe yes, maybe no. Where the hell is everyone getting the idea that I'm a decent human being, anyway?"

"Can't Jolie be here instead of me?"

"Jolie is…complicated." *To say the least.* Mitch wasn't sure where Jolie's head was at regarding Eden or what she might do if she found out about Chastity. "And you never know, she might wanna join in."

He shook his head. "I don't think so."

Mitch didn't think so either. "Eden needs you now, Carter. More than ever before." He knew when the Boy Scout had given up, resigned himself to a situation he wanted no part of but had no choice in. Kind of like all of them had. And who knew, maybe it would earn Carter another merit badge.

"I need a drink," he said.

"Get what you need. With two glasses. Then come straight back here. Don't make me have to hunt you down."

The kid nodded and headed downstairs with his head pointed at his feet. Still hearing shouts from the cage, Mitch grabbed a chair from another room and brought it back into Hyde's room. It was going to be a long night. He tried asking Chastity questions, but it was no use. She wasn't very happy with him.

Carter took his time, but eventually came back up with two glasses and a bottle of Jack. By the time Chastity stopped yelling, cajoling and trying to seduce her way out of her prison, they'd gone through half the bottle. She sat on the edge of the mattress, glaring at both of them.

"I have to do this every four days?" Carter asked, filling his glass again.

Mitch held his out for a top-off. "Get drunk?"

Carter shook his head. When he stopped, his body waved back and forth, trying to right itself. His tolerance had just been tested...and bested.

"No, we can trade off," Mitch said. "But I needed to know you could do it right and not run away."

"I'm not sure I can. They don't teach this shit in the Police Academy."

"You're in the regular academy? I thought they had standards." Mitch laughed into his drink.

Carter sat up a bit. "Did Jolie tell you that I was in the regular academy?"

"You mean, Eden."

"Huh?" He blinked. "Oh, yeah. I mean Eden."

"I don't remember what she told me. Tech School? Police School? Whatever."

Carter sighed. "I'm training to be a forensic tech, not an officer. I couldn't get into the regular academy." His words were slurring softly.

Mitch took the bottle away from him. "Because of your illness?"

Carter nodded.

"What's wrong with you?"

"Epilepsy."

"Epilepsy mixed with narcolepsy?"

"Among other things, epilepsy causes"—he made air-quotes—"'extreme fatigue.' So do some of the medications. My doc hasn't been able to get it right yet."

"Oh." Wow, weren't they just a perfect little family—sleep issues for everybody. "They teach you how to fight in tech school?"

"No, that's why I go to the gym."

"Think you could take me on?"

"I'd love to try."

Mitch smiled at the challenge in the guy's eyes. "When and where?"

"The gym I go to: Busted. We'd have to wear gloves, though."

"Too bad."

"Yeah."

They heard a whimper from the cage, bringing them both back to the cause of their animosity.

Chastity looked confused and miserable as she fell back onto the mattress and closed her eyes. When her body spasmed, both men quietly approached. As soon as they saw Eden's brown eyes open, Carter slammed the key he'd been clutching into the lock.

Throwing the blanket around herself, she rushed to him and touched his face. "You made it."

"*You* made it." He hugged her.

She grimaced. "And you smell awful. What have you boys been drinking?"

Mitch stayed with his back against the wall, struggling to subdue the pangs of jealousy toward Carter and the slugs of pain from Hyde.

CHAPTER XXX

Mitch kept his distance for the rest of the morning, unhappy that they both seemed so comfortable with the hospitality he was forced to offer. He wanted the Boy Scout to leave so he could be alone with Eden. But since that would be a huge mistake, Carter's hovering was probably a good thing.

After they left, he jumped into a cold shower and switched into work mode. It was a welcome respite. He got to the office late, his client waiting impatiently along with a pissy Jolie, who gave him a look that would've mortally wounded a lesser man and that Mitch blew off.

He cut the session short. He'd only been paying attention to every other word the V.P. of Fresh Visual said anyway. The guy was probably grateful he didn't get the whole hour he'd paid for. Mitch had really laid into him, pointing out every stupid thing he was doing in his professional life along with some personal jabs for good measure.

Then it was Jolie's turn to let Mitch have it. "You look like hell. Did you sleep at all?"

"No. Anybody else coming in today?"

She ignored his question. "What did you do last night?"

"There was a *Scream* marathon on—I couldn't put down

the remote."

"You're a terrible liar."

"No, I'm not." With as much practice as he'd had over the years, why was everyone just catching on now?

"Yes, you are."

"Drop it."

"Fine." She gave him one last glare and then put on her game face, studying her planner. "You leave for Atlanta on Thursday. I got a morning flight for you, returning Friday at noon. You'll pick up the car at—"

"Nope. I need to be back by Thursday night." He had a Thursday Night Smack down planned with Carter and Chastity.

Jolie looked up at him. "There are no flights."

"Find one."

"I tried."

"Try harder."

"What do you think I do all day, Mitchell?" The intensity of her voice increased with each word, climaxing with his name squeezed out of a stiff jaw. "While you are off doing who knows what, I have to cover for you. Lying to clients, buttering them up so they *stay* clients whenever you decide to play house with your new toy. I hope she's worth it."

Ahha, so it wasn't that he was flaking on work, it was *who* he was flaking on work with. "I pay you awfully well to do what you do. If that includes the occasional cover-up, you've never complained before."

They both understood which cover-up he was referring to.

"Maybe I should start complaining, then."

"Maybe you should." He tapped his pen against her desk hard enough to nearly break the thing. "Try to find an earlier flight back. *Please*." He let the word hover in the air between them. Fitting, since he doubted he'd ever said it before. "Even if I have a layover in Budapest. I need to be back by midnight."

"You're not going to tell me why, are you?"

"No."

She sighed. "Just tell me it's not about Hyde."

"It's not about Hyde."

"I'll try."

"Thank you." He nodded and went back into his office, slamming the door behind him. He flinched—not because of the sound but because of the violence he felt in himself. In the man, apart from the beast.

I will not *lose control.* He took a few deep breaths and then dialed Eden's cell phone, disgusted that he knew the number by heart having only called her, what, twice? He needed to up his game, be more aware of any signs Hyde was on his way out. He was being too fucking nice for the bastard to stay down much longer.

She answered on the second ring, like she was expecting him to call. Another bad sign. "Hi."

"Look, there's a chance I won't be there for your next transformation. I'm going out of town and might not be able to make it back."

"Carter knows what to do. We'll be fine."

"I had to get the guy drunk to keep his ass in the chair last night. I'm not convinced he understands or is even capable of sticking around for you."

"He's stuck around me for years. You can trust him."

Yeah, sure. Maybe he should restock his liquor cabinet before he left. "I'll be back in time. Just don't go to sleep until I'm there."

"You're worried about nothing."

"I don't think so."

After a long, awkward pause, they hung up before either of them said anything useful. Mitch wasn't sure which one of them hung up first. It was a relief either way. Talking about that kind of shit wasn't his forte, not that he had any experience with it. Feelings were for people *with* feelings. He'd always been pretty sure he didn't have any. Surprise, surprise.

━┼┼─┼┼─┼┼━

Jolie couldn't find an earlier flight. His speech for Bennett Financial stank. He couldn't focus and had never written an outline in his life. No doubt it would be the last time they fought to get him for any of their execs. Great, he was losing his mind and his clientele. *Good fucking times.*

He went to the airport directly after finishing the meeting, more impatient than a pregnant woman in her fourth trimester. Cursing himself for not carrying enough cash, he offered passengers on earlier flights a hundred bucks in tens and fives. No takers. He considered threatening a few of them, but knew he'd probably end up manhandling an Air Marshall and have to walk back to Florida.

"It's me," he said, tucking the phone between his shoulder and ear.

"I know. Caller ID." Eden's voice brought an uncomfortable clench in his gut. *Damn her.*

"I'm not going to make it. Did you talk to Carter?"

"He knows what to do. And what not to do. Don't worry."

"Thanks for the advice. Make sure he knows where the key is and—Shit!" He ignored the stares from travelers around him. "I didn't give you a key to my place." *Damn it, could you be any stupider, asshole?*

"Oh."

He imagined her brain working as quickly as his was trying to and hoped she was more successful with hers than he was with his. He had nothing.

"We can stay here," she said. "Carter can lock me into my room."

That wasn't good enough. "Break a window in my back door and let yourself in."

"And get arrested when one of your neighbors calls the cops? No, thanks. I'll be safer here than in the pokey."

What the hell is a pokey? "Give Carter a message for me,"

Lauren Stewart

he grumbled into the phone. "If he lets anything happen to you, he'll spend the rest of his life sleeping...in a coma."

"There's no need for violence, Mitch. I'll be fine. Promise."

Sadly, that was a promise she had no control over keeping. "Give him the message. And, Eden...be safe." Another thing she couldn't control.

"I will. Can you call when you get back?"

"I'll come by your place as soon as the plane touches down."

He sat in the first class waiting area, gripping his phone, waiting for...for what? And what the hell could he do if something went wrong anyway? At midnight, he cursed himself for not bringing Jolie into it, telling her about Chastity, and getting her to let them into the house. But it was too late now. He'd know if Carter had done his job in eight more hours. Eight motherfucking long hours.

CHAPTER XXXI

Eden woke up on the couch, Carter frantically clearing off the coffee table in front of her. He never cleaned. "What are you doing?"

He glanced up from the table and threw his hands behind his back. His eyes were in full panic mode, his mouth moving but no sound escaping.

"What's wrong?" Why wasn't she still in her bedroom? "Did she—" Eden saw the door to her bedroom. There were two large holes near the hinges and it was hanging at an odd angle, staying upright only because of the padlock on the outside. Then she looked to the front door, which was slightly ajar but still looked whole. She grabbed the throw blanket off the back of the couch and wrapped it and her arms around her naked body. "How did she get out?"

Carter shook his head, but said nothing.

Eden brought her hand up to rub her eyes. When she unclenched her fist, she saw a straw. Cut short. An inch, maybe two. Not something one would use for a daiquiri. Some kind of powder sticking to one end. Fear. Horror. The unimaginable. Swiping her nose with her other hand, she saw traces of the same white powder on her finger. She looked up to Carter in desperation.

"What happened? How did she get out?" Her voice was nearing hysterical.

He tucked his arms in tighter.

"Tell me what happened! Why did you let her out?"

His mouth opened. A second later, words tumbled out. "I didn't. She didn't get out."

"Then where did I get this?" Her heart rate was increasing exponentially. When he didn't respond, she asked again. "Carter! Where did this come from?" She held out her hands, palms up.

He didn't look at her. "I got it from a friend. I just…"

She clenched her fists, one still holding the straw. "What is it?"

Silence.

"What. Is. It." Her jaw was locked, and the words had to struggle their way out. How could he bring this into their home? *Her* home?

"It's not heroin, Eden. I swear."

A small part of her was relieved—the idea that the same drug that had killed her mother might be coursing through her veins was unbearable. But Chastity had snorted something and left Eden with all the repercussions. She looked at the straw in her hand again, not knowing if the racing beat of her heart was due to fear or the drug.

"It's not—" he stuttered. "It's medicine."

She stared at him, mouth agape, taking shallow breaths. "Medicine? Are you kidding me? Is that what you call it?" she spat, hurling the straw at him. It landed on the floor between them, fueling her anger even more. Inadequate. The toss had been inadequate. She was inadequate. And Carter was absolutely inadequate.

"How could you?" she screamed. "*Medicine* that just happens to look exactly like cocaine, huh? Does giving it another name make it okay? Do you think I'm stupid?"

He stepped back, his face red, his eyes shiny. "It was in my room. I never imagined she would find it. That *you* would find it. You *never* go in my room. I'm sorry."

"You're sorry?" Her voice filled the apartment. "Oh, well if you're *sorry*, then it's no big deal. We can both just turn into junkies. Since you're *sorry*." Her worst fear, and he had brought it into their home, a reminder of everything she'd fought against, everything she hated. And he *knew*. He *knew* how afraid she was to even be near it.

"I'm not a junkie, Eden, I swear."

"Is this what you've been taking all this time? Is this your 'medicine'?"

"No, it's not for me."

"Yeah, right." Rage burned through her chest, charring her belief in him and her trust in her own judgment.

"It's to help—"

"To help you focus, right? Sure it is." She looked around the room for something to throw at him, something heavy that would hurt. But he'd done such a thorough job of clearing off the table, there was nothing. So she tossed off the blanket and ran at him.

He stood still, accepting the pounding of her fists on his chest. But it was no use—she could never punish him enough.

She shoved him away and cried, "Well, I hope you are very focused while you get your stuff and get out!" *Leave me alone so my heart can finish breaking.*

"I'm sorry, Eden. I never would have…" He lifted his arms as if he wanted to hug her.

"Get! Out!" She pushed him with everything she had, wondering if the drugs in her system increased her strength as he stumbled back.

He caught himself and nodded. Moving slowly to grab a bag that was next to the door, he looked back at her. "I'm so sorry."

"I don't ever want to see you again."

She was weeping by the time the door closed behind him. Then her body started to shut down, close in on her until a welcomed feeling of numbness overtook her, her sobs becoming distant. As if they were coming from someone else's soul.

Mitch was out of breath from running from the airport to his car, screaming at traffic, and sprinting up to the second floor of her building. He slowed when he saw Carter leaning against the railing outside Eden's apartment. "How'd it go?"

Carter lifted his head, and Mitch saw the redness of his eyes. After a moment of recognition, the guy bolted toward the far stairway.

Mitch broke out into a run again, passed the door to Eden's place, and stopped. From over the railing, he watched Carter book across the lawn, a bag banging against his thigh.

He'd never catch him. Mitch jogged back to her door and pounded his fist against it, resisting the urge to break it down. That was when he heard her crying inside. Full-throttle waterworks, little gasps of air, then more crying. He grabbed the knob, ready to kick it in and possibly break a foot on the metal if he had to. He didn't care. He needed to get in there.

He needn't have worried—it wasn't even locked. Eden was curled up on the couch, completely naked, slowly rocking back and forth. What the fuck happened? He crossed the room in three strides, grabbing a throw blanket on the way, and slid onto the couch, covering her. "What happened?"

Tears flowed down her cheeks incessantly. Her eyes were puffy and red, her breath coming in shallow hiccups. But her face was peaceful, as if her body was reacting on autopilot without any input from her brain.

"Eden. Are you alright?" He lifted her chin, ignoring the wetness that made his hand slip slightly. "Say something."

She didn't.

His thumb brushed her lower lip, tugging at it slightly, wanting to somehow help it start working again. "Please say something." He stared at her lips, deciding whether he'd rather have them form words or cover them with his own.

She looked at him through lashes turned even darker from tears and shivered a shrug.

He needed words. And she wasn't going to give them to him. His anger pulsed when he thought of who would provide them instead, even if he had to do it through a toothless and bleeding mouth. "It was Carter, wasn't it?"

She neither agreed nor disagreed, but he knew.

"Did he hit you?"

The tiniest shake of her head came without change of her doll-like face.

He sighed. "Did he"—his throat clenched at the word—"*touch* you?"

Head shake, this time more adamantly.

He leaned backwards. "Then what the hell did he do?"

She bit the lip he'd just released but seemed incapable of speech.

"Where is he, Eden? Where did he go?" No, she needed yes-or-no questions. Carter had done something that turned her into a fucking magic eight ball of grief. "Is he at the station?"

Her expression turned into outright nervousness, probably knowing what Mitch would do to the guy when he found him. She wasn't going to tell him anything.

Then he remembered the bag Carter had been carrying when he'd fled. It was a gym bag. Mitch tried to keep the sneer off his face when he remembered the name of the gym where Carter had suggested they have their boxing match. Well, their duel would happen sooner than either of them thought. Should have happened weeks ago.

He stood, wrapped the blanket tighter around her, and lifted her from the couch. His hand touched skin, warming him. He ignored his need to melt into it, into her, and carried her to his car. Setting her down gently on the seat, he swung around and jumped in. The trip to his house took two minutes tops. She didn't say a word, just stared at him with blank eyes.

She might have been afraid of him, he didn't know. At this point, he didn't really care. He'd had a job to do, had left it to someone else to take care of, and would now make sure that mistake did not go unpunished. But *he* wasn't the first person who would be punished. No, there was an order here that needed to be maintained. How's that for leadership?

Chapter XXXII

You didn't think to get her some fucking clothes, asshole?
Mitch made sure the blanket was tucked tightly around her
and carried her inside his house without letting her put a foot
on the ground. After settling her into his bed, trying to make
her comfortable while he was anything *but*, Mitch said, "I'll
be back as soon as I can."

She clutched the arm of his jacket, her grip weak.
"Don't…hurt him, Mitch."

As thrilled as he was that her speech had returned, it was
too late. Flexibility had never been his strength. It was
decided. He peeled her fingers off and set her hand at her side.
"I'll be back soon."

"Please. He's not worth it."

True, but it will make me feel a lot better. "After I finish
talking to him, I promise that he'll still be standing, okay?"
Even if I have to prop up his unconscious body.

He knew right where the gym was—around the block from
the police station. Normally it would be the kind of place he'd
rather die than enter, but today was a special occasion.
There'd be cops, lots of them, but anger blocked out all
rational thoughts of self-preservation.

He parked in front of a hydrant, vaguely thinking how happy he'd made some ticket giver's day. Not a big concern right now.

The place was big. A sunken lobby with uncomfortable, cheap-looking chairs lining one wall. This was no country club, this was where muscles were bruised and worked to full capacity and no prisoners were taken. Perfect for what he had planned. Concrete floors matched the long reception desk. Yellow lines were painted along each wall, directing traffic up a flight of stairs to where he imagined the workout room would be. A hallway curving around the metal banister led off to…offices? Showers? He didn't really care.

Knowing that blasting through the reception area without more than a dirty look to the kid behind the counter would bring the attention of at least twenty sweating cops down on him, he stopped and tried to appear cordial. The pumped-up teenager smiled back, probably used to expressions like the one Mitch currently wore.

"I want a tour. Now."

"Okay, let me get someone." The guy picked up the phone.

"Now. You have thirty seconds to find someone or I leave."

His bluff worked. The guy glanced around him, sighed, and then came around the counter, his steps slightly bouncing and a salesman's smile on his face. "I'll show you around." He kept talking, but Mitch ignored him, making sure his feet were right behind the kid's, pressing him to move faster.

They walked upstairs into a huge room filled with equipment surrounding a boxing ring lifted about three feet off the ground. Two men wearing gloves were slamming each other, followed by kicks, jabs and prancing. Mitch found the violence encouraging. He scanned the room, searching for his personal, human punching bag. Not there.

"What are you doing here?" Landon's voice came from the side. He stood up from a bench press, wrapping a towel around his shoulders.

"Hello there, Officer. I'm thinking of joining your club." He was the last person Mitch wanted to see. This made things more complicated. It wasn't going to stop him from doing what needed to be done, but he'd have to be more careful. And didn't that just suck.

The cop lifted both eyebrows. "I wouldn't have thought you were a joiner, Mitch."

The gym employee glanced back and forth, from man to man, stepping out of the way. He was smarter than Mitch had given him credit for.

"I'm always on the lookout for a place to fit in," Mitch said.

"Don't know if this is the place for you, then." Landon flicked his head toward the ring. "Unless you're a fighter."

"Oh, I'm a fighter alright. But today I'm just taking the tour. I'll let you know if I end up becoming a member."

"You do that."

Mitch threw the same insincere smile back to the cop and turned to the teenager. "Continue the tour."

"Sure." The kid danced on his feet nervously and then led Mitch back down the stairs and into the locker room, spouting bullshit details about the benefits of membership.

Carter was standing in the middle of the empty locker room, his locker opened, stuffing his bag into it.

Mitch was on him in a heartbeat, pulling the kid's arm behind him and shoving him against the metal in a chokehold. "What did you do to her, asshole?" He heard a gasp and footsteps running for the door behind him. He needed answers. Now. He had maybe a minute before every cop in the place, including Landon, dragged him away. Not his most brilliant move, but his blinders had been finely-focused.

Carter didn't even fight. His body was limp and defeated before Mitch had touched him. "I didn't do anything to her, I swear. I didn't! Let me go!"

"Tell me what happened." He heard shouting and feet hitting stairs. "Damn it, tell me what happened."

"She got into…my stash."

"Your stash? You little piece of shit." Mitch relaxed his arm, gave one last brutal shove, and let the guy go. "They know about it?" He nodded toward the thunderous footsteps coming closer.

"You can't tell them! They won't understand. Please, Mitchell, don't tell them."

Three cops pushed the door open, more of them steps behind. Landon was in the lead, smiling when he saw Mitch.

Carter held out his hands to the intruders. "It's okay! We were just talking. No big deal."

They slid to a stop but didn't retreat.

"Really. It's just a misunderstanding." Carter smiled and shrugged. "It's a chick. But we're dealing." He nudged Mitch like it was a big joke.

The men took their time backing off.

Landon didn't even pretend to leave. "I've seen you at the station. You're a trainee or something, right?" he asked Carter.

"Yes, sir."

"How do you know my friend, Mitch?"

Mitch cut in before the Boy Scout said something stupid. "I'm trying to get into his ex's pants." Both men whipped their heads toward him. "What?" He held up his hands and shrugged. "Carter was telling me what her favorite position was, and I…lost my head for a minute. But I found it." He winked at the shocked detective and then knocked on his forehead. "See? Right where I left it."

"You're nuts, you know that?"

"I do now, Officer. Thanks." Mitch threw an arm around Carter, who was still stunned by the derailment of this conversation. "We're gonna keep talking now, right, Carter?"

"Yes," he whimpered, as Mitch's hold tightened.

It was a good thing Mitch had no intention of actually deceiving the cop, because it would have been a complete failure. However, his attempt at totally confusing the guy worked perfectly.

"If you want to talk, why not do it at the station, kid?"

"No, sir," Carter said quickly. "That's not necessary. We're just shooting the shit…sir." The forced smile didn't quite make it to both sides of his mouth.

"Uhhuh." Landon walked into the adjacent shower area, keeping his eyes on them until his neck would no longer allow that much rotation. "I'm gonna be in the shower. If I hear anything funny, it should take me about five seconds to get back here."

As soon as Landon turned the corner and the sounds of water hitting tile wafted in, Mitch separated from the kid and told him to sit with a quick nod of the head toward a long bench running along the aisle of lockers. Carter sat so hard, his ass would be bruised tomorrow.

Not the perfect place for the violent discussion Mitch planned on having, but if he dragged Carter out, he knew Landon would come up with a good enough reason to take him in. And with Eden still a wreck at his house, he couldn't afford any delays. So he resigned himself to no beating, but the Boy Scout didn't need to know that.

Mitch stood over him, keeping his voice low. "You think having that cop in the next room will keep me from pounding you, don't you?"

"I was hoping so, yes."

"Hope is nice. Fucking useless in this situation, but still nice. You have one sentence before you start bleeding. Make it good." He straddled the wood slats of the bench and waited, his arms crossed over his chest.

Carter glanced toward the shower area and leaned in close to whisper. "Chastity found something she shouldn't have. I guess she snorted some of it. Then when Eden—"

"Stop. I said one sentence." *And my patience is a little shorter than the rope I want to choke you with.* "Eden found your dope. So what did you do to her?"

"Shhh! I'll be kicked out. It wasn't dope." His eyes

searched for danger, having no idea that the biggest threat was right in front of him.

"I really don't give a shit about what you're putting up your nose, shooting into your veins, or shoving up your ass. I care even less about who you want to hide it from. What I *do* care about is why she's sobbing in my bed right now." Not sobbing, she wasn't sobbing. And that was the scariest part. He was afraid she wasn't feeling anything anymore. "So spill."

The naughty Boy Scout's brow furrowed. "You took her to your place?"

"Not the point. Stop thinking about *where* and start thinking about *what*. You have two minutes before I've decided where I'm going to stuff your body." Truth was, even *he* wasn't stupid enough to give the detective more fuel for his Mitch-burning crusade.

"Last night, after Eden...*you know*, I got a phone call from Jolie."

His eyes narrowed. "Jolie called you? Why?"

"She wanted to come over."

"Why?"

Carter shrugged, confused. "Because she wanted to see me."

"Why would she want to see you?"

"Because we're dating."

Mitch's laughter nearly threw him off the bench. "What?"

The little brat actually sneered at him, downright proud of himself. "You didn't know?"

"You're serious. Holy crap, you're serious."

Landon's bulky body appeared in the doorway, a towel hastily wrapped around his waist, eyes suspicious. But he wasn't wet. The guy probably wished he'd picked up his gun before hitting the *pretend* shower he *wasn't* taking.

Mitch didn't care. He just kept laughing. He looked at the cop, hysterical, and pointed to the kid. "He's fucking my ex!"

Carter's smile fell. "Jolie is your ex?"

Shit, the guy looked crushed. Which might actually make sense when confronted with the facts: The asshole who might be swiping Carter's girl also got to the woman he replaced her with before he did. Yeah, that had to sting a little.

"It wasn't a big deal, Scout. We experimented for a while early on, but I'm not—I don't—"*Jesus, what kind of guy am I?* "I don't commit."

Once Landon had given them both some kind of evil cop-eye and gone back to pretending to shower, Carter asked, "Whose idea was it? To break it off."

"It was a long time ago, so I don't remember." Mitch actually felt guilty. Weird. He'd been totally fine with killing the brat a few minutes ago, but now he was lying to save the guy's feelings? There was all kinds of wrong here. "Probably her...definitely her. She's a lot smarter than I am." That second part was probably true—Jolie was very smart. But the first part was definitely a lie. She'd understood but hadn't been happy about it right away. Or for a while after that.

Steam from Landon's absurdly long shower crept into the main locker area. Sucking in thick, humid air, Mitch searched his memory, not sure if he cared or not but feeling like he owed the guy as much as of the truth as possible. Why bother? Because Mitch had every intention in the world of possessing the guy's ex-girlfriend. And infatuation loves company just as much as misery does.

Jolie. Sure, he remembered bits and pieces. Beautiful girl. Still was, but they didn't match. Like peanut butter and rockets. Sexually they were more like animals, which was fine, but he'd felt her get too attached. It was an impossible situation. He needed her to keep an eye on Hyde when Shelly couldn't. And the mushiness she started to drench him in— being overly attentive beyond her job, touching him, dancing around with the idea of a future with him in it—was a deal breaker. Where she got the idea he'd ever be interested in that kind of relationship was a mystery. He was ninety percent sure they'd only fucked facing each other a handful of times.

How's that for noncommittal?

She'd taken it well. She was like that, a fine-let's-move-on kind of girl. He respected that. He respected *her*. So if she decided to aim all her charms at the kid sitting in front of him, self-doubt flooding his eyes, so be it.

"She's quite a lady, Scout. Treat her well and she'll treat you well."

"We'll see," Carter mumbled.

"Great. Don't care. So our only problem here seems to be that I don't know what happened after Jolie called you last night."

"She wanted to come over, but Eden was still awake, and I...You know how Jolie is—the word 'no' just makes her more insistent."

Mitch couldn't agree—he never really paid attention to what she did after he said no to her. So he gestured for the guy to continue.

"I thought I could leave and be back right away, making sure Jolie wouldn't decide to swing by while Eden was..."

"Let me guess. Saying no took the rest of the night."

Carter blushed, but his glare stayed put. "Yes."

"And the wreck of a girl at my house right now is because you don't keep your goodies to yourself well enough, drugs or otherwise."

"Yeah, I guess so."

Mitch sat back. Something in the way Carter was fidgeting made Mitch think the Boy Scout was lying. Or it might have been that the guy was starting to see a possible end to his mortality. Eden believed in Carter. He was just a confused, overwhelmed, in-way-over-his-head idiot. "Fine, you can live. Primarily because you won't have another chance to fuck up. You are not to see Eden again. Do you understand me?"

"I need her to know how sorry I am. To make it up to her somehow."

"Start by growing up and keeping your dick in your pants when someone you love is counting on you." He slapped him on the shoulder and stood. "How about that?"

"I need to do something for her, Mitchell. Ask her what I can do, please."

"We'll see, Scout. We'll see." Then he shouted, "We're all done talking, Detective. Would you like to come look for blood spatter?" He left Carter sitting dejectedly in the foggy room.

CHAPTER XXXIII

After Mitch left, Eden spent the next half-hour in a huge pool of self-pity—easily imaginable due to the amount of water that had fallen out of her eyes today. She looked at the clock again. Okay, make that an hour in pathetic-hood. More than enough. As she reawakened to her mind and body, she pushed away thoughts of how her life was *meant* to be and tried to focus on how it was. She couldn't spend eighty percent of her life dreading what Chastity was doing with the remaining twenty. She wiped her cheeks on the sheet covering her. Soft sheets that smelled like *him. Wait. First think about me,* then *him.*

She was smart. In school. Reaching for a goal no one would think someone with her past capable of, but she was proving them wrong. And she could create a future, during daylight hours at least.

She was tough. Look at what she'd overcome. Still mostly sane, still finding beauty in the world. She'd always considered herself a survivor, so this was just another thing to survive.

She was good.

That one stumped her. *Good.* What did that even *mean*?

Was it about polite word choices or being bluntly honest even when it hurt the people around her? Was that *good*? Giving instead of taking—even when she only hurt herself?

So her evil half might do something unimaginable. She couldn't do a thing about that other than stay locked up. And they weren't the same person, not where it counted. Her body was involved but not her soul. Her soul was still hers. And she wouldn't hide behind the trappings of a fake sense of selflessness anymore. What's wrong with taking? Being happy?

Something triggered inside of her. Respect? *If Mom could only see me now,* she thought with a bitter chuckle. She sat up in Mitch's bed, throwing off the sheet. She'd spent her life cowering under something. *Enough is beyond enough. Grow a pair, Eden.*

She was buck naked. It would be smart to tackle that little problem before Mitch came back. Standing tall, knowing it was a deliberate attempt to stay connected with her newfound ambition and strength, she wandered over to his dresser.

His clothes were stuffed in the drawers haphazardly—t-shirts mixed in with socks and small jewelry boxes she didn't open. There was a line, after all. A crooked one, but a line nonetheless. He'd invited her into his home, not his junk drawers.

She chose a black cotton t-shirt that hung down to the middle of her thighs, and then searched for some shorts. No boxers, he didn't wear them. Trying not to dwell on what was under his pants, she went into the large walk-in closet on the other side of the room. It was almost empty, all of his suits and shirts hanging neatly on one side. The other side was bare. As if he'd kept that section cleared for someone else. Gut clenching, she wondered who he was waiting for.

"Eden?"

She jumped back and dropped her hand from the rack of ties.

"You better not have left me." His voice. Quiet. Lacking

the anger that had filled it earlier, that it almost always held.

"In here." She peeked out and saw him, his shoulders relaxing when he saw her.

"I'm glad you found your voice. But you need to get back in bed."

"I'm okay now."

"You look like hell. When's the last time you slept?"

She shrugged. When she didn't move, he approached. She would only have to lift her hand to touch him.

"Do you want me to pick you up and throw you back in bed?" he asked.

Yes. "No."

He leaned down to slip an arm under her knees, like firemen do. Which would mean her butt would be very close to his—

"Okay! I'll go." Jogging over to the bed, she jumped in, the mattress bouncing under her.

He was beautiful. There was no other word for it. Strong jaw, straight nose, dark hair dangling onto his forehead. She recognized the look in his eyes, but it had never made her feel so adored before. And so warm.

"Nice shirt," he said.

She ran her hands down the cotton and smiled. "Better than yours."

He glanced down at the rumbled shirt, tie, and trousers he'd probably slept in and then shrugged. "I've been occupied."

With Carter. "You didn't hurt him, did you?" She didn't believe Mitch would do anything too stupid. Well, maybe 'believe' was too strong a word.

"Nah, we just had a talk." He ran a hand through his hair. "He said he'll do anything you want if you forgive him."

Forgiving Carter's betrayal hadn't been the priority, just his health. "I don't want to think about that right now. I want to—" Her eyes roamed over his body, and, suddenly, all she could think about was what was under his pants.

Say it, Eden. Say it. She took a deep breath. "I want to do something else."

"What?" His lips were tight, suspicious, all of their usual fullness tucked between his teeth.

"Could you come here? Please?"

He looked away, considering. Not afraid. Mitch was never afraid, but right now he looked it.

"I need you," she whispered.

His chest fell as the air rushed out. Taking the smallest steps known to man, he came over to the bed and sat down next to her feet.

"Don't make this any harder for me." She patted the spot next to her, the one he'd occupied the morning she'd first seen him.

He smirked. "Harder for *you*?" But he scooted further up on the mattress, sitting stiffly against the headboard, waiting. His face was tight, wary.

"Stop looking at me like that."

"Tell me what's going on, and I'll look at you accordingly."

"You're very difficult, you know that?"

"I think you've told me that before." He scratched his shoulder. "What's going on, Eden?"

"I've had a hell of a day...of a month. But I'd like to think I'm stronger for it."

"Listening." Their mutual discomfort seemed to relax him slightly.

"I need to see if I can do something. If you don't want me to, then tell me. That's fine. But if you'll let me..."

He squinted his eyes. "Are we talking about what I think we're talking about?"

"Lesson five."

He cringed. "Yeah, I thought so."

Why couldn't he be a regular man? The *one* time she puts herself out there, with someone she wants and trusts, and he rejects her. "Forget I mentioned it."

"I was hoping you just needed a shoulder to cry on. Holy shit, did I just say that?" He snapped his fingers in quick succession. "Look, I'm not what you need."

"You're exactly what I need. Except for the whole bastard part."

"Well said."

"I trust you. I'm attracted to you. I'd like to think you're attracted to me." She waited for him to respond. When he didn't, she said, "Okay, that hurts."

He stood and began pacing in front of the bed, not looking up from the floor. "Of course, I'm attracted to you. I'm an asshole, not an idiot."

She wished he would stop. Tell her what he was thinking, feeling, let her in just a little bit. But that wasn't how he worked. No, Mitch was closed off so tightly, it surprised both of them every time he had an emotional response he couldn't control.

"So what's the problem?" she asked softly.

He paused. "You've thought this whole thing through, right? But have you thought about what happens if one of us walks away from this with...*feelings*"—he grimaced at the word—"that are unrequited?"

"You think I'll fall in love with you?"

His expression was unreadable—somewhere between patronizing and wonder. "Or I with you."

She laughed. "Yeah, like that'll happen."

"To my knowledge, I am capable." He sounded offended. "Though the theory has never been tested."

"One night isn't enough for anyone to fall in love with anyone."

"One night," he mouthed, his eyes roaming down her body. He cleared his throat. "You sound so sure."

I'm not. One night of sex might not bring two people together in love, but a bunch of random moments of kindness, comfort, and trust, followed by one night of sex? Yeah, that might just do it. And she couldn't let that happen. If the tremors in her chest meant what she feared they might, she wouldn't be able to handle him tossing her away. "You know what? Never mind. I'll find someone else to practice on." Someone safer.

His eyes flared. "No. You won't."

She looked down, embarrassed, plucking the edge of her t-shirt like a harp. "I'd hoped you'd be the one. I was wrong. I'm sorry. Forget I mentioned it." This was humiliating beyond reason. What had she been thinking? That whenever he looked at her, she felt more worthy of a human being? That when he spoke—even with words meant to hurt—she melted at the timbre of his voice and wished it didn't have to end? Yeah, that was what she'd been thinking. Well, yippee for her. He obviously wasn't thinking the same thing.

"Why do you want to do this?" he asked. "With anyone, let alone me? After everything else that's happened to you lately, don't you think you should slow down in this particular area?"

Geez, it wasn't possible to slow down any more. Was she going to wait until she was sixty? "Why? My body's already done it. With you, for God's sake! It's my mind that hasn't." And so desperately wants to now. "Do you remember the look on my face when I woke up next to you? Do you have any idea how scary that was? Just the idea of it. You had your arm wrapped around me. It should have felt good."

"You woke up naked in a stranger's bed. No one would feel good under those conditions."

She conceded the point with a tilt of her head. "But I'm twenty-three and am terrified to let anyone touch me. There has been one time— No, two times. Two times in my entire life that I've wanted to be touched. The first was tainted by Chastity. The second was interrupted by Carter. And then you ran away from me." She hoped he'd wanted to stay there as much as she had. He *had* to have some feelings for her, not as strong as hers, but some. Didn't he? She'd seen the fear in his eyes, the panicked look on his face when they'd separated.

Carter's entrance hadn't caused that look. The kiss had. How that kiss had connected them. And it terrified him.

He studied her. "You're not afraid I'll hurt you?"

"You'd never hurt me." Not physically, at least.

Holding her eyes, he let out his breath in one puff, nodded and sat down on the bed. "What do you want from me?"

Her chest clenched, pulse quickened. She'd asked…and he'd agreed. Shocking. And frightening. "Um…only as much as you'll give me willingly. Never more than that. If you don't want this, please tell me."

"Want this? Abso-fucking-lutely. Think that everything will be the same afterwards? Not a chance in hell." With a twitch of his jaw, he said, "But I'm a gambler. So let's see who's right." He reclined into the pillow. She could tell he was struggling, his feet tapping an inaudible beat in the air. Air that was almost suffocating her with nervousness…and desire. "You sure you want to do this?"

She nodded at the man who was offering himself up to her. For her needs. Her wants. Giving over the control he coiled so tightly around himself. "Kind of awkward, isn't it?"

"You don't know the half of it." He glanced down to below his belt, carrying her gaze with his. He was already hard, his erection tenting his pants.

Holy crap, would that actually fit inside her? Yes, because it already had. She just hadn't been there to feel it. It was time to remedy that. "I want to see your body," she whispered, ready for him to change his mind at any moment, half of her hoping he would.

"Okay." Sighing, he wiped his hands on his pants and reached for his tie.

"Wait." She put her hands on top of his. "Can I do it?"

Nodding once, he didn't fight her exactly, but was so tense, even the guided movements were jerky and stiff.

She pressed his hands up onto the pillow he was leaning on. "Hold on to this." She considered giving him something to bite on, he looked so nervous.

He tucked his palms under the pillow, his arms straining against the fabric of his shirt, and gave her a look of self-determination…and outright challenge.

Still kneeling beside him, her breath shallow and quick, Eden leaned over to undo his tie. It slipped off and was tossed onto the floor. *Okay, I can do this.* One by one, she popped open the buttons of his shirt, spreading it to expose his smooth, muscular chest. Her hands shook only slightly as she pulled the ends from his pants. She felt his heart racing under her fingertips as she traced a line from his neck to his belly button, momentarily losing herself in the light dusting of hair beginning there and trailing further down. Before she got ahead of herself, she trailed her hand back up his side, eliciting a quiet moan from him.

"Can you…?" she asked, biting her lip.

He raised himself onto his hands, bringing his body closer to hers, so she could bring each shoulder to bare. Neither of them looked at the other—he avoided her eyes while she stared at the perfection within her reach. The crumpled button-down landed on top of his tie.

"Your shoes." Were off the second she suggested it, along with a sock nudged by the other foot and sent tumbling over the edge of the bed. She gently pushed his resistant body back down, hearing him swallow, seeing him shove his hands behind his head and the pillow crush in his grip.

She wouldn't stop, even if she gnawed off her upper lip before she was done. As her hand brushed the hot skin above his belt, he flinched slightly, then seemed to right himself and resumed his feigned pose of relaxation. He was breathing harder, perhaps as hard as she was, but he didn't move unless she asked, never hurrying or touching her.

She felt his erection tap her wrist through his pants as she undid his leather belt. Her eyes focused on his as she lowered his zipper. She could do this. This was her choice, no one else's. She wanted this to happen…with him.

With a gentle request of her eyes, he lifted his hips so she could pull off his trousers and throw them onto the almost-finished pile on the floor. Once the t-shirt she wore floated down, the pile was complete.

Her heart was pounding so hard she thought she might need medical attention. But not yet. She had lots to do before she'd stop to think about that. Looking at his body, hard and vulnerable, was difficult, but she knew she had to. She tried to take strength from his eyes, but that was no help—he looked terrified.

"Is this alright?" she whispered, praying he would say yes.

"This is…tough…but *very* alright." He sighed. "I've never let anyone…*in* like this."

"That makes two of us. Well, it *will* in a minute."

He groaned.

Smiling nervously, she glided her palms across his chest, down his taut abs. His body shuddered the whole way. She swallowed, steadying herself, and touched him. He jerked under her hand.

"Oh, shit." He yanked the pillow from behind his head and put it over his chest, clutching it, his arm muscles straining, almost as if he were in pain.

Her hands flew off. "I'm sorry."

Lifting the pillow so she could see his eyes, he asked, "Could you…um…could you come up here?"

She moved alongside him, stretching her body out so it snuggled close to his side, liking the way they fit.

Releasing his grip of the pillow with one hand, he brought her face to his. There was no tension in his lips as they brushed against hers, just warmth and softness. Once they connected, he removed his fingers from her chin. He was kissing her the same way he had before—slowly and patiently.

Her body had other ideas. She held his face, loving the scratch of his unshaven jaw, imagining what it would feel like on the rest of her body. Opening herself to him, she felt a wave of heat spread through her, a want she'd often read about but had never known was real or just something books *pretended* was real. It was. With any plans to linger in this moment quickly fading, her leg slipped over his body, rolling her on top of him.

He mumbled something into her mouth, or maybe it had just been a groan. Whatever it was helped her know how right this was. How right *they* were. She knew he was struggling to keep his hands off her—tendons straining, muscles bulging throughout his body. He was tight under her, pressing himself into the soft mattress as far as he could as if he was afraid to let his skin touch hers. His lips and tongue weren't the only things reaching out to her. As she moved against him, fitting further into him, she felt his erection brush her center.

Oasis. He was her oasis. After a very long walk through hell.

CHAPTER XXXIV

He was going to rip the fucking pillow apart. *This was a really bad idea.* Why did he think he could do this? Control himself?

Focus on the kiss. Not the part of her that was a centimeter away from his pulsing cock. He needed to stay still, needed her to decide *what* they would do and *when* they would do it. Asking for her lips had already crossed the line he'd set for himself. *Breathe, Mitch.* This was about her, not him. He would let her find herself, even if it killed him. Which was a serious possibility. She needed to learn what someone could offer her without just taking for themselves. He couldn't allow himself to touch her. It would all be over if he touched her—he'd scare her away. Or he'd come like a teenager without ever being inside of her. That might be worse.

Every muscle was cramped, aching to envelop her. *Shit.* He was so close to giving in, to press her down onto him. Or to flip them over and press his way into her. He was going to lose his mind. Truly lose his fucking mind to her.

Focus on the kiss. Ignore the warmth and wetness he felt just above his— *The kiss.* Her hands on his shoulders and sides, pressing, grasping. More quickly now. Her thighs were slick with her, sliding down so close to— *No, the kiss.* Her hair fell around them like a veil, closing them off from the outside world. It smelled like strawberries. Only reminding him of his own hunger. Not for food. For her. *Damn it.*

She needed to slow down. He knew it instinctively—she shouldn't be rushed, even if it was her own body that was hurrying. Jesus, she felt good, her weight pressing against him, filling him. Like he needed to fill her—*The kiss. Focus on the fucking kiss.*

He needed to say something. But at some point, he'd gotten lockjaw and was now very probably foaming at the mouth. Or at least drooling. He wanted to touch her breasts so fucking bad. Just the side. He'd be happy with a one-fingered brush against the fullness that wasn't already pressed so hard against his chest. *Just the side.* Yeah sure, like he needed a finger wandering off, knowing exactly where it would head next. *This was a very bad idea.*

"Slower," he managed to stammer out.

"I don't want to go slower." They were both breathing hard, panting. She reached behind her and wrapped her hand around his cock. "You don't want me to go slower either."

"Oh, fuck. No, really—"

She squeezed.

"I'm begging you to stop." He couldn't feel his legs. "We need to slow down."

"Why?"

He blinked. "Good question." There'd been a reason, right? Just not one he could remember presently. This wasn't his first rodeo. He'd been with lots of gorgeous women before, but Eden was... Eden was something completely different. It wasn't her outward beauty that drew him in. It was her strength, her fire, her desire to do what was right even when it wasn't easy, her ability to make him see himself as a worthy human being. How the hell did she do it?

When she sat up, all the air in his lungs went with her. He searched her face for signs of fear or regret. No, he couldn't let her regret this moment. It might destroy both of them.

She smiled, her eyes lighting up the room. "I'm doing pretty well, aren't I?"

Thank God. "Are you fucking kidding me? You're doing great."

"I feel great." She lowered herself, warming him again, and whispered, "*You* make me feel great."

His mouth moved, but his mind was blank. What do you say to that? The most amazing woman you've ever seen is naked on top of you, smiling with lips *your* lips have made fuller. What the hell do you say to that?

"I think I want you inside me, but…"

Oh shit, did she say "but"?

"Are you okay with this?" she asked.

"With what?" Her walking out of the room? Hell, no.

"With me"—her brow furrowed—"*using* you."

Once his heart stopped palpating and his cock stopped jerking, he allowed himself to caress her cheek. One quick touch before wrapping his fingers back together under his head. "I want this to be clear: I will enjoy every second of this you give me. Whatever you offer, whatever you take. I'm…yours."

She blinked rapidly. "Do you mean that?"

"You better fucking believe it." He watched the trepidation disappear from her face. "I will behave. But I might need another pillow." He lifted the disfigured pile of fluff he'd been choking the stuffing out of and enjoyed the melody of her laugh.

Her mouth moved to his neck and though he ached to return the favor, capturing the scent of her hair again, he couldn't move. He was her prisoner, a willing captor for her to touch, grasp, and play with for as long as she wanted to. Climbing off him, she traveled down to his chest, hands moving slightly ahead of her mouth, unpredictable, exploring.

He'd never felt so exposed, so vulnerable, so incredible. With every brush of her lips, she discovered him, tasted him, *knew* him. She dipped lower. To his abs, the crest of his hip.

Desire raced through his body, bouncing between the touch of her fingertips to the stroke of her tongue.

He couldn't control the arch of his hips, lifting to bring his cock closer to her lips, desperate to feel her take all of him in. But if she did that, he'd come. Abso-fucking-lutely. "No, don't—" *Oh shit, that was close.*

Her eyes were huge, brows close together. "Did I do something wrong?" How could she be so uncertain and so right at the same time?

"Nothing wrong. All amazing. But if you keep doing that, it's... I'm going to..." How do you find the right word when none you've ever used seemed soft enough for your lover's ears?

"Oh, sorry," she said with a look that proved otherwise. "I got carried away."

"Perhaps you could get carried away again later." Like when he could get more oxygen.

He felt the little vibrations of her laugh against his skin as she brought her lips up his torso and back to his mouth. He didn't need to remind himself to stay focused on the kiss anymore. It was everything. It was insanity and euphoria all rolled up by a beautiful little brunette who made life worth something.

Jesus, he wanted to touch her. But he had to wait, clutching the pillow or the headboard, his arms sore from the effort.

She straddled his hips again, rolling her core against his length. Face to face, even her moans were beautiful. It was excruciating for him to not be able to take her fully. She spread open his fisted hands with her fingers and intertwined them, but kept them pinned to the bed.

"Why didn't I talk you into this sooner?" she said with a smirk before sliding down his body, kisses trailing down his neck.

He jolted when he felt her silky warmth envelop the tip of his cock. "Wait," he groaned at the same time as he saw her eyes open wide in shock and her body stop, then retreat slightly. *Damn it.* How could he tell her all of the things he wanted to do? That he wanted to taste her, spend the rest of his life with his mouth between her thighs. This was supposed to be *her* show. His needs didn't matter. He couldn't tell her that, once his cock was inside her, the stopwatch until he came would start at about one minute, thirty seconds like a seventeen-year-old kid? He sighed. "Condoms, corner pocket."

"What does that mean?"

"Drawer. Corner. Condom."

She reached out and opened the drawer of the nightstand, pulling out a new box. Ripping it open, she fumbled, sending them everywhere but where they needed to be. She was going to fall off the bed—or worse *him*—if he didn't stop her.

He grabbed her wrist and rolled over her, unwilling to break contact for even a moment. He grabbed a long train of packets off the ground and presented them to her. In his excitement, he hadn't realized he was now on top of a naked woman he hadn't exactly been given permission to touch.

She didn't look like she cared much. Yeah, that was verified when she wrapped her legs around his waist and pressed her hips into his. Breathing would be a good idea right now. Sliding the inch it would take to be inside of her was also a good idea, but he could wait...about thirty more seconds. *Nice control, asshole.*

She took the condoms out of his hand and said, "I had to put one of these on a banana at a party once. It was a dare."

"Dare you to try it again."

"And if I can do it?"

"Anything you want."

She smiled. "And if I can't?"

"Anything you want. In addition to a how-to lesson."

"You got yourself a deal." She rolled them both over, her breasts pressed against his chest. "I like having control over you, Mitch."

"That makes two of us." Words he'd never imagined

coming out of his mouth.

For some reason, he decided to make it harder for her, turning his cock and hips away from her as she tried to aim. And he loved that she was game. Her smile and occasional glare were, unbelievably, worth the delay.

"I could keep you still with these." She bared her teeth.

He let her win, knowing he'd blow the second that mouth got anywhere near his cock—teeth involved or not. But before she could collect her prize—his prize—he'd make her work for it. They played, laughed, and teased until the moment she slid him inside of her. When his world stopped. Everything he'd ever known. Everything he'd ever *been* disappeared in that one movement.

Forcing his eyes open, he saw her. He cursed the pleasure he felt ripping through his body. Because it happened at the same moment as shock registered on her face. He needed to help her.

"Jesus, Eden, we can stop." His words were guttural and torn from him. The hardest thing he'd ever had to say. "Get off." He grabbed her hips and pushed her up, away.

She slapped her hands on top of his, her eyes wide. "Did I hurt you?"

"No. I—" He stopped. "Are you in pain right now?"

She started to move slowly. "I feel..." A smile spread on her face. "This is how it's supposed to feel, isn't it?"

He sat up halfway, leaning on his elbows as she rocked him, wanting to be near her flush breasts, her pounding heart. "Yeah, I think it is." Yep, he might get used to this, after three or four lifetimes.

This *was* how it should feel. She was tingling, vibrating, each time she lowered onto him, taking him deeper. She tried to keep her eyes open, but they *so* wanted to close, to allow every nerve to focus on the feel of him inside her. "Touch me." When she heard him inhale sharply, she looked at him.

"You sure?" His hands were inches from her hips, shaking. "Because it could change things…rapidly." When he shifted to sit up straighter, she felt him press further into her, rubbing against the wall of her core. Both of them moaned.

Oh, God. "I want you to touch me, Mitch." She rose slightly, tempting him into action. Given permission, his chest relaxed momentarily. Then he clutched her hips and pushed her down.

"Oh!" A spike of pleasure tore through her, lifting her up and slamming her back down again. She threw her head backwards, digging her fingers into his shoulders.

He kept the momentum, rocking her faster, pulling her forward so her center brushed against his skin with every thrust.

Her breath came out in gasps, matching his. Someone was moaning loudly, probably *her* since the sound continued as he dragged his teeth across her shoulder. Oh my God, she wanted him to bite her! Wait, reverse that. She wanted to bite him. Who would have ever thought she'd have it in her? Um…no one? Not wanting to break their rhythm, she carefully lifted his chin. She clenched her muscles, wanting to hold onto him forever, but the feeling was getting too strong. Too overpowering.

His eyes were glazed over, the vein in his neck pounding under her fingers. He blinked and opened his mouth to say something. At first, all he could get out were short moans in beat with their hips. Then his lips moved. "I—I—"

A cry broke free from her, sending her scream and euphoria bouncing off the sky, aftershocks bringing jolts of pleasure as if God himself was sending her a reward.

$$\sim\!\!\!\sqrt{}\!\!\sqrt{}\!\!\sqrt{}\!\!\sim$$

Mitch kept her moving above him, her legs shaking and limp, the ripples of gratification being prolonged with each movement.

Her chest lifted with every gasp as she started breathing again, her eyes shining. "Another thing I've never done—check."

Did she mean…? "Never?" His voice was hoarse, broken apart by the gift she'd given him.

She smiled, a question filling her eyes.

Was it over? Did he *deserve* to finish within her? He slowed her down, letting her recover, wondering what he should do.

"What were you going to say?" she asked breathlessly.

You mean, before you made me the luckiest bastard on earth? Who could never have earned this much happiness in twelve lifetimes? "Don't remember."

"Too bad." With one twitch of an eyebrow, she let him know how much she believed him. But she didn't push. Until she brought her hands to his chest and pressed him down. "You don't want to stop now, do you?"

"Stupid question, Eden." When she smiled, he felt the sudden need to wipe the grin off her face and replace it with the half-lidded look she'd worn earlier. He flipped them both over, trapping her underneath him, fighting the idea to take her fast and hard with everything he had. That would come later. If he was very fucking lucky. But she'd have to make that decision, not him.

Her eyes widened momentarily until he carefully started rocking into her. Then that smile disappeared and she moved against him, lifting her hips to meet his.

It was fairly traumatic for him to move so slowly. *Gentle. Be gentle.* Kissing her helped to calm his thrusts, the shake in his thighs and ass, the struggle to make this special for her. She was nothing like any of the other women he'd been with. She deserved nothing less than all the pleasure and care he had in him to give. And part of him hoped that, in return, she would accept him for who he was. If he could just show her that he was worthy of her.

He brought his hand under her ass, using it to lift her to him, to be deeper inside of her without bringing all his force down onto her. When her moans increased, he realized he'd sped up. Pressing into her, he wanted to claim her. In a way no other man would ever be able to do. His body, this experience, would be the yardstick she'd compare all future lovers to.

Whoa. His rhythm broke with the idea of her being with someone else. He stopped, heart pounding, body wanting, brain melting. His mind was overcome with images, nightmares of her being under any body but his. No, that couldn't happen. He couldn't let that happen.

Her hand brushed his cheek, then his shoulder. "Don't stop." Her voice was guttural with need. "Please, don't stop."

How incredibly hot is that? He lifted away from her, admiring her beauty, and all thoughts of anyone but her disappeared. In that moment, all he wanted was to block out the rest of the world for her, to be the only thing she saw, the only thing she felt.

Her legs tightened around him, her hips lifted higher, and her muscles clenched around his cock, sending out a moan he recognized as his. He picked up the slow, difficult rhythm of thrusts from earlier until he felt her nails dig into his back.

"Faster...please."

That, he could do. Their union sped, not to the maximum, just enough to appease her. His eyes never left her face, watching her enjoyment, searching for any signs she wasn't being fulfilled. *Looking good so far.* Her body arched under his, her arms pulling him deeper, demanding more speed. He tried to ignore the intensity of his own pleasure, the incredible feeling radiating through him. He slipped his hand in between them and helped her along, knowing how pissed off he'd be at himself if he came before she'd taken everything he had to give.

Her hand grasped the nape of his neck and yanked him forward, an inch away from her face. She swallowed and glared at him. "Stop. Being. Gentle."

Sweeter words were never spoken. He gave in to her, forcing his eyes to stay open to make sure she was still alright, but unable to ignore the sensations her body was sending scorching through him. She stopped breathing, squeezing him with more strength than he'd thought she had. Then her breath resumed as a gasp and she cried out, her body jerking as she came.

He couldn't hold back any longer, seeing her breathless smile, her eyes. With one final push, he felt himself release into her, holding onto something he'd never remembered feeling before. As if this moment would be burned in his memory for the rest of his life.

CHAPTER XXXV

For the next thirty-six hours, Mitch was numb to everything but her. The world was probably still turning, people were still living their lives—making bad decisions, getting into trouble, doing the occasional good deed. He imagined. But didn't really care.

Everything he cared about was curled into his arm, her leg still resting across his body, both of them breathless.

Did they eat? Not off of plates, but yeah, he remembered eating. He vaguely recalled going to the grocery store, not wanting to leave her but knowing he kept nothing in the house that was good enough for her. And she needed food. Between the amount of exercise they were getting and her previous stress-induced weight loss, she needed calories. He'd wandered through the aisles, looking for nutrient-dense foods, grabbing anything he thought she might like. Fruit, granola bars, chocolate, power drinks, more condoms.

She'd eaten most of the food off his body. Then wiggled and giggled incessantly while he snacked off her. They'd taken countless showers together and gone swimming a few times, so neither was sticky from the remnants their tongues hadn't reached.

Did they sleep? Yeah, catnaps wrapped around each other's bodies, waking up dazed, happy and still exhausted. Before starting to explore again.

He also remembered an angry call from Jolie when he didn't show up at work. He thought she might have jumped through the phone line and wrapped it around his neck if she could have. She was suspicious enough to know something was going on and then plain pissed off when he wouldn't tell her what it was. But he shrugged it off easily—he had no plans to share any part of Eden with anyone else ever again.

〜〜〜

"You're a very good teacher." She trailed a fingertip across his chest, still damp from the shower.

Laughing, he said, "You're a quick study."

She nodded. "You should see me do calculus."

"As long as you're naked, I'll watch you do anything."

"With regular study breaks, of course." She winked and kissed him. "Thank you, Mitch. For everything."

"Stop it or I'll blush."

"I'd love to make you blush, but I don't think that's possible."

He swept his lips across her forehead. "You must have missed it. I definitely blushed. A few times."

"That's not called *blushing*, Mitch." She laughed and then pushed up on her elbow, allowing the first bit of air between them all day. "Question."

Oh, boy. "Easy one or tough one?" The easy ones involved their bodies, trying different positions, testing new sensations. He hoped it wasn't a tough one—those involved speech. Questions about the past, sometimes the present. He wouldn't lie to her anymore, not if he could possibly help it. Second nature wasn't something he had any experience ignoring.

"An in-the-middle one," she said.

"Wait. Let me prepare myself." He stretched his neck from

side to side, muscles sore. "Okay, let 'er rip."

"Do you think your stamina has anything to do with Hyde?"

He flinched at the name he hadn't thought about—the creature he hadn't felt—for days. That never happened. More than the physical reminders, Hyde was usually a constant ache in his mind—transform for one night, dread for the next thirty-four days. A cycle with no end.

"Was that a tough one?" Her voice rang of regret, something he never wanted her to feel.

"No, not tough. Just—" He ran a hand through his hair and tried to bring her smile back. "Stamina? I'd like to think that's all me. But, honestly, I've never thought about it. Or had this many opportunities to test it."

"I'm glad I could help."

"Me too." He flipped over, rolling her onto her back. "Is it my turn now?" He kissed her neck and then dragged his tongue to her breast.

"Your turn for what?"

"You've been bossy for a day and a half, when do I get a turn?" *Not that I minded, of course.* His tease turned flat with a nervous twitch of her body. He stopped and looked at her.

Holding his eyes, she stretched out each arm, then each leg. "Give it your best shot, boss."

Holy shit. She had no idea what she'd just asked for. Free rein? Huh. Where should he start? His lips returned to her breast, his tongue tasting her taut nipple, cupping her fullness and bringing it into his mouth. The arch of her back making his job even easier. He took his time, listening to her light moans as he worked his way down her flat belly with his hands, then his mouth.

Running his teeth along her hipbone and kissing the hollow in between it and her belly button, he wrapped his hands around her and lifted her ass. Then he ran his palms down the back of her thighs, spreading her legs in front of him.

Glancing up to check on her, he saw her wide brown eyes and open mouth. "This too bossy?" he asked.

She shook her head so hard, her entire body moved with it.

Back to work. No, hobby. Yeah, this was the world's best hobby. He kissed the inside of her thigh, moving slowly upwards to where it met her center, pausing to admire her beauty. Considering how beautiful she was, how could this part of her be even more so?

When he touched her, she shivered. Then moaned. Another stroke. Another moan. *Amazing.* He could control her passion so simply. And she let him. *Fucking amazing.* As he parted her, he realized the discomfort he felt was his cock pressing into the bed like a hammer. Didn't matter. *She* mattered.

Her body jerked when he brought his tongue to her. He'd been gentle, he *knew* he'd been gentle. Because he was trying so fucking hard not to shove his face closer and lap her like a man dying of thirst at first sight of water. *Try harder, asshole.* He tried.

Her taste was like a condensed version of her, leaving him aching for more. Using his finger and his mouth, he was moaning along with her. He pressed a hand to her belly to keep her still and stroked her harder, sliding inside her, bringing more of her wetness to him.

Her hands were in his hair, pressing him deeper. "This too bossy?" She laughed, her voice breathless.

He didn't respond, not wanting to take his mouth off her, glad to feel it didn't matter to her as she pushed him closer. He clutched her hip as her body started to jerk against him. Damn it, he didn't want her to finish too soon. Then he'd have to stop. At least for a second. Then he'd get to start again. Yeah, that'd do.

He worked her harder, feeling her muscles clench under his tongue and fingers. She felt no shame in the volume of her cries. He used their rhythm to push her over the edge, bringing out one last prayer of thanks from her. Her fingers tugged his hair painfully and he smiled, not stopping his tongue until her legs went limp, their only movement a steady shiver.

He tossed a blanket over her, not wanting to cover her beautiful body, but wanting to protect her from everything, even the air around them. He kept his other hand on her, lightly stroking, until her legs stopped twitching.

Best hobby ever.

⫭⫭⫭

"Mitch, your phone." She shook him slightly. "It's been going off forever."

He ran a hand over his eyes and looked at the clock: 11:00. Did that mean a.m. or p.m.? Light peeked through the drapes. Oh, a.m. Sunday or Monday? Who the hell knew?

She kissed him, catching his lower lip in her teeth and tugging gently.

"Good morning," he mumbled.

"Someone really wants to talk to you. They've been calling nonstop."

When the phone started ringing again, he leaned over to the nightstand and grabbed it. "Why didn't I turn this thing off?"

She shrugged and dragged her body away from his. He blinked at the caller ID. Jolie. Yeah, he had to answer. It was better than her deciding to stop by and check up on him.

"Hey, Jolie. How ya doing?" He pulled the phone away from his head when she started yelling.

"Where have you been? I have been calling you every half an hour for…days!"

"I told you to cancel my appointments."

"That was three days ago! You said you would be back today. What is going on, Mitchell? Are you alright?"

"I'm very sick."

Eden laughed, covering her mouth when he put a finger to his lips to shush her.

"You'd better be dying," Jolie said. "No, scratch that. You better get healthy quick. If you cancel on Sprite, you won't only lose them, you'll lose every speaking engagement at every one of their offices. They don't understand the concept of sick days." She took a breath. "Are you really sick?"

He coughed lamely, and then shot a warning glance to Eden who seemed to find this funny. "Very." Damn it, he had to return to real life. It had taken him a long time to find a profession in which people would pay him to be an asshole. And now more than ever—because of the woman naked and smiling in front of him—he needed to have an outlet for his evil. He'd need to be twice the asshole at work so he could come home to her. Hell, maybe he should increase his fees. Twice the asshole, twice the price.

"Do you want me to come over?" Jolie asked.

"No!" He sniffled. "No, I'll be okay. One more day. That'll be enough."

Eden crawled across the bed on her hands and knees, mischief in her eyes, ignoring the shaking of his head.

"Have you taken any cold medicine? I could bring you something to make you feel better."

"I have what I need here. Thanks." Fake cough. Hand not fast enough to stop Eden from sliding her lips around his cock. Okay, they probably could have been faster, if he'd tried a little harder. When her tongue flicked out, he moaned.

"What's wrong?" Jolie's voice.

"Oh." *Damn it.* "I think I'm gonna be sick. Don't come over. Don't want you to get sick too." He pressed 'end' just as Eden wrapped her hand around the base of his erection. Running his hand through her hair and tossing the phone on the floor, he said, "You are in so much trouble." Thirty seconds later, he'd forgotten why.

CHAPTER XXXVI

From: "JCabot" <jcabot@theclinic.net>
　　To: "The Clinic" <rwhittley@theclinic.net>
　　Subject: Hyde 0016
　　Have not seen Mitchell Turner in seventy-two hours. He's holed up with Eden Colfax at his house. Both in their human states. My guess: They are copulating just like you wanted them to. Repeatedly.
　　Damn her. It should be me. Screw this. Time's up, slut.

　　Another nap. Another shower. They'd barely made it to the almost-empty box of condoms the last time.

　　He looked incredible, splayed out on his back, his breathing calm while he slept. Wanting to touch continually but knowing he needed the sleep, Eden settled for resting her head on his chest, listening to the rhythm of his heart.

　　She wondered if what they were doing was normal. But then, did it really matter? Worst case she was incredibly lucky.

Best case, she was still incredibly lucky. Every muscle was sore, along with many parts she didn't think were made from muscle. But the soreness just reminded her of what he'd done to make her feel that way, so she wasn't complaining. Her body had been vibrating for days, ready for more of what he gave her. Which was far more than she could have imagined. He was like a perfect gift, one that kept giving and giving.

He yawned, scratching his growing beard. It looked good on him. Everything looked good on him. *Nothing* on him was better.

"Hey, beautiful," he said, his voice gravely. "I'm guessing I have, like, two more hours until you've killed me."

"I've come to a decision."

He raised his head and an eyebrow, instantly alert. "I don't like it when you do that. Makes me nervous."

"You realize by admitting that, you've just quadrupled the likelihood of it happening again, right?" She laughed and snuggled closer.

"I do now. So are you going to tell me or draw my agony out for the last two hours of my life?"

"This"—she put her hand to the side of his neck—"is my favorite part of your body."

He laughed. "That? Why?"

"Because that's what tells me when your heart is racing. And these"—she pointed to his eyes—"let me know it's because of me. What about you?"

"My favorite part?" He sighed, looking up at the ceiling.

She knocked on his chest with her fist. "Still waiting here. And it better be good."

He chuckled. The backs of his fingers brushed along her hip, to the small hollow between the bone and her belly button, sending a shiver through her. "I'm a big fan of this one." His hand moved lower, two fingers caressing her core. "And I'd be remiss if I didn't mention this, of course."

"Of course," she said, her back arching slightly, disappointed when his hand moved away.

"But my absolute favorite is a toss-up. Between this"—he touched her chest, her heart—"and this." His finger poked her right in the middle of the forehead.

"You're smooth, my man. Very smooth."

"I am, aren't I? A talent I never knew I had." He laughed and rolled on top of her, his body hard and strong, yet giving and accepting of hers.

She knew he was ready again. She felt his erection pushing between her legs. But *he* wasn't pushing. She'd seen him struggle with keeping control since they began this journey and adored him for it. With a look into his eyes, she knew what he was thinking, saw herself reflected there. And it helped her see her own worth. Up until recently, he'd been an impossible sell—constantly pushing her away, belittling her. But no more. And he wasn't lying anymore. When Mitch looked at her like that, she knew it was true—he was as smitten as she was.

For right now. She sighed.

All of that would end once they put their clothes back on, layering themselves to keep distance from the world. And each other. It hurt to think about. She didn't want to live without his skin on hers. Maybe it couldn't last, maybe this *wasn't* normal. When would he start closing himself off to her? Would it be little by little like a slow death? No, not with Mitch. With Mitch, it would be fast. He wouldn't feel a thing.

Holding back a whimper, she held him tighter and kissed him deeply enough to stop her lip from trembling.

⌐⋀⋀⋀⌐

Mitch let the water pound on his shoulders, glad to be free of his sweat, less happy her scent had to go with it. He'd left her sleeping soundly, mouth hanging slightly open. Oddly adorable. Of course, for all he knew he snored like a pirate—he'd never thought to ask anyone. Never really let anyone stay the night either.

Until Eden, Jolie was probably the only one to see him asleep and before her, only his sister. But the few minutes of rest he had before Hyde woke up wasn't the same, now was it.

─╫─╫─╫─

Eden didn't want this to end, but as the light coming through the window turned from white to blue, she knew her four days of reprieve had ended. And with it, *him*. That's why she'd felt the need to claim him, draw his attention back to where it should stay, during the call from Jolie. But it had been a metaphorical wake-up call as well as a literal one. She'd asked for one experience, and he'd given her days. Her and Mitch's time together was running out.

She heard him quietly singing in the shower and headed downstairs, famished. This much action could make a girl hungry. Laughing at how far she'd come, she looked down at her naked body. Comfortable. Powerful. Complete. Starving and thirsty, too.

In the kitchen, she stuffed a croissant in her mouth and leaned into the fridge. *Oh, green flavor!* She grabbed the power drink and twisted off the cap, then took another for Mitch, tucking it under her arm. Contemplating the need for hydration versus how many she could carry, she took a few big gulps and then popped the croissant back into her mouth.

"Where. Is. Mitch?"

Eden turned toward the angry voice behind her, and mumbled, "Hi, Jolie," from the corner of her mouth.

Jolie apparently wasn't impressed by naked, multiple-juice-holding women with pastries between their teeth. Darn it. Holding a paper bag with tiny grease spots blooming on the bottom, Jolie stood with her other hand on her waist, hip jutting out, resentment in her eyes.

"I didn't realize you were a nurse too, Eden. Don't they usually wear clothes?"

Fumbling the bottles in a feeble attempt at covering her crotch and breasts, Eden held her ground. What did she have to prove to this woman? She wasn't doing anything wrong. Embarrassing, oh yeah. Wrong, no. She had more claim on Mitch than his assistant did. At least for the present moment.

"Are you mute?"

Eden set down the bottle that had been insufficiently covering her chest, took the croissant out of her mouth, and offered it to Jolie. "Are you hungry?" Her smile was forced and tight, but it was there. And that made Eden proud.

"You have no idea what you are doing to him." Jolie's entire body was taut. "He's screwing up his entire life, do you understand that?"

Eden cocked her head to the side. "Funny. I thought you were his assistant, not his mother. Mitch is a grown-up, *Mom*. He gets to make his own decisions."

"Probably screwing up your entire life too." Jolie plopped the bag on the counter, its liquid contents tipping over and darkening the bag. "Damn it!" She righted the bag, angrily scooting it away from the edge of the counter and grabbing a towel to wipe her hands.

"Get back up here." Mitch's fierce baritone sailed down the stairs into the kitchen. "Now."

The women held each other's gazes—Eden's uncomfortable, Jolie's spitting fire.

"I think he's talking to me." Eden grinned. "But I'll go get him for you." She hustled upstairs, hearing Jolie's heels clacking on the wood floors right behind her. When Eden entered the room, she nudged the door closed with a hip, tossed a power drink toward a smiling Mitch and grabbed the crumpled sheet off the bed to cover herself.

"What's wrong?" he asked.

Before Eden had a chance to speak or turn, she heard the soft squeak of the door and watched the corner of Mitch's mouth curl up in a sneer. "She's behind me, isn't she?"

"What are you doing here?" His voice was harsh, eyes

threatening, body buck naked and wet.

"I brought you soup, you bastard!" Jolie was close to tears. It was a heck of a reaction. Because he lied to her or because of what she'd found?

Mitch made a half shrug. "Thanks."

"Why did you lie to me?"

Oh, it was the lie. That was good. Eden decided she needed to go to the bathroom. To hide until the sparks stopped flying. As she crossed in front of Mitch to escape, he grabbed her arm, his fingers forcing dents into her skin.

"You stay." Then turned to Jolie. "You go. I'll call you later."

Jolie didn't move. Nobody moved. "So what? You guys have been playing house for the last four days? That's so…sweet."

Yeah, not believing she meant that.

Apparently Mitch didn't believe it either. "Yes, I lied. What's the problem? I lie all the time."

"Not to me, you don't."

"I'm not having this conversation with you right now. Thank you for your concern. I'll see you at the office tomorrow."

Jolie stared at him for about…forever. Tears welled in her eyes as she searched his face.

"I'll see you tomorrow, Jolie."

Her shoulders dropped. "I'm not sure you will." She spun on her heels and stormed out.

His eyes were stuck to the wall, unseeing, until they heard the front door slam. Then he relaxed his grip on her arm. "I think she might be mad at me."

"I think that's a good bet." Eden busied herself with the cap on her drink, not sure where the situation left them.

He reached out and tugged the sheet she was wrapped in. "Drop it."

She looked at him, wondering how long they could pretend everything hadn't changed, terrified how much it had.

Untucking her arms from her sides, she sent the barrier between them to the floor and stood, unabashed, before him.

"You're so fucking beautiful." His voice drowned in regret as he took her in his arms and clutched her to his chest.

His heartbeat filled her head, flashes of them bound together darting through her mind. It was over. *It was really over.* She stood on her tippy toes to kiss him. To thank him. "I should get dressed."

He held her away from him so he could look her in the eyes, confused. "No." His voice broke. "No, you shouldn't."

"Reality sucks, but that doesn't make it any less real." She wouldn't cry or beg him for more time. She'd just embarrass herself. He'd given her everything she'd asked him for. Make that, everything *period.* There was no chance for them to have a regular relationship. All they'd been doing was pretending they weren't what they were.

"I should go," she said. "Leave you alone."

$$\text{---}\math{-} \land\!\!\!\!\land\!\!\!-\!\land\!\!\!-$$

Oh, God. She'd come to her senses. He'd been believing in a fantasy in which he was actually *good* enough for her. He couldn't prove what wasn't true to begin with. What could *never* be true. There was no way to stop her from realizing the truth. To pretend Hyde didn't exist. Pretend he could have a normal—no, an *amazing* life with her.

Sooner or later Hyde would reappear, Mitch's feelings making him even more vicious. And someday, Hyde would hurt her. And Mitch wouldn't be able to stop it.

But he'd only gotten four days! Four fucking days of her. That wasn't fair. How was that fair? How was he supposed to go back and live with himself as he always had?

"No." He wouldn't let it happen. That was it. There was no choice here, nothing to decide. She was *his.* He'd find a way. Later. He'd find a way to deal with Hyde later. Not now. He picked her up and carried her to the bed.

She didn't struggle, her face tucked into his chest, her breath hiccupping slightly as he set her down and laid next to her. He caressed her arm, her neck, her face. Trying to reclaim what they'd had twenty minutes before, his hands were almost frantic.

She wouldn't look at him. Why wasn't she looking at him? His heart plummeted as he realized it was because she knew this dream was over. She knew that, even as a man, he would never be what she deserved. Any words he might use to express himself would be unworthy—unworthy of her ears, unworthy of her heart.

He'd been right—there was no choice. But *she* had been the one to choose, and she hadn't chosen him. *Wise decision.* He tried to turn her head to his, to receive his kiss, but she was stiff and unyielding.

"Please, Eden," he begged, his lips grazing her cheek. He'd die if he couldn't touch her again. Curl up and fucking wilt like an annual in the fall.

"One more time," he whispered.

$$\dashv\!\!\wedge\!\!-\!\!\dashv\!\!\wedge\!\!\dashv\!\!\wedge$$

Only one more time?

Looking into his breathtaking eyes, dark lashes, Eden realized she was addicted to him. But it took more hope than she could muster to imagine he felt the same. He'd given her a gift that had lasted four days. Still not long enough, but certainly more than she had asked for. Shouldn't bother wishing for more. And what could she say anyway? If she poured her heart out and told him what she really wanted, his expression might change to shock or horror. If she stayed silent, she wouldn't have to see the truth of his rejection.

He'd go back to his regular life, locking Chastity up until Eden could gather enough money to get her own cage. Unless he decided to buy her another gift just to hurry her out of his life. She couldn't blame him. Or be angry about it. She needed to suck it up and fake satisfaction as long as he chose to let her stick around, tell herself that she could be happy without him. She was good at that. She had lots of practice with denial. That's how she'd thank him for what he'd given her.

But right now, with his hands running across her skin, making her shudder, she could give him something he wanted. Something that might satisfy him, if not her. Without him next to her eternally, she'd never be satisfied.

One more time—that's what he was asking for. Before he walked away.

She opened herself up to him, wishing it didn't have to be the last time, and primed every nerve in her body for his touch. This was something she wanted to be able to remember when she was alone. Forever.

―ᶌ―ᶌ―ᶌ―

He didn't want to come. That would end it. Each orgasm he gave her, each time her body clenched around his, was almost unbearable. He wanted to fill her perpetually, hang onto her for as long as he could.

―ᶌ―ᶌ―ᶌ―

He was everywhere inside her, but it still wasn't enough. She couldn't open any more, couldn't give him what he needed. Because she just didn't know what it was. If she had, it would have been his. Instantly. If it was within her power to give, she would have given it to him. But it wasn't.

It hurt not to be enough for him. The pleasure he brought her was bittersweet with its goodbye.

―ᶌ―ᶌ―ᶌ―

When he could no longer hold himself back, he took her

mouth with his and released into her with a groan. It hurt. Incredible pleasure mixed with goodbye.

It has to be this way...for everyone's sake.

CHAPTER XXXVII

They stayed joined together for longer than they should have, still kissing. It wasn't going to get easier. With that in mind, Mitch shifted his weight off her, dragging his lips away from hers.

She let out a sigh and ducked her head as she rolled away from him, avoiding his eyes. "Can I borrow some clothes?"

"Yeah." He climbed out of their bed and rummaged through the dresser to find her something suitable.

"Mitch?" Her voice was small, uncertain.

He whipped his head around like he was expecting her to— He took a breath. To what? Tell him she didn't want to live without him? Tell him she felt the same way he did? That they'd make it work? "Yeah?"

"Is it alright if I use the cage tonight? For Chastity?" She shrugged. "If you'd rather I leave, I'll understand." She didn't meet his eyes, drawing into herself as if she was resuming the distant and unequal relationship they'd had before. As if nothing had changed. When, for him, *everything* had changed. Instantly anger churned in his stomach, piped though his veins, scorched his lungs. How could the four best days of his life mean nothing to her other than an experiment of "Can I or

Can't I"? How could she not *know* him after that?

"Of course, you can use the cage." His words came out in not much more than a growl. "Do whatever you want." He threw a white tank top and black shorts to her without turning, and then slipped another pair of shorts on his own body.

"Thanks. It's almost time, isn't it?"

He glanced at the clock. "Yeah. Almost time."

"I think I'll go there now. I'm tired." She grabbed her power drink from the nightstand and guzzled it. "Thirsty too."

He hated her smile at that moment. As if everything was normal. As if his life hadn't taken an unexpected detour into nirvana and now back into hell. No, deeper. Into an even deeper hell.

"You gonna have that?" She nodded toward the juice he'd dropped before tossing her on the bed.

"Have it. I need something stronger. Then I'll be back to lock the cage." He walked away before she answered and went to find the biggest bottle of whiskey he had. Out of her presence, he started running, running away from the room he never wanted to be inside of again, the woman he wanted to be inside of forever.

Not gonna happen, Mitch. Sorry, asshole, but you just don't measure up. What the hell had he been thinking? Picket fence and a happily ever after? No, the bad guy never gets a happily ever after. With stiff hands, he opened a bottle of Jack and took a swig directly from it. Then he grabbed a bottle of Jim Beam for good measure. And, sure, a glass might be necessary at some point.

Unless he put some food in his belly, he'd throw up all the coping device he planned on pouring down his throat very soon. He went into the kitchen and saw a paper bag on the counter. Jolie's soup. Sure, that'd work. He could stomach that. Healthy liquid followed by the toxic stuff. It would do. He ripped the bag open, tore the top from the container, and downed the chicken broth, coughing on a noodle.

As he dragged his feet back upstairs, he realized Hyde was

back, clawing at his belly. Huh. Too bad the pain didn't even compare to what he felt in his chest.

He heard his phone ring as he walked to the bedroom door and peeked in. Eden wasn't there. He found the phone after it had stopped ringing. He flipped it open and returned the last call, which was from the same number as the last five he *hadn't* heard. Didn't matter, they were all from Carter anyway.

"What's up, Scout?"

"Do you know where she is? I've been calling her cell for days and can't get hold of her. She isn't at the apartment, and you never answer your door and—"

"She's fine."

On the other end of the line, Carter blew out a breath. "Oh, okay."

There was a long pause, during which Mitch seriously considered hanging up. One pathetic man was really all he could handle right now. Sadly for Carter, at the moment, Mitch was the most pathetic and, therefore, most in need of some serious attention…from the two bottles of liquor in his arms. "That it?"

"No, wait! Is she still mad at me?"

"Not sure."

"She hasn't said anything?"

"Not about you."

"Oh." Disappointment dragged Carter's tone into the dust, slowing down a conversation that was already going nowhere.

"That it?"

"No! Do you need me to come over tonight?"

Nice offer, but, in the mood he was in, Mitch was just selfish enough to not want to see any kind of happy, let's-be-friends-again kind of crap. Okay, he was *way* too selfish to see that. If he saw any man's arms go around her right now, there was a good chance the guy would leave here bleeding. If at all.

"I got this one," Mitch said. "She may need you for the

next, though."

"Are you sure?"

He felt it the moment he lost control. "No, I'm not sure, you little shit!" His voice echoed through the room. "I am everything *but* sure right now! I don't know what the hell I am doing all of a sudden and I feel like I'm going insane! Aren't you glad you fucking asked?"

"I'm coming over."

Mitch clenched the phone, his volume lowering to a more reasonable level simply because his jaw allowed only a very narrow opening for the words to pass through. "Do not come over here. In fact, be very thankful you aren't here now. Eden is safe and sound in the cage, but *I* am not. You hearing me?"

"Tell her I really need to talk to her about something. She needs to call me. She needs to know."

"That you've given up snorting your dinner? Good for you. I'll tell her."

"No, it's not that. It's something else. Please, Mitchell, tell her to call me. I know—" There was desperation in the Boy Scout's voice. And, unless he was feeling the same pain Mitch was—which was impossible—something else was going on.

"What do you know, Carter?"

"I need to talk to her first, then you. Please tell her to call me."

"Fine." Mitch ended the call hard and threw the phone onto the bed.

When he went into Hyde's room, Eden was already sitting on the mattress inside the cage, hands resting in her lap. His clothes looked ridiculous on her. Even though she'd rolled the waistband of the shorts over multiple times, the elastic would never fit her slender waist. The sleeves on the tank top gaped, giving him a glimpse of her breast, making this even harder.

Her eyes widened and she grimaced at what he was carrying. "Are you gonna drink all that? Like, this week?" Her smile was encouraging, or maybe pitying.

He set the bottles on the table, and went to get the key to

the cage and a syringe—protocol for Hyde, not Chastity. Before she saw it, he replaced the syringe into the first drawer. Forcing his feet to move toward her was difficult. When he closed the door, Eden flinched at the metal-on-metal sound. Standing two feet away from her, the position seemed kind of fitting—what with the bars between them.

Eden stood and walked toward him, oddly calm. "Who were you screaming at?"

"Your boy, Carter, called."

"My boy?" She let whatever she was about to say pass. "What did he want?"

Mitch shrugged. "He asked you to call him. So I assume he wants to talk to you."

"I'm not sure I'm up for that yet, but whatever." She placed a hand against one of his, the bar between their palms, taking a deep breath. "Mitch, if you want to— If *she* wants to— Ugh, this is tough to say." She pressed her lips together briefly, and then her words started tumbling out as though they were escaping the confines of her mouth. "If you want to have sex with her, it's okay with me, I mean, you don't have to worry that I will wake up mad at you or anything because it's not my decision, well it is my decision, I guess, since I'm deciding right now and what I'm deciding is that it would be okay for you to sleep with her whenever she comes out, not just tonight but whenever you want to—"

He pulled his hands away from hers, horrified, and shot back from the bars. "You're giving me permission to use your body when you're not in it?"

She nodded, slightly out of breath from her rant. "Yeah, I guess so."

He grimaced at the idea. Have sex with someone who wasn't her? "Why would I want to do that?"

She flinched. "You don't have to look at me like that. I was just trying to be nice."

"*Nice?* Well, it's insulting. To both of us." What was she thinking?

"Sorry," she mumbled, turning away from him and grabbing her power drink off the mattress. She took a long gulp. "Thanks for getting these, they're really good."

"Are we going to just have shitty, normal conversations from now on? Because that's not something I'm really interested in doing with you."

She covered her mouth to keep her drink down. Then she started crying. Sobbing.

Mitch kept his feet planted where they were, even though his quads were twitching to go to her. He ran both hands through his hair and concentrated on the window. *Nice drapes. Blue. Little swirls.* The weeping continued. He tapped his foot on the hardwood. *Block the light. Energy efficient. Of course, the plywood behind them helps with that too. Shit.* Her breath was coming in little gasps. *Don't look. Don't look at her. Focus on something else.*

He scanned the room, making very sure he never faced her direction. *Let her cry it out. She'll be fine. Why is she crying? Did I do something wrong? A drink! Get a drink. Big, very big drink and wait for her to stop crying. Damn it!* "Why are you crying?"

Her eyes were red and leaking everywhere, as if she'd been caught in the rain with her face toward the sky and hadn't been able to look down. She wiped her cheeks with the edge of the tank top, flashing a flat belly and the bottom curve of her breast, reminding him of things that would never happen again.

"Christ." He was like a Pavlovian fucking dog. He moved behind the chair so she wouldn't see the twitching of his cock. Having a mood detector that made itself visible in the least opportune times was the worst part of being a man—even when that man's mind was in the foulest of moods.

"I think I should go," she whimpered.

"You can't. Not until your cage is delivered. Then we'll—"

"You bought me a cage?" For some reason, she looked

disappointed.

"Isn't that what every woman wants? I know most would prefer jewelry, but I thought this was more practical. I suppose I can have some bling installed on it, if you want."

She shook her head, her tears slowing. But not stopping. What did she want from him? "I'll pay you back."

"Consider it a gift."

After a brief sagging of her shoulders, she stood up straight and put her hands on her hips. "When will it come?"

"Not sure. I had Jolie order it before our little squabble. But it's being delivered and installed here. I couldn't tell Jolie about you. She was confused enough that I wanted another one. So unless you absolutely can't handle it, it should stay here. I think the bars on the windows brought enough attention to you already." He sneered, knowing she didn't deserve the sarcasm in his tone, but unable to stop it. "What would your neighbors think?"

"You're right—my apartment is probably the wrong spot for it. Maybe I can find a warehouse space or…"

"Why do you want to leave so badly?" He sat down in the armchair and poured himself a drink. Maybe he should bring his entire liquor cabinet up here. Then he'd never have to move. He could have the booze delivered too. Stay inside locked up for one night, stay shit-faced until the next transformation. Great idea. Just great.

"I think I've taken up more than my share of your time."

Is that what she thought it was—his time? His fucking time? "Let's get this over with." He wanted out. He wanted to get away from her before he turned into a weak, sobbing puddle on the floor.

She sank down onto the mattress and looked at her hands. After taking a deep breath, she turned to face him, bringing her legs up into a fetal position. "I'm sorry, Mitch."

His stomach tightened so hard, he had to lean his elbows on his knees. "Don't ever say that to me again." *Close your eyes before I break down. Please God, close them quick.*

She rolled over, putting her back to him. Her shoulders shook, but no sound came out. Or maybe his system had started to break down—first his hearing, then sight perhaps, smell next, as each sense was taken away. He hoped it was that.

Eventually her breathing evened out and the fatigue brought on by the last few days got the best of her. Mitch didn't move closer, didn't try to look at her face, tried not to stare at her body. Tried to get a grip and be a man. Shit, he was acting like a teenage girl after her first love broke up with her in a text message. Pathetic.

He didn't know what would happen when he saw Chastity. Sure, he'd desire her—that was kind of a given. Would it be better to flush Eden out of his system? Remove her scent by covering it up with someone else's? Maybe. But Chastity wasn't the one to try it with. It would be like wiping the water out of his eyes while he was drowning.

How long had it been? An hour? Two? Still no Chastity. Much less Scotch in the bottle, but no more Chastity. *What the hell?*

He spent the rest of the night watching her through the bars, never getting closer. Reveling in the fact that the pain from Hyde was finally overtaking the pain of losing Eden, he almost welcomed the bastard home.

Chapter XXXVIII

Eden jolted awake and looked for Mitch. He was still sitting in the chair, dark circles under eyes that looked as if they'd seen hell and didn't yet know they'd returned.

What had Chastity done to make him look like that? "What did she do?"

Mitch shook his head from side to side slowly. "She didn't show."

"What do you mean?" She looked down. She was still dressed in Mitch's clothes.

"Can't you tell? You finally got some sleep."

It was true—she *did* feel rested, but that meant... "It worked! The sex worked!" She jumped off the bed and bounced to the steel door. "How long do you think it will last?"

He pushed himself off the chair and semi-staggered over to unlock the cage. "I have no idea. I'm not even sure it was the"—he swallowed—"sex."

As soon as the lock was opened, she threw herself at him, giggling and absolutely unwilling to let his moody drunkenness ruin the good news. "Why'd you drink so much?"

Dang it. Being face to face, inches from his lips, was a stupid position to put herself in. But she couldn't seem to move away. His heart was hammering against her breasts. Or it could have just been the echo of hers. They stayed stuck together, searching each other's eyes, waiting to see which one would say something, who would move first.

He did. By unwrapping her arms from his neck and stepping backwards silently.

"I'll go…" *Home to cry.* She bowed her head and walked past him, careful not to brush against him. It took everything in her not to throw herself at him again or start spewing words of love and emoting all over him. *Grow up, Eden. Did you really expect him to start installing the picket fence?*

"When will you be back?" His voice was flat, clipped almost.

She stopped, didn't turn. "I don't know. I don't know when she'll come, so…" She couldn't ask. Couldn't offer herself up for more rejection.

"Tonight. Every ni— Oh!" He collapsed to his knees, grabbing his stomach.

She knew he'd had a lot to drink, but not that much. He was obviously paying for it. "Do you want some water or aspirin or something?"

"It's him, Eden. It's Hyde." He groaned, rolling onto his side with his eyes clenched shut, his chest convulsing as he fought for breath. "Get Jolie."

She ran to him and slipped her hand under his head. "Tell me what I should do."

"Get Jolie and get out." Anger mixed with the pain in his eyes. "I don't want you here," he said through gritted teeth. His words were like cement being poured around her heart. All he had to do was blow it dry and toss it into the ocean.

"Where's your phone?" she asked solemnly.

"Bedroom. Hurry."

That he still didn't trust her enough to want her help was like the lash of a belt. It made her feel even more pathetic for relying on him so much. But she'd dwell on that later.

She found the phone on his bed and went through the contacts to find Jolie's number. She saw her own name with a star next to it, right on the top of the list. *Probably an accident.* Jolie's was the second.

An angry voice answered. "I'm not talking to you."

"Jolie, it's me. Eden." Before Jolie could start in on her, she started explaining. "He needs you. Hyde's coming. You have to come over now."

"No. You're there. You take care of him."

"He doesn't want me, Jolie." She swallowed, readying the admission to a woman who would eat it up smiling. "He wants *you*. I'm supposed to call you and then leave." Eden imagined Jolie sitting up straighter in her chair, suddenly interested in hearing more.

"You're leaving?"

"After you get here, yes." And do what? Go to a movie? Get her nails done, knowing that the man she loves is being well taken care of by another woman, one who he actually trusts and wants beside him. What in the world could distract her from that?

"I'm on my way," Jolie said. "He's really turning in the daytime?"

"He's never done that before?"

"Not that I know of. His transformation isn't even due for another few weeks, so who knows what's going on. It's your fault, you know."

This wasn't the time to fight. Maybe later, when Mitch was okay. Or maybe never, when Eden was no longer a presence in his life.

"How long until you get here, Jolie?"

"Five minutes. Maybe ten, depending on traffic. So you can start packing your stuff up now."

Eden could hear the smile in the other woman's voice, like a cat with a milk mustache. "Not much to pack. But thanks." She wanted to throw the phone at the wall, smash it into little bits. Instead she ran down the hall to Hyde's room, hearing Mitch's groans get louder.

He was standing, barely, staggering into the cage.

"She's on her way." She went to him cautiously and took his arm, guiding him to the mattress.

"Help me get the straps out. Quick. I don't know how long we have."

Eden knelt between his legs and reached her hand underneath the foot of the bed and felt around. When her fingers touched metal, she yanked down. One. Two. Then the top corners.

"Put the cuffs on me. Then get out of here." When she didn't move, he said, "Please, Eden! For fuck's sake! This is different. I don't know what is going to happen. You need to strap me in and then leave."

Her hands shook as she closed each cuff. "I don't want to go."

"I don't want you to be here when *he* is." His eyes begged her to listen. "Don't want you to see me like that again. Not after—"With all four limbs bound, his body writhed on the bed helplessly, painfully. "Please, just listen to me. Hyde is dangerous. I need to stay in the cage. I can't—" His words were broken apart by a groan and a spasm that contracted the muscles in his neck and torso. "You have to call Carter and have him help you tonight, lock you up in case Chastity comes, too."

Eden nodded, agreeing without thinking.

"If you don't do it, I will."

"Okay, I'll call him. You just…take care of yourself." She leaned over him, her body reacting without thought, and kissed him.

He flinched briefly, and then met her lips with a shudder. Way before she was ready to let go of him, he turned his head, tearing his mouth from hers. "You need to leave before I transform, and you end up kissing him."

That thought broke through her need for him, allowing her

to regain control and put space between them.

He seemed calmer, the painful contractions of his body slowing. "It was a nice try, but I think that's what's bringing him out early."

"No, I don't believe that." Eden watched him struggle for a long time, his mouth moving as he counted his breaths with his eyes closed, going into himself and further away from her.

Jolie appeared at the door, glaring at her. "All packed up, dear?" She'd gotten there fast.

Eden glanced one last time at Mitch. "Please call me." She stepped out of the cage. "Jolie, please make sure he calls me as soon as he's…himself." Without waiting for a response she may or may *not* have gotten, she left.

CHAPTER XXXIX

Concentrating on slowing his breath, doing some messed-up, desperate kind of yoga, Mitch felt himself winning, gaining control over Hyde, pushing the bastard back into his ever-ready attack position. *How long will it last?*

Jolie approached the cage and peered in. "Jesus, Mitchell, you look like shit. When's the last time you ate?"

"Not sure."

"Well, did you have the soup I left for you?"

"It was delicious."

"Good. Do you want more? I could pour it down your throat."

He heard the venom in her voice, but didn't say anything. They both knew how dependent he was on her at this point, so he'd accept the verbal punishment.

"Maybe later, thank you, Jolie."

"You're...welcome." She paused. "Seriously, Mitchell, are you doing okay?"

He didn't look at her. "Am I forgiven?"

She hmphed. "That depends on your answers to my questions."

"How many?"

"Does it matter?"

"Maybe. Was that number one?"

"Don't be so goddamned difficult." She sighed. "Did you really ask her to leave?"

He stared at the ceiling. "Yes."

"Will you be playing house anymore?"

"No."

"By whose choice?"

He tried to avoid a pause in his answer, not sure which of them he wanted to convince more. "Both. Both of us decided it would be best." *For her. It would be best for her.* He wanted Eden out of his thoughts, but the fucking stubbornness of his own mind was keeping her front and center.

"So it was just sex?" Jolie asked.

"For one of us, yes."

She laughed. "Poor girl. You've ruined her for other men. I wish I could have seen her face when you let her down easy. Wait, you didn't let her down *too* easy, did you?"

"Don't want to talk about it." He readjusted his arms, shaking them to keep the blood flowing. "She's a nice girl. I didn't want to hurt her." *Did I? Did I hurt her?*

"So things go back to the way they were?"

"No."

"What does that mean?" she growled.

If he turned his head to look at her, he knew she'd be white knuckling the bars—he heard it reflected in her voice. "It means I may need a favor."

"You're already asking for favors? I haven't even forgiven you yet, and, in case you haven't noticed, you're kind of at my mercy right now. It's a particularly bad bargaining position, literally and figuratively."

"Eden once told me the reason she didn't lie was because she could never believe anything anyone said if she wasn't being honest with them."

"Eden's a moron."

He stiffened. "No, she's naive. Totally different. But right now, I think you might want to show a little respect because her naivety is about to make me try something I'm really bad at."

"I'm listening."

He took a breath. If Eden called Carter like she'd promised to, then all this was for naught. But if her pride got in the way and she decided *this* was the moment to prove her independence, then telling Jolie might be the only way to help her. He wouldn't let anything happen to Eden. Ever. Regardless of how she felt about him.

"Eden needs my help, but I can't. She needs Carter's help, but she may be too stubborn to ask. If that happens, she'll need yours."

"I would rather swallow glass."

"I need you to help me do something I can't do, Jolie. I've been a bastard to you and you never deserved any of it. You've always done what I demanded or ordered. Now I'm *asking*. Once it's done, then we figure out what happens next."

"What happens for…" Her voice floated up as if asking a question. "What do I do?"

"Get me my phone and uncuff one of my arms. Then step out of the room until I'm done." He wouldn't tell Jolie unless absolutely necessary. He'd meant it when he said it was Eden's secret to tell. Unless her safety was at risk. Then all bets were off and he'd do what he had to.

"Golly, thanks. Sounds like everything has changed." Sarcasm chilled the air. Didn't affect Mitch though—he was too used to hearing it come out of his own mouth. "I am at your beck and call and you tell me nothing."

"For now, Jolie. Only for now. I need to focus on this before Hyde shows up and I don't have the option."

"You seem fine."

"I know. That's what worries me. He hit me hard and fast a bit ago and now he's gone." *Mostly.* "But I can't trust it." Damn it, saying it out loud made it real. What if he would never be able to let himself roam free again? Always wondering when Hyde would strike? Mitch would be under a self-imposed house arrest, never venturing farther from the cage than he could stagger back if need be.

"Mitchell, what's wrong?"

Why bother to hide his frustration? Who knows, maybe it would stave Hyde off for a little longer. "Go get the fucking phone, Jolie."

She could be a good listener.

He'd reconsidered before Jolie brought him the phone. He shouldn't have a hand free if Hyde was this unpredictable, this close to the surface. And Jolie wouldn't be able to strap him in once he appeared. Mitch wouldn't even want her to open the door of the cage.

"Stop. I need you to dial Carter's number for me, put it on speaker, and set it over here." He pointed his chin to the side of the mattress. About two feet away from the bars. "Then I need you to leave. Go have a drink downstairs, whatever. After I speak to him, I'll call you back in. If I'm still me, can you slide your arm in between the bars and take the phone back?" He looked at her thin arms, judging their diameter. "I'd hate to lose the phone if Hyde decides to eat it or something."

She nodded and slipped her hand through as though she'd done it many times before, rotating her elbow when it touched the metal. It just made it through. She wiggled her fingers at him. "Ta-da."

"Nice work," he said.

"Thank you. I come in handy sometimes."

"Yes, you do." *If only you weren't such a pain in the ass so many other times.* "I'm assuming you know Carter's number."

"He told you." Not a question, a statement of mild regret.

"He mentioned you in passing. Call him. Use the speaker."

The number was buried in the call log, but she dialed it from memory without hesitation. They must be closer than Mitch had thought. She slipped the phone through the bars and stepped back, the sound of her footsteps in the hallway disappearing seconds later. Or maybe they were just covered up by the sound of the phone.

He wasn't taking any chances. "Out, Jolie. All the way. When you hear me screaming your name, you may return."

She huffed, heels clicking rapidly in the hallway.

I swear I'll kill her if she's just outside the door. He tugged against the straps around his wrists. *Frustrating as fuck.* He couldn't check where she was and he wouldn't be able to kick her ass until she freed him. *Charming.*

He let it go when Carter picked up at the other end of the line.

"Is she okay?" The beginnings of panic were apparent in his voice.

"I'm on your caller ID? How sweet." Mitch kept his voice as low as he could, not taking any chances of Jolie knowing anything until absolutely necessary.

Carter sighed. "What do you want?"

"First off, I want you to stop yelling. In addition to giving me a headache, you're on speaker. Secondly, I'm having a bad day. Need you to check on her."

"Where is she?"

"I hope she's going home to call you. But since our girl"— he paused at his slip—"since Eden is as stubborn as a donkey, I'm concerned she won't make that call."

"So *you* are."

"Indeed. Go over there tonight and make sure she stays home."

The delay in Carter's response was either due to his brain doing the math or trying to come up with an excuse to get out of it. Mitch hoped it wasn't the latter.

"The fourth night was last night. Is it every night now?"

"No. But nothing happened last night and both of our cycles seem to be in flux."

"*Both* of your cycles?"

Shit. "I misspoke. *Her* cycle. *Her* cycle is off." He filled Carter in on the previous night, trying to be as vague as possible, just in case Jolie was as nosey as he knew she was.

"Mitchell, I have some news about that girl's murder. The one in the alley."

Why did he need to qualify his first statement? Because they'd all been wrapped up in so many *other* murders lately? Mitch's heart contracted at the thought of the death that had left him half dead himself. Murder number one—Shelly's. Yeah, that was a biggie. How could he have forgotten that one? But he moved on. *Just keep swimming, asshole.*

"Talk," Mitch said.

"There's this guy…"

"Does he walk into a bar? I think I've heard it." His temper was tissue-paper thin and Carter wasn't helping.

"When I went into the station, someone had just turned in some cell phone footage of the club from that night. The receiving officer didn't think it was important and gave it to me to look at. It showed a dealer walking out into the alley where the dead girl was found. So I went and talked to him."

Not interested that the kid had fallen off the wagon, Mitch said, "Good for you for finding a new supplier. Is there a point coming soon?"

"The guy said something about the night that girl was killed. He was there. But he's not going to the cops because, well, because he's a dealer."

"What'd he see?"

"He was finishing up a meeting with a customer in the alley." Carter's words came out achingly slow. "And he says he…um…he saw a hot woman with long brown hair talking to the girl who got killed. Like, a half hour before someone found the body. I don't need to tell you which girl has long brown hair, do I?"

Mitch's mind filled with the memory of wrapping that hair around his fist, twirling it around his fingers, brushing it out of her flushed face while he was inside of her. He swallowed. "No."

"I want to see if the dealer can recognize her from a

picture. Then I need to talk to Eden."

Mitch kept his voice calm. "No, I don't think you do." The news would crush her. Eden had been so lost until she'd convinced herself Chastity hadn't done it. This would...destroy her, maybe make her do something stupid like turn herself in. "She doesn't need to know, Carter. We can make sure it doesn't happen again—you and I will make sure. Don't tell her." His biceps strained against the binds. Helplessness was not something he dealt with well.

"She's hurt enough people, Mitchell. This has to stop. Think about Eden."

Who the hell else would I be thinking of? "Don't." One word, one unspoken threat.

"I need to do something for Eden. Something to redeem myself." Carter sounded like he was about to cry.

"Then keep her safe tonight. Do that."

"Why isn't she at your house, using the cage?"

"I sent it out for polishing." He really needed to kick the sarcasm habit if he expected to get any help from anyone. *Needing help sucks.* There was one way to bring out Carter's protective side. "She thinks I'm only using her for sex."

Carter coughed. "What the hell? You guys are— Never mind, I don't want to know." He took a minute, probably to push images of a naked and sweating Eden under a naked and sweating Mitch out of his mind. Kind of like Mitch was trying to do. "Okay, I'll go over there tonight like you asked even though she probably is still furious with me. She may not let me inside, but I'll try. But if this is you deciding to bail on her permanently, I'm gonna kick your ass."

"No plans to bail on anyone, Carter, but feel free to try and kick my ass anyway." He looked down to his body, spread-eagle and bound. "If I'm available."

"I'm going to tell her everything, Mitchell. Everything I know. I can't keep doing this."

"No!" Mitch heard the click of Carter hanging up on him. What the fuck now? Damn it. At least Carter would take care of her tonight. He would be the hero. What would Eden do when he told her about the dead girl? Nothing Mitch could stop her from doing now.

And Hyde would either show up or not. He seemed to be dormant again—no testosterone spike running through Mitch's veins, no new pain, no muscle spasms. But he couldn't let his guard down. Couldn't walk too far away from the cage. Shouldn't really even be without the cuffs. Only one way that was going to happen. *Better to be severely sedated than to be bound.* He should make that into a fucking bumper sticker.

With a quick glance to the side table to make sure the syringe was still there, Mitch yelled for Jolie. A second later she entered the room. *Shit.* He hadn't heard any heels hitting the stairs—they'd started clicking from the hallway. Not a hell of a lot he could do about it now.

"Jolie, I want you to empty about half of what's in that syringe and give it to me."

She didn't say anything, just did what she was told, her back to him. "What's the goal here, Mitchell? Get just high enough so you can rush off to help your girlfriend?"

"Number one, she's not my girlfriend. Number two, I want out of these chains. Not the cage, only the chains."

Jolie smiled slightly, though he didn't know which point she found amusing. She unlocked the door and stuck him, all the while wearing that fucking smile. The sting of the needle in his arm was a surprise, something he wasn't used to. He hated the idea of using drugs almost as much as Eden did. Jolie pushed the plunger and then uncuffed him, stepping back to watch him sit up and rub the injection site.

"Thanks for the help," he said.

"I'm very useful to have around."

"Yeah, I've noticed."

"Took you long enough to remember."

His eyes shot to hers. There was something in the way she said that—something different, something hidden, something wrong.

"Remember what?" he asked.

"Remember us. Together."

Together? Them? Yeah, not what he meant at all. The drug hit him hard, sending a wave of heat down to his toes, up to his head. He wiped his face and put a hand out behind him for balance. Maybe a half dose was still too much. Hopefully what was too much for the man would be just right for the beast.

As she left the cage, she said, "I heard a bit of your conversation with Carter."

He was losing focus. "Just a bit? Gee, I would've thought your hearing was better than that." Her face was blurring slightly, but he saw her nod.

"Do you think she killed that girl? The one in the alley?"

"Seems so." He lay back onto the pillow feeling nauseas. *Just say 'fuck no' to drugs. Great, another bumper sticker.*

"Where is Carter going, Mitch? To talk to Eden or to the witness?"

There was a strong possibility he was going to throw up. *How could anyone enjoy this feeling? Do it willingly?* "Too much fucking narcotic."

Pure drug-induced fire radiated out of his belly as if it was the terminus and the morphine was being thrown out by centrifugal force into each cell of his body. The last thing he saw before passing out was stars.

CHAPTER XL

Even though he wouldn't be able to see her, Jolie put a smile on her face as she called him. "Carter?"

"What do you want, Jolie?" he grumbled.

"Wow. What'd *I* do? I just wanted to talk to you."

Tight sigh. "What about?"

This was going to be a tough sell, but she was confident she could do it. "I think I found a way to get you out of this and still keep your real medical file 'lost.'"

Silence.

"Did you hear me? You can still be a police officer. It was tough, but they agreed. A 'for services rendered' type of deal. And you won't have to do anything about Eden anymore."

"They'll take her to the clinic?"

She heard the relief in his voice and gave herself a pat on the back. "Yeah." *Just as soon as Mitchell knocks her up.* "So they win, and you win."

"What about you?"

"You're worried about me? That's sweet." Her smile grew...

"I know what you did to that girl, Jolie. I know you killed her."

…and then died. *Damn it.* Was it worth a strong denial? No, she was too tired of dealing with him. "Oh. Then you'll make a wonderful policeman." How the hell did he find out anyway? How the hell could she talk her way out of this? "What you don't know is that the girl was dangerous. I tried to help her. I did. But she attacked me," Jolie lied. "She didn't have anyone who cared enough about her to take care of her like Eden does."

That was true. The girl had been a body, someone to make sure the police stopped looking at Mitchell as a suspect. Jolie had made sure he was in public. Mitchell wasn't the kind of man people easily forgot. And the junkie was someone *everyone* had forgotten and no one would miss. Just a body. The Clinic had waited too long to do something. It wasn't Jolie's fault—it was theirs.

"I'm not sure I believe that."

"I have her file right in front of me, Carter." *Or I could, as soon as I make one up. What was her name again?* "I can show it to you, if you want. Tonight?"

"I'm busy."

"All night? What if we meet at your place? I can show you what I have and then I could tuck you into bed before I go." The other carrot she'd dangled in front of him—herself.

"Eden will be there. Mitchell said she might change."

"I'll help you babysit. After she goes to sleep, I can show you the other girl's file and the email from The Clinic that releases you from your obligations. Then I can take over watching Eden. You'll be free to do whatever, or whoever, you want to do for the rest of the night."

The pause was long enough so that Jolie started to wrack her brain for another way to get him to meet her. She had business to take care of. Sad, but undeniable. He could get her into a mountain of trouble.

"I want to see that file," he said. "In fact, I want to hear everything you know about the clinic before I allow Eden to go there. I've been researching them, Jolie. But I keep running into dead ends. Do they have as many secrets as you do?"

She sighed. *Poor boy.* He'd just guaranteed his fate. "I'll tell you what I know." *Yeah, right.*

"Bring the file, and we'll talk. But I'm not going to fuck you, Jolie."

"That's too bad, Carter." *'Cause I'm going to fuck you.*

Eden wasn't cured. She knew it without opening her eyes. She felt it in every muscle in her body, every aching brain cell. Her shoulder felt like it had been hit with a club. God, it hurt. She'd gotten no rest last night, which meant that Chastity had shown up after all. *What did she do to me locked up in my apartment? The P90X workout for 9 hours?*

Thankfully, Eden had locked herself in, cautious but hopeful she was worried for nothing. All she had to do was call the apartment's superintendent who she'd given a just-in-case-I-get-locked-*inside*-my-apartment key. Not something most people did, obvious by the look on the man's face when she'd asked him to lock her inside and told him to let her out in the morning. And, if he forgot, she had her cell phone. In the event he was a total creep, she'd checked the interior deadbolt ten times before falling asleep.

She stretched her usable arm to touch her bruised one. Then stopped. *What the heck?* There was something on her hand, on her shoulder. Something slightly sticky, slightly wet. Her eyes popped open to see her ceiling above where she laid. On the floor, her front door ajar. *Oh, man.*

She heard a sickly groan from a few feet away, turned her head and then screamed. Carter was splayed out on the floor, covered in blood. His blood. On his chest, his neck, his head, spilling onto the floor. He looked as though he'd been beaten with a baseball bat or a sledgehammer.

"No-no-no-no-no." She scrambled toward him, her knees sliding on his essence. She wanted to touch him, wanted to stop the blood from further escape, but didn't know where to begin. Her hands shook like the wings of a hummingbird, adrenaline causing her physical pain to disappear.

He was breathing, the blood snapping in his throat each time he in-or exhaled, as if it was filling his lungs.

"Carter, no. No." She put her hands on his wounds, but there were too many. "Carter, please. Don't die." Her voice came out in gasps, mixing with her sobs.

His eyes fluttered open. Recognition. He saw her.

"Carter, don't die. Don't die. I'm getting help. I'm going to get help." She tried to stand, tried to get a foothold on something other than blood. She felt his hand grip her ankle. "I'm so sorry, Carter. I'm so sorry." How could she have done this?

He pulled at her, wincing, his face distorting even more from the pain. "It. Wasn't. You." He coughed, droplets of blood spotting his cheek and chin.

She tugged from his grip, not wanting to hurt him anymore, but needing to be free of him. "Let go, Carter. Let go! I'll get—" His cell phone was a few feet away from his head. Next to an empty syringe. She leaned over him, his hand still on her ankle, and grabbed the phone, dialing 9-1-1.

Before the operator had finished his greeting, Eden started talking. "Please, send an ambulance. Please! There's been an—" *An accident? Really, Eden, was it an accident?* "A man needs help. He's been beaten, I think. Badly. He's covered in blood and can't breathe. Please!"

Carter's hand tightened around her ankle and he was shaking his head, though she knew it was causing him pain. "No, Eden. Go."

She ignored his protest and tried to focus on what the emergency operator was saying.

"…you located?"

She yelled the address into the phone with more pleas for them to hurry. "He's dying. Please help him! I don't know what to do."

The operator told her help was on the way and then guided her through the description of Carter's injuries, asking her what happened—"I don't know"—and telling her to apply pressure to any gushing wounds. When she pushed against the side of Carter's chest to stop the bleeding, the phone slipped out from under her chin, the battery shooting underneath the couch.

She was on her own until the paramedics got there. "Carter?" Her voice was shaking. "Carter, look at me. It's going to be alright. You're going to be fine."

He ducked his head slightly in a nod.

"I'm so sorry, Carter. I didn't—" *What? Mean for my evil side to try to beat you to death?* Why had she done it? "I'm so sorry."

"Go. Now." His voice sputtered, sending a fine mist of red into the air. "Tell. Mit— Jol— Not. You. Go." He pushed weakly against her leg to get her moving.

She wasn't going anywhere. She needed to stay—to make sure someone came to help him and because she deserved to be punished. They could do all the tests they wanted on her once they found out about Chastity. She'd be their guinea pig, as long as they promised to keep other people safely away from her.

Because she was a monster.

The paramedics arrived a few minutes later. Then the police came. Eden wept, one arm lying limp in her lap, the other wrapped tightly around her, as they took Carter away on a gurney and investigators studied the apartment. The only time she stopped crying was when she saw Detective Landon walk in, meeting his wide eyes before beginning to sob again.

"I know you, don't I?" he asked.

Eden let her shoulders shrug as part of the full-body shaking it was currently doing. Hopelessness was drowning her. Nothing mattered anymore. The possibility of her being capable of murder had been part of her unhealthy denial up to this point. Now it was a certainty.

Landon walked the perimeter of the room, his eyes darting from where Carter's body had been to the door, to her, to areas that hadn't been spattered with blood. He went through the kitchen with gloved hands, speaking softly to the other officers. She heard whispers as they showed Landon the syringe and a broken cane dripping with Carter's blood—maybe hers too.

He came back into the room and sat next to her on the couch. "They said you don't remember anything prior to waking up, is that true?"

She nodded.

"We need to bring you down to the station for questioning." His voice was reasonable, like he'd just asked her about the weather or what was on TV.

She started to stand, pushing herself up from the couch. Her shoulder gave out, shooting pain through the arm and into her chest. She fell backwards.

His eyebrows peaked. "Are you hurt?" He turned to the other cops while helping her ease farther back onto the couch. "Why didn't she get medical treatment?"

A few of them shrugged, looking bored. She guessed that dying men, massive amounts of blood, and hysterical women were commonplace in their world.

"Where does it hurt?" Landon asked softly.

She looked at her shoulder and brought the other hand to touch it gently.

Landon carefully lifted the sleeve of her blouse and grimaced at the bruised and bloody skin. Then he motioned to the forensic tech to take a picture of her shoulder. "How did you miss this?" he said to the room in general. He took her by her good arm and helped her stand, his hand gentle against her skin.

"Can you speak?" he asked.

No, she couldn't. Speaking, along with feeling and breathing at a regular rhythm were all things she just couldn't do.

CHAPTER XLI

Inside the frigid interrogation room, Detective Landon was far kinder to Eden than any of the cops she'd seen on television. His questions were concise, direct, and thorough.

Unfortunately for him, she didn't have a lot to say. Or anything, actually. Her voice was still out of her control. Her mind too. Images, feelings, sensations jumbled together, forming a whirlpool inside her head, swirling too quickly for her to catch one. When she ran out of tears, her cries were muffled, waterless, but never ending. She'd wait until they read her the Miranda Warning, and then find a way to ask for a lawyer. Maybe she could write them a note.

When he started asking her questions about another man, Eden was dumbfounded. *More* dumbfounded. *What other man?*

"Did you go to Static last night?" he asked.

Eden looked at him. Static. Chastity's favorite club. Maybe Mitch's too. Where he'd met Chastity. Taken her home from and—"No." She shook her head violently.

"When is the last time you were there?"

"I don't know." Even without law school, she knew better than to talk. Listening was better—find out as much as they knew so she could tell her lawyer when the time came. Which it would. Soon. She was shocked it hadn't already happened. Had she missed it during a stress-induced momentary blackout? No, sadly, she was now totally *her*.

"Ms. Colfax...Eden. The body of a man was found in the alley behind Static, the same alley where we met each other." He didn't need to remind her of how they met. They both knew. Their first meeting had been twenty feet away from another murder victim. "This victim was a known drug dealer and suffered similar wounds to Carter Poole. Do you know anything about how the man died?"

"No. Nothing." Once the flashbacks started, maybe Chastity would show Eden more. How much of that would she tell the detective? How much would he believe?

He sighed and stood. "I'll be back with someone else. Do you want some water?"

She didn't respond, vocally or physically.

He sighed again and left the interrogation room.

Next they sent in a woman who had her black hair tied in a low ponytail and wore the sort of clothes meant to be casual and inspire trust—khaki pants, a button-down shirt, no jewelry. She introduced herself with a name Eden forgot ten seconds later.

Sure, she's just like me.

The woman kept her head tilted to the side, mirroring the small sips of water Eden took from a FLPD coffee mug, posture open and inviting. Classic shrink. Eden had seen a lot of them. This one seemed to be focused on rape and leading Eden into a perfect self-defense plea. Was this the woman's first day on the job? "How did you know the man?" "Did he attack you?" "You had to defend yourself, didn't you?"

Eden found her voice once the idea that Carter might be accused of wrongdoing came up, unable to stop herself. But she only gave the briefest of answers: Carter was her best friend. She didn't remember what happened. He would never have attacked her. The cup of water had evidently refilled her tear ducts, because her eyes started overfilling again.

Detective Landon came in a short while later and whispered something in the shrink's ear. He shot Eden a quick, tight grin and walked out, the shrink following him.

Eden craned her neck to look at the gauze and tape the EMTs had wrapped around her shoulder. The sling they'd given her helped keep the muscles relaxed, but there wasn't much else they could do. She'd refused the painkillers they'd offered. She could deal with her shoulder. All she had to do was think about Carter and she knew it could be a lot worse.

Landon had told her they hadn't heard any news from the hospital. Since the other police officers mostly ignored her, she hoped that meant Carter was still alive. If he wasn't, surely it would have shown on the cops' faces or in their demeanor. As it was now, they were tense, waiting for something. To find out if they were dealing with a murder instead of just an attempted one?

A long while later, Landon stepped into the room and motioned for her to follow him with a flick of his head. She did. No questions, no hesitation. *Maybe this is when they read me my rights.* She walked a few strides behind the big cop through the station, passing meth addicts, prostitutes, and drunks. A well-put-together-looking woman, with eyes as big as the tires on the SUV she probably drove, was scared out of her mind, keeping her body as tightly wrapped as possible so as not to touch the undesirables.

Eden wasn't sure which one she most resembled—a terrified suburbanite or someone the suburbanite was terrified of.

The detective led her to a desk stacked high with paper and files, a few coffee cups, and a computer that might have been held together by all the Post-its surrounding the monitor.

Landon pulled out a dirty-looking fabric chair and sat down, and then held out his hand, indicating the seat she should take. He picked up his phone—not a cell phone, the old-fashioned, bulky landline one.

"You wanna call someone?" he asked.

This isn't his first day. Why is he doing this out of order? She didn't ask, not wanting to remind him if he'd simply forgotten. *Yeah, right. He forgot. Just make the call.* Her one phone call before they officially arrested her and put her in the slammer. There was only one person to call. But she needed to stop crying before she dialed.

"Tell whoever it is to pick you up in about twenty minutes. We need to get your signature on the statement but Processing is still getting the other paperwork together."

"I get to go home?" It wasn't a whine, but sounded like one.

He shook his head. "No, not home. Your apartment is a crime scene for now. You'll need to stay somewhere else."

"Why are you letting me go?"

"I was told to," he said with a humorless smile. "I was *told* to look into the drug dealing angle. I was *told* that the murder of the junkie and then last night's murder of the dealer in the alley, plus the attempted murder of your friend the rookie were all so similar, it was *probably* a fight over territory."

Landon put down the phone and leaned toward her, lowering his voice. "I'm not sure how much you're wrapped up with Mitchell Turner, but his friends must be watching out for you, too. I've checked you out, Eden. You're not like him or whoever is protecting him. You need to stay away from them. Because whatever is going on with him and his friends is not something you should be around. When I take them down—and I will, regardless of my orders—I don't want to have to take you with them."

She shook her head. "Mitch didn't know who called you. Neither of us know anyone in the police department who'd want to help us, other than Carter, and he's only a tech trainee."

"Carter? The kid who…" He shook his head. "No, Carter's not a tech. He's a new hire. Just took the rescue diver course, I think."

"You must be thinking of the wrong person. Carter, *my* Carter, just finished a forensics course at the Tech Academy in the Keys."

He grabbed a pen and scribbled something on a small pad of paper. "There is no Tech Academy in the Keys. It'd be way too expensive to have one there. The only thing that's down there is the dive school we send officers to once they pass the exam."

"No, that's impossible," she said, her voice gaining strength while her heart lost some. "He couldn't get into the Police Academy."

"I don't know what he told you, but there's no Tech Academy in the Keys. I could be wrong about *him*, though. I'll need to recheck his file."

She rubbed her forehead, thinking back on what exactly Carter had told her about the course. No, he'd— No. The detective must have gotten Carter mixed up with someone else.

He yanked on the telephone's cord and pulled the phone closer to her, ruffling the chaos on his desk. "Do you have someone who can pick you up?"

"I think so. Have you heard anything from the hospital? Any news about Carter?"

"No, not recently. But you can check up on him when you leave here."

"I will." If she could walk to North Broward Hospital, she would. Right now. She needed to know Carter was going to be alright. And then if—*when* he was better, he could tell the police what she'd done to him. Then they'd bring her back here and lock her up for good.

She picked up the receiver slowly and held it to her ear. *Wait, what's Mitch's phone number?* In the time of cell phones and speed dialing, did anyone even know anybody's phone number anymore? She closed her eyes to think. Landon must have taken that as a hint, because she heard him get up from the desk. When she looked, she saw him speaking to another officer across the room.

Mitch answered on the fourth ring, just before she gave up. "What?" His voice was just as she remembered it—gruff, mean, and amazing.

"Mitch?" *I will not cry, I will not cry, I will not cry. I'm crying, aren't I?*

"What's wrong, Eden?" His words flew through the phone lines in short succession—he was in panic mode.

"It's Carter. Carter. Oh God, Mitch, there was so much blood." She ignored a few stares of other civilians around her and focused on keeping her breath steady so Mitch would be able to understand what she was saying.

"Is he—No, never mind. You can tell me later. Where are you?"

"At the police station."

"Fuck." He blew out a quick puff of air. "Did you tell them anything?"

"No. But Carter. He told me—"

"Don't say anything else! You hear me? They could be listening."

They? Oh, the police. Yeah, that was a possibility. "Okay." Her brain was on autopilot, the plane was going down, and there were no parachutes. What does one do at that point? Panic. And, in Eden's case, apparently adding more dry weeping into the mix seemed like a good idea, too.

"Breathe, Eden. Breathe." He waited until the hiccupping of her breath had slowed down. "Do not say anything to them. Do you hear me? I'm going to call a lawyer."

"Why? Can't you pick me up?"

"What? Aren't they holding you?"

"No. They said I can go home. I wanna go home, Mitch," she whimpered.

"I'm coming." No pause, no question. He was coming. "No. Shit. I'll send Jolie." Or not.

"But I want *you*."

"You'll have me, okay? Just as soon as we get you home."

He yelled Jolie's name at the top of his lungs, and Eden flinched away from the phone.

"Mitch?"

"Yeah, babe."

She wasn't sure why he couldn't come himself but wasn't going to argue over the phone. She was too tired. "Tell Jolie to hurry."

"I'll be waiting for you. Be strong, Eden."

She'd try. Jolie would pick her up, and then Mitch could take her to the hospital to see Carter. Yeah, she'd need Mitch to be there too. So he could keep her standing. And strong.

CHAPTER XLII

Eden waited on a long row of plastic chairs set so close together, she had to tuck in her shoulders to avoid touching the people on either side of her. The man on her left looked as uncomfortable as she did, but she leaned closer to him anyway, just to get away from the man on her other side. *He* smelled like he'd had just had a tryst with a box of wine, his body slumping toward her.

She said a quiet prayer of thanks when Jolie walked in. The woman always looked perfect, which made the contrast between her and the rest of the lobby's occupants even greater. She looked so comfortable, as if she were in Nordstrom's doing a little shopping rather than in a place that smelled like sweat, nervousness, and captivity. Her hair was down, hitting the middle of her back, the front kept off her beautiful face with a clip. Crisply ironed gray pants and a flowing top completed the image of controlled sexiness, bringing every eye in the place to her.

Eden jumped up, entirely aware that, in comparison, she looked more like the drunk staring at Jolie than the object of his ogling. At least the blood was gone. The clothes she'd been wearing when she woke up were in a lab somewhere nearby being analyzed for trace evidence.

Jolie scowled at the girl who had caused her so much trouble. That trouble would all be washed away soon, though, as soon as Hyde appeared. "You look like hell, Eden."

"Then I guess I look better than I feel."

Jolie shrugged and ventured a glance around the room, grimacing. "Can we leave now?"

Eden nodded and followed Jolie out the station door to Mitch's car. She'd parked in front of a hydrant.

Jolie was silent as they drove, wondering how to ask why they'd let Eden go with so much evidence against her. But she had to be subtle, and Jolie didn't do subtle well.

"Why didn't Mitch come?" Eden asked.

"What?" Jolie was jolted from her planning. "He thought it might look suspicious. Even though they're not investigating Shelly's case anymore, they don't trust him. Cops." She rolled her eyes. "Oh yeah, and he's caged." Her smile was humorless.

"He's still in the cage? Did he change last night?"

"No. It was a false alarm, but he's still fighting Hyde off. He took a sedative to help."

The girl's lip curled slightly, and she nodded. "I need a phone. Could I use yours?"

"I left it at the house. You'll have to wait."

Jolie had never been more pissed off, more alone. She'd always felt someone had her back—The Clinic when she was dealing with Mitchell and Mitchell when she was dealing with The Clinic. Of course, Mitchell had no idea that he was actually supporting one of the people who were destroying any chance he had at a normal life. And now that Jolie had killed Carter—and in such a messy manner—The Clinic was going to be beyond angry with her. But she'd had no choice. Framing Eden for his death had been a perk.

Killing the drug-dealing witness didn't bother her at all. Like the junkie before him, the guy was probably going to die a violent death anyway. Jolie had just hurried up the inevitable. But Carter. Eden's handler. He'd been different. Had given Jolie pause. But she'd get over it.

She should have known Carter wasn't cut out for this type of work. "Losing" his medical file and getting him into the police academy hadn't been enough. Her skills with sexual and emotional manipulation hadn't been enough. Poor deluded Carter couldn't be trusted, so he'd had to go.

It was a sad realization, but sad realizations were a daily event in her life. She did horrible things to a man who, in another life, might have loved her. Instead, Mitchell was only hers when Hyde took over his body.

Life sucks. Everybody uses everybody. Everyone uses themselves to get what they want. Or to get the results they're told to get.

For Jolie, screwing Carter had been a mildly pleasurable part of that process. Screwing Mitchell—no, Hyde—after giving him a whopping dose of narcotic, had been even more pleasurable. But not nearly as much as what the girl now freaking out in the passenger seat next to her had experienced. No, Eden had the man, while Jolie had to make do with the beast.

Yeah, doesn't life just suck.

Jolie took her hand off the steering wheel and put it on Eden's arm. "I'm so sorry about Carter, Eden. He was a really nice guy."

Eden's lower lip started to shake. "Did he die?"

Jolie glanced at her, confused. What the hell did that mean? Didn't she wake up next to his body? When Jolie fled the apartment the night before, Chastity had been screaming at her. The bitch was pissed—not because Jolie had beaten someone, but because Jolie had beaten *Chastity's* someone. "He's mine," she'd yelled. "Why did you end what was mine?" Jolie hadn't answered. The look in Chastity's eyes had scared the shit out of her, and Jolie knew that if she didn't get out of there quickly, she'd end up a bloody mess right next to Carter.

"Is he dead?" Eden asked, her voice breaking.

"Isn't that why they were holding you?" Oh shit, why *had* the cops let her go? Jolie hadn't yet told The Clinic about Carter's death, so how had they found out? There was no way they'd have known it was once again time to grease whoever's palm it took to close the case. What the hell?

Eden shook her head. "Did you speak to someone at the hospital?"

Jolie looked back to the road before they veered off and crashed. "Why would I?"

"Carter wasn't dead. They sent him to the hospital. But I don't know if he's..."

Jolie's hand tightened on the wheel, her heartbeat picking up speed, her foot pressing harder on the gas pedal. *Oh, shit.* She was in trouble. "Was he conscious?"

"For a few seconds," Eden whimpered. "He told me to leave. He told me to leave him there. On the ground. Bleeding." The girl was pathetic.

Jolie blinked and swallowed. "He actually said that? Or did he just shoo you away?"

"He said it, and he told me to call you and Mitch."

Jolie nodded slightly and ran her teeth over her bottom lip. "He's a smart kid. What else?" She only risked a quick glance at the girl. If Eden saw the expression on Jolie's face, it would be a dead giveaway. Holy shit, did he tell her anything condemning? And what had Eden told the cops?

"He told me that I didn't do it."

Jolie flipped her head to look at Eden. "Really?"

She shook her head that was already starting to shake all by itself.

"Did he tell you who *did* do it?"

"No."

Jolie took a deep breath and flexed her foot to release its

pressure on the gas pedal. "Well, did the cops talk to him? Get any information from him?"

"They told me he was in surgery…because of what I did to him."

"But you just told me he said you didn't do it."

"Yeah, like that's something I believe."

Jolie relaxed into her seat for the rest of the drive to Mitch's, leaving Eden to her own thoughts. Her own nightmare. So Eden still believed she'd attacked Carter. That was very good. And the police didn't know any differently. But Carter being alive changed everything. Jolie needed to come up with a plan. She had to get to Carter before he woke up. *If* he woke up.

The Clinic was going to be furious. She'd been sloppy, in addition to drawing more attention to Hyde and Chastity. This needed to end.

If Eden died and Jolie made it look like Hyde had done it, part of her problem would go away. The Clinic couldn't blame her if their handsome guinea pig did what they'd basically created him to do. And if Mitchell believed he'd killed Eden, as well as his sister, maybe Jolie could convince him to go away with her. Somewhere the cops couldn't find them. The cops didn't scare her nearly as much as her bosses did.

Could she disappear well enough that The Clinic couldn't find her, either? Mitchell too. She had to take him with her. But without the serum, what would he be like? She'd never known him without it. The Clinic had approached her after Mitchell's father had died. She was ambitious and looked young enough to convince a sixteen-year-old boy she was just a friend. A friend they thought he would connect with, be attracted to, keep around. And he had. Jolie guessed they'd thought she could use her questionable sense of morality and do what she was told. And she had. Even after she realized she was in love with the bastard.

Fifteen years later, she still wasn't a hundred percent sure what the drug controlled—his cycle or his rage. Probably both. She could deal with him transforming more often. And maybe, with the evil appearing more often, he'd be more like Chastity. More like Eden. Easier to control when he was human, nicer even. She stifled a chuckle. Mitchell being nice. Yeah, she'd love to see that.

They pulled into Mitchell's driveway a few minutes later. Eden jumped out of the car and ran to the front door.

"Which hospital, Eden?" Jolie yelled at her.

"North Broward!" Then she threw the door open and bounded up the stairs.

Jolie walked into the house to look for her phone, hoping she'd hear good news from the hospital. Maybe one of her problems hadn't made it out of surgery alive.

⌁⌁⌁

The headaches were back, even though Mitch hadn't changed last night. He'd thought they were connected to his transformation, but maybe it was the cage—radon leaking out of the bars or something. *Yeah, sure, it was radon. Moron.* If the morphine wasn't still flowing through his system, he'd be in a fetal position clutching his head and crying right now.

Instead, he was sitting up on the mattress, wiping his eyes, when he heard Eden's shout from downstairs. His body waved back and forth slightly as he tried to find a good spot to balance in. When he heard the pounding of her footsteps in the hallway, he leaned forward and steadied himself with the bars, not trusting he could stand.

She plowed into the room and slid on the hardwood floor, her eyes puffy and red. *Too many tears.* The cage stopped her, and she knelt down to his level. Her fingers grasped his, the bar between their palms. She didn't say anything, just searched his eyes for help, understanding. But he didn't understand a damned thing. And help? How could he help her stuck in a prison cell?

When he realized that the only thing he could offer her was

to listen, he said, "Tell me what happened."

"Can you come out? Can I go in?" Her words were frantic, tumbling over each other in their haste.

Damn it, he wanted to hold her. Put his arms around her and press her hard against his chest as if that could force the fear out of her. "Yeah, get the key. But if I tell you to get out, you get out. Understand?"

She didn't nod, just turned and ran to the table for the key. Fumbling, she unlocked the cage and rushed to him, her body landing on his, knocking him backwards onto the mattress with her on top of him.

His cock immediately reacted to the position. He cursed it, cursed *her* for forcing his body to lose control so quickly. But with her arms around him, her cheek against his chest, her shoulders jerking slightly from her sobs, he ignored his desire and held her. He kissed her hair and ran his hands down her back. Comforting someone was completely foreign to him. He hoped like hell he was doing it right.

"He said I didn't do it, but I must have, Mitch. *She* must have done it." Her voice was muffled, her breath warm on his neck. "But they let me go. Why did they let me go?"

"Because you didn't do anything wrong, Eden. You didn't." Chastity did. And the woman in his arms wasn't Chastity.

She raised her face to look at him—so much anguish, so much doubt. He wiped her cheek, letting his hand trace down her face and rest on her trembling lip. When she inched higher up on him, he accepted her invitation. He very carefully put his lips on hers, sweeping them side to side, barely touching.

She moved even higher, opening to him, pulling him closer with the arms wrapped around his neck. Her tongue touching his, smooth, wet, warm.

His hips lifted by themselves, pressing his erection against her. She moaned into his mouth. What the hell was he doing? *Nice guy.* She's completely vulnerable and all he's thinking about is banging her...in a cage. *Yeah, nice fucking guy.*

He pushed her away, trying to break the kiss, but he'd have to push a lot harder to pry her off him. And that was something he couldn't do. Then he'd have to speak. Say something like: *Sorry you think you killed your boyfriend, but you need to get off me before I rip off your clothes and have at you.* Yeah, that'd be *just* what she needed to hear.

"Just in case you care, Eden, Carter's in a coma." The bitterness in Jolie's voice echoed off the ceiling and did something Mitch had been unable to do—remove Eden's lips from his.

Eden sat up, dazed but recovering, a dark blush appearing on her cheeks. "You called the hospital?" She stood and stepped out of the cage without looking back.

Mitch tried not to be disappointed at how quickly she seemed to forget about him. "Lock the door," he muttered, wiping his mouth but still tasting her.

She whipped her head around and went to close the padlock. "Sorry." She held his eyes until Jolie spoke.

"The surgery went okay, but he's still unconscious. They don't know much more than that. Something about, 'We'll wait and see.' Which is just brilliant." She rolled her eyes. "I didn't go to med school, and I could've made that diagnosis."

Eden spoke to Mitch. "I need to go see him."

He nodded. "Take my car. Do you know how to drive?"

"More or less."

Not encouraging. "Enough to not kill yourself? Maybe Jolie should go with you."

Jolie glared at him.

"Do you want to come, Jolie?" Eden asked. "I know you and Carter were…close."

Jolie looked at her feet for a minute before speaking. "Sure. But then I'm coming back here. Mitchell, you and I have more to discuss."

Yippee, I can't wait. "I'll be here." For how much longer? He felt a faint pull from Hyde in his gut as the drug's effects faded. Once it was entirely gone, he'd need the straps again.

But taking more before the last dose had been metabolized out of his system seemed tragically stupid, especially considering how drastically the first dose had affected him.

Eden's eyes were shy again, like she regretted her reaction to seeing him moments before. "See you later, Mitch."

He nodded, not knowing what to say. He wished *he* regretted her reaction earlier. Or his. It would make things a lot easier. He knew it had to end, knew *he'd* be the one to make it so. Did he want her with the caveat that he'd have to spend the rest of his life in a cage? Living only for her visits. Never trusting himself to be outside or around other people. Not that he cared about other people, aside from having a small problem with actually murdering them. But how would that be enough for either of them? With that danger always hanging over their heads. As unromantic as it was, the idea that he'd be unable to financially support himself was beyond what his oh-so-male ego could stand. What a lovely life they'd have together—he'd be a kept man. Literally. Kept in a cage until she came home after a long day at work. *Yeah, that'd be what every woman dreams of.*

Mitch avoided Eden's eyes. Too much to tell her, too little time in an already unfortunate moment. So he'd get to obsess about that discussion for a while longer. *Goody.*

"Don't be too long, Jolie. I may need you." He didn't apologize for taking her away from Carter's side. He knew she'd be happy to have an excuse to leave the hospital. She had no attachment to the guy and had probably agreed only because it would be the *proper* reaction for someone who actually cared about people. But not Jolie. No. At some point, Mitch had rubbed off on her.

Maybe the truth was that he'd rubbed everything off and had nothing left to hold him together.

CHAPTER XLIII

Carter was unmoving, his breath regulated by the machine at his side. It also tracked his heart rate and brainwaves, sending quiet, hollow beeps that echoed in Eden's ears. His head had been struck once. On the side, just above his ear. But the bandages were wrapped all the way around, covering his forehead, ears, and most of one eye. A bruise peeked out from under the gauze protecting a broken cheekbone. One arm was tucked neatly to his side, attaching him to tubes and tape to multiple bags of fluid and medicine. His other arm was loose, limp under her hand.

With her other hand, Eden picked at the edge of the sheet, reading the imprint left by the hospital supply company. Blue cursive lines she traced over and over with her eyes.

Jolie stood behind her, occasionally shifting from one foot to the other. It was better than the pacing she had done earlier, as if searching for an excuse to leave the room but not being able to think of an adequate one.

Eden wished she'd just go. The woman's nervous energy was bouncing off the walls, creating more tension in Eden to take along with it. She didn't know if Carter even knew they were there or what happened to someone's thoughts while they were comatose. But, just in case he felt them there, she didn't want him to know how terrified they were that he wouldn't make it back.

"Jolie, maybe you should go check on Mitch now."

"Really?" She sounded relieved. Not surprising.

"Yeah. I think he needs you more than Carter does at the moment."

"You're probably right. I should get back. Are you going to stay?"

Eden nodded, keeping her eyes on Carter, wondering if she should just sleep here. If the hospital staff would even let her. She wasn't a family member, not on paper at least, so they'd probably kick her out soon. But they were all either of them had. "For a while. I can get a cab back to the house later." She sighed. "I don't have any money."

Jolie rummaged around in her purse. "Here."

Eden took the twenty-dollar bill Jolie held out. "Thanks, I'll pay you back."

"Whatever. Take this too." She handed her a cell phone. "The code to unlock it is '6969.'"

How clever. Undoubtedly Jolie's favorite sexual position. *Put that on the list of 'Things I Never Wanted To Know About Jolie.'*

"Mitch's number is speed dial one," Jolie said. "Call me *immediately* if he wakes up."

If he wakes up. She'd said, 'if.' Eden swallowed. The doctor had repeated the 'We'll wait and see,' but his averted eyes had clued her in on his true diagnosis. "I'll see you later."

"Yep," Jolie said as she hightailed it down the hall.

Eden vowed to never, ever wear heels again. The sound of Jolie's clicking on the tile grated on Eden's nonexistent nerves. When the sound had faded, she laid her head down next to Carter's arm and closed her eyes. Maybe if she willed him to wake up, spoke to him in her dreams, he'd come back. But maybe her will wouldn't be enough.

The drug was out of Mitch's system now. And with its disappearance came more activity from Hyde, pushing at the wall of Mitch's flesh, trying to get free. Straight out of the movie *Aliens*, for fuck's sake. If Mitch looked at his belly, he wondered if he'd see Hyde's face break through his ribcage, growling and showing off his fangs.

When Mitch saw Jolie come into the room, he sat up quickly. "First shoot me up, then tell me about the Boy Scout."

Jolie picked up a vial and, with a practiced hand, filled the syringe with morphine.

"Half the dose of last night, Jolie. That was too much." He hadn't turned, which meant that all the drug's effects had been leveraged on the man, not the monster.

"I was thinking the same thing. I need you to be aware tonight."

Not sure what that meant. But the needle's pinch distracted him from his thoughts. *Tough guy's afraid of a tiny, little needle. Impressive.*

"How is the kid?" he asked to focus on something other than the push of the plunger.

"What?"

"Jesus, Jolie. At least *feign* some interest in him."

She looked offended…or guilty for being caught, Mitch couldn't tell which.

"He's in a coma. They don't know if he'll come out of it. Eden is crying a lot, slobbering a bit." She shrugged and pulled the needle out of his arm, rubbing it with a piece of gauze. "Does that make me a bad person? That I'm not more drooly over him?"

He looked her over from head to foot. How many years had they known each other? Seemed like forever. They'd worked together, partied together, slept together, but there was nothing *real* between them at all. He would have a hard time even calling her a friend. Everything he'd wanted—a beautiful woman who was just as emotionally cold and unwelcoming as he was. After. *After* he told her the sexual part of their relationship had to end. Before that, she'd been more clingy, needy, perhaps more drooly. But he'd been honest. And things had cooled down eventually and become exactly what he needed. Strangely, he'd never actually considered if it was what *she* needed. She would have said something if it wasn't. Jolie was hardly one to hold her tongue.

A wave of heat swept through him, not as harshly as the previous night, but definitely something uncomfortable. He blinked, trying to keep his eyes focused.

Jolie smiled at him. "You're feeling it, aren't you?"

"Yeah, I am." He heard the slur, recognized the timbre of his own voice, but felt detached, as if it didn't really belong to him.

Her face was beginning to fog, multiply. Eyes doubling, then tripling. Dark brown hair getting impossibly full as his vision blurred. He smiled. *Jolie is very beautiful. Not Eden-beautiful, but definitely beautiful. Eden is truly beautiful.* How many times had he repeated "beautiful"? He giggled and leaned back onto the mattress.

"...you've had enough, Mitchell...too much. You need to be awake...I need Hyde to..."

He couldn't catch her words or they weren't all being put together by his brain. But her lips were definitely moving, so she was saying something.

"What did you say, Joles?"

"Nothing, Hon. You...rest now."

His head sank into the pillow. Closing his eyes helped him concentrate a bit better. He thought about the kid. *Poor bastard. Didn't think Chastity would've done it, but it sure as hell looks that way. Wrong place, wrong time.* Mitch thought about what Carter had said. *Drug dealer. Eden. Chastity. A hot brunette was the last one to see the girl ali— Wait.*

Something didn't compute. What was it? His head was

fuzzy. He couldn't connect to the idea that was teetering at the edge of his mind. No, something was wrong. He couldn't grasp onto it. He wanted to catch hold of that detail, the one that danced around his brain, just out of reach. *Brunette. Chastity. No, that's wrong.* He opened his eyes and looked at the woman peering down at him, just outside the bars. Right before he lost consciousness, he said, "Chastity's hair...not brown. Jolie, what's—?"

CHAPTER XLIV

Nurses came into Carter's room regularly to check on the machines and take his vitals. They ignored Eden. She ignored them. With no windows in the room, she had no idea how much time had passed, how long she'd been by Carter's side, or how much longer it would be until he opened his eyes and saw her there.

Jolie's ringtone startled her. Eden unlocked the phone with Jolie's oh-so-creative code. The caller ID said: 'Mitchell,' with a picture of his irritated face looking back at her. She easily imagined his annoyance when Jolie took the photo. She'd seen it in person countless times in their relatively short relationship. *Relationship?* Could she actually call it that?

"Mitch?" she asked.

"It's me, Eden." Jolie spoke quickly, instantly setting Eden on edge.

"What's wrong?"

"Eden, hurry. You have to get back here. It's Hyde. He's— he's—Oh God! He's out!"

"Jolie?"

The phone clicked off. Eden shot out of the chair, sending it skidding out behind her. With a quick glance to Carter, she silently apologized for leaving him and ran out the door. She caught a cab outside the hospital, shouting the address at the cabbie and telling him to hurry. She tried calling back, but no one answered. *Oh God, what was happening?* What was she going to find when she got there?

The phone, gripped tightly in her hand, rang. *Thank God.* "What's going on?"

A male voice she didn't recognize responded. "I was just going to ask you the same thing, Cabot."

"No, this isn't—"

"Shut up! What the hell happened to Colfax's handler?"

"Handler?" she asked on an inhalation. What the heck was a 'handler' and why did the man know her last name?

"The kid, Carter Poole. What happened? Did Colfax's Hyde do it or did you?"

It was as if the cab had just entered a tunnel, the world outside disappearing from Eden's perception. All that was left was the cell phone against her ear and the man on the other end of the line. What should she say?

He rescued her from her indecision. "Where are you? Why didn't you send me a report as soon as her handler went down? If this is some kind of passive-aggressive bullshit about the emails, I'm not amused."

Eden took a deep breath. She needed to find out who this person was and how Jolie was involved with Carter and Chastity. "I haven't been near a computer." She tried to make her voice sound like Jolie's—sassy, snobbish, and bitchy.

"And, of course, you were about to use the smart phone that is currently stuck to your face to email me, right?" he spat.

Could she claim that she forgot her password? Would he believe that? "I couldn't get into my email on the phone. I forgot my password." When he didn't respond, she kept talking, getting sucked deeper into the lie. "It was auto-filled on my phone. I dropped the damned thing and the battery fell out."

"Are you kidding me, Cabot? How the hell do you forget four fucking digits?"

"What can I say? It's been a long day."

"Fine. Since you've got me on the phone, tell me what happened. Then, when you get a chance, I'd really appreciate a written report." His voice shot out bullets of sarcasm wrapped in a mocking tone. "But since you've been having a tough day, there's no rush."

"I can't talk right now. I'm in a cab. But, yes. The *kid*'—her voice broke—"is in the hospital. Unconscious. I don't know what happened, but I'm on my way to find out."

"So he wasn't another one of your little mistakes?"

"My little mistakes?" A spasm gripped the muscles of Eden's neck. "No."

"Well, if it *was* her Hyde, we need to bring her in until we can get her dosages right. We can't have her going around killing people, now can we?"

Eden didn't respond. Her mind was so overwhelmed that speech was impossible.

"We'll leave that to you." The man's laugh was dry and humorless. "I want a full report in my inbox twenty minutes *before* ASAP, so you better remember the goddamned password. Do you understand me?"

Jolie's password. "My four-digit password, right. Understood."

"Forgot your password. That's such bullshit. You just love being a pimple on my ass. But your playtime is running out." His voice thundered. "Do what you're supposed to and do it right. Last chance, Cabot. You hear me?"

"I hear you." After he hung up, Eden checked the phone log. There were only three numbers in it—the man she'd just spoken to's, Mitch's, and Carter's. *Oh my God, Carter.* Tears flowed down her cheeks.

The "medicine" I found wasn't cocaine, was it, Carter? It was for me. You'd been giving it to me. All this time she'd thought...

As the cab slowed down, Eden's attention was brought back to her more immediate problems. They were pulling into

Mitch's driveway. *Mitch.* Jolie was in there with him, and he had no idea what was going on. This time even Eden knew more than he did, which wasn't saying a lot. What if Jolie had already done something to him? Made him into one of her 'little mistakes'?

Eden tucked the phone into her pocket and repeated Jolie's password again. Later she would see if she could get into the email account, but right now she needed to focus on getting Jolie away from Mitch. *Or Hyde.* She hoped she didn't have to deal with Hyde too. For once, Jolie might have been telling the truth and Hyde might be out. Maybe Jolie was already dead. Eden threw the money in the front seat and opened the door before the cab had come to a stop.

The driver yelled, "You want any change?"

"Keep it!"

The door was unlocked so she didn't slow down, stumbling up the stairs, screaming Mitch's name. The door was closed. No sound from the other side. Eden took a deep breath before turning the knob. Shoot, she should have gotten a weapon or something. What the heck was she doing? *Be smart, Eden!* Eyes darting around the hallway, she saw a glass vase on a table, wilted flowers sagging out of it. She ripped the sling off her arm, ignoring the pain in her shoulder as she dumped the flowers onto the floor. Splashing brownish water onto the ornate rug and her pants, she tested the vase's weight. Heavy. But she could wield it. It might not do a lick of good against Hyde, but what would?

A yelp came from inside the room—Jolie. Eden had to move, had to try to help. She needed Jolie alive. So she could beat information out of her.

She cradled the vase in her arm and opened the door. The first thing she saw was Hyde, definitely Hyde. He was bigger than Mitch, coarser features, not as refined or as beautiful. His muscles bulging, his chest heaving, his face furious. His growl shattered any sense of adequacy Eden might have felt before she opened the door. His hands clenched the bars, two fitting into each palm.

She stepped into the room, her hands tight around the vase, eyes sweeping the room. She blinked. Hyde was still in the cage. Pissed off as hell to be there, but he was definitely still in the cage. The padlock was still closed. Yet another lie. Jolie didn't know Eden had spoken to Jolie's boss. So what was the game plan? Eden couldn't get Mitch away from Jolie, couldn't let him out, when he was Hyde.

She ignored the grunts coming from the cage. She could've sworn the yelp had sounded feminine. But Jolie wasn't there. Not unless...

S*tupid.* Behind the door.

A second too late, she flipped around and saw something moving fast, swinging toward her head. She jumped sideways. The cane clipped her bad shoulder, sending pain shooting into her hand and chest.

"Damn it, stay still!" Jolie slammed the door with her foot and stood in front of it, barring Eden's escape.

"What are you doing?" Eden screamed.

Jolie's eyes were wild, uncontrolled, and angry. "Should've used this." She looked down to what she held in her hand along with the cane. A syringe.

Eden backed away, gripping the vase with one hand but unsure she could risk getting close enough to use it. "Why are you doing this?"

Jolie smiled. "You're bleeding." Her tone sounded as if she'd just complimented Eden on what she was wearing.

Eden glanced to her shoulder. Yep, she was bleeding. Hand-to-hand combat with only one untrained hand. *We're off to a great start.*

"Hyde likes blood, don't you, hon? It excites him. Makes him even meaner." She took slow steps, swinging her hips as she approached Eden. Like a stroll through the freaking park.

Eden stepped backwards, keeping space between them, wondering how long she'd have until she hit the wall. "What is wrong with you?"

Jolie flinched, confused, and stopped. "There's nothing wrong with *me*. You two? Yeah, there's all sorts of wrong with you two."

"With me?" She shook her head. "No, I wasn't the one who hurt Carter, was I? Or the others?"

"Nope. To each. But I'm not a murderer. Self-defense isn't murder." She looked peaceful—hypocrisy and self-righteousness leaving no lines on her face.

"Self-defense? This is self-defense?" Adrenaline, fear, and anger filled Eden's veins, pumped by a heart that felt as if it were about to combust.

Hyde shook the bars of the cage. "Let me out, bitch!"

Oh my God, I'm going to die. I'm going to die now. Eden couldn't focus. Couldn't think of a way out of this. Couldn't slow her breath. Her pounding heart. Sweat making her grip on the vase slip.

"Why are you self-defensing people to death, Jolie?"

She blinked. "For him. I'm doing this for him. So Mitchell doesn't go to jail. Shelly was an accident, Eden, it really was. She was my friend." Her eyes pleaded for understanding. "I didn't mean to. She would have told him what I was doing while he was Hyde, and he would have been so mad at me. *So* mad at me."

"What were you doing, Jolie?"

"He liked it. I made him feel good. Nobody else could make him feel good." Her crazy was spilling out all over the place. "But when Mitchell saw her body, he felt so guilty that he called the police. So I had to give him an alibi. And then, I had to give him another. Because The Clinic wasn't doing anything to help." She switched direction and walked over to the cage, teasing the beast inside, but not getting too close. "I'm sorry about Carter, though, Eden. I'm really sorry about that. He was a good guy."

Is. He *is* a good guy. No, that's not quite right. "How long has he been drugging me, Jolie?"

She jerked her head to the side. "How did you know that?

Did he tell you? Did he wake up?"

Eden just stared at her. "Why did he do it?"

"Are you sad, Eden?" she mocked. "Would it make you feel better if I told you I had to coerce him into it? That I had to force him?" She smiled. "Bummer. It's too bad I'm not going to tell you."

Eden decided then and there that it didn't matter whether she lived through this or not. She was taking Jolie out with her.

"So what's the plan, Jolie? The same thing you did with Shelly—kill me and make Mitch think he did it?"

"No. He and I need closure. I thought it would be more poetic if he actually did the dirty work this time. And I really hate lying to him, you know." She leaned the cane against the side of the cage and fished the key out of her pocket. "You want to hurt her, don't you, big boy?" she said to Hyde. His huge hands gripped the bars. She petted his finger, keeping her body out of reach. "But not me. Nope, you and I understand each other." She was more delusional than Eden imagined if she thought the look on Hyde's face was that of understanding. He was studying Jolie, biding his time, waiting until she unlocked the cage. If he'd had a tail, it would have been twitching.

Eden inched toward the woman, terrified it meant nearing Hyde and getting farther away from the door as well. Jolie glanced back. And Eden froze in place. No need to feign terror, it had etched itself across her face all by itself.

Steady, Eden. You can do this. No, you have *to do this.*

Her expression seemed to bring pleasure to Jolie. She smiled and put the key in the lock. Eden was out of time. She ran at Jolie, the vase raised above her head, her shoulder screaming at her to stop.

Jolie's eyes widened. She stepped back from the bars, just as Hyde's hand swiped at her throat. Jolie's heels skidded across the floor, fleeing Eden's pursuit. She tripped and fell, sprawling out on the floor. Eden lifted the vase even higher and slammed it down, aiming for Jolie's head. Jolie flipped over onto her back, the glass shattering next to her ear. She covered her face to protect it from the shards and kicked at Eden's feet.

Eden's legs came out from under her. She hit the floor, pieces of glass piercing her legs and back. She refused to stop now. Jolie tried to scramble away. Eden grabbed her leg and pulled.

Jolie twisted around, the syringe in her fingers. Eden let go and scooted backwards, sliding through the glass, feeling it puncture her palms.

"I spoke to your boss, Jolie. He called."

She stopped crawling. "You what?"

"He thought I was you."

Jolie shook her head. "That's impossible. He doesn't call. He never calls."

The look on Jolie's face gave Eden confidence. "Well, he did. He seemed pretty pissed that you hadn't emailed him about my 'handler' being out of commission."

Her eyes were wild, scared. "What did you tell him?"

Think, Eden. Think. "He said something about 'playtime' being over. You should run for it, Jolie. Right now. He knows about Carter, and he's going to come for you. Run. Go into hiding."

Jolie started forward again, slower this time as if her fear and her stubbornness were fighting each other with each movement. "I can't leave. They'll find me. I know they will." Jolie held the syringe out, grimacing from pain and fear. "No, I can explain it to them. It was all your fault. *You* killed Carter. And Hyde killed you."

Eden shook her head. "They'll figure it out." She ignored the pain in her hands and slid farther away.

Jolie's eyes darted up above Eden. Her face turned into a mask of horror as if seeing the approach of her own demise.

Eden heard a growl from behind her. He was there. She felt it. Hyde was out of his cage and standing right behind her.

CHAPTER XLV

Hyde. Eden felt him, looming somewhere right behind her. No one moved. Eden didn't turn, didn't flee. She knew enough about wild animals to know running just encouraged them. If she dared move, she would have strangled Jolie. The woman in front of Eden, the one with a full view of the beast, was terrified—blinking like crazy, mouth an inch open. A few minutes ago, she'd been so sure he would never hurt her because they 'understood each other.'

A strange thought passed quickly through Eden's mind: *He'd better not just kill me. He'd better kill her, too.*

He hissed. No words. Just a hiss.

Eden saw Jolie's plan a second before she bolted. "Don't move," she mouthed to Jolie. Her warning came too late.

Jolie scrambled to her feet and ran for the door, heels slipping on the glass.

Hyde pounced.

"No!" Eden screamed.

He flew right over her and tackled Jolie just as she turned to look, her face seeming to visualize the death that was coming at her. He hit her hard, crushing her under his bulk. Jolie's scream was cut off by her grunt as their bodies smacked onto the floor.

Eden didn't want to see. She turned her head from Jolie's cries and saw the syringe that Jolie had dropped. She jumped up and grabbed it, her feet slipping on the glass and her own blood. She saw the cage, knew she'd be safe inside of it. She could wait it out until Hyde was gone and Mitch came back. And Jolie was dead. Oh God, what was she thinking of doing?

She held her hand steady, placing her thumb on the plunger. Ignoring Hyde's guttural laughter and Jolie's horrible begging, Eden sank to her knees. She had one shot. One chance to puncture his skin and push the drug into his body. No drug would be fast enough. She might very well die before it took effect. *If* it was enough. *Big frigging 'if,' Eden.* What the hell was she thinking? She called out to Chastity for strength, some sort of last-ditch plea for help from a side of her she didn't know, but someone she trusted had the strength to do what needed to be done.

Jolie was crying, covering her face with one hand and beating Hyde with the other. Her strikes had no effect on him. He looked like a cat playing with a bug, tossing her back and forth with easy slaps—nothing to him, but everything to his victim.

Eden crept closer on her knees, keeping her movements as small as possible. As if the smaller they were, the less likely he'd be to notice her. As if Jolie's pleas would fill his ears and her fear would keep him satisfied until Eden could get close enough. She took a deep breath, closed her eyes, and lunged toward his leg. As soon as she felt the needle enter flesh, she pushed down on the plunger and scrambled backwards.

Waiting for the arm that would strike her and throw her across the room. The one that would end all of this, at least for her. She couldn't look.

"What'd you do that for?" Hyde's gruff bass sounded muted, not angry, just confused. "I wasn't done."

Eden peered through one eye, not wanting to see her end coming.

Hyde was still sitting on top of Jolie. He batted her face as if trying to wake her up instead of kill her. But it didn't matter—Jolie was limp, lifeless. The syringe stuck out of Jolie's thigh, dangling to the side, bouncing slightly each time Hyde jostled the body beneath him.

"Oh, God," Eden moaned.

Cursing herself for making a sound, calling Hyde's attention to her, she ran the only direction she could—toward the cage. He was on her before she got through the door, nails clawing down her back, spinning her underneath him.

"Stop!"

His laugh was guttural, base. "Why should I?"

"Because of Mitch. Mitch wouldn't want me hurt."

"Why would I give a fuck about what Mitch wants?" He toyed with her hair, wrapping it around his finger and tugging until she cried out. "Huh?"

"He puts you in the cage, doesn't he?" She was panting, unable to get a deep enough breath with his weight pressing down on her chest. "I could speak to him, ask him not to tie you down."

Hyde cocked his head to the side in a very Mitch sort of way. It was the first similarity Eden had ever noticed between them. "He's smarter than that. He knows what I can do." He ground his hips into hers, rubbing himself against her pelvis. "Do *you* know what I can do?"

She wanted to press her body through the hardwood floor under her to get away. "I'd rather not. Thanks, though."

"I could fuck you until you bleed. Or I could fuck you and *then* make you bleed."

If she could breathe, she would've gasped. But at least he was talking, not just tearing her apart. "Are those my only options?" she whispered.

He snagged her bottom lip in between his teeth and yanked so hard tears appeared in Eden's eyes, the metallic taste of blood filling her mouth. But she didn't cry. She didn't scream. *Yay! Give yourself a pat on the back, Eden. Quick, before he kills you.*

"The fact that I'm giving you a choice at all is a big deal. I wouldn't have given her one." He flicked his head back to Jolie's body.

"So I should thank you then."

"Do or don't. I don't give a shit." His enormous shoulders shrugged, lifting his hands and pressing more of his bulk into her ribcage. "*He* doesn't either, you know, my little slut. He doesn't give a shit about you either." Hyde's lips tightened.

A faint dimple appeared on his cheek, grabbing Eden's focus. Her heart fluttered with the tiniest bit of hope.

"Say that again," she said.

He shoved his hand under her and squeezed her ass, smiling when she yelped. "You talk a lot."

"True." She risked a nod. "Tell me he doesn't give a shit about me. Come on, big boy, say it." *Why would he do what you want him to?* "You know what? Don't. It hurts too much."

His lip lifted in a snarl first, and then turned into a wicked grin. "It hurts you that he hates you? Sorry, bitch, but he does."

The dimple appeared again. Mitch's tell. Hyde was lying.

She lifted her head toward him and peered into the monster's eyes, looking for Mitch's color or something to recognize him by. "You're in there, aren't you?" she said breathlessly.

Hyde growled and pushed her back with a rough palm against her forehead, slamming her head into the floor. "Quit your yakking, or I'll kill you and *then* fuck you."

"No, you won't." She blinked the stars out of her eyes, praying she didn't lose consciousness.

He pushed himself off her, brows furrowed, eyes darting up and down her body, confused. "You think you know me, cunt?" He paced around her, the circles tight enough she had to curl her legs under her and sit up to avoid being stepped on.

"No." She couldn't try to escape—he'd just tackle her again. But she measured the distance to the cage anyway, trying to figure out how long she'd need to shut and lock the door. "You know me, though, don't you?"

Same look of confusion, Mitch-like tilt of the head, the dimple. Eden hoped Mitch was just under the surface of this creature, pulling Hyde back from hurting her until he could come back into himself.

"Maybe you recognize what we have in common," she said.

He let out a long sigh. "I'm bored of you. And he's going to be back soon, so it's now or never."

"Could we go with never? Or maybe a *next time*?"

He grabbed her by her shirt and hauled her to her feet like a momma cat with her young, except much harder, meaner and with a growl instead of a purr. Her clothes were already torn in places. It took only a small yank from Hyde and they were ripped from her body, leaving her exposed, in just her underwear and bra. The bra was the next thing to be taken from her, with one quick tug from Hyde.

She wrapped her arms around herself until, with one look up into his eyes, she understood that her humiliation just excited him. She dropped her arms and stood before him as confidently as she could, forcing herself to take deeper breaths.

He backed her up until the cold metal of the bars pressed grooves into her back. His fingers dug into her waist as he lifted her, setting her against him, her legs dangling a foot off the ground.

She cringed from a pain at her hip, heard the rip of her underwear, and felt the only barrier between them fall away.

He held her with absolutely no effort at all, one handed, while he adjusted himself to take her.

She turned her head and shut her eyes, waiting for the inevitable. Tears she didn't want him to see squeezed through her clenched eyelids.

"Yeah, I know exactly who you are," he said, his voice breaking slightly in anticipation.

"No, you don't." *I don't even know who I am, but I know who I want to be.* Bolting out of her box of denial back into this moment, she pushed him, refusing to continue being a victim. She kicked her legs out of his grip and squeezed her thighs together so he couldn't get in.

Why had she given up? Made it easier for him? She knew who she *wasn't*. She wasn't a scared little girl anymore. No, she had to fight. "Mitch! Come back! Come back to me, Mitch, I need you!" she screamed, hammering her fists against Hyde's chest.

He smiled at her childishness, pressed his body more firmly against hers, capturing her in between himself and the cage.

"Let me go! You have no idea what she's capable of! What *I'm* capable of!"

He grabbed her jaw and smashed his lips against hers, grinding against her teeth painfully.

She spoke into his mouth, cursing him, threatening him, fighting him. Until she felt his abs tighten severely. He released her jaw to grab onto the bars behind her and rocked against her. His groan was long and low, as if he'd had an orgasm.

Too scared to be disgusted, she pushed against his chest again. Less hair, smoother. Running her hands along his shoulders, she found their strength and size familiar, just like she remembered.

His mouth softened on hers, no longer pushing and greedy, just desperate and needing. He lowered her onto the ground, but held her lips. "Eden," he whimpered between the brief parting of their lips.

Mitch. She sighed and opened up to him. Wiping tears from his cheeks as they fell, she absorbed his goodness until the police came.

CHAPTER XLVI

Mitch would have killed to get in the shower. But it would have to wait. Police officers marched around his house like termites, led by their king—*or queen, wasn't it? Queen Landon. Yeah, he'd love me to call him that*—after 9-1-1 had received a frantic call from one of Mitch's neighbors about the violent screaming coming from his place. Landon wandered through the house, leaving the other cops to do their work in Hyde's room.

Mitch had gone downstairs with Eden and watched them patch up the damage Hyde and Jolie had inflicted on her. He'd barely spoken to her, ashamed of what he'd let happen. All of it. When he could no longer bear the way she stared at him, he went upstairs to see what—if anything—the cops had uncovered. It didn't matter now. Nothing mattered now. If they hauled his ass off, it would just be to a different prison cell, so who the hell cared anymore.

He stuck his head into Hyde's room. Jolie's body was on a gurney being rolled out of the room in a coroner's bag. Not wanting to look at her, dwell on *her* deceit and *his* stupidity, he kept his eyes on the two cops who remained inside the room.

"We got a timetable here, gentlemen?" he asked. "I need a nap."

"That's a nice cage you got there." Landon's voice was cordial, calm, unpleasant. Even knowing approximately where the detective was standing, Mitch was startled when he saw him, no more than two feet away, reclining against the wall. And Mitch hated to be startled. He was also too tired to react with more than a momentary flinch.

"Thank you kindly, Officer."

"It was mentioned in your sister's report, but the dimensions were off—inches instead of feet. Sounded more like a bird cage than what it actually is." Rolling his eyes, Landon pushed himself off the wall and crossed to the cage, stepping around the shattered glass. "What exactly do you use that for, Turner?"

"It's a sexual thing. You swing that way, Nick?"

"Experimented in college, but it didn't do it for me." He aimed a sarcastic sneer at Mitch.

Mitch didn't know if he liked this guy or hated him. *Probably hate. Yeah, almost definitely hate.*

"Who makes this? Reiner's?" He waited until Mitch nodded. "Yeah. Good company. Good customer service."

Damn it, that startled him again. To Mitch's knowledge, Reiner's made only one thing—animal cages. Did they make prison cages as well? "You have them at the station?"

Landon shook his head. "No, they're too expensive for the state to pay for. Humans don't need them that strong anyway." He gave Mitch a pointed glance and then continued his tour around the cage, brushing his hand along it. "I didn't know they made them with the one-and-a-half-inch pipe, though. Is that new?"

Mitch's eyes bulged. "What did you say?"

The detective brought his gaze to the two police officers and then walked toward Mitch. He stopped about five inches away from Mitch's face and whispered, "You think I don't know what you are, Mitch?"

His body tightened. "You don't know anything about me."

"No? Hmm… We'll have to chat." He took a few steps back. "Maybe that bar. Heavenly? You were right about the martinis. We should meet up there sometime soon."

Mitch nodded, not knowing how much the cop actually knew but eager to find out.

"Gentlemen," Landon called out to the men. "Are we about done for tonight?" He turned to Mitch and lowered his voice. "I got a hot lead on a case I'm working on. Off the clock."

"What case?" Mitch was suddenly warm, nervous. *What is this bastard up to?*

"Of course, we don't need to tell you that this room is off-limits for the time being, do we?" Landon said nonchalantly, glancing at the other police officers and then flicking his head toward the door.

Mitch followed him downstairs. Eden was still on the couch, gauze and bandages wrapped over so much of her body.

The detective stepped outside, letting the other cops pass him. When they'd all gone, he said, "Oh, and if you see Chastity again, say hello for me."

Mitch's stomach dove a foot lower. *Chastity knew this prick…* "How do you know Chastity?"

"We met at a club. I love that girl. She sure knows how to have a good time, doesn't she?"

"You know Chastity." Not sure why he was repeating himself, but somehow the idea was so surreal, he thought if he kept saying it out loud, eventually it would sound even remotely possible. Yeah, it wasn't working.

Landon nodded. "Of course, I had no idea she would get into so much trouble or I would've stuck around."

He wanted to wrap his hands around the cop's neck and shake him until his brain came loose for touching her. *If he touched her…* "You're *done* with Chastity."

"Is that a statement or a question?"

"Statement."

"Thought so." The detective sighed. "Now that I know who she is? Yeah, I'm done. I'm not a frigging rapist."

Glad that's clear. "You didn't know about her...*issues* until this morning?"

"Correct," Landon said with a nod.

"So why the hell didn't you get here sooner?" He could have asked, '*Why didn't you stop Hyde from almost raping or killing her?*' but he didn't. Good thing, too, or else he might have thrown the guy against the wall at the same time. Which wouldn't be smart. He was in enough trouble as it was.

Landon threw his hands up in the air. "I'm not omniscient." He looked shocked at the volume of his voice and quickly leaned in and whispered, "If I'd known fifteen minutes earlier, I never would have let Eden leave the station."

"What—?"

The cop held up his hand to silence Mitch. "I don't want to talk here. Later."

Mitch gritted his teeth. "And then we can stop all this vague bullshit and talk straight?"

He smirked. "That vague bullshit got me a detective badge."

"Well, it makes me want to beat it out of you."

"Then perhaps we should meet elsewhere."

Mitch paused. "You're not taking me in?"

"No way. I have too many things planned for you. Plus, I imagine your *friends* would have you out before I'd finished writing your name on the paperwork. So, don't worry, we'll have time for that beating."

"The gym." Mitch would have to find a way to discover who his 'friends' were. But, yeah, he could probably squeeze in a drink and a battle with the detective.

"Sounds lovely." The fucking cop actually winked at him. *Piece of—*

"Goodnight, Eden. Take care of yourself," he said, looking over Mitch's shoulder. "And stay in touch. Hopefully I'll be calling you with good news soon."

Mitch turned around to see her a few feet away. His body instinctually fought itself—part of it wanting to go to her and the other part wanting to back away as fast as his feet could carry him. Split down the middle.

When she saw his face, she tilted her head, confusion laying itself heavily on her brow. What did she see? She shook it off and smiled at Landon. "Thank you, Detective. I will."

"Do you need a ride somewhere?" He didn't bother to hide the suggestion that Eden would be safer elsewhere. In fact, Mitch agreed.

Mitch watched her eyes dart from his, to the floor, to the ceiling, to Landon's, trying to make up her mind on which way to go. He let her off easy. "Why don't you go see Carter for a while?"

"Are you sure?" she asked.

"Absolutely." As much as he hated the thought of her being less than ten feet away from the cop, he liked the idea of her staying away from *him* even more. It was time to say goodbye—for both their sakes.

Her nod was hesitant. "I have a lot to say to him when he wakes up. Then I'll come back here, and we can talk." When her eyes flashed at the word "talk," he knew it wouldn't all be about Carter. Or Jolie, for that matter.

"I'll be in my car," Landon said. "What I said before still holds true, Turner, don't worry. And I'll be in touch. Soon." He smiled insincerely to Mitch and walked toward his car.

Eden crossed the distance between them and pressed her body against his, wrapping her arms around him, wincing slightly as they made contact. When she stood on her tippy-toes to kiss him goodbye, he turned his face. Her lips grazed the corner of his mouth.

"Are you sure you don't need me to stay?"

He kept his hands on the few places on her arms that weren't covered in bandages, pushing her away gently, but she didn't seem to notice. "Why would I need you to stay?"

"Because you're in love with me."

Deer, meet headlights. *Say something. Say anything. It doesn't have to be sarcastic. Or even smart. Just say something, damn it!* "No, I'm not."

"You know, Mitch. The thing about liars is that they always have a tell." Though her eyes looked tired, wounded even, she smirked up at him, her full lips playing at a smile.

Focus on what's coming out of her mouth, not the mouth itself. "I don't have a tell. I'm not lying."

"Yes, you are."

He peeled his hands off of her. "What's my tell? I don't have a tell." He saw the slight bounce in her gait as she stepped outside and down the steps. *She can't leave like this.* "Stop!"

Across the driveway, he saw Landon's jump out of his car, his hand on his gun. For a moment their eyes met. Then Landon rolled his eyes dramatically, slid back into his seat, slammed the door, and looked down, shaking his head.

Eden turned around slowly, trying to hide her grin, looking up at him through her lashes. "Are you kidding? If I tell you that, you might stop and I'll never know when you're lying."

He threw his hands in the air. "You know what, fine. I have some feelings for you. Something like love, maybe." He shrugged. "I don't know what to call them."

Her teasing grin turned into a teeth-flashing, see-it-from-Pluto smile. She came back to the front step.

He held out his hand to stop her. *This was going to break her heart. But better it be broken than trapped.* "The thing is, Eden. I can't— I can't be with you." His chest fell at the look of bewilderment on her face.

"Why not?"

"Because…" For someone who claimed he was good with getting rid of people, he was doing a piss-poor job of thinking of any words to use. "Because, I can't live like this. *You* can't live like this."

She searched his face, as if looking for some indication that he was joking. "We could—"

"Make it work? Sure." His nod was exaggerated. "You'd come visit your boyfriend every few days who, oh yeah, lives in a cage. And we could lock each other up and spend our nights looking longingly at each other through the steel bars of our matching prison cells? That's a great fucking idea."

He pushed the words out of his mouth before he could think of an excuse to not say them. "Go be with Carter. He obviously loves you—he almost died for you, for shit's sake. Go try to make that work. He can take care of you."

She shook her head. "He was involved in all of this. Just because he tried to come clean—if that's what it really was—doesn't mean he made things right." Her face looked flushed, her eyes glassy. "And I don't want him to take care of me. I want *us* to take care of each other."

Much more of this would have him on his knees, recanting every phrase. "I don't want to spend my life not knowing who I am. I couldn't trust myself to be with you."

"But Hyde didn't hurt me."

Just get it over with, asshole. "Yeah, sure. Look at yourself, Eden. He could have killed you. I might not have been able to stop him." Mitch had been there. Saw her terrified face as she called out to him for help. Understood exactly what Hyde planned on doing to her. Didn't know what he'd done to stop the bastard, or if it would ever be possible again. And even if he could...

"What about everybody else? Do you think he wouldn't have killed Jolie if you hadn't done it first?" He ignored her flinch, ignored the fact that he'd reminded her of something best forgotten. "Do you think I can trust myself to be out of that cage knowing that you are the only one who is safe from him?"

The determination he'd grown to adore appeared on her face, in her stance. Making this all the more difficult.

"Wow, Mitch. I never thought you were a quitter."

"I'm not quitting, I'm acknowledging the truth."

"You just learned what truth *was* a day and a half ago!"

she yelled. "Of course there's a way. There's always a way. We have information. We know Carter and Jolie were making us transform."

"No, we know we were being manipulated, but that's not enough."

After the cops had shown up, Eden had whispered information in his ear, the caress of her lips only slightly distracting him from the knowledge of what Jolie and Carter had done to them. Fifteen years. Jolie had been doping him for the last *fifteen fucking years*. Probably in the damn coffee he drank every morning. In the soup she'd brought over. In the goddamn soda she always offered him when he was still in his teens. But he hadn't even known Jolie when Hyde first started showing up. No, there was too much Mitch had to learn before he would let himself live his so-called 'normal life' again.

"There's a lot more to figure out before we're free," he said. "If we're ever going to be free."

The calmness of his tone seemed to enrage her even further. But, thankfully, she kept her distance. "Mitch, please. We have a lead now. A big lead. Maybe a solution. You can't give up."

"I just did."

"No, that's unacceptable. You are mine, Mitch. All of you. *Both* of you are mine. If I have to prove it to you, then I will. I'm not giving up on us, even if you do. We can make our own freedom."

Mitch felt his heart shut down, go back into hibernation in response to the pain he saw he'd caused her. *That's really fucking healthy.* But she'd get over it. There was a chance *he* would too. A small chance. *More pain to keep the beast at bay, I guess.*

"I'm going to need you to check on me until I find another babysitter," he said. "And until we get you set up elsewhere, you will sleep here just in case." *Great, so we can relive this moment daily.* He couldn't look at her anymore. Just couldn't see the pleading of her eyes, the last bits of faith she had in him flushing away with her tears.

"Mitch, please don't—"

Ignoring the despair sweeping through his body, he shut the door and rested his forehead on the wood. Dying with each whimper coming from his doorstep. When he could no longer hear her sobs, imagining she'd driven away with the cop, he steeled himself and went back to his cage.

CHAPTER XLVII

By the time Eden stumbled to Landon's sedan and sagged into the seat, her tears were gone, leaving behind only salty trails on her cheeks. They prickled, itched. She didn't lift her hand to scratch, didn't have the strength to.

"What was that about?" Landon asked.

Her head moved slowly, a useless weight at the top of her neck. "He's afraid."

"He doesn't seem like the type. Afraid of what?"

"Of life. Of who he really is." Even her eyelids felt heavy.

"How very existential of him."

She shrugged and leaned back in the seat. "He's spent the last fifteen years believing he was in control of himself. Then he finds out that might not be the case. Believe me, it's a tough pill to swallow."

He gripped the steering wheel. "You mention this and I'll kill you."

She turned toward him. "Mention what?"

He reached under his seat and brought out a large manila envelope. "This," he said, handing it to her.

Landon's name was printed on the outside—no stamps, no address. It had been dropped off. By someone who spent time at the station. By someone whose handwriting she recognized the moment she saw it. Carter.

Before she unwound the tie keeping it closed, she stopped. "I'm not going to like this, am I?"

He shook his head. "It's from your boy, Carter."

"He's *not* my boy." Inside the envelope was another. She read Carter's message and stared at his neat signature below it, chuckling darkly. He always did things right, didn't he?

She pulled out a mixture of copy paper and lined paper Carter would have carefully separated from the notebook. Handing the envelopes to Landon to hold, she moved past the letter-sized envelope on top and flipped through written observations of herself, of Chastity. Dosage schedules. Then notes regarding her moods, her attitude. Personal things he had no right to judge, let alone notate.

"The frigging thing actually says, 'Do not open unless something happens to me,'" Landon said, tapping his finger on the envelope. "What the hell was he thinking? As if I wouldn't open it immediately. Doesn't he think I've ever seen a movie? It was just chance I went back to my desk today and saw it. You've seen my desk."

She had. And she imagined the envelope could have stayed in that mess for weeks. Could have been delivered weeks ago. Who knew? Did it make a difference? Not really. The damage was done. To her, by her—you name it. And now she was alone.

"What's this?" she asked, holding up the letter-sized envelope, afraid to open it and find something worse.

"It's a confession. Carter's confession."

With a shaking hand, she pulled the letter out. She put it down after reading the first few lines. She wasn't ready to read all of it. Not yet.

"Who is doing this?" she asked.

"I don't know. But I sure as hell am going to find out. That"—he pointed to the stack of papers in her lap—"will help. I hope."

She stared at the pages—Carter's notes, his justifications, his apology. It might help, that was true. But Carter himself was dead to her—figuratively, if not literally. His deceit had left her empty, void. She'd believed in him, thought he'd believed in her. Wrong on both counts. It stung, an electric jolt in her side she couldn't break free from. Given by the strong, muscular arms he'd wrapped around her so many times.

And Mitch? *Mitch.* Her belly and chest clenched. He was lost to her. Forever? If she didn't find the truth? Yes. If the truth didn't come with a solution? Yes. He would stay behind his bars, locked away from her permanently. He'd go back to thinking the evil inside of him *was* him. And maybe he'd be right.

A chill ran down her body, and she felt herself go blank, numb. Her emotions switching to the *off* position.

She took the first deep breath of her new life.

"I have more information. Jolie's password, but it'll need to be quick. Before they shut down the account," she heard herself say. Her voice sounded hollow, as if it was traveling down a long tunnel from her mouth to her ear. "I need your help, Landon. You think *you* want to know what's happening? Not half as much as I do."

Landon conceded with a nod.

"I need her cell phone."

He leaned in front of her, opened the glove compartment, and took out a phone. "You mean this one?"

"That's the one." She watched as her only ally—the cop, the stranger sitting next to her—put the phone into her outstretched hand. But she couldn't trust him. Not until he'd proven himself worthy. Not until she could trust her own judgment again. But he'd have to do for now. She'd be careful. Smart.

"Eden." He pulled away from her and swallowed.

"What?"

"Your eyes."

She yanked the visor down, and aimed the small mirror

toward her face. When she saw Chastity's eyes looking back at her, Eden's pulse sank, her heart stilled. Then it started a new rhythm. Four beats echoed in her ears, followed by a break. Something was definitely broken. But not her. No, she wasn't broken. She was power. Cold, undeniable power.

"Is it you...or...or her?" he asked.

"Oh, I'm still me." She slammed the visor closed and took one last look at the house in front of her. A house of voluntary bondage.

Feeling nothing, she curled her fingers around Jolie's cell phone and said, "We have work to do. Let's get the fuck out of here."

A moment before she heard the squeal of brakes behind the car and the tap on the window, she'd known something was wrong. But she still hadn't learned to trust herself. Not completely.

That needed to change. As Landon cursed and raised his hands in front of him, Eden slowly turned to the window and saw the gun pointed at her face. How many of the men could Chastity take down before they shot her?

EPILOGUE

Upstairs in Hyde's room, Mitch heard the pounding on his front door. Damn it. The sun wasn't even going down yet—too early for her to come back. And what was he going to do with her anyway? He imagined them staring at each other, both of them close to tears, anxiously waiting to see who would go to sleep first. Who would transform. Yippee, they could take turns. He could watch her nap, his eyes not leaving her face, keeping his sobs quiet so as not to wake her. Good fucking times.

The knock got louder. "Jesus, you're going to break your hand," he mumbled as he went downstairs to let her in. Hyde was subdued and had been since Mitch had come back into himself. But he couldn't trust it. Couldn't trust himself. He took a breath and opened the door.

"I told you not to—"

Landon stood scowling on the doorstep, his head tilted and his hand pressing the side. "Not to what, Turner?"

He walked away from the cop, leaving the door open. That was as much of an invitation as Landon was going to get. "What do you want?"

"They took her."

He whirled around. "What did you say?"

Landon lowered his hand and turned to the side, grimacing. Blood trickled down from his hairline just behind his ear. "I said, they took her. They must have been waiting for the others to clear out. When we were about to pull out of your driveway, they came out of nowhere and hauled both our asses from the car at gunpoint."

Mitch felt the anger take hold of him, filling his body. But it was all *his* this time—Hyde didn't push at all. "How did you let them take her?" He wanted to pound Landon through a brick wall.

"I didn't *let* them do shit! They took her, Turner. They took our girl."

He growled, "'Our girl?' *We* don't have a girl." His jealousy bloomed as he realized that Eden could belong more to the detective than him now. She might belong to anyone now.

No, she's mine. Always will be. He took a deep breath, trying to regain control. "Who are they?"

Landon took a wobbly step forward, blinking rapidly. He looked like he was going to fall over at any moment, without Mitch's help. Mitch grabbed the guy and brought him to the stairs, easing him down.

The cop put his hand to his head and closed his eyes. "She fought them. We both did. Then when I reached for my gun, one of the"—his voice broke—"one of those motherfuckers hit me from behind. When I opened my eyes, all of them were gone." Landon was still mumbling, but Mitch couldn't hear him, his mind narrowing in on one word.

Gone. She was gone. What he'd both wanted and feared, but not like this. Never, ever, ever like this. He had to get her back. He was *going* to get her back.

And if they hurt her…

He'd make them pay. Even if he had to let the beast out to do it.

~The End~

ACKNOWLEDGMENTS

On an emotional level, this story was difficult to write and even *more* difficult to let go of. I need to thank all the people who helped me through the ups and downs of this project, who were unendingly patient and supportive, and who I will never deserve. Especially Caroline Hanson, Christina McKnight, Roxanne Price, and my mom. And special thanks to Olivia Rivers for the amazing cover design.

ABOUT LAUREN STEWART

Lauren Stewart lives in Northern California with two of the most amazing children that the world has ever seen. She reads almost every genre so, naturally, her writing reflects that. With every book, every story, you'll find elements of other genres—fantasy, mystery, romance, paranormal, suspense, YA, women's literature, all with a touch of humor because what doesn't kill us should make us laugh.

CONTACT LAUREN

Sign up for my newsletter to get:
Behind the Scenes Looks at Your Favorite Characters
Updates about Coming Soon and New Releases
News about Contests and Giveaways
Teasers and Sneak Peaks
Book Signings, Conventions, and Appearances
Just go to: www.ReadLaurenS.com

Find me at:
www.facebook.com/LaurenStewartAuthor
Twitter: @ReadLaurenS
ReadLaurenS@gmail.com

OTHER TITLES BY LAUREN STEWART

Darker Water, Once and Forever #1
Unseen, The Heights Vol. 1
Unearthed, The Heights Vol. 2
Hyde, an Urban Fantasy
Jekyll, Hyde Book II
Strange Case, Hyde Book III
The Complete Hyde Series Box Set
No Experience Required, a Summer Rains Novel
Second Bite